STORIES FROM
THE BLUE MOON CAFÉ III

Edited by Sonny Brewer

MacAdam/Cage
155 Sansome Street, Suite 550
San Francisco, CA 94104
www.macadamcage.com

Library of Congress Cataloging-in-Publication Data

Stories from the Blue Moon Café III : anthology of southern writers /
Sonny Brewer, editor.
    p. cm.
    ISBN 1-931561-78-8 (alk. paper)
    1. Southern States—Social life and customs—Fiction. 2. Short stories, American—
Southern States. I. Brewer, Sonny.
    PS551.S74 2004
    813.' .0108975—dc22

                                                                        2004014323

Manufactured in the United States of America.
10 9 8 7 6 5 4 3 2 1

Book and cover design by Dorothy Carico Smith.

Several of these stories have appeared elsewhere, in some cases in a different form:
"Falling" by Bart Barton in *The Apalaches Review*; "Salt" by Barry Bradford in *The
Alabama Literary Review*; "Long Time Coming" by Rick Bragg in *Sports Illustrated*; "It
Wasn't All Dancing" by Mary Ward Brown in *It Wasn't All Dancing & Other Stories*;
"Geronimo" by Brock Clarke in *The Greensboro Review*; "Colored Glass" by Doug
Crandell in *Glimmer Train*; "Bayou Canot" by Joe Formichella in *The Wreck of the
Twilight Limited*, MacAdam/Cage; "People on the Empty Road" by Tim Gautreaux in
Same Place, Same Things, St. Martin's Press; "Charting the Territories of the Red" by
William Gay in *New Stories from the South*; "I'll Fly Away" by Wayne Greenhaw in *The
Spider's Web*, River City; "Waterwalkers" by Bret Anthony Johnston in *Corpus Christi*,
Random House; "Birdland" by Michael Knight in *Goodnight Nobody*, Grove-Atlantic;
"Hard to Remember, Hard to Forget" by Dayne Sherman in chapbook form, Over the
Transom; "The Joy of Funerals" by Alix Strauss in *The Joy of Funerals*, St. Martin's
Press; "Artifacts" by Brad Vice in *The Southern Review*.

STORIES FROM
THE BLUE MOON CAFÉ III

Edited by Sonny Brewer

MacAdam/Cage

TABLE OF CONTENTS

INTRODUCTION

Sonny Brewer

The Mississippi River is busy this morning. I'm in New Orleans for the Tennessee Williams Literary Festival, and from my eleventh-story window at the Monteleone Hotel in the French Quarter and by the light of a rose-tinted dawn, I'm able to count four tugboats struggling against the current in the bend at Algiers. One captain with a six-barge tow is holding her steady near midstream. The big river must be something to work against: the wheelwash boiling up astern of the tug is churning and cresting to heights of three or more feet and laying a troubled wake in the silvered course to the Gulf of Mexico. But the boat's not moving. Some business is holding him steady there while the other three big working boats are moving on out of sight past my window.

So I'm here this weekend to be on a couple of Tennessee Williams festival panels related to this Blue Moon Café anthology, and I'm wondering: with a jillion places to eat in this town that's known as the Crescent City, with an artful quarter-moon on the sidewalk water meter covers, how many joints in town would be called the Blue Moon Café?

None. Not one.

At least not according to the fat telephone book in the nightstand drawer in this hotel room. But, for the weekend at least, there's a Blue Moon Café in town. And that would be this third volume of our collection of Southern writing known as *Stories from the Blue Moon Café*. A moveable feast as its editor gets out there and sashays up and down Royal Street and Bienville and St. Peter and meanders around Jackson Square with his nose lifted for the tantalizing aroma of a good story for the next volume.

I might've found something right off the bat, soon as I checked into the hotel. Turns out the bellman, Ben, has been writing quietly for the last five years and has written three complete novels. And he doesn't have an agent, nor a publisher. Yet. The light on the desk phone is blinking red to let me know I've got a message. When I call down to the front desk, they tell me they're holding a package for me. It's Ben's manuscript pages. If the man knows how to write, you readers of *Stories from the Blue Moon Café* will be among the first to know. Let's keep our fingers crossed.

Some low clouds have rolled in down the river from nowhere and veil the rising sun so effectively that it looks like a giant white pearl floating six inches above the opposite shore. As my eye follows the silhouette of a jogger on the levee, the defiant sun burns a hole in the ragged clouds and pops through—tah-dahhh (like, did you really think you could keep me from my morning's business?)—with such a brilliant and shattering light I have to look away.

I didn't expect to awaken so early this morning—a little after five—since I was out kind of late last night with friends. It was not one of those famous Bourbon Street nights with too much Scotch whisky and mixing it up in the crazy push of people flowing up and down that surreal glitterway. It must have been a wake-up call from that Creole-spiced and pecan-crusted mahi mahi, topped with butter-and-white-wine sautéed crawfish tails followed by a cup of coffee with chicory so black and thick that writer Bev Marshall watched the waiter pouring mine into the heavy white china cup and said she'd changed her mind and would skip the coffee. I doused it with cream from the little silver pitcher and a teaspoon of sugar and it made a wonderful dessert.

This place has got so many good cafés and restaurants that I swear I can be at home in Fairhope, a hundred miles or so east of here in Alabama on the eastern shore of Mobile Bay, and something comes up about New Orleans and sooner than later the talk turns to some seafood and red wine recollection and my mouth will water and I'll find myself thinking it's only a couple hours' drive and why don't we head on over to the Quarter for dinner and a night of wandering along the streets taking off from Jackson Square. But our two boys have homework and baseball practice, and me and the mom have got stuff to do and we can't just pick up and run off into the night the way we once did.

Still, when we do get a big enough Creole craving to get us over to Orleans Parish, we know there'll be plenty of good places to eat. Fact is, if you aren't a good café you won't last long in New Orleans. It's a rule of the city in a city with few rules.

The French bread with my dinner at Brennan's last night was so warm and fresh, with a good light crust that crunched when you tore off a piece and slathered it with butter, that I asked Richard, our waiter, if it would be possible to get a few dozen loaves to take home with me. Seriously. Rick Bragg's moving to Fairhope for half a year to be our first writer-in-residence at the Fairhope Center for Writing Arts (into a cottage that was restored, in part, with money donated by the authors in this collection), and we're throwing a housewarming and welcome-to-town party where we'll serve some homemade gumbo. What better than good New Orleans Leidenheimer French bread to sop into a bowl of spicy shrimp and crabmeat and the fixings in a light brown tangy roux?

And maybe you can't get to New Orleans and have a jacketed waiter give you a phone number for the best French bread around, but you can keep *Stories from the Blue Moon Café III* on your table so you won't go hungry for good Southern writing. And New Orleans ain't got a lock on that. We've got entrées from Mobile, Nashville, Chapel Hill, Tuscaloosa, Natalbany, Bayou La Batre, Molino, Jacksonville, Chattanooga, Oxford, Selma, Montgomery, Fairhope—man, all over the South! I can't be sure, but there might even be a Yankee or two slid up to the table in here if they've set their story below the Mason-Dixon.

It's getting on up around 7:30 now and it's going to be a fine Friday in New Orleans. The weatherman promised. I've counted three runs of the ferry bringing people and cars from the other bank to a dock on this side of the river so folks can go about their business in the city. I was going to make a couple of phone calls before I get out there bopping around with the gang doing the Tennessee Williams fest, but I'll let that slide for now. I'm going to go grab a table

SONNY BREWER

and pull up a chair in the alley at the Royal Street Internet café, and have a cup of sweet chicoried coffee with milk and a hot buttered cathead muffin.

Then, after a day of attending TW festival sessions with Robert Morgan and Tim Gautreaux and some more good writers, when night comes on in this city where Anne Rice found the vampire Lestat peering out of her imagination, I'll make for Lounge Lizards, an all-night bar down on Decatur, and catch the acoustic rock-blues of the Stump-Knockers. New Orleans has got food, and New Orleans has got music.

And this time around, our Blue Moon Café mix has got music. I know you didn't fail to notice the CD in the pocket inside the front cover. There's music on it, original songs performed by Grayson Capps, who leads the StumpKnockers and sometimes does an acoustic solo performance on the road. He graduated from high school in Fairhope. (Read his bio/essay on page 87.) He's twice been our troubadour at Southern Writers Reading, the annual November literary slugfest out of which this anthology grew. He's also warmed up the author reading stage in my bookstore, Over the Transom Books, on several Thursday nights. When you stick this CD sampler into your music machine, you'll find out why we hang around with the dude.

And why our "good café" philosophy here at the Blue Moon includes not only Southern-flavored fresh hot fiction and essays and a poem or two, but a tune or three or four of foot-stompin' original music by a singer whose lyrics are stories in themselves. It's all about hoping you keep coming back to the Blue Moon Café for more of what we serve up. A good café ain't about taking your money and sending you down the street, it's about making sure we set on the table the best we've got to offer, and always greeting you with a nod and a smile when you swing open our door. Have a seat and kick back. We've been in the kitchen stirring up a plateful of good reading. No parsley sprigs to fork over to the side. You might even cut into a line or character that'll trouble your sleep, snatch your eyes open at dawn, and drag you out on the street for a cup of coffee. Don't worry. We've got a cozy back booth for you. And we never close. Because when it comes to storytelling, Southern appetites will not be kept waiting for long.

And here's a postscript: I liked what I read from Ben Fant. Turns out he's a Mississippi State grad. Look for his first published story in the next *Stories from the Blue Moon Café*.

—*Sonny Brewer*

BAILEY FAMILY RESTING PLACE

Matt Baggett

The Bailey family lies there
forgotten in the woods.
Unkempt cedar trees, too
big to hug, crowd over the
walls of the small plot.
The midday sun kinks
in the canopy overhead.
The knobby, rough concrete lies
over, lazy and cracked, holding
in the people below.
Death once came by dirges
swinging a pickax to turn
this earth. Now the houses
pop up like mushrooms after
a warm shower.
Their farm gobbled up by backhoes
and bulldozers only to excrete
a neighborhood.
The last one came home in 1974,
planted among family in the clay.
Squirrels chatter and gnaw at shells.
Moss grows where grass can't.
Wrought iron gate, rusted,
bearing the surname, hung in
honeysuckle at mid-swing.
Marching forth only in the long
branches of a gusty midnight wind.
Swaying and singing their lonely song,
they catch in the cedars and go
underground.

Humps covered in periwinkle mark
the spots where they have gone
to meet eternity.
Believing one day that the houses and
shallow plots will be wrenched open
like at the third day of the Ascension
and whole bodies will fly up into
the open arms of Jesus.

For Those Who Ride the Dog

Nikki Barranger

There were half a dozen souls who rode the dog on that November day as the big Greyhound bopped up the Causeway high-rise to the drawbridge just at the very split moment when the Kohncke shell-barge toppled the bridge's piling legs, sending the whole slam-crumple misery into twenty-five feet of brackish Lake Pontchartrain swell. It must have been more than thirty-five years back, but I have thought much about it since then. In fact I think about it maybe once a day and meditate about it every time the window badge on my car trips a switch at the Southbound Causeway toll-gate plaza, and the yellow-green sign winks with the message that says PAID GO. What I think about is how the bus went charging up that fifty-foot hill of concrete slabbing to find a great big gap of nothing at the top. I think of how the wheels must have gone from the sound of *blap-a-lap-a* to a sudden spinning whine as the dual side-by-sided tire treads had naught to grab by way of footprint, and the giant streamlined rolling box sailed tumbling up into the sunlit air to hit the far-side rim of broken bridge.

It was certainly a surprise for me when Otis Appleyard, president of the St. Agnes Scuba Lancers, called me at my law office an hour after and told me, "Drop what you are doing and dress out in wetsuit gear and meet up by the Prestressed Company boat-launch pronto. We got a dive to do."

"Otis," I said, "I'm due in court in half an hour."

"Screw court," said Otis. "There's a Greyhound Stratocruiser on the bottom of the lake. It lies at the five-mile bascule by the drawbridge. There's a Kohncke gravel barge towboat knocked down a hundred yards of arch, and us Lancers are the closest ones with gear can maybe help." Otis is a watchmaker and tends to be terse and precise. "So," said Otis, "get your ass to stirring!"

Lucky my date in court was only a confirmation in Everett's

uncontested divorce and he was ambivalent about it anyway. He even offered to drive me. When big news like this hits town, everybody wants to get into the act. On the way down to meet the Lancers, all Everett could talk about at sixty miles per hour was whether this might be something providential, and how it was likely God's way of whispering in his hopeful ear how he should give it another chance with Blanchie who was his adulterous bitch of a wife.

The whole time Everett was rattling on about Blanchie, all I could think about was how I had first met Everett, when he was working on building concrete forms for the construction of the very Causeway we were aimed at. Both of us had worked on the building of that twenty-four-mile ribbon of expansion-jointed Portland cement that connects the New Orleans south shore of Lake Pontchartrain to the north shore at Lewisburg just by Mandeville. He was a carpenter, and I was fresh out of law school handling "first line" of all the workman's compensation on the project for the United States Fidelity and Guarantee Company. If anybody got a leg broken or went into the drink by mistake, they knew I was the first one to call. That's what I mean by handling first line. I had met Everett when he was a witness in one of those cases. His cousin had lost an arm putting it where it didn't belong to be, inside the hydraulic scissors lifters on a front-end loader. But that is another story for another time. Everett's boss had not taken it kindly when he testified, however, and Everett got fired, even though I objected. I had liked Everett from the first because, interviewing him, I found out we both played bluegrass, and we got to be friends. I'd stood groomsman when he and Blanchie got married. And then he got to be something else. He got to be a matrimonial client when Blanchie took up with rough sex among the plumbing trades. Another big irony in all of this had been that the day the bridge opened, all of the workman's comp work on the north shore went to New Orleans lawyers and they would travel the bridge Everett and I built to try the cases I used to get. So on that November day, and for some time before, our joint respective Causeway connections had been very much a thing of the past. Final irony: when our bridge gets knocked down, it's me and Everett are the ones that get called back into the act to do something about it. So here we were in the throes of all this first-line providential nostalgia, speeding to a boat launch, all because we live in an unlikely world of coincidence where strangers get together to play bluegrass. All, except blue wasn't the only kind of grass Everett was into.

One thing I hadn't thought about until we were standing on the boat-launch was Dramamine. As the crew boat pulled through the foamy winter chop, when it bounced and bumped its fenders up to the pier extension for us to get on, I thought *plenty* about Dramamine. The fact is, I am a helpless victim of seasickness. And here was Lake Pontchartrain in the happiness of a playful squall—flinging white-caps all about the horizon and me with a chance to be a photo-op-type hero in a wetsuit with no seasick prevention.

"Everett," I said. "Have you got any Dramamine in your car?"

"Nope," said Everett. "What you want that for?"

"You ever been seasick?"

"Nope. What's it like?"

"Nausea. It's like, first you're afraid you're gonna die."

"Oh."

"And then you are afraid you *won't*."

"I don't hardly never travel with no Dramamine," said Everett.

"Oh well," I said. "It was a long shot."

"Tough tacos," said Everett.

"I make it a standing rule to dive in only mild weather." Now this was frankly bragging on my part since this wetsuit had been in salt water only a scant three times.

"That is a rule about to get broke," said Everett.

"Unless one of us can come up with Dramamine."

"No help," said Everett. "But I got half a lid of Blanchie's leftover mary-jane in the glove box."

"What good is that gonna do?"

"It will serve, I betcha. It kept the morning sickness plumb out of sight all the whole time she was knocked up with Emily."

Thinking no doubt how little Emily had come into this world stoned to the very gills, Everett sighed and looked off into space.

"Get it."

He got it. He passed me a penny matchbox and I remember the picture of an Indian in profile on the top and the message *CLOSE BEFORE STRIKING*. But it wasn't matches. Inside was something rusty green and leafy.

"You sure this will help?" I asked.

"Tickfaw *Red!*" said Everett, as though this answered all arguments. Everett, being a carpenter, knows about these things. "And I will pray," he added, "to Jesus who calmed the Red Sea waters."

"I think it was the Sea of Galilee," I said, "but let it pass."

"Whatever floats your inner tube."

"What do I do with it?" I asked, looking from the matchbox to the end of the pier where stood the wetsuited backs of five other Lancers (two CPAs, a real estate salesman, and our fearless watch-maker leader), all of whom were loading air tanks onto the stern of the crew boat.

"You smoke it is the usual thing," said Everett.

"Not, I think—in front of the Chamber of Commerce," I nodded to the end of the pier.

"I take your point. You can eat it..." he paused "...in brownies. Blanchie makes the best pot-bottom-brownies south of the Carville Leprosarium. Of course, brownies take some time to whip up. And plus which you need an oven."

"Eating is eating." I shook the contents into my hand and pressed the hand to my mouth, an orifice which was already feeling queasy in the spray. One chomp and I realized with stunning clarity just why they call it *grass*. I slid closed the box and went to put it in my pocket and remembered that there are no pockets in a wetsuit.

"Chew," said Everett. "Chew hard!"

I chewed while walking toward the Lancers.

"And try to make some spit before you swallow," Everett added.

We tumbled into the crew boat and made for the five-mile bascule. A *bascule*, in case you don't know, is the drawbridge gadget that counterweights the draw. As the boat pitched to and fro and fro and to, I wondered what morning sickness must be like—because what worked for *it* was certainly not working for those in the turbid throes of oil-rig crew-boatly *mal-de-mer*. I had reached the point when I was afraid I was going to die as I strapped on the tank and then I thought of those poor people in that bus and then, from thinking of them as I strapped on the weight belt and tugged at the flippers, I reached the stage where I was afraid I *wouldn't*. I tried to concentrate on the rising image of the broken bridge coming up on our starboard bow. It was an impressive sight to see. The center section of the fifty-foot rise was simply not there. It was gone—solid gone! What was there instead was a gap of nothing. That was the first time I imagined what it must have been like for the driver with half a dozen souls behind him, tooling along at seventy miles an hour on that clear sunny day like any other clear and sunny day. And as your magic diesel sled goes whiffling above the salty broth, you spot the Friday towboat *Capt. Minos Gautreaux*, in its altogether usual progress nudging the rust-buckety barge toward the tunnel underneath the high-rise draw, and you wonder still another time if they'll have to raise the draw-grill, and you start to shift down for a stop, and you know that they never have before, and you take your hand off the stick and wave a jaunty greeting to the sleepy captain of the tow. And everything seems altogether usual and as it ought to be as you think of getting off home in time for lunch.

We sat on the starboard gun'l of the boat, our tanks on our backs just above the water.

"We are going to have to find it first," said Otis. "First man to see an underwater bus, rap on your tank like this with your knife butt." He tapped three times and paused and then three times again. "Then everybody gather to the sound and then try and see if there's something down there—something we can *help*. In this chop, it's going to be hard to see stuff. And for Christ sake be careful. Over you go."

And over we went. Seasick beyond the point of actively wishing for death—just when one feels things inside the woe-laden body can't get worse but one has set one's mind upon a November swim in an effort to be the photo-op hero, when the vagrant seed of Tickfaw Red still lingers between lip and gum and a belch that carries you-know-not-what rises behind the SCUBA mouthpiece: backwards you lean, and toes over nose—into the murk and down. There was only about twenty-five feet of water, but it felt diesel-dark enough to be a hundred fathoms. I had to swim with hands stretched out in front instead of trailing at the usual hips, just to keep from bumping into drawbridges and pilings. I could only see about as far as my knuckles on arms extended. At first, the heave of the water keeps you in the prison of the ocean motion as you say goodbye to the boat bottom. But then at ten feet down, a miracle: as though touched by a magic wand, the world grows still and there is only the hiss of air and the sound of comforting bubbles. And miracle of all miracles: the heave stops and the nausea is no more. The suddenness of the relief is an unexpected pleasure like topping a hill in a car to find yourself driving at speed through a meadow full of bluebells, or the comfort of a hibernating sleep. But there is no time to marvel—get to work and be a hero.

The first thing I found was a piece of concrete pylon-leg, all jagged from its fall, and I had to get right up close to see how it was bashed and shattered. I cleared the mask and tasted diesel oil. I remember seeing that somebody—who knows, maybe it was Everett—had scratched into the side of it *Jesus Saves! But I'm gonna spend mine!* It was balanced against another piece of piling leaning back toward the south and it suddenly occurred to me that I was right under it. This was an uncomfortable place to be. It was wobbling and if it became *un*balanced, it would come down and be a very big and heavy scrunching weight smack on top of *me*, so I swam out from under it. Even there, feeling that jaggety piletop, I could start to build the notion of what must have happened with that bus, and as I turned to look south in the direction of New Orleans where it had been speeding from, I heard the three sharp signal pings and then another three. They were dead ahead of me and after two smart straight knee kicks, first thing I knew I had Otis Appleyard's left flipper up against my mask where I could see him tapping with his knife on his yellow tank, so I did the same with my knife and felt Stanley Gardener (photo-op hero of the real estate bourse) come up behind me just the way I had come up behind Otis. We drew together, shoulder to shoulder, and found ourselves feeling serrated edges of glass and a twisted piece of steel and rubber: the bent and corkscrewed remains of a windshield wiper, the first bit of bus to hit that cement pylon.

We peered past the mangled window frame into the opaque seethe of mud, blood, and diesel fuel beyond. I started to find a way past the opening, and I was halfway through the pretzel-bent steering wheel before Otis grabbed my ankle and pulled me back to tap me on the mask and motion me back and up to break water. I found that as I drew past the frame in answer to his tug, there was something in my hand, but I couldn't tell just what it was. As we rose to the surface, once more the discomforting heave of water brought back the yaw and pitch of nausea.

Otis pulled up his mask as we huddled in a circle. "They are, I think, past help. It looks like the bus must have hit that edge of the bridge…"

"Either that or one of the pylons," said Stanley squinting.

"And the bus must have bounced back after."

"Either that or it fell straight down flat," said Stanley.

"Anyway," said Otis, "we don't know just what we're going to find back up inside there besides a whole bunch of dead folks and their suitcases, and if we go in, we could find it hard to get back out, specially if we all go in together."

"Either that or we could get tangled," said Stanley.

"Riiight," said Morris, a hero of comptometry and ledgers: one of the CPAs. "I don't care for tight places."

"I suggest I go in alone," said Otis, "and see who can I find and bring back out and you all form a line and pass them up to the boat. What you got?" They all looked at me and for the first time I realized I was holding something in my hand. It was a driver's hat with a

patent leather sun visor and a smashed silver badge in the center with
writing that said:

> *It's such a pleasure*
> *To Take the Bus*
> *And Leave*
> *the driving*
> *to us*
> *!*

The crown of that hat glittered with sparkly shards of rearview
mirror glass in the sunlight. I threw it up to the boatman.

"Let's go," said Otis, "catch that anchor chain and bring it to the
front window. We can use it as a guide to the top."

Even in water that shallow we had no more than about forty-five
minutes of air. In that time we were barely able to bring up the driver
and the passengers but no luggage to speak of. I was the first man by
the window to take the forms of the lifeless as Otis passed them back.
First was a little girl who had goldy-blond hair and pigtails with soggy
red ribbons. One of her patent leather Mary Janes was missing and so
was its sock. As I passed her upwards, I made a cross with my thumb
on her pearly forehead, greased with diesel chrism. I couldn't say
why—I just did it. Next was a lady, probably her mother, in a camel's
hair coat with a gold locket around her neck that had sprung open.
Next behind her there was a soldier and, ironically, there was a sailor
in full bell bottoms (his glasses were still on his face—the grandpa
kind with gold temples and no rims). What made his presence so
peculiar was that the sailor wore the nose-nuzzling twin dolphins of
the submariner over his left pec. Then came a nun who held us up a
lot because of the rosary and the flowing robes. Let me tell you, under
twenty feet of diesely mud-water, the flowing robes of the Order of St.
Benedict don't flow—and rosaries on a belt can get tangled up to beat
hell in corkscrewy windscreen wipers. Last among the passengers was
a lady with a collie dog, the leash still wound around her right wrist
nearly up to the elbow when we brought them both aboard. We laid
them side by side still attached.

We gathered at the surface and Otis said, "Where's the driver?"

"He must still be down there," I said.

"Either that or maybe he got out," said Stanley.

"No way," said Otis. "He must have hit the window glass and then been swept back by the rush of the water. I'm going back down and look at the back of the bus."

"I'll come too," I said. I'm not sure why I was so all-fired eager except maybe it was to make the nausea stop by getting under deep and out from the heave of those waves.

"Take my flashlight," said Stanley, who was glad to stay topside.

And down the anchor chain we went, Otis and I with Stanley's hard rubber Eveready, pitching a short, bright pole of light for about four feet ahead of its lens. Since I had the light, I went first and it wasn't but about fifteen seconds before I wished I had passed the light to Otis because being first, I very quickly found, was not a real great position to be in as we swam, bumbled, and otherwise groped through the front window and down the aisle-way toward the Jim Crow section of that Stratocruiser. The farther we got toward the back, the more stuff we ran into that we didn't necessarily want to deal with. There were suitcases that had come out of the luggage racks. There was what appeared to be the contents of a bag of groceries someone must have been bringing home from Solari's because there were all these parcels of delicatessen wrap swimming by in front of a drifty brown paper bag with the famous logo on the side. It slapped tight across my face mask and for a panicky moment I couldn't see anything but flapping sack. Peeling it off caused me to drop the flashlight —and that was even less helpful to a sense of security, since I then had to feel around for it on the floor and when I found it, the beam was shining into the face of a giant two-foot Winnie-the-Pooh teddy bear with a blue ribbon round its neck. It was a bear big enough to wave its articulated arms as though it was saying *Hullo, Piglet.* For some crazy reason I grabbed that waving arm and held on with my flashlight-free hand. That was when the bus shifted.

There was a grinding sound behind us and then a *tonk-tunk!*

sound that seemed to go right through the whole length of the metal shell surrounding us. And with the sound the bus shuddered and moved, like a big mama bear rolling over in a deep December sleep. It was an eerie feeling as we made our backward way over a duffel bag and past somebody's umbrella floating by like chaos come again. With that *tonk*ing sound I called to mind the wobbling balanced piling that had proclaimed in scratchy cursive *Jesus Saves*, and judged the distance which that jagged end had been from the bus front where we had come scraping in. I reckoned it out as being just the right length for that piling to come drifting down to block that narrow windshield opening. Following these disquieting thoughts came a deep scrunch-grinding noise like a giant dentist's drill on a sick molar. The only thing that stopped me from making an immediate guppy-in-a-fish-bowl sprint for that front opening was the intervening bulk of watch-making Otis, but as I looked back over my shoulder to make sure he was there, I caught sight of my air gauge and that up-close view was enough to freeze the blood, for it was showing almost only five more pounds of pressure left. I waved the gauge at Otis, shining the light beam on it to indicate how we'd best be thinking about the surface and home, when I realized that the hand doing the gauge waving was also gripping the paw of that Pooh-bear. All of a sudden in the midst of panic and pain, it seemed just plain old funny. Otis nodded at the gauge and looked at his own, and then back at me with staring eyes wide open. Then the eyes of Otis focused on something behind me and he gestured with his hand to a place over my shoulder. I looked back and there was the thing we had come for, drifting up behind me and just in reach of the flashlight beam: the bus driver, or at least a part of him: it was his extended hand floating upwards from the floor in an undulating motion, an almost-dance, and I remember thinking that the wristwatch on that hand would not keep time again. I turned loose my air gauge and passed the light to Otis, and reached and took the hand in mine and tugged. And up came the battered face and form of Vincent Hahn.

Amongst all the folks who had been on that bus, that driver, dear old Vincent, was the only one I knew. He had been driving that route for years and years and used to take good care of me when I rode with him before the Causeway was built, before the coming of Stratocruisers. I rode with him back in the old high school days—when his old bus took two and a half hours to get me to the New Orleans dermatologist's office every other Saturday morning. We'd used to chat, and every time I climbed the steps, he'd punch my ticket as he'd say, "Come to ride the Dog again. Welcome. Welcome." And then he'd pull the swivel handle and the door to the bus would swing shut with a *whoosh*, and we'd be off and down the road heading for Irish Bayou and the old Watson-Williams Bridge. It wasn't much of a bridge, the Watson-Williams: next to no shoulder, narrow as a rabbit track, and full of potholes, but at least it stayed together. And then at evening on the round trip home, he'd be doing his last run of the weekend and say, "Thank Gracious God it's Saturday night—and we can all go home and sleep like Hahnville Christians." And he'd push that swivel handle and the door would swing wide in the twilight with that same *whoosh* and the trip would be over. Vincent had always worn a prodigious silver belt buckle with a stamped relief of a locomotive on the front. Funny how you remember things like how that buckle always marked his middle, right over the belly button. It was on those trips I got through reading sophomore year's *David Copperfield*. All those recollections rippled back as I followed Otis and his stubby flashlight beam, hauling vast Vincent Hahn with his big silver belt buckle back down the aisle, dodging parcels and luggage, parasols and duffel bags, still with that Pooh-bear in my forward hand, seeking that blessed window hole where we'd come squeezing in. And there it was—not the escape hole we'd left behind but that *tonk-tunk*, scrunching, jagged-end piling side, right where the windshield wiper used to be—right where we ought to have been swimming out with Vincent. The bus had shifted and our front-window exit hole was blocked. And there was that waggish concrete wall message: *I'm gonna spend mine!*

Otis reached out a hand and pushed the cement barrier. It did not budge. It did not so much as wiggle. That piling was nudging up to the bus-front like they were making love. Otis turned and looked at me with the light shining upwards between us. I could see his air gauge and the scary-looking shadows through the mask that made his face look even more scared than we both were—like something in a midnight movie when they do the lights from under the vampire's face. But the scariest thing wasn't the underlit horror on the wide-eyed expression of Otis. It was the air gauge by his shoulder reading two pounds of pressure. The needle was bingo in the middle of the red mark. I didn't even bother to look at *my* gauge. And all of a sudden things were very calm. I stopped listening to the bubble and hiss of our failing air and heard in my head again the voice of good old Vincent saying "Come to ride my dog again. Welcome. Welcome…" And I reached my Pooh-bear hand past Otis's air hose to the swivel handle in the center of the console and pulled. It gave just a little but it gave enough to say *pull harder*. Otis looked down and saw what I was doing and grabbed with both hands on top of mine and we yanked together like crazy men with three hands. It was Otis and me and Winnie-the-Pooh while my other clutching fist behind drew David Copperfield–courage out of poor dead Vincent Hahn. And the passenger gate of that Stratocruiser swung wide open like God and General Motors had intended it to do. In my head I could hear the comforting *whoosh* of going home in the twilight on the Watson-Williams Bridge as I tugged the hand of Vincent close behind me. And through the beautiful doorway we drew him, light as dandelion fleece up to the surface. It was Otis Appleyard on the right and me upon the left. I felt like an angel bringing someone up to Heaven as the sunshine surface brightened up the oil-slicky water topside. And as it will happen, the first absurd thing that broke to daylight through the last of our rust-sucking bubbles was the waving wiggly arm of that two-foot teddy bear with a streaming blue ribbon round its Winnie-the-Pooh neck.

When we were all back aboard, the crew boat made a roar and a great swooping portside turn, and we headed home. In our haste we had forgotten to bring towels, and we shivered and shook in the wind all the way back to the pier. To make discomfort bleaker still, there was nothing to cover our sad cargo, all those rueful folks lying side by side on the pounding floor of the vessel. None of us could bear to look. And none of us could drag up either inclination or energy to talk to one another, we were so turning-blue-cold and goose-bumped under the neoprene suits. So we looked over the edge of the boat or back at the wounded bridge. And to complete our comfort level, we were mired in a slick of diesel. Later on, I had to scrub the fins with pumice soap, and still even today they smell like truck stop.

Perhaps it was that chewy half-lid of Everett's Tickfaw Red that colors how I remember that bouncy trip home, looking back again at the fractured arch above the water and feeling a sense of being a high-rising eye, sailing over and out of the boat and looking down on it as though I were flying into New Orleans on a jet. And I remember seeing the bus go straining up that ramp as the topmost span splashed down. And then I felt myself as though I was another all-seeing eye, diving from air to being deep inside that Greyhound box with all those shocky folks and with them seeing sudden nothing from out of the window front as Vincent's foot stirs from a footrest to seek a brake. And a sailor's arm rises to the back of the next seat just ahead. And the panic of a nun, feeling the missing sensation of no rhythm of road underneath the tires, and then looking once again to know— the forecast of the bash of bridge edge and pylon lip, leaping to strike the front of the graceful flight. I know the certainty of a physical world stopping and stunned, without an expectation of a future, and the happy laws of nature turned so hostile to our innocent aim of getting on for home and fixing lunch. I feel with all of them the dense and sudden knowledge that *this is the way things are, and thus they have to be*—this is the way the world is put together. And with the mighty shock of the great slamming bump of bus on bridge edge, there is the dreadful smiting yaw of helpless uncontrol—a rolled-out pout of backward slinging of time—and out of time—a ticking backward on a wristwatch that will never work again—back to the awesome moment of your borning birth, the first and last instant when such a numinous grief can be encompassed down the swallow of the bite of self. And all of it's inside this little box of knowing. And all of it's come down to intersect this battle in the blunder-brawling moment of the metal-concrete slap. The pucker of the instant hangs—a razor-strap thunder in the air. Time sits cracking, like a baseball on a bat. And the world is falling upwards with another dreadful thump, blundering from below. The bus cleaves water and rises, and sinks, and rises and sinks as the seas rush in with the justice of the way things are—to push with mighty waters, so much more gently back—so much more gently but so irresistible—a force that says to all of us *you are mine, little one—you are mine*. And all of us inside this bus—we know that it is true. And the physics of the world we love has turned to waterstone, and turned, and turned against us once again.

For this is death and this is dying. With one shoe off and one shoe on.

I stepped from the crew boat across the water to find Everett on the Prestressed pier with a hot bath sheet he had scampered off and borrowed from the YMCA. There was a towel for each of us. Those toasty towels were almost like a welcome back to life. And later on I burned mine up, together with the slick, anointed wetsuit—we could never get them clean—they were that greasy. The smoke went up to heaven in a black and grateful bang mark against the sunset. Strange, the uncleansability of that towel—for, scoffing at all that diesel oil, the two-foot Winnie-the-Pooh came diesel-free and sweet from the Maytag wash water. I gave it, clean and pretty, to little Emily and she has it still.

Everett called me the following week to say that he and Blanchie had gone back both together. He asked if I would stand godfather to Emily. And naturally I said I would, even if it might make Blanchie nervous—to have the family divorce lawyer holding the new-named baby at the font. Well, at least by then Emily wouldn't be so stoned.

"She'll just have to suck it up," said Everett. And suck it up she did.

And I remember all of that, whenever there comes back to me the PAID GO inkling of the doings of that diving day—of the rising falling diving, under the broken bridge. Funny and ironic: finally what I most of all remember is the comfort and the welcome pleasure of that warm embracing towel on the dock. And never *was* a towel so warm and welcome—as welcome as the last suck of the rusty-bubble air in your tank. As welcome as the opening whoosh and gurgle of a swivel-handled door. As welcome as the sleepy sleep of sleeping winter bears.

FALLING

Marlin Barton

for Jimmy Rhodes

I must have been a fool like no other in Demarville, Alabama, to think that I could save my marriage to Juanita by chasing after the grand prize at the Belmont Chicken Drop. But I guess I was just as desperate as those chickens must have felt as they dropped out of that airplane door from three hundred feet above ground, all of them looking like a string of feathered skydivers without parachutes. You've got to remember, though, that chickens, or at least game chickens, can fly—when they absolutely have to. So none of them crashed and burned like my marriage was about to, or like that airplane did later.

Juanita didn't really want to go at first, but I talked her into it. Told her it would be something unusual, something people would be talking about for a long time. The poster I'd seen said there was going to be a parade before the main event, and we drove on over early Saturday morning so that we could get a good spot on Main Street, which is where I knew the parade would have to come since it's pretty much the only street in Belmont. We ended up parking in a vacant lot and had to pay a man two dollars to squeeze into a space between a beat-up van and an old dented Cadillac with expired Tennessee plates.

"Exactly what kind of parade is it?" Juanita said before we got out of the truck. She checked her lipstick in the mirror.

"Just a parade. With floats, maybe a band. I don't know for sure."

"Well, there's all kinds of parades. Christmas parades, Thanksgiving Day parades, Fourth of July parades. What's this one? Seems like you'd know since you're the one who wanted to come so bad."

"It's a Chicken parade, I guess."

"You're not telling me that they're going to try to march a bunch of damn chickens down the street?"

If I hadn't known better, I would have thought that she was beginning to get a little mad at me. But I did know better. We never got mad at each other anymore, not really, which wasn't all that good a thing, believe it or not. If you ask me, people who don't fight don't love. Or at least one of them doesn't. We used to have awful fights, world-champion events, but no more.

"I doubt they're going to march chickens," I said. "Maybe it'll be a bunch of floats in the shape of chickens."

"Why would they want to do that? Parades are to celebrate things."

"I guess they're going to celebrate the mighty chicken."

"Why?" she said, like all this was something to take as serious as a funeral.

"Because of the big event later," I told her. "It'll just be something fun. Come on."

We climbed out of the truck and I grabbed the two lawn chairs we'd brought. Juanita got the little cooler filled with Cokes. We found a good spot in front of the post office and sat down. Sure enough, after a while I heard some firecrackers way down at the other end of the street and people started standing up. I figured the parade was beginning and kind of wanted to see if there *was* a big chicken float. I looked over at Juanita for a second. She didn't seem to have heard the firecrackers. She just stared across the street, like maybe she was thinking about some good time she'd had years ago—with someone other than me.

Like I said, we'd had our problems. Maybe more than most, to be honest. Daddy used to say you've got to keep a woman off balance. "If she don't cook," he'd say, "raise hell. If she cooks, don't eat." I used to follow that advice. And I used to drink a good bit. If I was drunk enough, I'd fight sometimes. I never hurt anybody bad though, except myself. Once, back when things got real rough between us about two years ago—I mean one day when Juanita and me had had some kind of screaming match about my drinking and about whether or not we could stay married—I took off out of the house, and after a crazy night of drinking and fighting and showing everybody how I didn't give a damn about anything, I ended up wrecking a friend's truck and almost killing myself. Juanita finally came to see me in the hospital after I'd given up on her. I told her I was a new man. I stayed home, got a little raise at the paper mill, and quit taking my daddy's advice. I did all the right things, and Juanita bragged on me to her friends. She was a satisfied woman. She'd finally turned me into a good man, she said, like she'd been trying to for all those years. Things were good, at least for a while.

The firecrackers started getting louder now. A few went *pop, pop, pop* real close by. Then whole long strings fired off, sounding like machine guns too hot to touch. In a minute, the first float rolled by, but it wasn't in the shape of a chicken. It was only a green pickup truck jacked way off the ground with a bunch of guys in back drinking beer and wearing feathers glued to T-shirts. They looked more like molted chickens than anything you'd see at a 4-H show. All of them strutted, flapped their arms, and squawked. I did think it was kind of funny, but Juanita looked at me and didn't even bother to roll her eyes or say a word. She could have been listening to her mother tell her how to rearrange the kitchen cabinets for the look on her face. All it did was make me think again how far from each other we'd gotten. At least when we were fighting, we knew the other one was *there*.

We had done real well for a while though, after I quit drinking and carrying on. We'd lived like normal people. At least I guessed we had. I'd never really known any well enough to be sure, only seen them on television. Then after about six months something started happening. First the sex went downhill. I could still satisfy her, though it did take a little more work on my part, but I didn't mind. The thing is, after a while, she just stopped wanting it. I wondered if she was sick, maybe had some kind of female problem. I was plenty worried. But she said, "No, that's not it." She couldn't explain. "I'm just never in the mood anymore," she said. "I don't know why." And she stopped keeping the house clean the way she used to. Even let the kitchen get dirty, which she'd *never* done before. She always took pride in how she kept the place. I'd never cared much one way or the other about how the house looked.

Another truck went by now, pulling a flatbed wagon with a big cage on it. A rooster was inside perched on a wooden box. Above the cage a sign said, "Behold a Mighty Cock," but someone had crossed out the "Be" in "Behold." Juanita shook her head without looking toward me.

Finally, after she convinced me she didn't have a female problem, it was like we just got to be strangers with each other. We'd drive somewhere, maybe to Tuscaloosa or over to Meridian to go see a movie, and wouldn't have anything to say. Things would be the same in the living room at night or at the breakfast table in the morning, depending on what shift I was working. I didn't know what to think. It seemed like if we didn't have anything to yell at each other about, then we didn't have anything to say at all. That's the way we started living. I knew we couldn't last. I'd always thought if we ended it would be in the middle of a terrible storm full of lightning and thunder, both of us shouting above it all, but here it looked like we were just going to let things die of some disease we couldn't name, something you might catch from bad chicken.

Another wagon came rolling past then, this one pulled by an old International tractor. It had a sign above it, too, "Chicken Drop Prizes," written in great big letters. Everyone started clapping and yelling real loud, like at a football game where the home team has just scored. Third prize sat on a little table at the front. It was a toolbox, bright red and opened up so that you could see new tools sticking out of it. Second prize was a washer and dryer. And then there was the grand prize, which is why everybody was clapping so hard. A redhead in a black bikini held up a sign and kept turning around and around. "Gulf Shores or Bust," the sign said. "Three Nights, All Expenses." I didn't know if people were clapping for the grand prize or the redhead. Probably both. She sure looked good, though, just like Juanita did on our honeymoon down at Orange Beach. And Juanita *still* looked good I'm here to tell you. If she'd been up on that wagon, people would have clapped just as loud, or maybe louder, and I would have been leading the cheer. I've never been the jealous type. I say be proud of what's yours. Of course, I was afraid that I wasn't going to have her much longer. If someone stops wanting you, doesn't care to lay claim anymore, there's not much hope. I knew that.

But I hadn't given up, not yet. Even though I'd gotten that raise at work, Juanita and I hadn't been able to afford any kind of real trip in a few years. If I could get lucky and win that grand prize, we could go down and maybe have a second honeymoon, walk on the hot sand in the daytime and warm up the sheets at night. Hell, maybe we'd even get into some big old fight about something and then cool ourselves off in the midnight waves with our clothes lying up on the beach. It was a dream, I know. A long shot. A crap shoot. But sometimes you just have to believe. You've got to fool yourself. And if I couldn't win her the grand prize, then maybe at least I could get ahold of the washer and dryer and have *something* to give to her other than just my love, which she didn't seem to want anymore. Maybe a new washer and dryer would look good to her, I thought.

It was all a matter of catching the right chicken.

I'd told Juanita that maybe there would be a band playing, but I didn't hear or see one. The next couple of floats were nothing but flatbed wagons stacked with chickens in cages. There were probably about thirty or so of them altogether, looking like maybe they were on their way to market. They couldn't know that they were about to soar from a great windy height, like a circle of buzzards. I figured it would be the most thrilling event in their dumb lives and wished that I could do something like it.

"Look who's coming next," Juanita said then, and I heard something extra in her voice that hadn't been there in a while. So I looked and wasn't too happy with what I saw. It was Charlie Armstrong standing in the back of a long-bed pickup, throwing one of those big Styrofoam airplanes in a loop over his head—catching it, throwing it, catching it again—and when he missed, someone on the street would hand it back up to him. Along the side of the truck was a sign that said, "Our Fearless Pilot." People started cheering, like he was some war hero back from glory.

I'd known him a long time, since high school, and always liked him all right. He was still about as crazy as I used to be, people said. Maybe crazier. Back when I heard he was learning how to fly, I figured he'd kill himself doing something dumb, like trying to fly under a telephone wire or land on the highway. He'd never gotten married, but word was he had a couple of yard children. And back right before Christmas, he'd spent a few nights in jail for fighting. I told Juanita about it. "That figures," she said, sounding real disgusted. "He never will grow up." But something in her voice had sounded like a high school girl.

She'd known him a long time, too. In fact, she'd been one of his girlfriends back in school. Every once in a while she'd mention him, and he was probably the only person she could make me jealous about.

He came riding by us then and spotted Juanita. "Hey, girl," he hollered, then threw the airplane right toward her and she yelled, thinking it was going to hit her. But of course it turned up into its loop all of a sudden and he caught it just as smooth as could be when it came back around.

"You're still crazy, ain't you?" she said.

"You know it," he hollered. Then he waved at me, grinning, and I waved back. Hell, you couldn't help but like him.

The parade passed on by and went out of sight then. Everybody started picking up their chairs and their coolers—and their babies, which is one thing Juanita and I didn't have, and never would. She'd told me before we got married that she couldn't have any. She used to cry about it some. I always told her it was all right with me if we didn't have any. But from the way she'd cry, I could tell that she wanted to be somebody's mama.

Everyone along the sides of the street headed in a slow walk to the big field outside of town. Some people put down blankets after they picked a good spot. Then they broke open their coolers and started eating fried chicken and potato salad and all sorts of picnic food. Juanita and I bought some hot dogs from a stand nearby and sat down in our chairs and ate and drank our Cokes. Maybe it was because of the way we were sitting, with our chairs a little too far apart, but we didn't look like the other couples sitting around us. Or maybe it was just because we didn't have a blanket spread out between us, one with a baby crawling around on it.

We got through eating, and I started wondering just when the big event was going to begin. I got up and stretched the muscles in my legs and tightened the strings on my tennis shoes. I hoped I wasn't too out of shape.

"What do you call yourself doing?" Juanita said. "You look silly as hell."

"I'm getting ready for the Chicken Drop. I want to be able to run and cut back and forth real quick. What I really want is to win us that grand prize. Wouldn't you like that?" I said, and found myself holding my breath.

"It would be all right, I reckon. We haven't really been anywhere in a long time." She sure didn't sound too excited about it. I let my breath out real slow.

"I got to go register and pay the entrance fee," I said, then walked over to a table not far from the hot dog stand. The old man there told me they'd line us all up in a little while, as soon as the plane came over. Then they'd shoot a pistol to signal that it was time to go after the chickens, once they started dropping, that is.

"Check the tag around its foot," he said. "The prizes are written on there. Of course, most ain't got nothing written on them except 'chicken,' which means you can take it home and eat it, but that's all. It's a consolation prize. Some of them do look like some pretty good eating, though, even if they are small."

I walked on back toward Juanita, and about that time heard an airplane engine wound out like a chain saw. I wondered why they weren't trying to get us lined up. Then Charlie Armstrong came zooming over the tops of the trees in his crop duster, a long white scarf around his neck, looking like some fighter pilot back in World War I. He turned a tall loop, just like that Styrofoam plane he'd been throwing, then when he came out of it, he climbed fast and rolled out. It was air show time. The chickens would have to wait their turn for glory. And so would I.

"Would you just look at him?" Juanita said. "He's acting like a fool. Like some kid who ain't got any better sense. He's going to get himself killed."

"Like I almost did when I wrecked that truck?" I said. "Or like when I used to stand in the doorway of a bar and yell, 'Everybody here is a son of a bitch and ain't none of you son of a bitches leaving?'"

She turned and looked at me funny. "What do you want to bring all that up for? That's in the past."

I didn't answer, just drank the last of my Coke, wishing for a minute it was a beer, or something stronger.

Old Charlie made another loop and rollout, this time even tighter than before. Then he flew so low over the field none of us thought he was going to clear the tops of the trees at the edge. He barely did make it. His wheels even touched one high limb. I saw Juanita hold her breath, but she didn't say anything. She held it again when he made a sharp dive from way up and came down so fast and hard it looked like he was going to bury the nose of the plane, and himself, three feet into the ground, but he pulled it out and made it over the trees again. He flew two more passes, finally dipped his wings at us, waved, then he was gone.

"That was something," Juanita said. But I could see that she was relieved more than anything.

"I've seen better air shows. Seems like he might have done a little more," I said, not sure at all why I said it.

She looked at me a second time, like I'd cussed in church.

In a little bit, we could hear the sound of a plane again. But it wasn't the same one. The engine ran so much lower and smoother, and then we saw it over the field flying in a big circle with its door wide open. It was the plane Charlie took skydivers up in, somebody said. I figured while Charlie had been putting on the air show, other people had been loading the chickens. I stood up and stretched again, then started getting nervous. Maybe I didn't have much to gain by all this, but I knew how much I had to lose.

"Let me have your registration slips," a big fellow called out. He carried a pistol in one hand, looked like a .22 revolver, and a couple of registration slips in the other.

"You going to wish me luck?" I said to Juanita.

"Break a leg," she said. She tried to smile. Ever notice how when somebody *tries* to smile it's worse than when they don't?

We all gave the man with the pistol our slips. There were maybe about fifty of us, including a few women. The big man and the fellow who'd been selling hot dogs took a long piece of string and stretched it out on the ground. "All right," the big man said, "everybody get behind this. Don't run 'til you hear me shoot, and don't worry, I ain't going to kill nobody."

The plane came back around again and I could see someone standing in the door. My hands started sweating and I crouched down like a runner at a track meet, then took a couple of deep breaths and cocked my head sideways so I could see the plane. The first chicken came dropping out, a second one right after.

"Ready!" the man shouted. Then he shot and my stomach tightened so you would have thought the bullet had hit me.

All fifty of us ran to the middle of the field like some crazy herd, and the chickens dropped out fast, fell hard, then must have figured out where the hell they were—higher above the world than they'd ever been—and something in their tiny yardbird brains told them to stretch out their wings. After that, they started spiraling down, one after another, like strange-looking buzzards all the wrong colors. Meanwhile, the crowd spread out, everybody sighting in on a bird and waiting for it to touch down. Only problem was, for each bird, there were about three of us waiting. The one above my little crowd got close and before it landed down among us it cut to the right and hit the ground running. I went after it, bent down, and scooped it up just as a woman and some kid grabbed at it. I got a good grip on it and held it to my chest while its wings flapped the hell out of my face. Let me tell you, a mouthful of feathers don't taste too good.

Finally I looked at its tag. All it said was "chicken." I threw it up in the air and of course neither the woman or the kid went after it, knowing that it couldn't be one of the prize-marked birds or I would have kept it.

When I looked up again the sky seemed to be raining chickens. Charlie made another pass over the field and chickens streamed out of the door, long lines of them, and they'd flap their wings, catch themselves on the air, and start the long ride down.

A white chicken, I mean pearl white, ran right past me then, like some sweet young thing worried about her virtue. I grabbed at it, but the woman got to it first and caught it by the leg. That thing squawked and fought like a hungry fox had it in its jaws. The woman read the tag and let it go with such a look on her face that somehow it made me think about Juanita. It was the same kind of expression I'd seen for so long from her that it had gotten to be natural, something I didn't even hardly notice, but on another woman I could see so easy what it was, nothing but disappointment.

I saw another bird about to touch down now at the edge of the field and nobody else seemed to see it at first. I took off running, but even though I had a good head start, another fellow saw the bird, then me, and closed in. I poured on the juice, though, and got to the chicken a good ten yards ahead of him. I made a fine grab, checked the tag, and could hardly believe it didn't say "chicken." Instead there were the words "tool box." For a second I felt like a winner. I'd never won any kind of prize in my life, and here I had one in my hand, but it wasn't what I wanted, or needed, rather.

"Hey," I hollered to the fellow walking away. He turned around and adjusted the cap on his head, then looked at me like I'd stolen something of his. "This one's the tool box," I said. "You want it?"

He grinned at me. "You serious?"

"Yeah."

"Bring it on, partner."

I started running with it and handed the bird off to him as I went past, heading back to the scattered, stampeding herd as fast as I could.

"Thanks," he yelled. "This is what I wanted. The hell with the beach."

At least one of us is getting what he wants, I thought.

I found a spot back among the crowd. Most all of the chickens had landed by this time, and everyone was running after them, picking them up, and throwing them down, except one older woman who was walking away with one under each arm.

"What you got, Granny?" a man in cut-off jeans hollered.

"Sunday dinner," she said, and seemed just as satisfied as she could be, like she had two prizes that were better than anything that had been on the parade wagon. I envied her in a way I couldn't explain.

Four last birds swooped down now. Then two of them turned in my direction and came zeroing in for a landing, but there were about ten or fifteen of us, waiting to make it a rough one for them. One of the birds got caught before it touched down, but the other hit the ground in stride, ran past the legs of a tall skinny fellow who seemed just too tall to reach down and grab it in time, and then it made for the tree line like we were all after it with evil in our hearts or a notion of unhealthy love on our minds.

I took off quick and had the lead again, but two guys, big guys, came on fast and bumped me from both sides and sent me sprawling over about ten yards of hard ground. I watched from the dirt cussing and hollering as they ran on into the woods after it. One of those last four birds must have been the grand prize chicken because nobody had hollered out yet that they'd caught it. Just my luck, I thought. I might have been right behind the prize bird—that close to a trip to the beach and maybe back into Juanita's heart—but there I was sitting in the dirt, like some kid wishing he had a toy truck to play with but all he's got is an old bent spoon his mama threw out.

I thought about jumping up then and going after those guys who had knocked me down, fighting them maybe and finding that chicken for myself. But I didn't know if they'd knocked me down on purpose or not. And if they hadn't caught that chicken yet, it was probably already roosting in some tree, way out of their reach, and mine. Besides, I didn't want to start back fighting and carrying on like I used to. I was through with all that. Old Charlie could keep on if he wanted, but not me.

As it turned out though, whether or not I'd gone after those two guys or the chicken didn't really matter. Because as I sat there with my hands in the dirt, thinking about Juanita and all we'd once had and all I still wanted from her, any chance for my marriage to last started falling from out of the sky.

First there was just a sound, like some terrible coughing, and I thought, "What's that noise? I should know what that noise is." And maybe I did know, but wouldn't let myself answer. Then from over the tops of the trees at the far end of the field, I saw Charlie's plane coming in low and fast, too fast, and I could see the propeller—*see* it, understand? It sat at a dead angle. No more coughing sound.

The airplane's nose was too low and the tail too high, like Charlie was trying to do a flip to impress everybody, not caring that he would land flat on his back, his wheels stuck in the air, maybe leaving him trapped inside a dead metal bird. But instead of flipping, Charlie got the plane to drop hard, like some mean hawk diving, only he managed to flatten the plane out at the last. He touched down, then the plane went spinning sideways, the tip of one wing digging into the ground, the tail still in the air, swinging out of control, the other wing coming around shaking and at such an angle that I thought it would break off. The whole plane looked like a wild, sick bird completely out of its head.

Men started running toward it just as the plane came to a stop. Then I woke up from some kind of drunk daydream it seemed like, finally believing what I'd seen. I got to my feet and started for the plane, too, not even thinking about Juanita anymore—where she might be or how scared she was feeling for her old boyfriend.

By the time I got to the plane, a couple of fellows had opened the door and crawled in. I stood there sweating with my hands on my sides and watched as they pulled out first one guy, then another. Both of their faces were cut and bloody, but they started moving enough there on the ground that I could see they were alive.

I knew somebody had to go in and get Charlie, and I hoped he was still alive, too. It's hard to imagine a man like him really dying. People want to believe some men are just too tough and crazy, that death can't touch them. But it can happen. I know. I'd come close myself in a totaled-out pickup truck at the end of a wild, stupid night. I knew how easy a man can die.

I took a breath then and started toward the door of the plane, but just as I got close, the same two fellows went back in. I can't say I wasn't relieved at the sight of them. Seemed like they were in there for a long time, and I was imagining all kinds of things, but finally here they came, carrying Charlie out. One had him by his feet and the other was at his shoulders. He wasn't moving. My stomach just sank.

Somebody hollered "fire" real loud then and we all looked and saw flames coming out around the engine. Just as quick as anything, though, a boy I knew named Luke, who raced stock cars over in Meridian, came running with a fire extinguisher from out of his truck. He sprayed the flames out before they got dangerous.

The two guys had Charlie stretched out on the ground now, and Charlie moved a little and blinked his eyes real hard. Thank the Lord, I thought, and suddenly felt a whole lot better about the world and everybody in it.

Then I saw something I don't guess I expected, but it made sense in a sad sort of way. Juanita came walking out of the crowd. It was at just the moment I'd started thinking about her again, wondering where I could find her and what I could say to her to make her feel better and maybe calm her down. But she wasn't looking for me. I saw that clear. She went right to Charlie and kneeled down at the top of his head. Then she took her hands and put them to the sides of his face and bent close over him. She whispered to him and he opened his eyes again and said something. The way Juanita looked there, holding Charlie's head in her hands, rubbing him so gently, was just like she was his mama, come to take care of her wild boy. And I felt like a forgotten son.

She finally looked up at the crowd and found me. She didn't have to say anything. My marriage had fallen right out of the sky along with Charlie, and no dumb prize could make it rise to the air again. It's almost funny. I'd become what Juanita had thought she wanted, but she'd found out different. Or at least I had. I couldn't hold it against her. She needed Charlie, or someone like him, just as much as he needed her, even if he didn't know it. It had sure taken me a long time to know how much *I'd* needed her.

In a minute or so I heard a siren way in the distance. It sounded like some kind of signal. I walked up to Juanita and Charlie then. "I'm going with him in the ambulance," she said to me.

"I know."

"But it don't mean anything. He just needs help."

"It's all right," I said and bent over and put my hand on her shoulder. She looked at me for another second, like she needed to explain more. I just slowly walked away. What was clear to me wasn't clear to Juanita yet, but I knew it would be.

When I got to my truck I saw a chicken walking by the side of it and pecking at the ground. I don't know what possessed me exactly, but I picked it up and looked at its tag. It just said "chicken." I knew it would. I took out an old croaker sack from behind my truck seat and wrapped the chicken in it, then put it in the cab and took the chicken on home with me. I'd have to go to the hospital later and get Juanita, and I figured on the way home I could stop and get a little feed out at the co-op. That's what I did. Juanita didn't even ask why I was buying chicken feed. She didn't really have much to say about anything. Neither did I.

I heard later, a few weeks later, that somebody found the grand prize chicken out in the woods the next day. I guess they took the trip. I hope they had a good time.

Juanita left me not long after that. It was a relief more than anything. Sometimes your heart carries even more than you know. She married Charlie about a year later. They sent me an invitation, but I didn't go. Sometimes I'd pass Charlie on the street. He limped for a while after that crash. Not bad, though. Then I heard that Juanita and Charlie adopted a kid. Somebody said it was really one of Charlie's and that there hadn't been any adoption at all. Who knows the truth of something like that?

I've still got the chicken I took home. She's a Black-Breasted Red, I found out, a fine bird. I don't ever plan on eating her. I even built a little coop for her, and she spends her days strutting around the backyard in fine style. I named her Queen. I treat her just like one.

SALT

Barry Bradford

I remember a hundred biscuits in the oven and hungry niggers on the ground outside with a fire and some sausage; raw-boned niggers that worked for food. Before daylight they hauled themselves onto the wagon and rode down into the woods with Daddy, facing a hard day of work already paid for.

I remember the day the drummer came. I was in the yard. It was noon when he stood on the road and looked at me and the house and said his name, which I forgot. He had a bag on his shoulder that was dark with shiny greases and paint and made a noise when he walked. Momma came out to the porch. She asked him who he was, I think, and he said he was a seller of things. He hauled two pans out of his bag saying they were cheap, then a Bible, and offered to read to us for a meal. Momma said it was okay and went in.

It was cold and rain began. He bent down and asked me how old I was. Five, I said. He asked something about Daddy and looked at the clouds, which were black. I told him about the storm pit Daddy and the niggers built in the bank behind the house. He asked me to show him.

It had a wooden door at an angle that led to nothing more than a hole in the earth with some supporting timbers. I watched the drummer go into the dark. He turned and all I could see was his face in what little light there was in there. He stretched out his hand to take mine. I looked at the house and back at him.

He said there were wonders in there, things that I should see, that I could only see as a child. I told him I was afraid of the pit, that it had caved in on a nigger when they were digging it. He said darkness and fear were brothers and they were his friends. He had seen their faces and I could see them, too. Take his hand, he said. I stepped to the mouth of the pit.

Momma called and told me to get in out of the rain.

He dropped his bag by the door and took up a large Bible. He told me he had others, smaller ones that were new for fifty cents. Where he came from he was known for his readings, he said, and could stop bleedings by pronouncing certain words of scripture. He had gotten this gift from his father, an evangelist, a man who could take up serpents without being hurt, who once stopped a flooding river, drying up the water with a verse and a scattering of salt.

I asked him if his father still read the Bible. He said he did not know. His father had gone into the woods to baptize a young woman and they had not come back. The town searched for them, but all they found was his Bible, on a stump beside the creek. This very Bible, he said. On the book lay a moccasin that he himself removed, the drummer said, without being bitten. Upon reading the passage, which lay open before him, he was in a moment given eyes to see his work. It was this work that he now performed, he said. He began to read.

The smell of pork mixed with words from the Law. The drummer moved in great strides across the front of the house, becoming louder and gesturing often with his hand. His voice was deep and rich. He chuckled, glancing at me with a smirk before moving to the other end of the room, then back and stopping in front of me. He squatted and squinted, holding the Bible out, and I looked carefully at the cover of bluish, pitted leather. I opened it and turned through the pages. In some places great red marks were drawn across passages. In others words were written in the margin or over the print.

His father never read another book in his life, he said. The old man's only work had been his study of the Bible and these notes. No one had seen those notes before but his father and himself. Now he had shown them to me.

The storm beat down on the tin roof. I sat down while Momma moved around the kitchen pulling together our meal of biscuits, salt pork, and turnips. Then she went into the back of the house. The drummer came in and laid the Bible beside his plate.

The drummer followed the creek for three days after finding the Bible. There had been no other sign of his father. But after the third day he came upon a black man deep in the woods. The nigger was half-naked, crouched near the cold waters. He gripped a cross made of pan handles and said the Beast was in the creek. But God had sent the Prophet to chain the Beast. The Prophet gave the nigger watch over the Beast until he returned with the hosts of Heaven. Before he left, the Prophet gave him a box and said a certain young man would come for it. He was to say to the young man, "With this do God's work."

The drummer reached into his shirt pocket and pulled out his hand in a fist. He reached across the table and opened his hand slightly, letting something fine and white fall into the turnips. He then went to relieve himself in the yard. Momma came back and began to salt the turnips. I told her she didn't need to because the drummer had already salted them. She looked at me until the drummer came in and sat down. He asked to say a prayer, raised his hands, and gave loud thanks for God's gift to him of this meal. He then went to work bringing biscuits and pork to his plate.

Momma asked him if he would have some turnips. He thanked her but said he could not eat greens as the juices made him bilious. Momma then produced my daddy's old navy revolver from her apron. She held it steady in the drummer's face and said he would have some greens.

He didn't move until she cocked it, and then spooned a small helping onto his plate. He looked at the turnips, then stood and said he would be going. Momma stood. He would eat the greens or be shot. He ate them and died on the kitchen floor.

We tried to drag him out to the yard but he was too heavy. Momma sent me to her room and closed the doors to the kitchen. Daddy didn't come home that night and I slept with Momma behind a locked door. The rain went on. I thought I could hear the drummer walking through the house and the pans clanging in his bag. I dreamed the drummer was knocking on the door and reading scriptures to bring the waters to a flood. I woke Momma and we crept with a candle to the front room. Momma felt in the dark for his bag. I took the pans back to bed and slept with the handles crossed on my chest.

The rain went on through the next day. The wind grew stronger. In the afternoon Momma looked out the front door. The rain had stopped and it was quiet. She picked me up and ran through the house, out the back door and to the pit. We went in and sat in the blackness listening to the roar of a tornado.

The rain returned. The yard was already a great pond. We sat in Momma's room and chewed stale biscuits. Toward dark Momma said she had to go back to the kitchen. I followed her and looked in. She took down a large bag of salt and carefully poured it over the drummer, beginning with his feet. His face was twisted on one side and his eyes were open. She covered it with a great mound of salt.

Daddy and the niggers got home the next day. The sun was out. The swollen Alabama had kept them away. They loaded the body onto the wagon and started back into the woods. One of the niggers climbed on with the bag and began to hand around the new Bibles. Another took up the large one and read aloud until the wagon disappeared into the trees.

LONG TIME COMING

Rick Bragg

History really was made here, in the college town of Starkville, Mississippi, not far from the Alabama line. One of the last unwritten taboos in college sports was busted here, amid the dark pine barrens and clear-cut timber and nowhere roads, when Sylvester Croom became the first man of his color hired as a head football coach in the storied Southeastern Conference. Yet four months later if you ask players, fans, or university officials whether history has been made, they tend to say much the same thing, at first: Mississippi State hired a coach, not a color.

"We have never once mentioned in a press release that he is the first black coach in the SEC," says Mike Nemeth, the school's associate director for media relations. People at the school say that Croom's race had nothing to do with his hiring, where the respected longtime college and professional assistant coach is being asked to snatch up a sliding program—one that may slip deeper still, as the NCAA mulls punishment for alleged recruiting violations under former coach Jackie Sherrill—and shake it into something people can be proud of again. The university's president and its athletic director, praised for their courage, almost shrug. "The university could not have bought this publicity for a million dollars," says the president, J. Charles Lee. Still, "That courage issue was never a significant factor for me."

It is the same in the community. "Well, I asked my boyfriend, Buster, about him, and Buster said, 'He's going to be a good one,'" says Louise Ming, who is 78 and has sewn a maroon sweater for his toy bulldog on the shelf. Croom can win, people are saying. Too much time has passed to yammer on about color. Mississippi State has an A-plus football man, they say, and by God, that is all that matters.

"Same thing as if he was white," agrees Howard (Buster) Hood, who is retired from the dairy business and food industry and already has paid for his season tickets. "We give him a chance. He can't do the job, we don't need him."

But something odd happens the more you let people talk, the more you ask them who they are, where they are from, what they remember about life before integration—or, if they're very young, what they were told about that time—and it becomes clear, as a Mississippi writer once said, that the past is not dead here, nor even past. Croom himself, sitting in a spacious office with still-bare shelves, first swears that maroon and white, not black and white, are the colors of *this* football team, the only colors that concern him now.

Then the 49-year-old coach drifts back in his mind to the people who bled and died in a struggle he remembers mostly through the eyes of a child and teenage boy—people who absorbed genuine hatred, who changed his society and made it possible for him to play his way onto the Alabama football team in 1971, the second year that Paul (Bear) Bryant allowed black players on his squad. And he begins to cry.

His father, in the late 1940s, feared being lynched. Croom himself attended a newly integrated junior high school where students refused to talk to him, where a spit wad spattered on his face the first day of classes.

But none of that is worth crying over, for Croom. It is the memory of a white woman that is causing him to break down, a 39-year-old homemaker and mother of five from Detroit who volunteered to drive protesters during the historic Selma-to-Montgomery voting rights march in 1965. Three Ku Klux Klansmen pulled up beside her as she drove down a stretch of road, a black man in the seat beside her. It was more than the Klansmen could stand.

"Viola Liuzzo," says Croom, and he takes off his glasses and wipes his eyes. It looks a little strange, to see hands that big wiping at tears. "When she got shot…all that lady was trying to do was help someone. Just plain ol' people, trying to do the right thing, and they killed her."

That was perhaps the first time the young Sylvester Croom realized the awful cost of the change that was taking place around him. And suddenly it very much matters that a black man is the head coach at a school in the conference of the Bear, the Big Orange, Death Valley, and the Loveliest Village on the Plain. Because if it doesn't matter, then what was all that suffering for?

"It was coming, sooner or later," says Ming, who is white, a few days after she approached Croom in a Starkville diner and asked him for his autograph, for Buster. She even had her picture taken with him. Not too long ago, this would have been scandalous. Now the autograph—a black man's name—is in a frame, a thing of value. Southerners get where they need to go, Ming says sweetly, "but we don't like to be pushed."

Nearly 40 years have passed since the first black scholarship athlete took the field in the SEC. And a lifetime, it seems, has passed since Sylvester Croom kicked a field goal over the clothesline in his yard in Tuscaloosa and dreamed about being swept up into glory on the Crimson Tide. But even as he entered high school, the only players wearing Alabama jerseys were white. "No way I should be sitting here," he says from his MSU office, his mind hung up—for just a moment—on that clothesline.

Then, that quickly, he is standing before a team of SEC athletes—his boys—in the Mississippi State field house. He's one of only five black head football coaches in Division IA, five out of 117. His players sit straight and tense, and you get the feeling that if he told them to jump off a roof, they would balk only long enought to write notes to their mamas.

"We're kind of tickled with him," says Jimmy Cowan, class of 1959, a retired engineer who lives in Aberdeen, Mississippi, and drives his recreational vehicle to all the Bulldogs' home and away games and—like most white Mississippians of his generation—went to all-white schools.

"It was a chance to do the right thing," Douglas Brinkley, historian, author, and director of the Eisenhower Center for American Studies in New Orleans, says of Croom's hiring. But, because of the coach's credentials, "it was also a safe thing."

Head football coach of a state school in the South is a position whose prestige rivals, and in some places exceeds, that of the governor. In the increasingly conservative, increasingly Republican South, the first black coach in the SEC had to be someone too solid to question, too deserving to deny. "We have to be able to say we were looking for the best football coach, not to cure the ills of our state," Brinkley says of the Southern mindset.

Croom wishes, of course, that his father had lived to see this. The Reverend Sylvester Croom Sr. passed in January 2000, but not before he saw many of the barriers that he once peered through knocked to the ground. His sons, Kelvin and Sylvester Jr., both played for the Bear, and Croom Sr. became the Alabama football team's chaplain, invoking God on behalf of whites and blacks (but rarely Auburn). He died too soon to see his older son take over an SEC program. But Kelvin, the baby brother, knows what their father probably would have done. He would have placed a hand on Sylvester's shoulder and, in a voice that always seemed to be dropping down from a mountain, told him something you had to know Croom Sr. to understand: "Son, you had the best ice cream."

In the glow of the stage lights, in a community theater in Tuscaloosa, a wrongly accused black man stood trial for his life. It was only theater, only another local interpretation of the classic *To Kill a Mockingbird*, but in the pitch dark of the auditorium, sweat beaded on the Reverend Dr. Kelvin Croom's face. In his mind he did not see an actor, a stage, or the curtain that could drop and cover the ugliness of the story with thick, soft velvet. "In my mind," he says, "I saw my father."

He saw the same South, the same story, but this one unfolded in Holt, Alabama, not Harper Lee's Maycomb, in the mid-1940s. A white woman had been raped and told authorities that three black men had done it. Justice had to be swift, for the sake of society. It did not need to be accurate.

Sylvester Croom Sr. had been out rabbit hunting with two of his brothers. They had blood and hair on their clothes when police went for them, acting on a tip from a black woman who said she had seen the Croom boys splashed with red.

Police arrested them and put them in jail, even as local clergymen tried to convince authorities that the boys were innocent. A short time later, fearing for the safety of their prisoners, officials spirited the boys out of the local jail and took them to a Birmingham lockup.

All this happened before Kelvin and Sylvester Jr. were born, and the story would be told and retold, sharpened every time, an old razor that still draws blood. How close, Kelvin would always think. How close his father had come to being another victim of a doomed, hateful way of life. "It was hard to sit through that play," Kelvin says.

The elder Croom's arrest might have cowed some men, might have made some men walk with their eyes glued to the tops of their shoes. Sylvester Croom Sr. straightened up tall in the service of God and took to wearing a cowboy hat. "You can't keep a good man down," he would boom from his pulpit at Beautiful Zion A.M.E. Zion Church in southwest Tuscaloosa, "and you can't keep a bad man up."

He was 6' 4", 290 pounds, and on the football field at all-black Alabama A&M he had hit like a pickup truck. The stories he told and the ones told about him made his boys want to be him. "Against South Carolina State, in about 1950, he picked up a ball on the one or two and ran it all the way back for a touchdown," says Sylvester Jr. "I'd always liked that story, and in my head I always saw myself doing that."

In the pulpit Sylvester Sr. was demanding, unbending. If he saw his sons acting a fool or just not paying attention, he would point one big finger at them, silently passing sentence, and it augered right into their hearts. "You didn't enjoy any of the rest of that sermon," Kelvin says. "You knew what was coming when you got home."

As the civil rights movement took hold of Alabama, Sylvester Sr. lived the nonviolence that the Reverend Dr. Martin Luther King Jr. preached, but in the afternoons he would stand at the practice field fence and stare at the vaunted all-white Alabama football team, and dream. His sons stood with him, dreaming too.

To work beside a man or share a lunch counter with him or sit with him on a bus, that meant something. But to line up across from him in full pads and slam into him with all the power in your body, without any consequence beyond the outcome of a play, a game? When was a man more free than that?

Tuscaloosa, like the rest of Alabama, was rigidly segregated, with an insidious Klan presence. The Alabama campus was off-limits—Sylvester Croom Jr. never strolled across it, or even walked past it. He saw it from the windows of cars.

Once, in the midst of the civil rights movement, an ice cream vendor came to Croom Sr. for counsel. "He was having difficulty," Kelvin says. It was a matter of conscience. The vendor was known to have the best ice cream in Tuscaloosa, and people—blacks and whites—lined up for it. He served whites through the front door and blacks through the back door. His business thrived, within the conventions of society. But it was a time to question convention, and the vendor, who was white, wanted to do something revolutionary. He wanted to serve blacks and whites through one door. "He knew what was right, but he needed someone to lean on," Kelvin says.

"You do have the best ice cream in town," Croom Sr. told the vendor. The people would have to decide if it was worth standing beside someone of another color to get some. "Serve it from one door," he told the vendor, and make it about flavor, not about color.

There is a Southern tradition of lamentation when it comes to daddies. Men have been known to drink too much and talk and cry all night, remembering. But a sober man sings the best songs of praise.

"I guess the best sermon he preached was the one he lived," Kelvin says. "If anybody did without in our house, it was him. It was important to him what Mom, me, and Sly thought of him. He always told us to love people, to never hold grudges." It would have been just words if Kelvin and Sylvester Jr. had not known that their father had a reason to hate.

"He always said, 'You got to do right every day,'" Sylvester Jr. says.

"Work within the system when you can," Kelvin says.

"Fight by the rules," Sylvester Jr. says.

"And," Kelvin says, "have the best ice cream."

The spit wad caught Sylvester Jr. square in the face. It was his welcome to the overwhelmingly white junior high school in Tuscaloosa that he, and later his brother, attended.

He did not do a thing except wipe it off. "I look around, and I'm ticked, and I see who did it," Croom says.

"Follow Dr. King's teachings, no matter what happens," his father had said.

Later that day, at football practice, Sylvester Jr. saw the boy who had thrown the spit wad—across the line from him in pads. "I hit him as hard as I could," Croom says, and he laughs out loud. It was a bone-numbing hit. "I would find a way to hit him…every day."

But is that in keeping with Dr. King's teachings? "Sometimes," Kelvin says, "you slip."

White students refused to be Sylvester Jr.'s study partners, to share a locker with him, to let him into groups formed for class projects. He was not so much mistreated as ignored. The thing he hated most was the silence, which he endured even in a hallway that rang with voices and pounding feet and banging lockers. "The biggest fear I had was just being isolated," he says. For all the interaction he had with students in some classes, "I might as well have been a tree."

But kindnesses, and courage, filled the silence. The practice field was three miles from the school, and the ninth-grade football players had to get there as best they could. The handful of black players did not have a ride, and it took time to walk three miles. They would have to miss part of practice. But the first week of football a car pulled up, and a white player, a quarterback named Stan Bradford, motioned the black players over. There was not room enough for all of them to sit in the backseat, so a couple of them squeezed into the front, beside Bradford's mother.

Every one of them knew that this was taboo, that people had been killed for less. "You just didn't sit with no white lady," Croom says. "It seems like a little thing, but that lady did something that wasn't supposed to be done in that time, and it changed my world."

Another challenge to convention came from the Tuscaloosa High football coach, Billy Henderson. Other Alabama coaches had black players, but they left them at home or on the bench when they played in racially charged places such as Montgomery—or across the state line in Mississippi. But no one was going to tell Henderson who could start on his football team. "It took courage, but he believed in us," says Kelvin. "He was some man."

Sylvester Jr. played practically every position—even did some kicking. He was a big, strong, 5' 11" and 195 pounds, and while his team won only about six games his whole high school career, he caught the attention of colleges. One day a recruiter from Alabama stood at the Crooms' door.

Sylvester Jr. had believed that Alabama was for dreaming, and that A&M was for playing. But Wilbur Jackson had broken the color line as the Crimson Tide's first black recruit in 1970, and Croom followed him there the next year. He remembers his first day of college. White players, knowing he was from Tuscaloosa, asked him how to find this place or that on campus.

"How would I know?" he said. "I never been here."

"I wanted one thing," Croom says. "I was sick of losing. I wanted to win." At that time all Alabama did was win. "And I wanted to stand there at the foot of Denny Chimes as the captain of the football team." His teammates, predominantly white, made him that in 1974.

As a center of the wishbone Croom won honors—he was on Kodak's All-America team and voted the best offensive lineman in the SEC—and signed with the New Orleans Saints, for whom he would play one game. But coaching would be Croom's football future, and he was an assistant for 10 years at Alabama before moving on to the pros, where he was an assistant coach at Tampa Bay, Indianapolis, San Diego, Detroit, and finally Green Bay. Then, last May, Alabama fired coach Mike Price. Mama called, as Bryant liked to say, but the door closed in Croom's face before he could step inside.

"At one point I thought I had the job," Croom says, and Alabama—by all accounts—strongly considered him before settling on former Tide quarterback Mike Shula, who was nearly 11 years younger than Croom and that much less experienced.

Croom loves Alabama. His brother, who took over their father's place at Tuscaloosa's College Hill Baptist Church, leads the devotion before every Crimson Tide home basketball game. Not getting the Tide football job hurt Sylvester, says Kelvin. "He had been successful at every juncture. He was All-America. Why not bring him back?"

But Sylvester would no more badmouth Alabama than he would his family. Asked about not getting the job, he thinks a minute. Then he says, "I just remember something Coach Bryant said: 'Go where they want you.'

"The interest Alabama showed probably opened this door for me," he says of Mississippi State. "They wanted me. Not a black coach. They wanted *me*."

The MSU athletic director, Larry Templeton, is not worried that Croom will leave for Alabama if things go badly for Shula and Mama calls again. "Not the least bit," he says. "Mississippi State gave him the opportunity, and he will remember that."

He will have every chance to succeed and will not be penalized for transgressions that may have been committed by his predecessors. His new contract would be extended for each year the school might be on probation. "If there are NCAA sanctions, his four years will begin when those sanctions are over," Templeton says.

Any backlash to the hiring of a black coach has been minuscule, says Lee, the MSU president. "We got mail from Ole Miss graduates" praising MSU—and some from Alabama, expressing regret that Alabama didn't get him. The response "reaffirms that [people] just accepted that it is time. Private giving for athletics has increased. We're quite happy."

Mississippi State, at least for now, has more pressing problems than its place in civil rights history. "The program has to be above reproach," Lee says. He felt Croom would guarantee that. But then, of course, he also has to win in the SEC. Recruiting has gone better than expected for a team under an NCAA cloud, but the players will have to line up against faster, stronger, more talented teams, such as LSU, and bleed. They need a reason to do that. They say they will do it for Bulldog pride and a place in history. Everyone says color doesn't matter, at first. Then you ask them who they are, where they are from, and...

Delijuan Robinson's mama mopped floors and drove a school bus and worked every other job she could find to give her four sons a chance. "She raised us by herself," said Robinson, a 6' 4", 295-pound defensive lineman from Hernando, Mississippi. "She made us finish school. Wasn't nothin' easy about that." If growing up poor and black wasn't a deep enough hole, the 19-year-old Robinson found out two years ago that he had a leaky heart valve. A scar from open-heart surgery bisects his chest. Now a black man will succeed or fail as a head coach in the SEC based in part on how Robinson performs. "I'll be proud to take on a role like that," Robinson says. "She'll be proud, too," he says of his mom.

Quarterback Omarr Conner's father is on dialysis, and his mother used to work at a chicken plant and now works at a fish plant in Macon, Mississippi, about 30 minutes southeast of Starkville. College football was supposed to be a ticket to something better. Conner watched his first season, under former Bulldogs coach Jackie Sherrill, collapse into a 2–10 agony.

Conner will never forget the first team meeting under Croom. "I thought, God has sent us someone to save us. I am fixing to play for Coach Croom, and Coach Croom played under Bear Bryant. And I can tell my child, 'I was part of history. I made history with the first black coach in the SEC.'"

Croom knows how hard it is to keep believing when the things you want seem so far away. He is uncomfortable being a symbol. But there is no denying it, really.

Somewhere, in a backyard in Alabama or Mississippi, a boy is kicking field goals over the clothesline and throwing touchdown passes to himself, lobbing the ball so high that he can be quarterback and receiver all in one.

"He needs to know," Croom says, "that things do change."

SQUIRREL'S CHAIR

Matthew Brock

S quirrel had a glass eye. Mama used to make him sleep on the couch because he snored so bad. Me and John Earl would wait until we heard him in there, then sneak in on our hands and knees. We'd poke our heads over the edge of the couch, and there it would be, shiny and blue, staring us down while his good eye dreamed. One time John Earl reached out and touched it. As soon as his finger hit the glass, Squirrel opened his good eye like he wasn't sleeping at all and grabbed John Earl's wrist. John Earl hollered. He jerked away and we ran back to our bedrooms, never messed with Squirrel's glass eye again.

He lived with us for as long as I can remember. For a while I thought Mama called him Squirrel because his cheeks looked like they were full of nuts, but she said it was just because he was squirrelly. I thought he was our dad until I was seven. Mama told me then that our real dad was probably somewhere called Tijuana, peddling wristwatches made of fool's gold. She said Squirrel was the next best thing.

Our next best thing dug through the dumpster behind Goodwill. He brought home Chinese checkerboards, wax grapes and bananas, bluegrass eight-tracks, World's Fair Coke bottles—whatever wasn't rotten or broke too bad. Sometimes he took me and John Earl, loaded us in the Flintstone Mobile, made us help him. John Earl was lookout. He squatted beside the corner of the building watching for pigs or anybody suspicious. I climbed inside the dumpster, threw things out to Squirrel. Once I found a 1956 *Funk & Wagnalls* words RHOD through SHAK stuck under a wad of wet pantyhose. Squirrel and John Earl didn't see any use for it, so I got to keep it. I took it to the bathroom that night when the apartment was quiet. I sat on the commode and turned to page 7940. That's how I know about ovums and sperm and a condition called hermaphroditism.

When I heard Mama bitching in the kitchen the other day, I rolled over to face John Earl. His orange rattail was a sea serpent. "What's going on?" I said.

"Your breath stinks."

Squirrel pounded down the hall and threw open our door. He stared at me and John Earl, his T-shirt too short to cover his whole hairy belly. He said, "If you two ain't up three seconds from goddamn now, I'm gonna yank you out of there by your hairless asses."

I got out of bed, and John Earl moaned. This shithole apartment, Richview. The walls are the same color as Mama's teeth and so thin you can hear our neighbors hacking. The place smelled like cats for months, even after Mama sprayed three cans of Lysol. Now it smells like cigarettes. It's smaller than our old place is why me and John Earl have to share a bed. We used to live closer to the good side of town, near the Square Dance Center, where wrinkled geezers barn jived all night, but Squirrel had an argument with our landlord. Squirrel said he couldn't respect a man that didn't believe in IOUs. We had to live with Uncle Jimbo until Mama and him could find another place.

Anyhow, I got dressed in a pair of holey swimming trunks I found in the dumpster last summer. I followed John Earl down the hall, past the picture of pretty Jesus under a halo, and into the kitchen. Mama sat at the table slurping cereal. A skinny cigarette burned in the ashtray. She wore the worn-out yellow nightgown I hated, nipples showing through, scattered browns I couldn't help but see.

I know it's gross to say, but she was fine when she was younger. There's a picture where she's wearing a cheerleading outfit. She's standing at the top of a pyramid of girls with her arms out, her skin as smooth as Aphrodite's sculpture. Now it's all loosey-goosey like a fishing net. She said the picture was took five years before her car wreck. The winter she was pregnant with me she slid on a patch of ice and collided with a cement truck. She broke a leg and I came out early, smack on the cold pavement. The doctors had to twist screws into her bones. I had to live under plastic so I could breathe pure air. I turned out okay, but the wreck caused Mama to walk with a funny-foot.

"What's Squirrel want?" said John Earl.

"He's found something and needs your help getting it up here," Mama said. "He's downstairs waiting."

"Why can't *he* do it?"

"Don't ask stupid questions."

John Earl let out a breath, then stepped outside onto the balcony. I stopped beside Mama. Her cigarette was a long ash. I said, "There's an island across the world called Sangir where they grow grapes the size of car tires. Folks don't know what a cigarette smells like. I swear."

"Don't start your nonsense with me, Mac, son, boy."

The morning was hot and gray. Across the street, Manny sung some Mexican song as he took down chains from the door of his pawnshop. A woman in a miniskirt walked by the Baptist church that used to be a gas station. Down on the corner, the bums burned time around the Richview Apartments sign. Two hundred yards away I-40 was a blur of traffic and smog. Cars and big rigs rumbled toward Asheville and Nashville almost invisible. Squirrel was in the parking lot, scratching his pecker, leaning against the hood of our Flintstone Mobile.

We call the station wagon that because the floor in the back used to be so rusted out we could see pavement rush under us. One time Mama picked up John Earl and a girl from the arcade. On their way home John Earl and her were playing footsie, and her sandal slipped through a hole. Mama turned around, but they never found the shoe. They came home bitching at Squirrel. Mama said the car was a death-trap and somebody would fall through and be run over. John Earl said he wasn't ever gonna get any mud for his turtle if Squirrel didn't get a better ride. Squirrel got so mad I thought he would jack them both in the jaw. He spent all night under the car with a flashlight, fixed the holes with a piece of plywood.

He straightened up when he saw us coming. He swallowed the last of his beer and fired the can over the chain-link fence between our apartments and the interstate. He met us behind the car. A green chair was in the back. "I think it's my best find yet," he said, looking me and John Earl in the face with his good eye, his glass eye going toward our feet. "It's hard to believe what people give away these days. At this rate I'll never have to work again."

Squirrel had a heart that didn't pump strong enough, or something. He said it meant he could die at any minute, but I figure we all could die at any minute. It got him out of work at the Levi Strauss factory though. He passed out one day while he was loading boxes of jeans into a truck. A doctor at the emergency room put him through all kinds of tests and found the problem. He gave Squirrel a letter saying he wasn't supposed to exert himself until he got a special surgery. The government sent him a check every month, so we had to make sure nobody caught him exerting himself.

He put a hand on my shoulder and said, "We're living large. Ain't we, Mac?"

"It's just a chair, nothing to get all schizophrenic about."

"Quit trying to act smart with those queer words."

Me and John Earl dragged the chair from the car. I dropped my end and the chair fell on the concrete, scuffing one of its corners. Squirrel cussed and took my place. He told me to watch for anybody suspicious, but there isn't anybody suspicious. You might see a woman with a bruise on her face from some man's fist. You might see a guy with a beard to his knees, yelling at somebody not there. You might see a hood rat making gang signs at a pig when he drives by. You might see that same pig pressing somebody's face against the sidewalk. You might see a suit from downtown stopped at the corner in his slicked-up car, waiting for a whore or a fix. Hell, but that's normal around here.

They lugged the chair up the three flights of stairs. When we reached our apartment, I opened the door and watched them cram the chair through, landing it on the kitchen floor. I thought Squirrel was about to die. He fell against the wall wheezing and holding his chest. John Earl plunked down on the linoleum. Mama limped in from the back, still with her scattered browns. She bent close and studied the chair. She made lines in its fabric with her nails. She said,

"You didn't find this behind Goodwill. What did you do, rob Heilig-Meyers?"

"Hell no I didn't rob anybody, Legs." (Squirrel called Mama Legs because she had long ones. He said they were as beautiful as handlebars on a Harley even with the scars.) "It was sitting at the drop-off door like it fell from the sky."

"Manny will pay good money for this," Mama said.

"I'm not selling it. I've been needing a good chair, something I can kick back in when I watch baseball."

"Then what are we gonna to do about this month's rent? You already pissed your check away at the pool hall."

"I told you this morning, we'll pay it when we can. Why are you always worrying about tomorrow?"

"My family's not getting thrown out on the street again. It's embarrassing is why, moving from one apartment to the next."

"They don't have apartments in Samoa," I said. "They live in huts. They don't wear clothes either. They walk around, wieners and boobies flopping everywhere. I'm not lying."

John Earl laughed. Mama gave me a look and said, "You boys go do something. We're talking grownup."

We went to the couch. John Earl turned on the TV, but I kept my eyes on the grownups. "We'll sell the car if we have to," Squirrel said. "We don't drive much anyhow."

"Nobody would buy that deathtrap," Mama said.

"I'm not selling the chair. I never had luxuries growing up. When I was Mac and John Earl's age, I shoveled manure for the man next door and gave my pay to my dad. These two sleep all day. If I want to keep the chair, it's staying."

"We'll be homeless again, but that won't matter as long as you have a chair for your bad heart and your lard ass."

Squirrel flashed his teeth like a saber-toothed tiger. He grabbed Mama's gown and pulled her to him. He squashed her face between his hands until she was a rock bass sucking aquarium glass. "I'm keeping the chair," he said and burped.

"You're so romantic," she said.

She jerked away from him and stormed into her bedroom. Squirrel watched until she shut the door, then laughed and looked at his chair. "Romance is a crock of shit," he said.

I said, "Actually, romance is a passion for the strange and marvelous."

"Shut up, Mac, before I slap your head off."

The chair was genuine suede and had a wooden handle that made it recline. Mama couldn't figure why somebody would get rid of such a perfectly good piece of furniture. She thought it must've been a lawyer's or doctor's in its previous life. Squirrel said it probably cost somebody a thousand bucks. He bragged about it to Uncle Jimbo and his new girlfriend.

Uncle Jimbo came over some Saturday nights to get fixed with Mama and Squirrel. He's Mama's brother, runs a junkyard out of his yard in Union County. He wears a hunting cap with flaps like a dog's ears. He always carries a new woman on his arm and a wad of money in his pocket.

He called Squirrel a bargain hunter, then threw a plastic bag of crystal on the coffee table. Squirrel picked it up and said, "You know I can't afford this much glass, bro."

"This here's a new recipe I'm wanting you to try," Uncle Jimbo said. "I know you're good for it."

He came into the kitchen, where I was sitting doing nothing, took a beer from the fridge. He said, "Mac, why ain't you out hunting splittail on a Saturday night?"

"If you're oily you must have seborrhea."

"Damn, boy, what drugs *you* on?"

I thought back to one night when we were staying at his house. He took me to the video store in Maynardville in his El Camino. He waited until the salesclerk's head was turned, then snuck me into the 18+ ONLY! room. I saw some shit in there: naked women tonguing each other, black women as fat as Squirrel and holding plastic dongs, a blonde with shaving cream between her legs. Uncle Jimbo offered to rent one for me, but I said no.

His new girlfriend looked close to a woman on one of those boxes: her shiny pink lips, her tube top digging into her melons, the black pants sticking to her hips. Uncle Jimbo sat close to her, smoothing her hair against her neck, sucking smoke through a straw hooked to a plastic Jack Daniel's bottle. Mama and Squirrel took turns hitting an empty Blue Ribbon can, passing it back and forth until the hot crystal disappeared from its crushed center and they were all loony.

Squirrel went to the stereo and looked through his stack of eight-tracks. He put in an Emmylou Harris tape. My poor mama started to sing along with that sick crow voice of hers, but she saw me sitting at the kitchen table and quit. She gave me a look like she'd forgot I was there. "Mac," she said. "Run on, now. Go find your brother." And then Squirrel handed the can her way and she didn't say anything else.

It wasn't long before everyone was flashed. Squirrel switched on the strobe light and said, "This is damn goooood shat Jimson."

Jimson toasted Squirrel with his pipe. Squirrel turned the stereo's volume up and grabbed Mama, twirled her in mad circles. He bumped the TV with his belly, causing its rabbit ears to drop to the floor in slow motion. Uncle Jimbo and his new girlfriend danced in a wild daze. I watched the way he tickled his fingers along her spine, and the way his tongue flickered in the crazy light when he leaned to kiss her. I would've give all the sapphire in the world to crawl inside his mouth and hide, come out later that night when he got down to the goodies.

John Earl was at the arcade. He went with Mears, the big-eared boy from next door. They're best buddies, plan on joining the navy when they turn eighteen. Mears has a moped, and they go on dates together. They get stupid on whippets, ride to the arcade and meet girls, then take turns driving them to the shop on Coster Street beside the railroad tracks for hand jobs, blowjobs—whatever.

Mama couldn't quit smiling. Both of Squirrel's eyes looked the same. Uncle Jimbo had his shirt off, and his girlfriend was twisting his chest hairs with her long fingers. The apartment smelt like burnt plastic. My hands were going tingly. I went to my bedroom, opened the window and watched headlights go by like rockets on I-40. I took my encyclopedia from my sock drawer. I held it, thought about more books, how in the fall I'd be allowed back into school, maybe. I was expelled in the spring for carrying a knife. An older boy with freckles, who sat behind me in science class, threw spitballs in my hair when the teacher's head was turned. It wasn't so bad until the rest of the class joined in, and by the time the bell rang my head was covered with gooey wads of notebook paper. I told John Earl about it and he told Squirrel. Squirrel told me to quit being a pussy. He gave me a rusty survival knife, told me to use it to scare the boy. I tried to one day while the teacher was at the board explaining mitosis, but I dropped it on the floor. The whole class went nuts. The boy jumped on me and held me down until the principal came. Mama still has to go in front of the school board, but I think I have a good chance of getting back in if she's not stoned out of her brain.

I sat on the bed and turned through pages. I stopped when anything new caught my eye. I read about Rome and saw a picture of Saint Peter's with its tremendous dome. I read about a man named Samson who strangled a lion and slew a thousand men with a mule's jawbone. I read about a Roman named Romulus who killed his brother Remus for jumping over a wall. I read about Greek spirits called satyrs that live in the forest and drink wine with Dionysus. I read about Russian literature and a man named Anton Chekhov. He wrote about lovelessness.

Rain against the roof woke me the next day. John Earl snored beside me with a gob of red marks that looked like ringworm on his neck. I got up and went to the living room, sat on the couch. Squirrel was in his chair drinking and watching the Rangers play the Yankees. Mama was in the kitchen opening a package of headache powder. "We gotta quit letting him come over," she said. "We gotta get healthy. I need to lose about twenty pounds and not to mention your heart."

Squirrel coughed and said, "I've lived thirty-nine years with this heart and it's done me fine."

Mama shook her head, poured the medicine on her tongue, took a sip of water, and swallowed. She grabbed a black umbrella from beside the front door and left for work. She took the bus uptown five days a week to clean hotel rooms at the Hyatt. There were times when I wondered if she would walk out the door and I'd never see her again. I could tell she wasn't happy. She never smiled except when she was on Uncle Jimbo's drugs, and that was fake happiness. The one time I saw her smile for real was when Squirrel came home with a vase of flowers and a honey ham. But after dinner they got in a fight and Squirrel left for most of the night, went down to the pool hall.

I asked Mama once why we didn't find a better place to live, a place with a yard and a tree or two to climb. She said we were broke. I asked her why she didn't go with somebody richer than Squirrel. She said she owed Squirrel for sticking with her through the hard times, like when she was so sick her hair kept falling out.

On TV, Nolan Ryan threw a slider that barely missed the outside corner, walking the bases loaded with Yankees. Squirrel almost choked on his beer. "I'll be glad when that skinny son of a bitch retires," he said. "He's not thrown but five strikes all day. I could get out there right now and put one down the pike. Couldn't I, Mac?"

"I don't know," I said.

"You don't know?" he said, cocking his head to the side like a yellow-bellied sapsucker. "You don't know much, boy."

Before Squirrel caught a Greyhound north, he lived in Arlington, Texas. When he was John Earl's age, he pitched baseball for his high school. He used to tell us about how pro scouts would come just to watch him adjust his jockstrap, how he would've went far had a horse not kicked him in his right eye. After that he wasn't able to see good enough to pitch strikes the same or throw out runners at second.

I looked at the living room window and the Coke bottles lining its windowsill. I wished I'd been alive when the World's Fair was in town. Mama said people came in from every country on earth. She said there was boxed milk you didn't have to keep cold, robots that talked to you, games, rides, dancing, and singing for six straight months. She said they served food in the Sunsphere. She said it was the most colorful she's ever seen the city. Squirrel said it was all a big mistake and wouldn't be back because everybody found out we didn't have a thing to offer the rest of the world. Beyond the window I saw the interstate and the cloud of mist that hovered over the passersby as they whizzed along in an eternal procession of traffic and people always with somewhere to go: San Antonio, St. Louis, the Rocky Mountains, Rivière Du Loup, wherever, and the planes always up high, above all the bad air, packed with folks heading someplace.

During a commercial John Earl shuffled into the living room smearing his face. He sat next to me. Squirrel glanced over and saw the red marks on his neck. "What the hell's wrong with your neck, boy? Looks like the measles. Who did that?"

"Elena."

"The girl who lost her shoe? She's a wildcat ain't she?"

John Earl couldn't hide his proud grin. Squirrel turned his can up, looked at me. "What's wrong with you, Mac? I never seen any hickeys on your neck. You ain't fag are you?"

"No," I said. "I'm a Satanist."

"He's a fag," said John Earl.

"I'm not fag," I said.

"You never got no mud for your turtle."

"You don't know."

Squirrel stood up and patted his belly. "I gotta get my mind off this bad excuse for a ballgame," he said. "You shits stay out of my chair."

He took a beer can from the trash and went to his bedroom. As soon as he closed the door I said to John Earl, "You ever think about killing that asshole?"

"Why would I wanna do that?"

"To make things better around here."

"I won't be here much longer. In two years me and Mears are

sailing the world on a submarine."

"What about until then?"

"How would you kill him anyhow?" John Earl said and hopped into Squirrel's chair. His rattail fell over his shoulder and lay against one side of his chest.

"I don't know. We could scalp him or use poison darts like the Sans. If there were scorpions around here, we could drop a bunch of them in his covers at night."

"Man, you need to get your nose out of that book. Come with me and Mears one night, and you'll be so happy you won't worry about killing nobody."

"I might."

"You'd rather sit in your room and read your sissy book. That's what fags do—read," he said and put his hands up like he was holding a book. He licked his thumb, acted like he was turning pages. "Let's see," he said in a girl's voice. "Is the word 'cock' in here?"

"'Cock' don't start with a *R* or *S*, dumbass. At least I *can* read."

"Least I ain't fag. You've never even had a girlfriend."

"Uh-huh."

"Who, Rachel? Man, she don't count. You didn't even kiss her."

Rachel was a Jewish girl from Seattle. Squirrel called her a Heeb, whatever that means, but she was the nicest person I ever met. She stayed at the motel a few blocks down from our old apartment. She had hair the color of the Rosetta stone, and she always smelled like Ivory soap. One day when I was screwing around in the parking lot, kicking rocks, I saw her on the sidewalk. She was riding a bicycle with purple pompons coming out of the handles. She tried to pop wheelies but kept falling off, dropping the bicycle against the sidewalk and giggling to herself. She noticed me watching and hollered, asked if I knew how to do it. I did, so I went over and showed her. I spent the rest of the day showing her, and by that night we were friends.

She didn't know her mother, and her dad was always working, so we'd sit on the bed of her motel room, looking at my encyclopedia until late at night. I liked the way her voice sounded when she read, and she didn't have problems with words like *schnauzer* or *samurai*. Sometimes she leaned in close to me and looked up for a minute like she wanted me to do something. I know now that she wanted me to kiss her, but then I didn't, so I sung the Star-Spangled Banner way off key until she laughed so hard she fell over on the bed.

Rachel said there were more encyclopedias at the library in town, and we planned on catching a bus, but her dad found another job in Nashville and we never got to. The night before she left, I pulled a honeysuckle vine from the ditch and took it to her. She almost cried when I gave it to her. She said it was better than flowers from a florist because it was took straight from the wild. She wrote a note on the inside cover of my encyclopedia:

Dear Mac,
I love the pretty honeysuckles. I'll never forget the times we spent reading about Robin Goodfellow, Rotterdam, and scabies (ouch!). I'll think of you every time I hear the Star-Spangled Banner.
Love,
Rachel

Afterward she lay stretched across the bed for a long time, looking at the ceiling. The room was quiet except for the rattling air conditioner and the interstate traffic outside. Rachel looked like a seraph with her soft white skin and her dad's T-shirt hanging past her knees. When she fell asleep, I didn't feel her tits or slide my hand down her silky panties, no, I leaned over and put my cheek against hers, breathed her in for the last time.

Me and John Earl were on the floor playing Chinese checkers when Mama came home from work. Squirrel was in his chair with his hat tilted over his face. Mama's hair was tangled and wet. "It's pouring out there," she said, stomping at the door. She put two boxes from KFC on the table beside the wax grapes and bananas. She said, "Come eat, boys," and went to her bedroom.

Me and John Earl hadn't ate all day. We ran to the kitchen, took paper plates from the pantry. One box had six fried chicken breasts in it and the other mashed potatoes and biscuits. Mama came back with a towel on her head. She grabbed a plate, sat beside me. She looked at Squirrel. "All that man does is play pool, watch baseball, drink, and sleep," she said. "Squirrel, wake up and come eat."

"When's he gonna get that surgery?" John Earl said.

"When we find an insurance company to pay for it."

I searched the box for a chicken breast. "Where's all the chicken?" I said.

"Your brother's hogging it," she said. "John Earl, give Mac a breast and put the others back in the box."

John Earl threw a breast at me, and I caught it just before it fell to the floor. "Dumbass," I said.

"I'll show you dumbass," he said and stood up with his fists at his sides.

"Sit down and eat," Mama said. "You two are at the dinner table."

John Earl gave me a look and sat down. I said, "In Camelot they sit at a round table so everybody's equal."

"Where the hell's Camelot? Canada?" Mama said.

"Yeah, Canada," I said.

"That don't make sense," John Earl said. "This world's round and nobody's equal."

"It's not round like a table," I said.

Mama took a breast between her fingers. She licked her thumb, looked at Squirrel. "Squirrel, come eat."

"We can hide the boxes and tell him we ate Beanie Weenies," John Earl said.

"That's all you'll be eating if you don't get a job," Mama said. "It'd help if you cut that hair and quit running with Mears."

"I'll get me a job," I said.

"Maybe next year when you turn fourteen."

John Earl finished his chicken and reached into the box for more. Mama slapped his hand. "Wait for Squirrel," she said. "He'll be hungry when he wakes up."

"I wish he wouldn't wake up," I said.

"You'd feel horrible," Mama said and looked in Squirrel's direction. "Squirrel, come eat."

It wasn't unusual for him to sleep two or three hours straight on Sundays, but when there was food in the house he was usually awake. Mama spit gristle into her napkin. "I can't believe this food's not waking him up. Squirrel, wake up." She waited a minute. "That chair must be comfortable," she said and started for the living room.

When her back was turned, John Earl snatched the rest of my chicken breast and wolfed it down. I threw a biscuit at him. It missed, went sliding across the floor. He sprang up and started for my face with a spoonful of potatoes. I grabbed his wrist with one hand and reared back to throw a punch with the other. This surprised him so much he stood there for a minute, looking at me like he thought I was Maximilien Robespierre back from the guillotine or something. But I didn't hit him. I knew he would pound me. He dropped the spoon and jerked his hand away. He went for my neck, but before he reached it, we heard Mama. She was hunkered beside Squirrel's chair. "Hush, damn it," she said, raising a trembling fist at us.

She lifted Squirrel's Rangers cap. I couldn't see his face from the kitchen, but something about it scared her so bad she let his hat fall back to his face, squealed, and circled the living room in a panic. "What's wrong?" I said to John Earl.

He shrugged his shoulders. Mama's eyes were desperate. She breathed like she couldn't swallow enough air. She went to the phone on the kitchen wall, but her hands shook so bad she couldn't hold it. She left it hanging and put her hands to her face like she was praying. She started circling the living room again, making the Coke bottles on the windowsill chime together. She stopped and looked at Squirrel, the skin on her cheeks getting tight over her jawbones like her face was about to bust. "You son of a bitch," she hollered. "You fat son of a bitch."

She tore the waterlogged towel from her head and threw it at him. It hit his chest with a thud, but he didn't move. John Earl dropped his chicken, and we watched Mama march around the living room yanking her hair. She fell to the couch and buried her face in its cushions. I hurried to her. "Mama, what's the matter?" I said.

She wouldn't look at me. Her color had left, and her whole body shook like she had the spotted-fever chills. I looked at John Earl. He was fixed to his seat, lips polished with grease, pointing at me. I stepped toward Squirrel. I heard Mama on the couch, her cries muffled by the cushions. When I was close enough, I reached out and touched his hand. I felt coldness. I took another step and lifted his hat. His good eye was huge and red, covered by a film of slime and staring dead at the ceiling. His other eye was as blue as it had always been, staring straight at me. His mouth was opened, his swollen tongue pushing his lower lip forward. A stream of drool ran down his chin. I reached to touch his glass eye, and when I did a tear bubbled up out of its corner. I jumped back. I dropped his Rangers cap and fell to the carpet. I couldn't cry. I couldn't speak. I couldn't blink my eyes. I don't know why, but all I could think about was the three rings of Saturn.

I was able to drag Squirrel's chair over to Manny's. Getting it down the stairs and across the street alone wasn't easy, but I'm getting strong these days, muscles like my daddy's, I bet. I had to do it myself because John Earl wasn't around, and Mama was still in her room. Since the funeral, John Earl was staying with Mears, and Mama had locked herself in her bedroom, not even coming out when her boss called or when the smoke alarm went off from me burning a pot of soup.

Of course, I'm not the one that killed Squirrel. His heart just finally gave out. John Earl couldn't quit looking into the casket. When Mama went to the bathroom, I told him, "You just wait. Any minute now a bunch of scarab beetles will roll him away."

He didn't get it, and I felt awful after saying it because Squirrel wasn't all that bad. He'd just had some bad luck in life, like anybody might.

Uncle Jimbo sent flowers. Squirrel's pool hall buddies was all that showed. They're the ones who got up the money for the casket and headstone. None of them was as upset as Mama. She reached into the coffin fifty times, fixing Squirrel's clip-on tie and stuttering about how handsome he was in his new suit, how he could just as well have been a doctor or lawyer if it wasn't for his bad heart. I kept feeling like I barely knew her.

Manny gave me fifty dollars and a buck knife for the chair. When I got home, Mama was in the living room smoking a cigarette, looking at the outline in the carpet where the chair used to sit. John Earl had come home from Mears's and was on the couch twiddling his thumbs. I walked over behind him with the knife, said, "Rodentia is the fag name for rats."

I took his rattail in my hand and before he could budge, sliced right through it. I dropped it in his lap, said, "Here's your Rodenti-atail."

I threw the money at Mama, said, "Go buy another nightgown."

Before I left, I stopped at the door and looked at them. Their mouths were Cheerios because they never saw it in me. I walked onto the balcony where I'm talking to you now and shut the door.

Look. Across the street Manny sings some Mexican song as he puts chains on the door of his pawnshop. A woman in a miniskirt walks past the Baptist church that used to be a gas station. Down on the corner the bums burn time around the Richview Apartments sign. Two hundred yards away I-40 is a blur of traffic and smog. Nobody stops because there's no reason to—no Roman wall or Sahara Desert, no Jericho roses anywhere.

The sun dips behind the mirrored bank building of the city. Sagittarius blooms in the south. Tomorrow I'll ride a bus to the library, read some books. I'll hop a train to Nashville, find my black-haired honey. I'll catch a midnight plane, fly to Tijuana, sell dope and call it rubies. Or maybe I'll stroll down to the arcade, get me some mud for my turtle. Nothing changes, only gets older. I swear.

It Wasn't All Dancing

Mary Ward Brown

In the morning a strange black girl in white uniform stood by Rose Merriweather's bed. Even her shoes and stockings were white. Like a fly in a bucket of buttermilk, Rose's mother would have said years ago. Rose's mother had been a St. Clair of Mobile, who had married a Pardue from the Canebrake, a family just as good or better.

"I'm Rose Pardue, of Rosemont," Rose had introduced herself as a girl. It had been her open sesame all over the Black Belt of Alabama. She fixed her once-famous eyes on the girl by her bed.

"Who are you, may I ask?"

"Your new nurse," the girl said pleasantly.

Rose pushed herself up on the pillow. The girl had a confident smile, quick eyes, small hard-muscled body.

"What became of the other one?" Rose asked.

"Your daughter let her go." The girl picked up a Kleenex from the rug, dropped it into the wastebasket Rose had missed.

Rose sighed. No sooner did she become used to one than Catherine fired her or she quit.

"Help me to the bathroom, please," she said.

This trip was the hardest of the day, since her muscles and joints had stiffened while she slept; but the girl was strong, steady, and kept her mouth shut. Once inside, Rose held onto the safety rail put up when she broke her hip.

"You can step out and shut the door now," she said.

The girl didn't move. "You daughter said to don't never leave you."

"My daughter's not here, though, is she?" Rose raised one eyebrow and wiggled it, an old trick of hers. She was a beauty, people had said in her day, but also fun. In demand every minute. Her father, a tease, had called her the "Sigma Chi Sweetie," though her hair wasn't gold, her eyes not the blue of the song, and her beaus mostly SAEs and Phi Delta Thetas. Her eyes had been "dark and mysterious." Like sapphires, she'd been told.

The girl turned and went out, closing the door behind her. Straight face. No smile.

Back in bed, a cup of steaming coffee in her hand, Rose watched her new companion transfer a small Spode coffeepot from tray to bedside table. The pot was from a breakfast set Rose had forgotten she ever owned.

Nervy of the girl to get it out, though, she thought. And what if she broke it? Well, Catherine wouldn't want those dishes anyway, just because they'd been hers. Might as well use and enjoy them.

"What's your name, new nurse?" she asked.

"Etta. Etta Mae Jones." Slight pause. "You ready for some breakfast?"

Rose had already placed herself for the day. This was her own tester bed in her own house—hers and Allen's, though Allen had been dead for years now. Some days she thought she was back in the country, back in the home of her childhood, in spite of the fact that she knew very well that house was no longer even in the family. At other times, her problem was worse. She'd wake up to find several days had gone by without her knowing anything about it. There would be Monday and Tuesday, then nothing at all until Friday. Wednesday and Thursday would be wiped out completely.

The doctor wouldn't tell her what was wrong with her, if he knew, except that he thought it was age-related.

"How old did you say you were?" he would ask, a sudden twinkle in his eyes.

She would look at him, as over the edge of a fan. "I didn't say," she would tell him.

She'd get a new pill of a different color. "Don't worry, sweetheart. You're all right. You could outlive us all."

The tray Etta brought was set with more Spode, and good silver. There was orange juice in a pressed-glass tumbler, a soft-boiled egg with toast and crisp bacon. Everything just right, as in the days of trained servants, and Rose was suddenly hungry. Starving.

"Very good!" she said, when Etta came back for the well-cleaned tray. "Thank you." She pointed to the egg cup. "I haven't seen one of these in years. I'm surprised you knew what it was."

Etta looked at her directly. "Mrs. Fitzhugh Greene, that I stayed with so long, wouldn't have her egg no other way," she said.

"But where'd you find all these dishes?"

"You don't know?" Tiny nightlights seemed to come on in the dark of Etta's eyes. Her face lit up. "You got a jewe'ry store, right there in your kitchen. All kinds of stuff up in them cabinets. I been with rich folks before, but they didn't have what you got."

Rose had stopped breathing to listen, her mouth half-open. "It's old stuff, too, some of it," she said. "Handed down in the family. It couldn't be replaced at any price, ever. Besides the sentimental value…. Did my daughter tell you?"

Across a gulf of sudden silence, they looked at each other. Only their eyes seemed involved.

"You thinking about do I steal," Etta said, unexpectedly.

Rose's mouth went dry. She had no idea what to say.

"You don't have to worry, Mrs. Merriweather." Etta flashed out the words like a switchblade. "I don't take nothing. And on top of that, you don't have nothing I want."

She picked up the tray without rattling a dish, but her mouth was set, her eyes wide open. Holding the tray up protectively, she gave the door to the hall, which stood halfway open, a jab of her hip like a boxer's punch. Without looking back, she sailed out of sight.

Heavenly days! Rose thought. How did that come about? And what if she quit? Rose was ready to explain, apologize, beg if necessary. Anything not to lose her.

Down the hall, pots and pans began to rattle. Water ran through pipes. A dishwasher was turned on. When Etta came back, the expression she'd worn from the room had been erased. She picked up a nightgown as if nothing had happened.

So talent was touchy, Rose thought; and now black was touchy too, it seemed.

At last she got up the nerve to ask, "Etta, if there's nothing here that you want, what do you want in this world?"

"Nothing in nobody's house," said Etta, her interest obviously leftover and cold by now. Her attention was on all the pill bottles, empty glasses, and neglected laundry scattered about.

"That girl left this place in a mess," she said.

Later in the day, as part of the routine, Rose sat up in a chair. Once settled, she turned her face toward the window. It was October and the leaves outside, though doomed, were still on the trees. Through blue autumn haze, the sky was like the tinted windshield of a car. She sat for a while without speaking, a far-centered look in her eyes.

"You think I'm rich, Etta?" she said at last, her voice like that of an old blues singer, saying a few words on the side. "To tell you the truth, I don't have any money. I've lived so long, I'm sure it's all gone. Catherine hasn't said so yet, but I expect to hear it any day. What will become of me then, I don't know."

Etta didn't waste any time. Empty pill bottles clattered into wastebaskets. Old magazines and newspapers were stacked up and carried out. Nightgowns were checked, refolded, and put back in the drawer. While Etta worked, they talked.

"You don't have no other chirren, just that one girl?"

"That's all. I didn't want any more at the time. My husband did, but I didn't. I should have tried for a boy at least, to carry on the name. What about you?"

"I don't have none at all."

"You didn't want any either?"

"Not unless I was settled down—good husband and all."

"You're not married?"

"That's right."

"No boyfriend?"

"Oh, yeah. I got one of those."

Rose drew a quick half-breath. "I don't guess you could say 'yes ma'am,' could you? Would that set back the whole Movement?"

The silence that followed was dense with resistance.

"Ah, well," said Rose. "Forget it."

Rose bathed herself sitting up in a chair. In a fresh gown, she watched Etta take away the pan of water and clean up the spills. A bed bath would have been easier on both, but would have cost Rose independence. When Etta had combed and brushed what was left of her hair, she asked for a mirror.

"Time to view the ruins," she said.

Once a day, in a silver mirror with her initials on the back, she looked at herself. As if to hide nothing, she no longer put on makeup. Her hair was drawn back in a thin ponytail. Her face had changed even in shape, had seemed to let go and fall, settling down along the jaw line and pulling everything with it. When she turned her head to the side, she saw jowls. Beneath her chin, loose skin hung like an old stretched sweater. Her eyes, above depressing gray circles, looked out as from a scene of disaster. The eyes themselves, once large and arresting, had shrunk and faded but were still familiar, her lifelong eyes. Her nose, too, though thinner and sharper, was the same. Otherwise no trace remained of the vivid girl or dark-haired matron she had been.

All in all, what she saw was a stranger, as much male as female, in whom she was disappearing day by day.

She handed back the mirror in silence.

One morning Rose fixed her eyes on Etta, who was dusting a carved chest of drawers. "You know something?" she said. "The name 'Etta' doesn't suit you. I don't care for that name at all. What if I call you something else, something cute, like Marietta? Or Henrietta?"

Etta shook her head as if humoring a child. "Don't make no nevermind to me."

"You could call me 'Miss Rose.'"

Etta straightened up and turned the dust rag over in her hand. "Naw, I just call you Mrs. Merriweather right on," she said. "That stuff all over with now."

On the mantel a clock began to strike, its measured strokes tamping down a silence that seemed about to fill the room. Rose drew a deep breath.

"I see," she said. "Then you be Henrietta. Marietta won't do, with Mrs. Merriweather. Too many M's."

Each day brought new questions and answers.

"How come your phone don't never ring?"

"Out of sight, out of mind, I guess," Rose said, in a moment. "Also, most of my old buddies don't have phones where they are.... My daughter calls up sometimes, doesn't she?"

"Yeah, but she times it to when you be sleep, look like."

"That figures."

"You got two grands. They don't never call?"

"Oh, no. They were turned against me years ago, Henrietta. I could be dead as far as they're concerned."

As if targeted, their questions and answers moved past ever-decreasing circles of facts.

"You had just that one husband?"

"Yes, just Allen. A lovely man, a cotton broker." Rose gave a deep sigh. "He deserved better than he got from me. For years I was nothing but a butterfly, just here, there, yonder. A husband and child were the least of my worries. Something finally brought me down, but it was a long time coming, I'm afraid."

Henrietta had stopped pushing the dust mop to listen. She looked at Rose. "You must have kept the house nice, though, and all like that, didn't you?"

"Well, I had a full-time cook and a housemaid. But to answer your question, yes, I did keep it nice. I had a flair for decorating—a 'touch,' people said; and I had something to work with. Furniture from my side of the family, and a collection of silver from Allen's. Big tureens on trays, wine coolers, a writing set. Even a pair of silver peacocks." She smiled, remembering. "The house was lovely, if I do say so, and I looked after it religiously. We polished that silver 'til it all but put your eyes out. My mother used to say, 'Before you sit down to read your Bible, sweep your front porch.'"

Henrietta was grinning. "Where your Bible at now?"

"Well, where do you want it? Out by my bed for show?"

Henrietta looked down at the mop, moved it absently back and forth. "You pleasured your husband at night, didn't you?"

"Pleasured him?" Rose was taken by surprise. "I guess I did, sometimes."

"You didn't cheat on him, did you?"

She had flirted, Rose thought, with too many; but it was only a game. To test her powers, she supposed. Once, though, it hadn't been flirting, and it hadn't been a game. She didn't answer the question. "I was wild enough, Lord knows," she said, instead. "I was what they called 'fast' back then, a 'fast girl.' Always restless until…"

"Unh-uh!" Henrietta interrupted. "Now I know what you was. A flapper!"

Rose laughed. She laughed often now, she'd noticed, and it made her feel good again. At times, almost happy. Dear, sweet Jesus, she thought in the afterglow, please let her stay. Just let her stay 'til it's over.

The next day she asked for her lap desk and wrote a note to Catherine. "Dear daughter: I like the new nurse you got me very much. She's the best one I've had so far. Please don't let her go without my consent. I'm doing fine now and don't need a thing. Lots of love, Mama." Her writing was large and shaky, but as carefully legible as a second-grade child's.

Then, without warning, she lost a few days. It was like falling asleep at a concert, except that when she woke up the concert was over and everyone had gone.

All but life itself had been stripped away from her. She had no self and no name. Through mental fog she thought of as hell, she had to get back to the bed in which she lay. Across the room, a chest of drawers appeared like someone from the past, someone she ought to know, saying expectantly, "You know me!" She knew nothing. She might have just been born. A blue velvet rocker, with a bathrobe on the back, drew the same kind of blank. Though she shut her eyes tight, tears seeped out and rolled down.

"Look at choo!" The voice was familiar, but she couldn't place it. A hand took hold of hers.

Holding to the hand, Rose opened her eyes. "Oh, God," she said. "God…"

The black girl smiled. "You better call on somebody knows you, hadn't you?"

In a flash, the name was back. Henrietta!

"Like who?" Rose said, trying to smile in return. "Who would you suggest?"

Henrietta brought a bowl of homemade soup, a glass of milk, and toast made in the oven. Strengthened, propped up on pillows, Rose waited to hear what had gone on during what she would call, when feeling good, her "temporary demise."

"Your daughter been here," Henrietta said at last. She was sitting in a chair beside the bed.

"Oh? And what did she 'llow?"

"She 'llowed as how we better stop having these spells, or she have to make a change-up."

"Change-up?" Rose looked hard at Henrietta, then lowered her eyes. "Did she say what was wrong with me?"

"It's nothing to say, like I tell you. You comes and goes, and that's it. When you wake up you fine, so quit worrying. Your new style magazine just come. Want to see it?"

"No, thank you."

Henrietta sat on a straight, cane-bottomed chair, a braided wool pad on the seat. Idly, she smoothed the uniform over one compact thigh, then the other. At last she broke the silence.

"Your daughter's not good-looking like you was, is she?"

Rose looked up quickly. "What makes you think I was good-looking?"

"Because you still got them ways. Airish. And your picture bes out, in different rooms."

"It could be my fault she's not more attractive," Rose said. "I was no mother, to anybody. I was out being the belle of the ball myself. I went off and left her with any black woman who'd sleep on a cot in her room. She has every reason to feel the way she does toward me."

The clock struck seven. It was dark outside. Henrietta got up and drew the curtains, then came back to sit by Rose's bed.

"Some chirren come up worse than that," she said, "and don't blame nobody. Besides, she don't have to be stout, and all like that. You didn't give her them weak-sighted eyes. You don't even wear no glasses."

"Do you know what she remembers most about me, as a child." Rose fixed her eyes on Henrietta. "A few smells, she says. Gardenias from my corsages. Hot cheese in the canapés I served at parties." She looked down. "Chanel No. 5 as I went out the door, then alcohol and cigarettes when I came in her room late at night…"

Both were silent, thinking.

Henrietta sighed. "She got a pretty face, though. She could get her some contacts, and fix herself up if she wanted to. Unless she don't care. She got a nice husband, like she is."

"Oh, yes. She's a good wife and mother. Very domestic, wonderful cook. Everything I wasn't."

"You fault yourself too much, Mrs. Merriweather. You all right— a nice lady. Everybody make mistakes in life. You ought to see some I have stayed with. Complaining every minute, couldn't please them for nothing. Your folks just don't know how to 'preciate you."

"You didn't know me when I was young, though, Henrietta. 'Spoiled' is not the word."

In the matte blackness of her face, Henrietta's eyes began to twinkle. "You had lots of slaves back then?" she asked.

Rose's eyes twinkled dimly in return. "Ho, ho," she said.

She wasn't feeling jolly underneath. The threat of a "change-up" was still in her mind, like the threat of death itself. Both would be coming soon, she knew. Just not tomorrow or the next day, she hoped.

Breakfast was cantaloupe, cheese grits, little sausages and biscuits. Why so special? Rose wondered. She took her time and enjoyed it all, good food on a pretty tray, thanks in part to Mrs. Fitzhugh Greene, the late Mrs. Fitzhugh Greene. "I was with her 'til she passed," said Henrietta.

As she leaned over to pour a second cup of coffee, Henrietta delivered the news she'd held back overnight.

"She thinking about selling some stuff out the parlor."

Rose was holding the cup in her hand. She set it carefully back on the table by her bed. "What stuff?"

"Furniture. Mirrors."

Rose waited. "No silver?"

"Just furniture, far as I know, and big gold mirrors. Antique lady coming tomorrow. Not to buy, just look."

Rose said nothing. While Henrietta got things ready for her bath—clean gown, towels, bar of English soap—she stared out the window.

"That's Pardue furniture," she said at last. "My Grandfather Pardue lived on a plantation and had twelve children. He had that sofa and chairs made in North Carolina for his wife. They shipped it down by boat, my father said." She paused. "As a child, I loved to sit on that sofa and feel the velvet with my hands. I thought all velvet was that faded blue color."

Henrietta brought a pan of hot water and a fresh bath rag. She tested the water with her fingers and flipped them dry over the pan, not touching Rose's towels.

"Tomorrow, you say?" Rose asked. "Could we keep my door shut? I don't want to see her unless I have to."

"You don't have to do nothing. That's how come I'm here."

For the rest of the day Rose was quiet. All afternoon she lay in the darkening room without turning on a reading light. She couldn't eat her supper when it came.

At bedtime Henrietta brought a cup of Ovaltine and sat down by the bed. "Everything be all right," she said, like a spoken lullaby. "She won't do it 'less she have to, she say. Your money getting low."

"I know," Rose said. "Now run on to bed and let me think."

After breakfast, with Henrietta still in the kitchen, Rose propped herself up in bed without help. When Henrietta came back, she was waiting.

"You know what comes next, don't you?" she asked.

"I'm fixing to cook us some collards. That's what come next. Frost done fell on 'em now, and they'll be good."

"I'll wake up in the nursing home, and you'll be looking for a job."

Henrietta bent down to pick up a pair of bedroom slippers. She placed them neatly by the bed, toes pointing under the mahogany frame.

"We have to be ready, that's all," Rose went on. "So let everything go, and listen. I want you to get something for me out of the bottom of my closet. It's in a round hatbox, under an old fur hat. Way back in the back."

She watched Henrietta shoulder her way past dresses on a rod and begin to set out boxes. Boxes of shoes came first: Delman, Amalfi, Bally, I. Miller. Beside them, Henrietta placed a pair of high-heeled black boots. The tops, lightly dusted with mold, flopped over on the floor. There were dated silver sandals, boudoir pillows rewrapped in gift wrappings, purses stuffed with paper to help hold their shapes, and a large pasteboard box labeled "Letters." Finally, Henrietta brought out the hatbox and crushed mink hat. Under the hat was a jewelry case of red Chinese brocade.

"She doesn't know about this," Rose said, untying the cord that held the rolled-up case together. From a pocketlike compartment, she took a charm bracelet heavy with charms, gave it a quick look, and laid it on the bed beside her.

Next came a pair of Victorian earrings of thin yellow gold. She held them up briefly, shook the fancy dangles.

"Mama wore these in the Seminary," she said, and put them down by the bracelet.

When she took out a round baby locket, she paused. "Ah!" She looked at the dented tooth marks, turned the locket over in her hand, tried to remember what was in it. She would open it later and see, she decided, and laid it down by the earrings.

Last she brought out a ring box of faded morocco. Inside, against a background of what once had been white satin, a large square sapphire caught the morning light. The stone, of deep but brilliant blue, was surrounded by diamonds like a frame. When it wouldn't go on the ring finger of her arthritic right hand, a hard push got it over the one on her left. On her hand, with its splotches like bruises and navy-blue veins, she looked at the ring and sighed.

"A man not my husband gave me this, years ago." She held out her hand for Henrietta to see. "I never wore it, wasn't supposed to have it; but he said it was the color of my eyes.... He wanted me to marry him, leave Allen."

Henrietta sat like a listening child. "You didn't love him?"

"Oh, yes." Rose looked at her. "I love him today, in his grave. But he was married already, with a wife and three children. And I had my own little family. Our paths didn't cross until too late, that's all."

She took off the ring and slipped it back into its slot. Silence fell like an intermission. Overhead, the sound of a plane grew loud, then faded.

"Wear your ring now," said Henrietta.

"No, I want you to give it to Catherine to sell. It could help a little." She snapped the box shut. "You can tell her I don't know where it came from. Just say I can't remember."

When Henrietta came back with Rose's noon meal, she was smiling. She put down the tray, adjusted Rose's pillows, and set the tray on her lap. Under a metal warming top, beside a slice of ham, was a bowl of collard greens, dark and shiny from the salt pork cooked in them, not too much but not too little for flavor. There was an ear of boiled corn, a crisp brown cornstick, two spring onions, and a small cruet of hot pepper sauce. A spring of fresh mint bobbed about on top of a glass of iced tea.

Rose looked at the tray. How many times had she sat down to a meal such as this at her own table? From his place at the head, Allen had served the plates. From the foot, she had seen to seconds, refills, and bread hot enough to melt butter on contact. For this she had rung a silver bell to the right of her plate. And always, as her mother had taught her, she'd tried to make mealtimes pleasant. "Shoot somebody later," her mother had said.

Looking back, she'd done a few things right, Rose thought. She'd stood by Allen 'til the end and hadn't faltered. She'd watched him go down year after year, no matter what they did or didn't do, and had braced him up as best she could. Though he couldn't speak at the last, his eyes had lit up when she came into the room. It hadn't all been dancing.

"Thank you, Henrietta," she said. "I don't know when I've had any collards."

"Give you strength," said Henrietta.

Rose ate collards, cornbread, everything, including a piece of pound cake rich with butter and eggs for dessert.

When Henrietta came back for the tray, Rose asked her to sit.

"How long before I 'goes' again, do you think?" she asked.

Henrietta was slow to answer. "Can't nobody tell about that," she said.

"What will become of you?"

"I be taking care of somebody right on. I don't have no trouble finding jobs."

They sat in silence, looking out the window.

"You never told me what you want in this world," Rose said at last. "I'd like to know before we part."

"What I want?" Henrietta frowned. "My mama told me to don't want nothing, just take what God send and be thankful." She stood up and took the tray. "Sometime He send a little satisfaction along. I be looking out for that."

Rose propped up on an elbow. "That's what you've been to me," she cried, staring at Henrietta with wide naked eyes. "A satisfaction!" She opened her mouth to say more, but something closed in her throat.

On the tray, dishes began to slide, and Henrietta had to stop them. "Naptime," she said quickly, with everything back in place.

Rose watched her leave the room, heard her rubber soles squeak down the hall. The kitchen door swung open and shut.

Rose made her way to the edge of the bed. Careful not to lose her balance, she opened the drawer to the table beside it and took out the jewelry case there.

Inside the locket there was nothing. No picture, no baby hair, nothing. As it lay in her palm, she could hear again a fat girl sobbing, bubbles on her braces. "Leave me alone, Mama! You don't care about me. All you want is for me to be alive." And later, the same girl, older and calmer but the same. "Why can't you understand, Mama? I don't want to wear your wedding dress. If Jesus came down and made it fit me, I still wouldn't wear it."

Briefly, Rose looked over the charms on the bracelet. One of her father's cufflinks; a gold cross from her grandmother Rose—Rose Lanier St. Clair, she was, a model of virtue but plain; a round disc engraved in old-fashioned script—Rose Pardue, Black Belt Cotton Queen, 1917; an eighteen-karat gold number 1.

Carefully, she put it all back in the drawer.

Stretched out at last, flat on her back except for her head on a pillow, she turned her face toward the window and thought of the blank from which she'd so far returned. A long shudder possessed her. She fought it off with a full deep breath, which she let out by degrees, and fixed her mind on the ring, the furniture, and a possible happy ending. The ring could save the furniture, Catherine could somehow forgive her, then she could forgive herself, and so on.

She didn't hear the doorbell when the antique dealer came, nor Henrietta hurrying down the hall to let her in.

When, on their way to the parlor, Henrietta looked in before closing the door, Rose was asleep. Pale, thin, neatly covered by the bedspread, she was almost like a wrinkle on the big Pardue bed, something a hand could smooth out.

ALL ABOUT THE MUSIC

Grayson Capps

I was conceived in the back seat of a Pontiac Tempest in Brewton, Alabama, and I first saw the light of this world in a delivery room in Opelika, Alabama. It was the morning of April 17, 1967. The year Woody Guthrie and Otis Redding died and the year of the Summer of Love.

My daddy was not long home from the Army and was preaching at a Baptist church in Augusta, Georgia. My mama was a pretty co-ed at Auburn University. When they found out about me they got married, and Daddy quit the church and became a student, too. They both got their degrees and certified to teach high school and we moved back to Brewton after they graduated.

The '60s hit Alabama in the '70s and something of those days is forever leftover in my brain. Weekends were an array of eccentrics, channeling Cannery Row or Greenwich Village, in and out of my life. I'm talking about at home with my daddy and my mama. Writers, painters, musicians, vagrants, and ne'er-do-wells reciting poetry, philosophizing, singing, dancing, and drinking.

I remember a man named Fred Stokes used to come by with his beat-up Martin guitar. Fred and a man named Bobby Long and my daddy would sit in front of a Realistic tape recorder drinking and smoking and singing, trying to get down a perfect recording, in three-part harmony, of Glen Campbell's hit "Break My Mind." Or some other song. Bearing down on it, trying to get it right. Without laughing before the end. Fred had this beautiful baritone voice that melded with the strings of his old guitar. Bobby had a high almost-pretty voice. My daddy had a full mid-range voice. It was all about the music. But then out of nowhere Bobby would stand up and recite "The Love Song of J. Alfred Prufrock" or something. He had a playlist of poems so long it would take a notebook-and-a-half to write all the titles down. Bobby would raise a toast to the poem or the poet or the night or my daddy and Fred with his glass of vodka and orange juice, and sit back down. My living room was a theater. "Life is a Cabaret" was what was playing.

We moved to Fairhope, Alabama, when I was in about the seventh grade and, *what else?* I got involved with theater. I got a partial scholarship to Tulane University in New Orleans. I majored in theater, and I studied acting. I graduated in 1989 with a BFA.

At the same time, after class I started playing guitar with Pete Ficht, a bass player who was also a grad student. We kicked-in a drummer, another Tulane acting student, Sterling Roig. The music was together enough that we started a band called the House Levellers. We called our music "thrash-folk." Within a year following graduation, we signed with Tipitina's record label in New Orleans.

We bought a 1977 Plymouth Voyager van and toured America for three years nonstop. We were on the cover of USA *Today*, we were in *Sassy Magazine*. We were opening up for Crowded House. We were getting famous. We were mostly flat broke, sleeping on people's floors or in the van, barely able to afford gas to get to the next gig. We were theater majors acting like musicians. Too much junk food, too much time on the road, and too little money climaxed in a huge blowout in Charleston, West Virginia. I quit the band. I was twenty-two going on fifty.

Back in New Orleans without two nickels to rub together, wondering what to do, when my friends John Lawrence and John Dawson discovered a stretch of houses on the railroad tracks off Tchoupitoulas Street in New Orleans. Sign on the street corner said South Front Street. But it was Cannery Row, at least for me.

Allen Crane was our landlord, a one-legged man who drove a rusted-out station wagon. He went bankrupt and died soon after we moved in. We weren't sure what would come next. We waited. There were these two shotgun doubles next door to us that Allen owned and after his death nobody claimed them. No signs went up. Nobody came around to check them out. So we moved in. We stayed there rent-free for a couple of years. We played music on the streets for food and ran extension cords to Dawson's shotgun for electricity. We tapped into the water main for running water and in-door plumbing. I had the gas hook-up, so we cooked at my house. John Lawrence had a wood-burning stove that kept us warm in the wintertime. It would glow red and you could light cigarettes off of it. Lawrence practiced his guitar and I was writing songs and playing my guitar and we got our street corner act on stage. We called our band Stavin' Chain.

In Stavin' Chain, I sung lead vocals and played rhythm guitar. John Lawrence played lead guitar. We hired rhythm sections. The music was slide-driven roots rock. Our lyrics told stories about characters full of desperation, nicotine, loneliness, and alcohol.

One night after a show at the Maple Leaf Bar, two young women introduced themselves to us: Shainee Gabel and Kristin Hahn. They were filming a documentary called *Anthem* and they wanted us to do the music. Shainee and Kristin said we were part of the Americana they wanted to portray in their film. They used five of our songs in *Anthem* and we went to L.A. and New York to promote the movie's debut.

During those months we were also opening for bands like the Wallflowers, Koko Taylor, and Jeff Buckley. Back in New Orleans one night at Tipitina's in walked Ron Wood and Mick Jagger. The Rolling Stones were in town. And so Ron Wood sat in with us for a twenty-minute version of "Hideaway" while Mick Jagger sat at the bar drinking water. It seemed like success was just kind of sneaking up on us, encircling us like cigarette smoke from an ashtray. We got signed to Ruf Records, a German label. We put out a CD distributed by Polygram Records. Our rhythm section had played on the Stones' record *Bridges to Babylon* and in Keith Richards' band the Expensive Winos. We had international distribution and a full-page ad in the *Village Voice*. We toured the United States and Europe. Success seemed inevitable.

Then Polygram merged with Universal and dropped our record along with many others across the country. *Wall of Sound* magazine called our record "the best 1999 album you never heard of." Our record label went bankrupt, and my girlfriend was pregnant. South Front Street was a million miles away. This was Reality Check 101. Our flash of fame and fortune shrunk like the silver glow of an old TV picture tube. All that was left was a ghostly little point of light in the middle of a fat olive-drab screen. I can hear Dawson saying, "Feed me!" Our band broke up, and, all over again it was just me writing my songs and playing my guitar.

I was still in touch with Shainee, and I remember asking her what she was going to do after *Anthem* played itself out. She said she wanted to write and direct a film that was set in New Orleans. Said she'd look for a story that caught and conveyed the town. I told her about a book my daddy wrote that I believed did that. His novel was based on Bobby Long and Fred Stokes, had never been published, and their story was placed right in the middle of New Orleans. When I gave it to her, she fell in love with the book and wrote a screenplay based on it. Shainee told me if it ever made it into production, she would want me to help with the music in the film. This was 1997, 1998 or so. I forgot about it. I played my music when I could, worked a day job when I had to. Then, this past June 2003 she called and said she found backing for the movie, the film crew would hit New Orleans in July, and wants me to work on the soundtrack and be in the movie. She said John Travolta would be playing Bobby Long and Scarlett Johansson would be playing the girl from my daddy's novel.

In the music business, you hear lots of talk about stuff that might happen. Hopes get up high like a kite caught in the wind along the levee. Then the string breaks. But *A Love Song for Bobby Long* was filmed from late July through August, and I am in the movie singing and playing my guitar. The movie is named after a song I wrote in defense of Bobby called "A Love Song for Bobby Long." I taught John Travolta some of the songs I remember Fred Stokes singing with Bobby Long and my daddy. The film is supposed to be released this year, in the summer or fall of 2004. I've got six songs in the movie. Much of the set for the film was a re-creation of South Front Street.

I've been playing guitar and singing for nearly twenty years now.

I've played theaters, festivals, radio shows, TV shows, whiskey-and-beer-stinking barrooms, living rooms, and campfires. I write songs that seem to raise the voice of dead prophets masquerading as town drunks screaming, "Look at us—we're pretty, too!" People come up to me when the band's on break, or when we're breaking it down and packing it up, and they sometimes call me a preacher, or somebody says I'm a poet, I'm a singer, or a guitar player. Maybe I'm just an actor strutting and fretting across the stage. Catch me on my day job and I'm a landscaper. I still have to use a shovel if I want to eat. I still have to dig in the dirt if I want to keep up the mortgage. And I don't mind. I tell you what, I've got a beautiful daughter named Sadie, and I've got a house on Music Street, and I've got my first solo record coming out in the spring. Bobby Long and Fred Stokes are dead, but my daddy is alive and well in Alabama and about to have his first novel published. Nobody knows how long their kite's going to fly, but good songs are written when the wind lies low, and as long as I'm alive I'll still be singing them.

The Dog House

Jan Chabreck

Jay made a big deal about the dog again that morning when Marcy was leaving for work. Marcy brushed past her husband and bent down to pet Sadie. But Sadie was not content with the small bit of affection Marcy was willing to show. The dog jumped up on her leg, scratched at her black stretch pants, and stared up at her with a whine. "Jay, could you just hold her 'til I get out the door? I'm going to be late."

"This stupid dog is a pain in the ass," he said. He glared down at the dog and bit at the plastic mouthpiece on the cigar that was hanging out of the right corner of his mouth. Jay was tall and thin with a swollen belly, and his sparse blond hair had receded until it resembled a monk's. The smoke made his soft blue eyes squint, but he didn't take the cigar out of his mouth.

"Don't start with the dog. Just hold her until I get in the car, please." Marcy hated to ask Jay to do her any favors.

Sadie lay on her back, wagging the whole bottom half of her body on the blue and gray linoleum between Marcy and the door. The cocker spaniel ears contrasted with the dog's thin snout and short straight hair. Sadie had a collie face and a Labrador retriever body attached to bulldog legs. Pieces of blonde fur floated around and landed on Marcy's pants.

Finally, Jay took the cigar out of his mouth. "You know, she was lying on top of the clothes on the couch last night when I got home. I hate a dog in the house. My mother never would let us have a dog in the house." He said this while scratching his chest with his thumb and knocking ashes from his white T-shirt onto the speckled floor tile.

Marcy bumped Jay with her elbow as she headed for the kitchen door. She yanked it open and pushed the dog back with her foot. If she had given in last night and made love, he wouldn't be so grouchy. Marcy thought of his jumbled teeth smiling at her. "How about some,

Sugar?" he had said.

Walking to the car, she looked around the yard at all the trinkets she had made (venting her anger in constructive ways as the counselor put it). She had made ceramic dwarfs, little plastic windmills, and fiberboard cutouts of women bent over doing the gardening. The three cement Marys she had poured into molds herself were in the middle of the yard, encircled with rocks she had collected. All the little figures weren't that bad, but they tipped one way or the other from Sadie barreling through the yard. And the trailer needed washing. Green and black streaked the maroon and beige exterior.

The sound of Sadie's barking pricked at Marcy like a rash as she backed out of the driveway. By the time she made it to her job at Head Hunters Styling Salon, she was ready for a nap. She searched the black-and-white-checkered walls of the shop until she saw Angie. Angie had gotten her a job washing hair.

"Hey Marcy, I'm glad you're early. Want to try this new color? I don't have an appointment 'til ten." Angie was tall and her silver hair stuck straight up on top of her head in little spikes that resembled the Statue of Liberty's crown. She held out a box of Golden Goddess Hair Color and Shine. The girl on the box was smiling about her beautiful hair. Marcy tried to visualize her own face with Golden Goddess Hair. She didn't really want to try anything new since her spiral perm had just grown out, but Angie had always helped her.

She had stayed all night at Marcy's house the night they found out Steve—Marcy's first husband—had gotten killed in an Army training exercise, and when Walter—Marcy's second husband—and the cashier from Time Saver had slammed into the main dock at Guntersville Lake without any clothes on, Angie had been right there to ward off the gossips. Angie was a true friend, so whenever she needed a model, Marcy felt compelled to cooperate…even if it meant looking like someone's sex-crazed teenage daughter on a talk show.

"I just went to a workshop on this new color. I think it'll look good with your eyes, and they gave me six free boxes. You're in luck today," Angie said patting the seat of her chair.

What luck, Marcy thought as she pulled on the pink plastic cape, sat down, and held onto the arms of Angie's chair.

When Jay got ready to leave for his job at the Coca-Cola plant, he let Sadie run out into the yard. Dogs belonged outside. Sadie raced through the grass, tipping two of the dwarfs and pushing one of the fiberboard figures forward. Dead leaves flew behind the dog's feet like grass from a lawn mower. Jay threw a garbage can lid in the dog's direction, but it tipped the dog's tail and landed in front of one of the Marys. He picked up the garbage cans and propped them against the sidewall of the trailer before getting into his pickup truck.

As he backed out of the driveway, Jay rested his arm on the truck seat and looked out his rear window. Just before he reached the street, the truck stopped with a jerk. For a minute, Jay thought that maybe the transmission had jumped out of gear, again. But when he popped the hood and got out to look, he saw that the rear tires had tripped Sadie and crushed her chest before the truck had stopped. Sadie lifted her head a couple of inches off the gravel and wagged her tail weakly.

The dog wouldn't make it to the vet's. He would have to kill it. He took a short-handled shovel from the truck and knocked the dog in the head. He had to look to make sure he hit it in the right spot, but he avoided Sadie's eyes. Stupid dog.

Marcy would never believe that this was an accident. He would have to get rid of the body. He took off his red baseball hat and fanned himself. Maybe he should bury it, but where? Marcy would see a grave if she went looking for Sadie, and she would have to look because Sadie was definitely going to be missing.

He thought about looking into Marcy's yellow-green eyes and telling her that her dog was dead. She might let him put his arms around her and hold her the way he used to when they first met. When she was grieving over Walter, he had known what to do. But now things had changed. Now he knew Walter was nothing compared to Steve...Steve was the real heartbreak.

He had agreed to a marriage counselor, hoping they could talk, but they never talked about anything important. For one thing, she

JAN CHABRECK

was always gone to a class or a group or something, and when she was home, she was painting something or fixing something. The counselor had said she needed creative outlets, but she never stuck with anything.

Jay got a black garbage bag from behind the truck seat and scooped the dog up into it. Its head rolled over toward him, so he pushed it down into the bag first. Even though the dog weighed only thirty pounds, he had trouble holding the thing away from his chest and swinging it up into the truck bed. When he finally laid the dog down, he rubbed his chest and shoulders and tried to think of a story that Marcy would buy.

He decided to dump the dog in a ditch somewhere, so he rode around the trailer park. But kids and women were everywhere between the trailers and the gravel parking lot, and he didn't want to answer any questions about the bag. Maybe he should just bury the thing behind someone else's trailer. As he made another circle around the block, he spotted Star Baby staggering along the side of the highway across from the park.

Star Baby was the town drunk. He wore an unzipped mustard-colored jacket with no shirt and brown double-knit pants that looked like they belonged to someone's grandmother. His dark, matted hair sat on his head like a cheap Halloween wig. Every day Jay saw him wandering through the neighborhoods, mumbling and looking off into the distance. People said he had fought in Vietnam and had never recovered from the trauma, but it was hard to imagine him standing up straight, much less fighting a battle. The high school kids passed by him in their fancy cars and blew their horns to watch him jump in the ditch for cover. The guy needed a break.

Jay drove his truck to the highway and pulled over on the shoulder behind Star Baby. When Jay reached across the seat to roll the window down, Star Baby stumbled and fell back onto a mile marker.

"Hey, Buddy, you want to make a couple of bucks?" Jay said from the truck window.

96

Star Baby walked cautiously toward the truck and stopped a safe distance from the door. He swayed back and forth with his eyes focused on something unseen, but finally he directed his stare toward Jay.

"You want ten bucks, man? I got a job here. I need you to bury this dog." Jay put the truck in Park and walked around to the truck bed. He wondered if he should have kept the contents of the bag to himself.

Star Baby shook his head as though he could hear music. His eyes moved from Jay to the passing traffic and back, but he didn't answer. He shoved one of his hands deep into his pocket as if he were searching from something.

"You need some money, don't you, Star Baby? Well, just take this dog and bury it, or do whatever you want with it, and I'll give you ten dollars. I'll even let you use my shovel." Jay picked up the shovel and stuck it in the grass in front of Star Baby. He tapped the side of the truck with his knuckles. He was going to be late for work.

Star Baby walked around the pickup and pulled the bag over the tailgate. He smiled as he held the package to this bare chest like a trophy. He didn't seem to notice how heavy the bag was.

Jay stuck the ten dollars between the bag and the man's sweaty arm. "I'll leave you the shovel," he said again. Then he turned his truck around and sped toward the Coke plant. Maybe he should just call in sick. He'd already missed five days this quarter. One more day wouldn't matter.

Marcy volunteered on Thursday nights at the Seamen's Center, serving dinner to men in need. Most of the men were merchant marines (not real servicemen, according to Jay). But they reminded her of Steve, her soldier. Sometimes, as she scooped the vegetables onto the trays, she pretended that she was still married to Steve. She and Steve would be living in his daddy's house on the highway by now, and he would be working for the postal service. They had had it all planned. She winced as she thought of the two of them sitting on the porch of their own little house, holding hands and talking.

Today, she felt self-conscious with her new orange-blonde hair.

She wondered vaguely what Jay would say when he saw her. The counselor had suggested that she fantasize to improve her feelings about sex. Fantasizing, it seemed, was the best way to work out a person's hang-ups. She scanned the room, searching for a subject. Usually, no one at the mission offered her much of a sensual image, but she tried to detach herself from her problems and invent something pleasurable. She let her eyes lose focus as she looked across the tables at the men. Their rumpled shirts and mismatched pants were a hurdle for her, but their greasy hair and unshaved faces didn't really matter. She had, after all, slept with Jay for three years. The only real requirement was that their shapes had to be similar to Steve's. They couldn't have bulging middles or narrow shoulders. Absolutely no bird legs or spaghetti arms. And they could not weigh less than she did. She couldn't imagine anything if they were too thin because then they were Jay. If they had big middles, they were Walter. They had to be tall and well built to be Steve...even for an evening.

A heavy man sat at the end of the first table stooped over his turquoise tray...too large-framed. Another man sat against the wall and held his tray in his lap as if someone might take it. He was thinner, but he wasn't tall enough to work for her. She wondered where Star Baby was tonight. He was a real army man even if life hadn't worked out for him. Marcy always tried to talk to him. Shellshock had made him difficult to understand, but he was the right height. She could focus on him, and he could be Steve for an hour or so.

Tonight, no one looked remotely attractive, so she played out conversations with Steve by herself. Every day Marcy found it harder and harder to remember what Steve's voice sounded like. At first she could imagine exactly what he would say, but now she had to invent something to soothe herself. Tonight he would mention her hair. "You look mighty good tonight, Babe," he would say. "That blonde hair makes you look just like Olivia Newton-John."

On the way home, she had to slam on her brakes to miss Star Baby, who was shuffling along the shoulder of the highway that ran in front of her house. He was dragging a black bag and weaving on and off the road. She pulled over just past the man and rolled the window down to talk to him. "What are you doing, Star Baby? Is that garbage?" She nodded toward the bag.

He smiled and fell forward before steadying himself. He hoisted the bag up to his chest and stood as straight as Marcy had ever seen him stand.

"Why didn't you come eat tonight? They had lasagna. It wasn't bad. You might still get some if you go in," she said.

"I'm burying this. Or whatever I want." He seemed proud of himself.

"Burying what, Star Baby?" Marcy could not see the man's features clearly. Maybe she would sit there for a few minutes.

"I'm taking care of it," he said, as though he knew exactly what he was doing. Then he moved his left arm under the bag, revealing a patch of fur poking out of a hole.

"What is that?" she asked, feeling suddenly cold. She thought she could still smell the food trays from the center on her clothes.

The man started walking down the road again, his arms wrapped tightly around his package. "Are you coming?" he asked. Marcy wasn't sure he was talking to her, but she watched him as he made his way to the strip of ground directly across from her trailer park. He stopped and let the bag roll out of his arms and onto the grass. She rode along the shoulder until she was close enough to see what he was doing. He was digging a hole, right next to the road.

"What are you doing? I don't think you can dig a hole here," she said, keeping an eye on the passing traffic. The air was dead still as he dug, and she watched. Finally, she got out of her car and walked in front of the headlights. For the first time, she could see a dog's foot hanging from the shredded bag. A warm, tingling sensation ran up her back.

The man continued to dig, bringing up perfect squares of clay and piling them next to the hole. Then he tucked his head into the lapel of his coat and laughed, snorted, and started circling the hole. Marcy had started to walk back to her car when she saw the dog collar,

Sadie's collar. She had made it in a macramé class.

Pounding anger turned to energy as she tried to grab hold of the man's arm. How had he gotten her dog? He wouldn't answer her, probably didn't know what she was talking about. He murmured to himself and wiped his face with his arm. After a few minutes, she grabbed the shovel from his grip. It was Jay's shovel. Had he been to her house? Did he know she had been watching him, using him?

As she turned to walk back to the truck, she could hear his footsteps following her. She whirled around to face him. He could not be Steve, not for a minute. She swung the shovel at his head, but hitting a man with a shovel was not as easy as she thought it should have been. When she swung the second time, she hit the metal against his head. He staggered, but he didn't fall. She felt a grabbing in her shoulder that gave way to a cool tingle in her elbow.

When she climbed into her car, she realized she had not let go of the shovel. She didn't want to let go. Clumps of dirt fell on the floorboard. As she drove away, she could see the man swaying down the road as though nothing had happened. The dog lay somewhere on the shoulder, still uncovered.

As she neared the driveway, she thought about passing her trailer, but Jay's bald head was positioned in the middle of the living room window, reflecting the light from the TV. He must have missed work again…another small paycheck. She pulled in the drive and turned off the car lights. What was she going to do with this shovel?

Jay walked out onto the driveway, leaned against an aluminum post, and stooped to see inside the car window. "Got a new hairdo?" he asked. His lips were stretched over his teeth; he probably wanted sex.

Marcy looked at his pink, freckled face and imagined what he would look like with pieces of grass and dirt growing from every crease. Then she looked around the yard at all her figures. Sadie wouldn't be knocking them over anymore. Marcy's eyes washed over with tears. She held the shovel to her chest and stepped out of the car.

"I swear it was an accident. I didn't meant to hit her," he said.

What was he talking about? Hit who? Marcy walked through the yard, batting over the dwarfs and the windmills. She pounded a cement Mary with the flat of her shovel. Jay stayed behind her, ducking each time she swung.

"Marcy, come on. I'm sorry. I wasn't paying attention."

She turned and jabbed at him, nicking his cheek under his eye. A thick line of blood filled the gash instantly. He put his hand up to his face and blinked. Marcy felt her knees bending beneath her. She threw the shovel down, and Jay backed away as she walked toward the house.

"You're crazy, girl. I think you've really lost it now."

She went inside and slammed the flimsy metal door. The paneled walls of the trailer reminded her of the Seamen's Center. She could hear Jay's voice from outside, ringing in her ears like an unanswered phone. "I don't approve of dogs in the house," she yelled to him. She turned out the lights and watched him wander through the yard, stumbling from one dwarf to another until he was out of the yard.

GERONIMO

Brock Clarke

Geronimo's scooter was dead and his real name was not Geronimo: it was Dale Lerner. Dale Lerner was a senior football player at Clemson University. "Geronimo" was Dale's nickname, but his teammates had not given it to him, nor had his coach. In fact, the coach had repeatedly refused to give Dale a nickname over the four-plus years of their association. The coach's logic eluded Dale, but as near as he could figure, the coach didn't let him have a nickname because Dale didn't play enough to *deserve* a nickname. This was a cruel piece of irony to Dale Lerner, who was convinced he didn't play enough only because the coach himself didn't allow Dale to do anything but run down the field on special teams once, maybe twice a game. When Dale ran down the field on special teams, he screamed like an Indian. Dale wasn't sure whether this screaming-like-an-Indian business was the reason for his lack of playing time, or whether it was unrelated. He didn't care. Screaming like an Indian was his thing, and he wasn't going to stop for anyone.

On account of his signature behavior, Dale thought his nickname should be Geronimo. And so for the fall of his senior year he thought of himself privately as Geronimo, introduced himself as Geronimo, and people—teammates, teachers, regular students, graduate assistants, mascots—had laughed at his nickname and at how he had just gone ahead and *given* it to himself (which even Geronimo suspected he could not really do because of laws and etiquette and things). The nickname had not earned him invitations to team parties or earned him more playing time or caused even a single reporter to interview him. The whole experiment had turned out disastrously and Geronimo felt even more pathetic than he had when he was just a bench-warming senior with no nickname. Now it was the day before Geronimo's last game and he could not start his scooter.

It was a Japanese scooter, a Honda Aero. Geronimo had had it for five months. Geronimo told everyone that the booster club had given him the scooter, but they had not. The booster club had never given him anything. Geronimo had purchased the scooter from a blonde Kappa Alpha Theta sister for sixty dollars. The scooter was designed to bear the weight of the sorority sister, who weighed one hundred pounds, not Geronimo, who weighed two hundred and eighty. When Geronimo rode the Aero, the scooter looked not like it would collapse but like it would be pulverized. If Geronimo were the mortar and the ground the pestle, then the Aero would soon be dust. The scooter was bright yellow, the color of a canary or close to it.

Geronimo had a theory on why the booster club had never given him a scooter or anything else. The booster club's name was IPTAY, which to Geronimo sounded faintly Indian. Perhaps, then, the booster club was offended by his screaming-like-an-Indian routine. You could never tell who you were going to offend these days. In retaliation for the booster club's thin skin, Geronimo named the scooter *IPTAY* and chanted the word every time he approached his scooter or parked it or thought about it. Geronimo had said *IPTAY* so often that he began to think of the scooter as more of a companion than a mode of transportation.

Earlier that morning, Geronimo's mother had called him, and they had had an argument about his future plans.

She had said, "Dale"—Geronimo had not told his mother about his nickname and she would not have used the nickname if she had been informed of it, which was why he had not told her—"Dale, you are graduating next month, am I right?"

"Yes'm."

"Let me hear your plans."

Geronimo had no plans, really. He had the vague notion that he would someday become a police officer and visit local schools and tell the kids not to do drugs and scare them straight if he had to, and then hand out signed, glossy pictures of himself frozen in a three-point stance, which no one at the school had ever taken. He'd have to hire someone himself. Until Geronimo had that picture taken, he would have to keep his plans simple.

"IPTAY and me are moving home to be with you."

"No, you are not," his mother said. She was a muscular, sun-burned woman who worked on the county road crew, and she did not see the need for nicknames much and did not understand scooters at all. She loved her son but thought him dopey and a little dangerous. This was the way she had felt about Geronimo's father as well, and she had kicked him out and then let him come home several times too often before she had finally divorced him. She was not going to make that mistake again.

"What's your problem, Momma?" Geronimo asked. "Is it IPTAY?"

"That's part of it."

"But I *need* him."

"It is not a *him*," Geronimo's mother said. "Not a she either. It is an *it*, and an *it* is less important than a he, she, or *they*."

Geronimo immediately felt like he was in a class—English probably.

"You gonna be an English teacher on me?"

"What?"

"You *conjugating* me or something?"

"Yes," his mother said.

This response made Geronimo uncomfortable in the extreme: getting *conjugated* by his mother sounded much more taboo then he had first thought it would. He decided to retreat to his original position.

"I'm going to graduate in December, and then we're coming home," Geronimo said.

"Grow up," his mother said, and then slammed down the phone.

Once the phone had been slammed, Geronimo felt as if it had been slammed on *him*—on his toes or fingers or head. He felt like crying, which would have been bullshit, and besides, he was already late for class. So Geronimo went outside and tried to start his scooter. It would not start. Geronimo felt even closer to crying. He did a cursory check of the scooter's vital parts, which he knew nothing about, and then the gas gauge, which he could at least *read*. The needle was on empty. He had forgotten to fill IPTAY with gas. Geronimo kicked the scooter and in doing so he actually *did* hurt his toe and actually *did* start shedding these little sniffling, childish tears because his mother had hurt him and so had his scooter and now he had no other choice but to just *grow the fuck up*. What growing up entailed, he had no idea. And so Geronimo cried and did not try to even hide the tears. He just picked up his dead moped and walked it to class. The walking cleared Geronimo's head some. It occurred to him that if someone were watching him—which there was not—but if there were then they might have found the sight quite moving, this nearly-three-hundred-pound man walking his scooter to class and crying and not afraid to show it. The thought made Geronimo feel somewhat better. There was no one watching him, but if there were, there was no telling what they might see. They might see a *grown* man walking his scooter with *dignity*. Conjugate *that*.

The class for which Geronimo was late was his senior seminar in Modern European History. By some caprice of the university administration, history had become Geronimo's major. He didn't particularly like history, didn't know who had decided it would be his major, and didn't know why he didn't have a say in the matter. All Geronimo knew was that he had to get a C in this class if he was to graduate in December.

By the time Geronimo reached the building, parked the scooter, and entered the classroom, the class was more than half over.

"Mr. Lerner, you are late," the history professor said as Geronimo entered the classroom and sat in his seat. The professor—Geronimo could never remember his name—had been lecturing on post-Stalin Russia.

"Mr. Lerner," the professor repeated.

"Geronimo."

"Of course," the professor said. "Mr. *Geronimo*."

Geronimo and the professor went through this same routine at least once a week. The professor seemed to take great pleasure in being corrected, too much pleasure, so Geronimo thought, to ever respect Geronimo enough to give him the C he needed to graduate.

"Mr. Geronimo," the professor said. "Why are you so late?"

Geronimo told him.

"A scooter?" the professor said. "You have a scooter?"

"The booster club gave it to me."

"We're talking about the same thing, are we not?" the professor asked, scratching the very top of his curly head of hair. He was a slight, well-dressed man who squinted constantly. The professor did not wear glasses to class, but Geronimo suspected he was the kind of vain man who probably only wore them at home, while he was poring over his manuscripts or lecturing his wife about how awfully good Gulag caviar was. "A scooter is a very small motorcycle. Is that your definition as well?"

Geronimo said that it was.

"Is it right outside?"

"You know it."

The professor said that he did *not* know it until this very moment. He also said that there were certain things more important than Khrushchev, Gorbachev, etc., and that the class would now drop everything and take a small field trip to see Geronimo's scooter parked out in front of the building.

The class did not move for a second, to see if the professor was kidding. He was not kidding. The professor walked right out of the classroom. Geronimo, who hadn't wanted to be in the classroom in the first place, was happy to follow.

"You heard the man," Geronimo said to the class. It was the first time he had ever spoken to any of them, as a group or individually. It was also the closest he'd ever come to being in a press conference. It felt good, these eyes on him, and Geronimo did not want the feeling ruined. And so before he had to face his classmates' lack of response, he walked out of the classroom. The rest of the seminar followed.

Four floors down, they found their professor considering the spectacle of Geronimo's bright yellow scooter.

"Mr. Geronimo," the professor said, slowly, formally, in a way that seemed very European to Geronimo, and which infuriated him, "Mr.

Geronimo, your scooter is bright yellow."

"Canary," Geronimo said.

"You are exactly right," the professor said. "Canary. It is the color of a canary."

This remark drew a small, nervous laugh from the rest of the class, but the professor ignored the laughter. The fact that the scooter was *canary* and that Geronimo said so seemed to decide something for the professor. He smiled very thinly at Geronimo, and patted him on the back.

"Mr. Geronimo," he said, "you do not strike me as a man who is about to graduate from this university."

That said, the professor turned his back to Geronimo, and walked away from him and the rest of the class, his leather satchel swinging and bouncing against his bony little hip.

Despite the fact that class was over, which was good news, Geronimo did not like the professor's ambiguous sendoff one bit. Did the professor mean that he wasn't going to allow Geronimo to graduate, or that he couldn't believe Geronimo actually was graduating *already?* Was this merely the professor's egghead way of saying: *Time flies?* Geronimo couldn't be sure. He turned to consult his fourteen fellow seniors, who were gathered around his beat-up canary scooter like it was a dead dog that they had just found in the road and didn't know what to do with.

Geronimo surveyed the faces of his classmates. He knew none of them, even though they were all seniors and had been in many of the same classes together. He didn't even know their names. There *was* this short blond guy standing next to him who always wore cheap plastic flip-flops to class, even in the winter. Geronimo remembered something about this guy's name being Phil, and that he was from Connecticut. Connecticut, Geronimo knew, was one of the smaller states.

"Phil," Geronimo said to the blond guy.

"Yes?"

"Nothing." Now that Geronimo had gotten Phil's name right, he had reached the far edge of their relationship.

"Did the booster club really give you this thing?" Phil said, pointing at the scooter.

"IPTAY!" Geronimo said happily. The boundaries of his and Phil's relationship seemed to stretch a little.

Like the canary comment, this happy outburst of *IPTAY* seemed to be a definitive moment in the minds of Geronimo's classmates. A couple of them gave him distracted half-smiles. They cast one final look at his pulverized scooter. A girl giggled and then put her hand over her mouth. Then, all fourteen of his classmates simply turned their backs on Geronimo and walked away. Geronimo watched them, strolling in small groups of two and three toward the library or their dorms or the campus bar.

"IPTAY," Geronimo said sadly, softly, as he put his hands on his scooter and began walking to the gas station. Geronimo felt the world was collapsing around him. But was this possible? Could the world actually collapse? And could you arrest the collapsing once it started? His father, before his mother kicked him out for good, had once stopped their cellar from collapsing by using large floor jacks to brace the ceiling. It had worked, for about two months. Geronimo thought two months sounded pretty damn good. "I'd take two months," Geronimo said out loud. But a cellar was not the world, and if the world *could* collapse then it *would*, and there was nothing you could do about it. No, there was not.

Geronimo put gas in his scooter and drove over to a team meeting, which was convening on the main floor of the student union. The coach met each year with his graduating seniors, so that he could impart some wisdom that would do them some good off the football field.

"Fellows," the coach said, "if a man cannot be moved by the sight of young Christian women eating soft ice cream, then a man cannot be moved."

Coach was referring to the dozens of women swirling and pacing around the student union, licking soft ice cream cones.

"Men," the coach said. "It is some wonderful twist of fate that the offices of the Fellowship of Young Christian Women were placed next to the Polar Freeze Tastee Stand. And it is some even more wonderful twist of fate that Young Christian Women take an extraordinarily great pleasure in some soft ice cream after their weekly meeting. But it is plain miraculous that today, November 23, the day I set out to teach you something about the way the world works, that it should be so ungodly hot, and that soft ice cream should be so desperately needed. Men, you have had a perfectly awful season and frankly, I'm ashamed of you. But at least you have this."

With that, the coach grabbed each of his graduating seniors in a tight, back-pounding hug, and then walked away.

Geronimo knew there was something wrong with his coach, who was a short, perverted bald man who looked more like a doorknob than a human being, and who, after all, refused to play Geronimo more than twice a game even though the team had gone winless that season. This was clearly a sign of the coach's dementia. But Geronimo had to admit that there was something mysterious and wonderful about these young, straw-thin women with crucifixes dangling just above the scoop necks of their tank tops, walking two by two, licking their soft ice cream very quickly so that it would not melt and trying to talk to each other at the same time and thereby almost losing some of the ice cream, which forced them into taking this gulping emergency action with their mouths. In their attempt to save their ice cream, the women often put their hands underneath the cones, and whatever they caught they would lick off their fingers, off their palms, the back of their hands, whatever bodily surface the ice cream happened to drip on.

Geronimo found all this licking so beautiful, so *artful*, that he did something he rarely ever did: he spoke to one of his black teammates.

"You see that?" Geronimo said to the guy standing next to him, a black strong safety nicknamed Cheetah.

"What?"

Geronimo then pointed at one girl wearing a white tank top. The girl, incredibly enough, seemed to have her whole hand inside her mouth.

"I see a white girl with her fist in her mouth," Cheetah said back. "Yeah!"

"A white girl sucking on her *fist*," Cheetah said. "What'm I supposed to learn from *that?*"

Cheetah then stared at Geronimo, as if he had an answer to the question. Geronimo did not.

"Yeah!" he said again.

Cheetah turned away from Geronimo, back to his black teammates, with whom he conferred in whispers. The black seniors, about fifteen total, looked in the direction their coach had departed. When it appeared certain that the coach would not return, the black players simply walked away.

After the black players' departure, Geronimo joined the white players, who were for the most part still standing there. Unlike the black players, the white players appeared very content in their ogling of the Young Christian Women. Geronimo punched a boulder-shaped back-up center nicknamed Herkie on the shoulder. The punch startled Herkie out of his ogling.

"What do you want?"

"What do you think of that?" Geronimo said, this time gesturing at a redheaded girl with a green, ribbed sweater tank top who was slowly, deliberately licking each individual finger.

"I think," Herkie said, "that she likes you, Lerner."

Geronimo cringed at the use of his proper name, but he decided to let it pass in pursuit of the truth. The truth, Geronimo knew, was that the girl did not like him. The girl didn't even notice him standing there. Geronimo knew that the redheaded Christian girl was more in love with her ice cream than with him.

"She's not in love with me," Geronimo said. "She's in love with her ice cream."

"What?"

"She's a *Christian.*"

"What are you talking about, Lerner?"

Geronimo explained to Herkie that, as a Christian, the girl was not allowed to desire a man to whom she was not married; but she was allowed to love someone or thing *non*-sexually. This is where the ice cream came into play. Geronimo told Herkie that if the woman were allowed to love someone sexually, of course, then he would be a prime candidate.

This struck Geronimo as a beautiful, profound piece of rationalization. He was surprised it had come out of his mouth, his brain. He just stood there and admired the rationalization as if it were an expensive car, a Ferrari perhaps, or a Mustang, a kind of car to which Geronimo had always been partial.

"Bullshit," Herkie finally said. "She wants you."

Immediately, the profundity of Geronimo's rationalization disappeared, and he was forced to admit two things: Herkie was lying, and yet Geronimo wanted Herkie to be telling the truth.

So he allowed himself to believe that Herkie was telling the truth.

"Are you sure?"

"Absofuckinglutely," Herkie said. He pointed back to the redheaded woman, who had finished licking her fingers and was back working on the cone proper. "You go talk to her before she leaves."

"I can't do it."

"Are you not in your last month in college?" Herkie asked. "Do you actually have anything to lose?"

Geronimo admitted that he did not having anything to lose. "But what should I say?" he asked.

"Speak directly," Herkie told him.

This seemed like useful advice. Geronimo walked up to the girl, who was considering the sight of this two-hundred-eighty-pound man advancing upon her, his size fourteen shoes pounding and flapping on the student union's brick floor.

"Yes?" she said.

"I was wondering," Geronimo said, "if you would lick me the way you lick that ice cream cone." This was not something he normally would say, but after all, he was speaking directly. Geronimo looked back to Herkie, who gave him a sly, waist-level thumbs up.

The girl asked him to repeat the question.

"Would you lick me like ice cream?"

"Yes."

This was so surprising that Geronimo bent over slightly and made an involuntary caveman-like sound, something approximating an *oof*! Geronimo looked around to get Herkie's reaction, but he had disappeared into the pack of his hulking teammates, who were leering at the last stragglers among the ice cream eaters.

"Listen," the girl said after Geronimo made another involuntary *oof* when he saw that Herkie was not around to give him any further encouragement. "I'm almost done with this." The girl held up her ice cream cone: there was no ice cream visible, only the cone itself left. The girl took a loud, teeth-grinding *chomp* out of it.

"Yes," Geronimo said, barely getting the word out of his throat, past his dry, chalky lips

"Well, do you want to go somewhere?" the girl said, finishing the cone with one last snapping bite. "I've got beer back at my apartment."

Geronimo nearly made the *oof* sound again, but reined himself in. He was not sure what kind of Christian girl he had on his hands here, but Geronimo knew enough not to further jeopardize this good thing with more involuntary caveman-like sounds. After all, here he was, about to get laid by a Christian girl with beer and all he had to do to secure such a thing was to speak directly. Such a man did not do things involuntarily.

"I go with you willingly," Geronimo said. "We'll take my scooter."

"It's not good beer," the girl said, grabbing his hand. "But it's got alcohol in it."

The beer did have alcohol in it, and Geronimo, who did not drink much by virtue of certain team rules, drank two beers quickly and felt drunk. Drunk, he felt compelled to say something romantic to the girl, who sitting on her couch next to him, drinking her third beer, looking a little bored.

What Geronimo did not know was that she *was* bored, which was why she had picked up Geronimo in the first place. The girl, who was a school psychology major, was about to graduate in December as well. Immediately after graduation, the girl was to become a psychologist for a Beaufort, South Carolina, middle school, where her sole duty would be to dispense advice to acne victims and anorexic girls whose only sustenance was *gum*. The girl was bored already with her job and was ready to do something reckless. Sleeping with this oafish football player who wanted to be licked like ice cream and *said so* fit that bill.

"Your shirt, sweater, *whatever*, looks like a potato chip," Geronimo finally said, finding his romantic sentiment in the ridges and grooves of the girl's sweater tank top. When he got no response from the girl, he elaborated. "I'm talking about the good kind. The ones with deep ridges."

"What are you saying?"

"Your shirt," Geronimo said as he reached over and stroked the material. "It's interesting."

"Fuck all," the girl said, sticking her beer in between the couch seat cushions and taking off her shirt and throwing it in the corner of the room. The girl had on a peach-colored bra and her skin was peach-colored as well. Geronimo noticed that she even had a little barely visible peach fuzz of hair on her forearms.

"You look like a peach," Geronimo said.

The girl looked down at herself.

"Christ almighty," she said, and then unsnapped her bra, and threw it in the corner next to her shirt.

"How about that?" the girl asked him, her hands resting on her stomach, which was absurdly flat, more like a back than a stomach. "Am I done looking like food?"

The girl, topless, looked more like food—like a pair of peaches balancing on top of a graham cracker—than before, but Geronimo did not say so. He just sat there, feeling a little breathless and tight in the chest, looking at this bare-chested girl who was staring at him. She seemed to expect something, some sort of action. So Geronimo took off his shirt and threw it in the corner, and immediately felt very stupid for doing so. He crossed his arms over his chest, the way he had seen girls do when they were cold. The girl sitting next to him did not cover her chest. She just kept staring.

"My name is Geronimo," he finally said.

"Laura Ann," the girl said.

"Laura Ann, what exactly are we doing here?" Geronimo asked. The question triggered something in Laura Ann. She stopped staring and scooted over on the couch, sat in Geronimo's lap, and began kissing him, first on the mouth and then on the chest and then she began licking him *like he was ice cream*, as promised. All Geronimo could think was that this was exactly why he had never taken steroids. Many of his teammates took steroids and all the starting defensive and offensive linemen did. Geronimo suspected that he would have played more in his four years if he'd taken steroids himself. But he had learned from the literature the coaching staff handed out at the beginning of each season that *doping*—this is what the literature called it—led to certain *erectile difficulties*. Geronimo didn't like the sound of that at all. Nor did he like the sight of the pimpled topography of his teammates' backs, which Geronimo also knew to be a direct product of *doping*. And now here he was with his shirt off and no back acne to speak of and no erectile difficulties whatsoever and Laura Ann licking him like ice cream *wished* it would be licked.

For the first time, perhaps ever, Geronimo felt lucky.

It was, of course, only a momentary feeling. In the next moment, Geronimo wished he *had* erectile difficulties, for Laura Ann, while treating him like ice cream, brushed the back of her hand up against his crotch. This was the unexpected final straw for Geronimo. He came. Laura Ann knew it. She looked up at him wide-eyed and scooted back off his lap and back on the couch and, in doing so, purposely knocked over her beer onto the spoo stain on Geronimo's shorts, thereby saving them both the agony of talking about it.

"I'm so sorry," Laura Ann said, jumping up to get Geronimo a paper towel. But she wasn't sorry. Even before Geronimo's early ejaculation, she began to feel this whole ice cream treatment was not so much reckless as it was *silly*. Once she had worked her way down to licking Geronimo's navel region, she longed for school psychology the way she had longed for recklessness moments earlier.

As for Geronimo, his only thought was that if his teammates ever found out about his early ejaculation, he would finally have an officially sanctioned nickname. That nickname would be: Oops!

"Oops," Geronimo said out loud.

"What?" Laura Ann asked, sitting back down on the couch and handing him a paper towel.

"Nothing."

Laura Ann nodded and decided to make small talk. "You're a football player, right?"

Geronimo delicately blotted his crotch and said: "Not too much of one."

"You graduating this year?"

"History teacher on my back," Geronimo said. "I'm *supposed* to graduate in December."

"Me, too," Laura Ann said. "Come January, I'll be a middle-school headshrinker in Beaufort."

"I don't know what I'll be," Geronimo said. "IPTAY ran out of gas and I've got mother problems, too. It's been a disappointing day."

"I see."

"It's been a disappointing *life*," he told Laura Ann.

Laura Ann shifted uncomfortably. If licking this big booger like an ice cream cone had been silly, then sitting here on the couch with no top on, listening to Geronimo tell her how life was *disappointing* was out-and-out ridiculous.

So she tried to switch the topic.

"You ever watch people in the stands?" she asked him.

"Say again?"

"While you're on the field, the sideline, wherever," Laura Ann said. "Don't you ever watch what people in the stands are doing?"

Geronimo *did* watch people in the stands and told Laura Ann so. By watching people in the stands for four years, he'd come to the following conclusion: what people in the stands like to do is wave their T-shirts. They like to go to the souvenir stand and buy two Clemson Tiger T-shirts for fourteen dollars a pop and then run right up to the railing, a T-shirt in each hand, and wave the shirts above their heads and bug their eyes out at the television cameras and scream at the players.

"They really do that?" Laura Ann had never actually been to a game and thought it was a wonderful story. Inexplicably, she felt like having another go at licking Geronimo.

"They sure do."

"What do you say to someone like that?" she asked.

"What do I *say?*"

"Yes," Laura Ann said. "The guy in the stands waving the T-shirts over his head and screaming. What do you say to him?"

Geronimo had never thought to say *anything* to the shirt-wavers before. But now, by the tone in Laura Ann's voice, Geronimo knew that the right answer might lead her to reconsider her sexual retreat.

Finally, after some thought, Geronimo told Laura Ann: "There is only one thing to say to that guy in the stands. You say: 'I'm going to burn you like wood.'"

Geronimo had heard this line from one of his black teammates, a wide receiver talking trash with an opposing cornerback. It didn't make sense to Geronimo when he first heard it, and it didn't make sense to Laura Ann either. She eyed him for second, then put her bra and shirt back on, and fiddled around some, throwing away beer bottles and stacking dishes, until it was clear to Geronimo that it was time for him to leave. So he left.

Geronimo's mother was waiting for him back at his room. It was first time she had ever been to campus to visit him. Their house in Florida was six hours away by car.

"Son."

"Momma."

"Where's your roommate?" his mother asked. Geronimo had no roommate, but he had once told her that he did. His roommate, Geronimo had told her, was from California, Nevada, somewhere, and they were the best of friends and sometimes engaged in impromptu drunken wrestling matches, which Geronimo let the roommate win.

"He's out," Geronimo said. "You come to apologize?"

"I came to do this," she said. She walked over to Geronimo and demanded his keys. He gave them to her. His mother then took the key to her house off the ring and returned the rest of his keys to her son.

"What'd you do *that* for?" Geronimo asked once he'd realized which key she'd taken. He was flat-out *pissed*, and felt like turning over a desk or a table, but he owned neither. There was just his mother, the couch she was sitting on, and himself. And you could not turn over yourself or your mother, could you? A mother was not a desk and her boy was not a table.

"I did it out of love."

"*Love.*"

"You need a job, friends, people," his mother said. "Not me and not that little-bitty bike of yours."

"*Love,*" Geronimo repeated.

His mother sighed, rubbed her cheeks with her large, leathery hands. Geronimo thought his mother looked like some kind of fish, the way she moved her cheeks back and forth.

"You really gonna graduate next month?" she asked.

"Might."

"Might *what?*"

"Might fail history."

"Dale."

"I *know.*"

"Come here," she said and walked toward the bathroom. He followed her. She turned on the light. They stood in front of the mirror together and she held up his hands, palms out. The hands were meaty and red and he felt very stupid just standing there, examining his fleshy mitts. So he made his left hand into the shape of Michigan, a state and a school that had not offered him a full scholarship.

"Your history teacher have hands like these?"

Geronimo admitted that his teacher did not.

"He has dainty hands," Geronimo said.

"You know what to do," she said. "I'll see you at graduation."

His mother kissed him on the cheek and left him standing there, looking at the Michigan of his left hand. Michigan had not given him a full ride, but his hands were big and his teacher's were small, and that was something better than a state or a school.

The history professor was wearing gray sweatpants when he answered the door. His house was made entirely of stone, as in a fairy tale.

"Are Hansel and Gretel home?" Geronimo asked and then laughed and then thought better of it and scowled.

"They're both out, Mr. Geronimo," the teacher said, not smiling, not seeming especially superior or European, not wearing wire-rimmed glasses like Geronimo thought he would be. Geronimo pressed on.

"I want my C."

"Why?"

Geronimo held up his big hands.

"I didn't ask why I should *give* you a C," the teacher said. His hands were in the pockets of his sweatpants and he was flapping the pockets in a way that made Geronimo think of a parachute not opening all the way and the parachutist getting skewered by a tree. "I asked you why you *wanted* a C."

"What?" Geronimo asked, not quite getting it. "You think I'm not strong enough?" He punched his left palm with his right fist, making a wet *smack*.

"Come on in."

Geronimo came in. The house was a disaster of books and blaring

TV and beer cans and Berber carpet. Geronimo had assumed that his teacher was married, probably to someone much better looking than the teacher himself. But now it was clear to Geronimo that his teacher lived alone and probably rented the house. The beer scattered around was cheap.

"You by yourself?" Geronimo asked.

The professor didn't answer. He sat down on the couch. Geronimo sat next to him. Two white men were playing Ping-Pong on the TV, moving quickly but stiffly, as if they were arthritic dervishes.

"It's the goddamned Olympic trials," the professor said. "I can't stop watching them." It occurred to Geronimo that his professor was drunk, and that now was the perfect time to plead his case.

"I want my C."

"Table tennis is an Olympic sport," the professor said. "Football is not."

"The world is broken."

"Fix it."

"I will. Give me my C."

"Why?"

Geronimo had an answer this time. "So I can graduate."

"Why would you want to do that?"

This was another question Geronimo had failed to anticipate. He gave the professor a panicked look. The professor handed Geronimo a Pabst from a cooler next to the couch, and opened another one for himself.

"Let me guess. You want to graduate so you can get a job, for which you are not qualified."

"I'm qualified."

"No, you are not. Why did you come to this school in the first place?"

"Why?"

"Yes. Why did you want to play football?"

Geronimo paused for a moment. He thought the professor was

looking for a profound answer and he wanted to give the professor one. But he could not think of anything except for the answer all his teammates would give, which Geronimo did not think was true in his case. But he gave it anyway.

"Coach said he would let me hit people."

"Fine. And have you hit people?"

"Not too many."

"Correct. So now there is no more football and you are only qualified to drink beer and let your body go to shit. Before you are graduated, you are allowed to do this; after you've graduated, you are not allowed. If you do what you're not allowed to, which you will, then you will end up alone." The professor made a circling gesture of the house with his beer, spilling some on Geronimo's head. The beer on his head caused Geronimo to feel as if he'd just woken from a dream.

"I understand, I do. I don't want to graduate. Please fail me."

"Alone, Mr. Geronimo. Get used to it. I don't care whether you want the grade or not. You will get your C. This is how the world works."

"I know it is," Geronimo said. He realized that the professor was right, and that he would be alone for the rest of his life and there was little he could do about it. Geronimo thought about hitting the professor, just reaching around with his right hand and slapping the professor on the right side of the head, directly above the ear. But even this, Geronimo suspected, would not make him feel any better.

"All alone," the professor said. He drank the rest of his beer, opened another one, and drank that beer, too. Then the professor got up and ran to the bathroom and began retching loudly, so loudly that he drowned out the sounds of the Ping-Pong match on TV.

Twenty minutes later the professor came back from the bathroom.

"You feel all right?"

"I feel good," the professor said, sitting back down on the couch and opening another beer. "Tomorrow I will feel bad."

"Tomorrow I'll feel *real* bad," Geronimo said, thinking about the abyss of his final game and the larger, more terrifying abyss that lay on the other side of it. "You sure you won't fail me?"

"Positive."

"Then what am I supposed to do?" Geronimo yelled. "Just tell me what I'm supposed to do!"

"Tomorrow we will feel bad, Mr. Geronimo. There is nothing we can do about it. Let us feel good tonight." With that, the professor offered him another beer and Geronimo took it.

It was halftime and Clemson was down three touchdowns and a safety to Florida State. After his talk with the professor, Geronimo was determined to make himself feel as good as possible during this, his last game, despite his ringing hangover. So Geronimo had sat on the bench for the first half and dispensed advice to the freshmen, many of whom actually played more than twice a game. Geronimo's advice to the freshmen was this: Don't even think about screaming like an Indian out there. The team's place kicker had tried it once during a kickoff, the year before. Geronimo explained to the freshmen that the kicker, who had since graduated and gone on to the NFL, was from Slavia or somewhere and knew nothing about being on the warpath and didn't he have some balls to think that he *did* know something about it? So Geronimo had head-butted the kicker and then lectured him on his sole ownership of the kickoff whoop and war cry while the kicker was staggering around, trying to take off his helmet and get the bees out of his ears.

"What I do?" the kicker had asked once he'd removed his helmet and silenced the bees.

"There are no Indians in Slavia," Geronimo had told him.

"What?"

"I'm from fucking *Texas*," Geronimo had explained to the kicker, and he also explained this fact to the freshmen. This was not true, of course—Dale Lerner was actually from Florida, from the panhandle. But *Geronimo* was clearly from Texas, and being from Texas, thought that being from Texas explained everything that one needed explaining.

"Understand?" he asked the freshmen. They did. The freshmen

understood that they had played poorly, so poorly that coach had sent them down to the end of the bench to be lectured about Indians and whooping and Texas and Slavia, which didn't even exist, they didn't think. It was a bad day for the freshmen.

And it was a bad day for everyone, including the baton twirlers. It was halftime, and the twirlers were out there on the field of play, throwing their shiny little sticks up toward heaven and then dropping them and distracting the marching band, who kept having to break step and avoid the batons, some of which were on fire. These miscues made Geronimo feel very good about himself indeed. One girl dropped three in a row and started crying right there *on the football field*. Dale might have sympathized with her crying on the field, but Geronimo did not suffer it.

So Geronimo sidled up next to one of the male cheerleaders, who was watching all this from the sideline.

"She's a disgrace out there," Geronimo told him.

"Janine's dropped a few," he admitted.

"An absolute disgrace."

"What are you doing out here?" the cheerleader asked. "Shouldn't you be back in the locker room?"

It was true. Geronimo should have been back in the locker room with the rest of the team, listening to coach tell them how Florida State was tearing them a new asshole out there. This wasn't exactly Geronimo's favorite expression. To be true, Geronimo got extremely agitated just thinking about it. As he was standing there on the sideline, Geronimo kept whirling around, as if someone were sneaking up behind him. Geronimo could just *hear* Coach at that moment: "Do you know that they are tearing you a new asshole out there?" he would be saying back in the locker room. Then, the coach would pause—he was a master of this sickening, foot-tapping, dramatic pause-and-stare number—until a majority of his teammates would admit that Yes, they did know that Florida State was tearing them, etc.

"*All right*", the coach would finally say. "They are fucking you up the butt and you have said it yourselves. Now what are you going to *do* about it?"

What Geronimo was going to do about it was stand on the sideline and not admit anything and badmouth the baton twirlers. Of course, he couldn't exactly tell all this to the male cheerleader, who was still standing there, waiting for an answer. In the olden days, everything would be different and Geronimo could tell the cheerleader whatever the hell he wanted. In the olden days, you could accuse male cheerleaders of all sorts of offenses—homosexuality, lassitude, piss-poor spirit—whether the cheerleaders were actually guilty of these things or not. But it was not the olden days anymore and Geronimo knew it, and so he kept his mouth shut.

"Well?" the male cheerleader said. "Are you going back to the locker room or aren't you?"

At the mere mention of the words *locker room*, Geronimo once again whirled around, giving the male cheerleader a good look at the name on the back of his jersey.

"*Lerner*, what are you *doing* out here?"

"Call me Geronimo."

"No."

Then the cheerleader did the same dramatic, toe-tapping number that the coach did. What has happened here? Geronimo asked himself. Have our cheerleaders become our coaches? Have times changed that much?

So Geronimo, who was not wearing his helmet, head-butted the cheerleader. Just up and head-butted the cheerleader and let out this weak little dribbling war whoop. The whoop was so weak because the head-butting hurt, which it didn't when you were wearing a helmet. Geronimo closed his eyes so he didn't throw up from the pain. He wanted to throw up. He wanted to cry again, too. The pain was severe—sharp, nauseating electric volts shooting up toward his scalp, around his ears and down his neck.

When Geronimo opened his eyes, he was surprised to see the cheerleader sitting on the ground. The cheerleader didn't seem so much hurt as he was mad. He wasn't even rubbing his forehead; the cheerleader was just sitting there, glaring up at Geronimo. Geronimo recognized for the first time that the cheerleader was nearly as big as Geronimo himself, and that he might not take being knocked on his ass lightly. But still, the cheerleader *was on the ground* and Geronimo had put him there. He forgot all about crying. The olden days were back.

"What the hell was that for?" the cheerleader wanted to know from his position of sitting on the ground.

"That was for the olden days."

"What are you talking about?"

"I'm from fucking *Texas*," he said, and let out another whoop.

"I don't care where you're from, Lerner," the cheerleader said as he picked himself off the ground. "I'm not going to forget about this."

Geronimo didn't like the sound of that at all. But luckily, just then, his teammates came roaring out of the locker room. No one said anything about Geronimo not being in the locker room, and his teammates swept him along as they tore onto the field. Geronimo found himself whooping and beating on the freshmen's shoulder pads, and there was so much good feeling out there on the field that it was as if they were not twenty-three points behind; as if the cheerleader whom Geronimo had head-butted would not get up and exact his revenge; as if Geronimo himself had not been a scrub for four straight years and would not be alone for the rest of his life. Things became very clear for Geronimo. He knew that while he felt good at the moment, he would feel awful tomorrow, and would probably even regret the memory of all this good feeling. But so what? He wished his professor were in the stands so that Geronimo could point at himself, jumping around the field with his teammates who, for the moment, had forgiven his severe limitations or forgotten them or just did not care about them. Yes, Geronimo wanted to get the professor's attention and shout: *I am not alone, not yet.* The professor would understand, he was sure of it. Because he was having his moment—the fans were on their feet, eighty thousand yahoos screaming for him, and they did not distinguish him from his teammates; as far as the crowd was concerned they were all the same steroided warriors happily beating on each other—and for that moment, it did not pain Geronimo that he was a final-game senior with no nickname except for the one he had given himself. It simply did not hurt.

COLORED GLASS

Doug Crandell

She holds a shard of ocher up to the fluttering leaves; tinged light flashes from above, as if the sun has changed colors. Is it a piece from an old milk bottle, yellowed from the soil's rich phosphates? Next to the dump is a hog pasture; a whiff of manure is carried by the wind to the edge of the woods. Harper says, "Pew-ee!" as she fans the air below her nose, overacting, more like a child than a middle-aged woman. She places the glass over her right eye and giggles, a sound Leslie has begun to associate with a certain type of crazy.

"Oh, my," says Harper, plucking something from inside a rusty and nearly squashed saucepan. "Look, Leslie, this one is from a Milk of Magnesia bottle."

His mother's been full of contradictions since the operation, a trait that the boy thinks is repeated in her hair: some streaks of reddish-brown, loose strands of gray and white, and jet black spots along the crown, none of it following any pattern or predictability. She is just as inconsistent as her hair, he decides. At times she cries so hard she laughs and at others she chuckles until she tears up and runs from the house, descends into a deep depression for twenty minutes only to reappear from outdoors, clutching a bundle of dead phlox tied tightly with jute rope and carrying the desiccated weeds, scurf falling onto her coat, to the sink for water.

The boy doesn't look at his mother. He is too busy with his own glass. Leslie peers through his slice of amber at the hogs inside the fence. They look like they've already been butchered and cooked: the four white shoats appear reddish. Stick an apple in their mouths, the boy thinks, and they're goners. Leslie hates his name and that it sounds like a girl's; he wishes he and his mother could trade. Harper, he says over and over in his head, that's a man's name. Lately, as he's tried to grow up and accept it, the thought has occurred to him that his mother may have been cruel, giving him a girl name because she'd suffered a life with a man's.

Harper Royal, only months after her hysterectomy at age forty-five, has drug him to the old dump on the farm to search for colored glass. She'd met Leslie at the end of the lane as he got off a Friday bus ride home from school. Now in tow is her father, Basil, a man who can't remember his last name, let alone why the three of them are digging with hand spades through piles of garbage from the late '40s.

The old man has left the trash pile and is now standing near the hogs, whispering something to them; the sound of it drifts over the stinging winds of a Central Indiana March. He kneels down to feed them grass through the fence. Even though they have a pasture full of it, the pigs gobble down the fescue, root ball and all, from the old man's fingers as if it were candied blades of truffles. He stops suddenly from whispering and stands up as straight as his slumped back will permit. He is looking out across the steep incline of the hill, a swarm of sparrows dipping down in a rush, then upward again, flying sideways out of view.

"Good morning, colonel!" he shouts, saluting the pigs, the crisp bend of his elbow slicing the air as he weakly claps his feet together. Leslie tosses his glass to the mucky heap and walks to his grandfather's side.

"Grandpa, come on. Come look at this piece Mom found." He takes the old man by the arm and escorts him back to the pile. Leslie makes sure his grandfather doesn't stumble over the loose clods and metal limbs sticking up from the heap of dark loam. Once the two are next to Harper, the old man quickly reaches out and snatches the glass from his daughter's hand.

"Give me that," he demands, a big grin framing his stubbed teeth. Leslie wonders if the old man's face has always looked so womanly, with its soft rosy cheeks and full lips, the brow delicate and smooth. Maybe that's why he was given a girly name? Because sooner or later he'd look like his grandfather? He'd gladly compare his teenage face to his father's, but that would require a shovel and one of those computer-generated face experts, someone who could use technology to remake the features of a dead man, to portray him as he once was, Leslie thinks.

He watches to make certain that a squabble doesn't start between his mother and grandfather over the glass. Since Harper's hospital stay, many moments have required him to intervene, pulling father off of daughter over everything from the last Pop-Tart to joint sobbing sessions started from one or the other's memory of this farm near Fort Wayne. When they talk about it, it's referred to romantically as the Duffey Place. A name they used before it was their own, when they cash-rented the farm and the woman they loved was still alive. Rebecca was Leslie's grandmother's name, a name he finds shouldn't fit an old woman, because he's not yet able to conceive that we are not always young and can sometimes grow to be eternally old.

Harper doesn't even blink when the glass has been filched from her. She smiles and winks at Leslie, an inside joke about how nutty family can be, how we must trust our love for them and not doubt, or cause waves or think of the remedies for such behavior.

The pigs behind them get spooked when Basil cheers wildly after placing the colored glass over his ear. He shouts, "I can hear the ocean in this blue shell. I can. I know I can, I know I can!"

Leslie turns to watch the hogs sprint up the hummock in the pasture. The four pigs stand together at the crest, puffing and grunting, the warm air from inside them visible as it streams from their frightened lungs. The boy thinks what their pulmonary arteries must look like now. In his seventh-grade biology book with a blue amoeba on the cover, he is required to memorize lungs, their maroon filigree and subtle weaknesses. The old man laughs and tosses the glass over the head of his daughter; it pings off a metal bed frame behind her. They all three watch as the shoats disappear over the green swell.

The dump pile is quiet now. Harper walks to the edge and picks up a wicker basket she's brought along. She begins to sniffle and pout. She gathers up shards of colored glass: saffron, purple, clear, milky, sienna, and others, all of it from the medicine cabinets of Basil and the dead wife of forty years ago. Leslie has a picture of Rebecca in his bedroom. She looks out at him from a black frame, her face like his mother's, sad and drawn tightly around the lips, a look of disbelief in her eyes. Sometimes he thinks the woman's face to be on the verge of laughing. When he notices it, after staring at the picture for a long while, he puts it down on his nightstand. He thinks, how can a woman the age of my mother be my grandmother?

Harper piles colored glass into the basket until the handle bows from the weight. She has stopped crying and is now singing a song. Her father joins in as Leslie takes the brimming basket from her dirty hands. They creep back to the house. Leslie walks behind them, the pieces of color falling over the edges of the basket and onto the cold green ground. He watches as ahead of him his mother and grandfather, arm in arm, sing songs that are wholly made up. He reaches down to the basket and finds a piece of amber like the one he fingered earlier, puts it to his eye. The glass is cold around his socket, and it smells of damp earth. Through the middle of the glass they look like thin, red lines, vertical and swaying. At the outer edges of the lens, muted landscape flicks past. As he views the morning through the glass, Leslie thinks of a new name for himself. Butch sounds good, a bully; so does Randall: it has the sound of importance. Finally, he settles for the time being on Scott, a nice, regular name, like an older boy he knows at school.

The old man stops abruptly in the grassy lane, pulling his arm free of his daughter's as if about to escape. Harper turns to speak over her shoulder. "Honey, don't drop so much of the glass." She points to the basket in Leslie's hand. He thinks she sounds almost like her old self.

His grandfather is now standing stock-still. He stares straight-ahead, not peering back from where they've come, but rather pointing toward the house. He says to Harper and Leslie, "I think I left my seashell back there." Leslie hands the old man a blunt triangle of blue from the basket.

"Ahh," he sighs, putting the glass to his long ear as if it were a warm compress, "There she is. There she is."

Months ago, during an ice storm in November, Harper had

knocked on her son's bedroom door, crying. She wore a cream-colored nightgown, a tail of crimson in the middle, wet with some blood. She gasped, "I'm sorry, baby. You shouldn't have to see this at your age. I'm sick. I need to go to the hospital. Your grandfather can't drive."

Leslie drove the best he could into the city limits and parked the station wagon under the port to the emergency room, neon red flashing above the automatic doors as he brought his mother to the nurses' station. Later, a woman doctor would tell him something had burst inside his mother, that she needed a quick operation, but that she'd be fine, which he assumed meant normal; which he now understands to be wrong. Since then, his mother has been weird in any number of ways. Sometimes up so high she wants to dance with Leslie in the living room to his indie music on the stereo and other times so low all she wants to do is stay in bed and call the help-lines the hospital gave her at discharge. For a couple of weeks she took some pills that made her the way she used to be, but after they ran out, she wouldn't get them refilled, even though Leslie has tried and tried to get her to go back to the doctor.

On Saturday morning, Harper sits at the kitchen table with the basket of glass in front of her. She is sorting it into various piles based on size, shape and color. All the glass is safe, thick and rounded at the edges, made dull from the many years in the dump. Basil is next to her lightly chewing on a piece of toast, a steaming cup of tea between them. Leslie walks into the kitchen, dressed already in jeans and a thick sweatshirt. His hair is combed back, wet from a hot shower the boy has snatched before his mother and grandfather were awake and up.

He goes to the cupboard and pulls out two packets of instant oatmeal, brown sugar and cinnamon. At the sink he uses hot tap water to mix the dry cereal into a paste. He turns from the sink and speaks.

"Good morning."

Harper looks shocked that he can talk, or that someone else is in the room.

"Well, hello to you, young man," she says, her eyes brimming with energy from the sorting task. She turns quickly back to arranging the piles of glass. The old man smiles as he nibbles on the crust hanging off the toast.

Leslie gulps down the oatmeal off a large spoon. He puts the bowl in the sink and floods it with water and several pumps of dish soap. He watches the bits of food floating in the bubbles, not liking how they seem to be moving on their own, like bugs trying to survive, floundering and swirling about. He must remind himself that it's just food, not poor creatures in danger. Leslie turns and goes to the front door, unhooks a jeans jacket from a nail next to the jamb. He talks loudly so they know he's leaving.

"I'm going to walk into town. See the lights at the courthouse." His grandfather stands up as if to come along, then slowly slides back down into the chair, a perfect gesture denoting: *on second thought.*

Harper smiles broadly. "Wait." She gets up from the table and paces to the center of the room. "Take this," she says, tossing him a piece of reddish glass. "See what that big light bulb looks like through it." In an instant, she is back at the table, flicking through other pieces. As Leslie puts the glass in his pocket and opens the door, he hears his mother's work: *clink, clink, clink.*

His grandfather says, "That kid looked familiar. What's his name?"

The farm Leslie lives on is just outside the city limits of Wabash, the first electrically lighted city in the world. It sits on top of a hill, so close to the town that from anywhere on its intricate plats the city lights are easily visible, like living in both worlds, Harper used to tell Leslie when he was a child. Every spring to commemorate the day Charles Brush first lit the city with a carbon-arc light bulb, the town holds a festival. Leslie's elementary school teachers all recited the same speech: "When the crude electrical switch was thrown in March of 1880, the Miami Indians watched from the banks of the river in lit dismay. It has been said that when our forbears were first introduced to electric light, they had the tendency to stare at them and then report with disdain that the lights had caused them not to be able to see *anything at all.*" The teacher would continue, a broad smile beaming warmly, "You guys are lucky—you're from the same town where electric light and Crystal Gayle were born."

People come from all over the state to eat funnel cakes, drink cider, and don caps with glowing bulbs on the bill, little stuffed things perched there like a Tweety Bird, yellow and round, plush. Every year, the same hats, thousands of them, made up again and again, Leslie thinks, always just alike, as if they'd all been created way before time ever began, before light was on the surface of the earth. On Sunday there's the grand finale: a staged blackout to remind the town what couldn't be seen before the discovery.

Leslie walks briskly along a ditch beside the road. He can see the cupola of the courthouse, its many strings of light teepeed from a weather vane down to the ring of black metal circling just under the oval windows. In his pants pocket he lets his fingers tickle the glass. For a moment he thinks of fishing it out and hurling it toward a passing car, but the thought fades away, like his grandpa did earlier in the chair: raring to move, then thinking better of it and accepting his limitations, sitting down to let it all go.

The streets running off the town square are lined with all varieties of booths and stands. There is one for the credit union, circled by three competing grocery store chains handing out toothpicks heavy with cheese and meat; next to those are booth upon booth of farm machinery dealers and seed corn distributors. There is the high school band and Spanish club, along with an assortment of computer dealers and cell phone companies. People milling about, nearly all chewing on something, carry plastic tote bags to lug all their loot home. The bags have a mascot light bulb on them named Sparky. A dialogue balloon floating from his electric smile says: *Energy is a Bright Idea!*

Leslie floats among the booths, looking at how happy all the people appear. They sit behind the skirted two-by-fours and plywood structures and smile and wave at the crowd passing by. Leslie thinks a man with a cowboy hat selling riding equipment, counter lined with rope and saddles, the smell of leather pungent, is waving at him. Leslie pulls his hand from his pocket and holds it up just as a man behind him, out of his sight, yells, "Dan Frazier? Is that you over there? Well, I'll be damned!" Leslie puts his hand down quickly, as if the answer he thought he knew had gotten away from him. The man behind him rushes by, charges the cowboy man's booth, shaking his head and repeating, "Well, I'll be damned!"

The boy walks on, now careful not to assume anyone is making an effort to connect with him. He keeps his head down and follows the broken sidewalks to the center of town. The courthouse is surrounded by hordes of people, all waiting to countdown, like at New Year's, the sixty seconds before a switch is thrown on the lawn and a giant replica of Charles Brush's light bulb is surged with electricity, the same light that on the next day, at dusk, will be ceremoniously extinguished for the blackout. A whole night, the brochure from the tourist office states, of how the Miami Indians must've seen this area before the dawn of electrical energy.

Leslie begins to lift his head some, looking around for kids from school. Next to a saltwater taffy wagon he spots Scott, the kid three years ahead of him, his namesake. Leslie watches him as he flirts with two girls in droopy letter jackets popping bubble gum, their jeans unlike Leslie's snug ones; the butt of theirs so saggy they must hold the waist with a clenched fist. Automatically he feels out of place, wishing he'd just stayed home and gone to the dump with his mother and grandfather. More people start to encircle the courthouse. In colorful throngs that remind Leslie of his mother's basket of glass, more and more festival-goers crowd in around him, one older woman accidentally goosing him with a John Deere yardstick. Leslie allows himself to laugh some over the incident as the lady creeps on by, clearing her throat, expecting people to let her get closer because of her age. From somewhere behind him a marching band plays and then stops, plays again, horns and tubas hacking through a snippet of a John Philip Sousa piece, then abruptly ending, a snare drum now rolling, readying the crowd for the big event.

Leslie clamps his elbows in closer to his side as a family with three small children riding in one long baby carriage squash in beside him, the father smiling, mouthing: *Sorry*, a look of genuine apology under his wide-set eyes. The enormous light bulb is hoisted off a wooden platform, lifted by several strands of steel cable into the air so that everyone can see it now. Leslie turns his head to find out if Scott is still where he was, but the spot is vacant, only a man with a washrag wiping down a veneered table is visible. Leslie spots the two girls near a trash barrel, spitting their gum out and quickly unwrapping more, pushing the pink hunks into their mouths, fixing their hair at the same time. Leslie realizes he is staring, so he pretends to look past them, surveying the crowd, he hopes, like a man looking for some complex indication that he's not the only one finding the event shoddily pulled together. Once the heat of a slight embarrassment has subsided from his cheeks, he turns his attention back to the light bulb twisting in the breeze, the official countdown beginning. The crowd is already on fifty-one before Leslie joins in softly.

The girls and their bubble gum edge closer to him. He allows himself to catch the upturned whites of their eyes, lashes batting, the two of them whispering, oddly pointing at Leslie as they approach, not caring if they step on toes or knock over packages. He turns away, trying to appear uninterested. The crowd is on forty seconds now and counting. One of the girls taps him on the shoulder. Leslie turns, giddy in his limbs, a sense of nascent power flooding his brain, all of it rare for him, brand-new to his body and mind. The girl speaks but Leslie cannot hear what she's said. Her mouth, lovely and red, lips so glossy they appear greased, is moving, but the crowd is ultrasonic now; it's down to ten seconds before the bulb will come alive, pop into an achy glow and cause those on the front rows to shield their eyes from light they can't see.

The girl gives up, gives in, and puts her mouth to his ear, standing on the tips of her toes, she forgets and whispers, still not giving Leslie any clue about what she is proposing, stating, wishing, telling, demanding. The crowd cheers; a communal *oooh!* is chanted. Leslie can't decide on how to behave. He tries to clap along with the multitude; his hands form a jagged wedge, and cannot come together evenly. The girl falls away from him, her face backing up as she and her friend smile and retreat, walking backwards, looking past Leslie, their faces unsure, as if they've interrupted something.

Leslie feels stupid, like he's again assumed more than he can accept. He detects someone at his side, standing too close, almost on his feet. It is a shock to see his grandfather next to him, a look of childish delight in his red eyes. Next to the old man is Harper, the basket of glass dangling at her knee, as she hands out pieces to the crowd, shouting over the drone of celebration, "Look at it through this!" She is happy one second, handing a fat little boy a hunk of green, and crying the next, never looking at her son, as she kisses her father on his smiling cheek. The basket dumps at her feet, other people's children rummaging through it, being scolded for doing so by parents who disapprove of Harper's actions. Leslie waits until the children recede, then bends to the ground to sort it out. He inspects the feet of his family, untied work boots gaping at the tongue, as he plucks the ugly glass from the ground. Leslie hopes the girls think he's helping a couple of strangers; he prays his hot face is not noticeable. When he's finished picking up the mess, he spots a piece of clear glass inside his mother's boot, stuck between her ankle and the leather upper. Leslie keeps his head down as he takes it out, the warmth from her body on his fingertips. He stands, leaving the full basket at her feet and walks away, needing them not to follow him closely home.

Sunday afternoon, almost evening, the weather outside harsh and erratic: bright sunshine in temps just over forty. Leslie watches through the kitchen window as the sunlight bears down from out of nowhere for a few seconds, and is sucked back up into the sky in an instant. Over and over it happens, as he sips soda from a paper cup, leaning on the sink waiting for his mother and grandfather to finish putting on their coats. The plan is to hit the dump, then head into Wabash for the end of the festival.

In the brisk weather they walk slowly to the rear of the farm, visiting the dump twice in as many days. Instead of spades, Harper has asked cheerfully if Leslie would mind getting a wheelbarrow with several long-handled shovels in it from the shed. Leslie pushes it behind Harper and the old man until he must slow to a crawl, a stance that makes his back hurt. He waits for them to get ahead some before resuming. The pigs have gotten a whiff of the human bodies; they've come to the fence, sniffing along the row and oinking as Harper and Leslie and the old man make their way down the lane to the dump. The pigs expect to be handfed again, desiring something from outside their world that also exists in it. The sun from earlier has completely vanished; it's now gray and solemn, the sky heavy with dark clouds, moisture that will become snow.

At the edge of the dump, Leslie peers through the dimness, over the drop of the hill toward the town as more lights are switched on, an act from the business owners which is supposed to make the fake blackout more striking. He wonders if the girls will be back, if they'd laugh at him if he tried to be polite and approach them to find out what they wanted yesterday.

The old man is tired. He ignores the pigs grunting at the fence. He sits down on a stump near the trash and watches as Leslie and Harper pull the shovels from the wheelbarrow and drag them to the pile. Without asking why they've brought heftier tools this time, Leslie uses his foot to plant the tip of the shovel into the ground; he jumps onto the metal lip with both feet, jamming it into the earth with some force. When he bends the shovel back, soft dirt flowers outward, spills onto the old ground, displaying rusty bolts and the brittle sheaves of corroded cans. He takes another dig and another, moving quickly around the pile, until it appears as though the entire heap had been loosened at the edges and could be peeled from the woods like a sticker. He focuses and works hard.

When Leslie looks up, sweaty and unaware from throwing himself into the thrust of the shovel, he sees that his grandfather and mother have disappeared. They are gone. He pulls his sleeve from his watch; time has passed him by. It is getting dark. He looks to the fence where the pigs should be, thinking the two of them might be feeding the shoats grass again: nothing, only the soft swish of friable weeds, the faint clicking of their heavy seed heads against one another, tapping, pecking out a coded song Leslie thinks he should know. He begins to holler for them; twisting around in circles he calls their names again and again. He stops and listens to the wind blowing past his ears, the trees creaking, the town just over the ridge talking to him, saying the festivities are getting closer, that darkness is real and will be forever, that it cannot be changed, and that age and blood and family make up the darkest parts of our lives. The sound is Leslie's first understanding of his obligations, of how he must watch over this family until he has his own, until the light from these years makes all the difference, and he can use it to brighten his way.

He finds them in the grass of the lane, sitting down like children, talking about Rebecca, of the farm before they owned it, and crying. Leslie plops down near them, the rut of the road on his tailbone. He tells them to watch the sky above the town, points to just over some dark trees. He smiles when the blackout is ordered; they can't actually see the town, but he knows the big light bulb goes first and that there's more to come, sort of like fireworks in reverse, he decides. His mother and grandfather say, "Ooohhh!" when the rest of the town goes black, the night sky their only view. The two of them cuddle up together, the old man stiff as he tries to hold his baby. Leslie settles in beside them, ready for how long they will stay.

BAYOU CANOT

Joe Formichella

"**N**o one knew where it was," Tommy says to Michael. They sit anchored along the east bank of Mobile River, across from the mouth of Bayou Canot. Tommy had stopped short of the turn in the river toward the site, cut the engine, and dropped anchor. He sits there studying the entrance to the bayou, the bend in the river that obscures the railroad bridge, as if the scene itself has a secret to be divined.

Michael looks at the wilderness up close, all around them. Sentinel cypress trees loom over the embankment where delicate white- and pink-topped pitcher plants poke their heads out of the lush green reeds, low branches hovering protectively. Behind that grow palmettos, and oak and swamp tupelo hardwoods. Tiny green-fly orchids sprout from the trees like accessories. Michael watches a solitary orange and black monarch butterfly flit among the vegetation. Dragonflies dart back and forth, hover in the air. It all looks like anything *but* a disaster scene.

"The first calls we got put us in Bayou Sara, more than a mile downriver," Tommy says, pointing to the south. "No one knew, not until they finally hijacked an engine out of Siebert and took it up the rails after the Limited."

Once they found the wreck, the rescue team came back up the line pulling three passenger cars, one for a communications center, a dining car transformed into a rolling ER for the seriously wounded, and a coach car to carry survivors from the scene. In place of the dinnerware and place settings, they stocked the treatment car with first aid kits, splints for broken bones, sterile dressing for burn victims, and bags of IV fluid for those in shock.

Within a hundred yards of the Limited on that return trip, surviving passengers started walking toward the headlamp of the train approaching through the gloom. They appeared out of the fog like something from a horror movie. More than two hours after the wreck, they were exhausted. They moved like zombies into another rail car, taking up seats without hesitation.

"I don't know if I could have gotten on another of those things," Tommy says. "Suppose I would have done anything to get away from this place, though."

Half an hour later, the rescue team had evacuated two carloads, over a hundred survivors, the walking wounded, as they were called. Back at the paper mill staging area, they were met by medical workers, triaged, and whisked off to area hospitals. Three nurses swarmed over William when he disembarked, spying his bloodied shirt.

"It's not mine," he told them, "not my blood." Patty was the one who needed help, he said.

Red Cross workers got him a new shirt, bused them both to a hospital, along with the others.

Charles was treated where he lay on a bench in the dining car, until he could be stabilized and ambulanced to the Medical Center cath lab. He was the only emergent patient to be extracted from the scene.

Back up the river, rescue boats started arriving, first a Baldwin County sheriff's airfoil, and a skiff off another tug in the water that night. Soon enough there was a small armada in the bayou. Tommy was among the first.

"When we turned that corner," he says, still anchored, "it was like a war zone, with the fire, the people screaming, the smell of diesel."

The chief on the scene, Chief Sullivan, was trying to find out how many people had been on the train, receiving varying reports from Amtrak officials. Dedicated ECS lines were crackling with calls from the different response agencies, dispatchers, feds, and soon enough, media outlets. The story broke across the wire services almost as quickly as the awful news had rung in Amtrak and CSX offices.

People were still in the water, clinging to floating debris. The fire from the ruptured fuel cell raged, setting the scene aglow in yellow and orange. More boats arrived, from other jurisdictions. A Coast Guard fireboat steamed up the river. And fishermen motored toward Canot from camps embedded all over the delta. Everyone anchored in the bayou a couple hundred feet back from the wreckage and the debris and the fire. That was the scene the first muted rays of daylight broke upon.

"Why *did* it take so long?" Michael asks, from their vantage point, bobbing out on the main river.

Tommy frowns at the impossibility of the question, a pain he's felt for years. He can only answer the way he was taught, "Wouldn't have made any difference," though that never makes the question go away.

"How can you say that?"

With the land rescue nearly done, Sully commandeered a ride on the Chickasaw City police boat and maneuvered about the scene, getting in close to the cars in the water, keeping all the other vessels at a distance. He directed official boats toward people still in the water like he was running a school car line, so no one would do any more damage in their eagerness to help. He had the cutter go to work on the fire, which was spreading up the shoreline.

Once they'd pulled everyone out of the water, had emptied the cars still up on the track, and ferried all those survivors from the scene by boat, or rail, even a few by helicopter, Sully called to his divers. "Suit up," he radioed to the teams. Task Force One had been on the scene for less than an hour, and their rescue operation turned into a recovery effort almost as soon as it began. This was the test.

Tommy and the rest of the divers zipped up their suits, pulled on masks and tanks, maneuvered closer. Up near the submerged cars, a greasy sheen from leaking fuel had spread across the surface of the water. It was a wonder the whole bayou wasn't aflame. Beneath that surface, the water was cool as it seeped inside their suits through gaps around the Velcro neck fastening, the cuffs about their wrists and ankles.

The team split into two once in the water, confirming procedure with hand signals given face to face, in front of headlamps. Three divers kicked to one end of each coach in the water.

The first task was to inspect the length of the cars, the divers feeling along the outside as they flippered from one end to the other, looking for breach points, signs of survival. They looked for air pockets, the only hope for passengers trapped inside the cars, and did not rush through the inspection. All that was visible, though, as they progressed down the length of the cars, was bodies stilled in the water, some even strapped in their seats, staring out the windows back at them.

Two of the divers surfaced for torch equipment, to the anticipation of other workers and respondents, Chief Sully up near the perimeter. They shook their heads to the question on every face. The mood of the scene changed in that instant, emptying it of all urgency, as everyone set about the task of recovery and cleanup.

A bright red switching engine returned up the tracks, hookup linkages on both ends, pulling a platform car loaded with railroad workers huddled around a tall crane fixed to the bed. They had to lift the sleeper cars that had jumped the rails and set them back on the tracks in order to haul them away.

The Coast Guard fireboat was gaining control of the fire, the column of black smoke rising from the scene like a beacon diminishing. Sully turned from that to the flickering of the blowtorch beneath the surface of the bayou. He was managing the scene one sure step at a time. He'd been with the department more than twenty years and still ran a ladder company by choice. He would be a cinch for the promotion to the administrative position everyone addressed him by, but he remained in a captain's slot.

Normally, he could arrive on a site and see all the moves, like a chess match, and guide his men calmly through each of the steps until the people were rescued, the fire out, the site secure. This one was different.

"We'll use one of those barges as a floating morgue," he told a lieutenant. And then a little bit later told the same aide, "Get me some sheets."

They would need sheets to wrap up the bodies once they were out of the water and on the barge. And those bodies would need to be identified as soon as possible.

Sully radioed dispatch and asked, "Can we get Rickert up here?" The county coroner.

One team had already gained entry through a broken window and had opened a hatch from the inside. They pulled the first body from that car, a young man with blond hair, in shorts and a T-shirt.

"Take me to that barge," Sully told the pilot of the police boat, pointing to where he planned to assemble the recovered bodies until refrigerated space could be found somewhere. That team of divers brought up a second, then a third body out of the water to be ferried over to the barge.

Sully commanded other agency boats into shuttle service out on the water, idling near enough at a spot where the divers could get to them, receive the victim and bring the body toward the barge. Those who wouldn't be drafted into that service, who were only really on the scene for the spectacle, drifted away rather than participate in Sully's parade of the dead. Some even went back to their fishing.

A certain quiet settled over the scene. The only sounds were those of utility, the two-stroke boat engines, the grinding of the winch up on the rail bed, the creaking of rail cars being moved about or the snap and pop of the remains of the fire. There were no natural sounds, no precious human sounds except the occasional crackle of radio transmissions.

Tommy was on the other team, going into the coach on the bottom of the bayou. In the first row of seats, they found a middle-aged couple, holding hands. Row by row the gruesome process continued, the search for and extraction of victims. At one point they found an empty baby's car seat, unhooked it and brought it to the surface out of habit. The county sheriff waiting next in the receiving line saw that and said, "Jesus Christ, what'd you bring that up for?"

"Hey!" Sully shouted down at him.

"It was a rule of Sully's," Tommy tells Michael.

"What?"

"No profanity."

"Why?"

"Why? I don't know. He never said. Was just a rule."

"Dumb-ass rule, if you ask me," Michael says, and turns back toward the bayou.

Then he feels the boat rock, to his left, and then the right. His fear of water never very far away, Michael first grasps the aluminum seat beneath him. It rocks again and he turns to see Tommy stepping over the bench nearest him, standing over him with his feet set wide, a pointed finger almost touching the bridge of Michael's nose.

"Nobody fucking asked."

"Goddamn, Tommy, what's wrong with you?"

Tommy opens his hand, draws it back a little, and slaps him. Not hard, just enough for Michael to snap his head back. Then he closes his hand again, and points. "Out here, no profanity."

"You fucking nuts?" Michael starts, even reaching to push himself from the seat, into Tommy's face, before Tommy draws his hand back again, a little farther this time. "All right, all right," Michael says then, holding his hands up.

"It's just a rule, Rogers. Can't you understand that? On the job, you ignore the rules, question the chief, people die."

While the *Pineda* motored the seventeen survivors they'd pulled from the water downriver, the crew brought those passengers in groups of one or two up to the wheelhouse, let them use the ship-to-shore. Captain Frank had radioed the harbormaster, the Gulf Navigational dispatcher, reporting the barges grounded back in the bayou, that they were returning to port. The rest of the crew, in turn, checked in with their families.

"Breeny," W. C. said when he reached home, "You shoulda seen it." He told her about the fire, the screaming.

Charlie told his wife, "We were heroes."

They turned off the river short of the Cochrane, under a CSX trestle and into a channel dredged out of the marsh adjacent to the

Scott Mill property. They were met by Red Cross and EMS personnel, survivors teetering down the gangway one by one, swallowed up in dry blankets, awaiting arms, ushered into idling buses.

Once the crew had shut down and secured the *Pineda*, they were met by four white sedans, each of them ordered into a separate back seat and whisked away to the hotel, which had become the ops center.

"What's going on?" Frank asked.

"Necessary precaution," was all he was told.

The other three got less of an explanation than that.

The switching engine pulled the two sleeper cars back down the length of track and parked them at the nearby state docks rail yard. Passenger belongings were retrieved and brought to the ballroom of the Terraces, reunited with owners.

Out on the bayou, twelve more bodies had been recovered and lined up along the barge. Sully was still trying to get a final passenger count. The rail service didn't count unticketed riders on its manifest, he found out. They were trying to determine how many of those children had been aboard, how many they should expect to find. Three such small bundles were already wrapped up in white on the barge, including the baby, who looked to be three, four months old.

"Does *anyone* know how many kids were aboard?" Sully was asking into the phone.

Tommy's team had progressed about halfway into their car. He unbuckled another woman slumped over in her seat and lifted her free. The bodies were getting heavier, the more time they spent in the water. But the faces were almost always the same, frozen in time. He felt his way back up the aisle toward the forward breach, holding the body close. He handed her body over to a partner, turned back for another.

Sully radioed that they were going to need an oilrig crane big enough to lift the railroad cars from the water. One was dispatched from New Orleans. He didn't know what they'd do about the lead locomotive still sticking rear-ended out of the shore. There'd be at least two bodies in there. That left three crewmembers unaccounted for. The fire was mostly under control. The remains of the crew dormitory car was charred and smoking. There'd be more in there, no doubt.

That's why this job was different. It had all the things Sully dreaded to encounter. People dying in the course of ordinary duties bothered him. He put his life on the line so that others wouldn't have to. When they died, people like Sully took responsibility. He wasn't sure why, and had maybe wished otherwise at times over the last twenty years, but he did. And kids dying. Nobody took that well. He'd have to talk to his men. Get them off this river as soon as possible and talk to them before they left the site. He'd sit them down in a train car, overlooking the site, their feelings near and raw, and remind them, "People die. There was no helping most of those folks today."

Media from around the country converged on the Terraces, interviewing survivors, rescue workers, investigators. W. C. watched the reports in his isolated room. Passengers talked about the horror, and the heroes out on the river. The guard stationed outside W. C.'s door let himself into the room when he heard the television set and told him, "You don't want to be watching that." W. C. didn't understand, but switched it off anyway. He'd seen the aerial footage a hundred times, the cars in the water, the fire. It didn't get any easier.

When they pulled the last coach off the remains of the bridge, NTSB took over, to determine exactly how the wreck had occurred. The fog had all but burned off by that time. Sully had come back to the near shore. He took off his helmet and replaced it with a Mobile Fire Department ball cap, running his hand through thin, graying hair. Then he rubbed the back of his neck, twisting his head about to try and work out a kink that had settled there. Deep lines etched the brown skin above his collar, from years of sun and stress.

"What you got, Chief?" they asked, coming up on Sully.

"Jumped the rails here," Sully told them, standing out on the precipice of the shorn bridge.

They looked over the scene, gauging the trajectory the engines would have taken. The right-hand rail there at the joint of the bridge abutment was rolled over, and pushed about eighteen inches inward.

"Rolled over," Tommy tells Michael, his hand held up perpendicularly, then rotating it about sixty degrees.

"Impact from the side," one NTSB agent said, both of them squatted down, inspecting the rail, leaning and looking over the side of the trestle. A fresh collision mark could be seen in the concrete a couple of feet below the track. Then they looked up the shoreline to the Gulf Navigation barges grounded there.

They stood up and checked the other side of the trestle before retracing their steps back to land and clambering down the embankment. They checked the leading edge of the barges for damage, measuring its height, taking notes. In the clear light of day it all seemed so perfectly obvious, as one of them pulled a phone from his pocket.

Only moments later two suited agents and a uniformed policeman entered Captain Frank's room at the Terraces.

"When exactly did you put in the mayday call?" they asked him.

He still hadn't quite realized what had happened.

Sabrina, at home with Willie, watched the portable television set propped up on the kitchen counter. Reports were starting to speculate that a barge had collided with the bridge before the train arrived. She hadn't heard from W. C. for hours.

A different agent accompanied by a different policeman asked W. C., "You were in the wheelhouse when you hit the bridge?"

"Hit what bridge?"

"There was no way he could have avoided hitting the bridge," Tommy says. "Not once he'd turned in there. Momentum alone would have carried him into the bridge. Pushing ten thousand tons on the water, it takes a mile to stop.

"Imagine a mile, Rogers," Tommy tells him.

Michael looks upriver, down. He looks into Bayou Canot. The farthest he can see is a hundred yards, maybe.

"Imagine putting your brakes on and the car not coming to a complete rest until a mile later."

Michael tries to think of where that landmark would be on his approach to Houston Street. "There's no way."

Frank never made the connection between the bump in his sleep and the wreck until he was told about it there in the hotel room of the Terraces. "Good God," he said, once they'd informed him.

In his room, W. C. told investigators he thought he'd hit another barge. "Either that or ran aground," he said.

The company rep who'd been called in told W. C. he probably shouldn't talk to anyone about what happened. "There might be a criminal investigation."

"Criminal?" W. C. said. "I didn't do nothing wrong, Mr. Teague."

"Just go home, for now. Keep to yourself."

They'd pulled thirty-eight bodies from the water. The midday sun was peaking, another thing for Sully to worry about, while they waited on state permission to use an air-conditioned hangar nearby to identify and store the remains. Two crewman were found in the burned-out dormitory car, and then a thirty-ninth passenger in the lower level of the same car, the smoking room. The best guess was that two engineers and a brakeman were in the lead locomotive, still buried along the shore.

"Figure, three more passengers," Sully told his divers, after they'd asked to stay on the job until it was done.

"What else would I do?" Tommy asks. "Sit around the house wondering how many we missed?"

They reentered both cars. At the very back of the top car they found a woman wedged up under a seat, clutching the framework. It took two of the three divers to pry her grip loose and pull her out of that small space. Curled up in a fetal position under the seat like that, they'd actually mistaken her for a little girl at first, which would have meant they were *still* three bodies short. Once they could straighten her out some, they realized otherwise.

She wasn't too old, they could see when they brought her to the surface, into daylight. She had a face that would always look eighteen, nineteen years old, with tight, delicate features. They lifted her to the barge, checked her jeans for any kind of identification, found nothing but an Amtrak cap jammed into a back pocket, then rolled her up in a sheet.

In the other submerged car, Tommy's team found no one else in the seats, swimming down the aisle slowly, then returning to the breach. The lower level was a baggage compartment, they'd been told, but they entered it anyway. At the very end of the car was a small, unmarked door. Tommy turned to the diver behind him and shrugged, as if to ask, "What's this?" The other diver shrugged back.

The door was jammed, or locked, and no amount of tugging on the doorknob would budge it. A diver went back to the surface for a crowbar.

Tommy wedged the fangs of the bar into the latch, leveraging the handle one way, then another, finally popping the door free of the frame. Another young woman tumbled out of the room when the door swung open. Behind her, a little boy still sat on the commode of the small, cramped restroom.

"Jesus Christ," Tommy said, then and now.

"Thought you said no profanity."

Tommy looks at Michael like he really could kill him, or die himself, his face void of any human feeling. "Weigh anchor," he says.

"Do what?"

"Pull the fucking anchor up."

The other two divers brought the woman back through the compartment, out, and to the surface, where the grim routine of checking for identification and then wrapping her up was repeated.

"One more," they called to Sully. "But it's a kid."

Sully rubbed at the back of his neck again. "That's all right," he decided. "After that, we're done."

Counting from when they'd first gotten the 911 dispatch, shortly after three that morning, they'd been at it eight long hours. "Long enough," Sully said.

Tommy found the boy fastened to the seat by a harness. He cut him loose and then took the time to pull his pants back up and buckle them.

"Just because," he says to Michael.

He lifted the boy from the seat, holding him close his chest, reached back and felt for the door opening behind him, squeezing both of them through at once. The boy couldn't have been more than four, five years old. He still had that baby blond hair that rippled in the current. One of his shoes had been wedged loose on the way out the door and finally fell from the boy's foot. It arced its way back downward, gravity pulling it toward what had been the ceiling of the lower level of the car forever ago in this world turned inside out. When the shoe settled again, the slight impact set off a little red light in the heel that blinked on and off for three, four seconds, and then stopped.

People on the Empty Road

Tim Gautreaux

Wesley and his girlfriend were parked in his father's driveway on Pecan Street, arguing in his old Pontiac Tempest. Bonita was a sulky brunette with a voice as hard as a file. She wanted him to get the forty-dollar tickets to the Travis Tritt concert, and he tried to explain that the twenty-dollar tickets were a better deal. He looked down the humpback asphalt lane to where it turned off at Le Phong's Country Boy Cash Grocery and ground his teeth. He sensed he was going to lose his temper again, the way a drunk feels in his darkened vision that he is about to fall off a stool. Bonita crossed her arms and called him the cheapest date in Pine Oil, Louisiana, and Wesley crushed the accelerator, leaving the car in neutral, letting the racket do his talking. The engine whined up into a mechanical fury until a detonation under the hood caused everything to stop dead, as if all the moving parts had welded together. Wesley cursed and got out, followed by Bonita, who spat her gum against a pin oak and put her hands on her hips. "Now you done it," she told him. "When are you gonna calm down?"

Wesley examined a volcano-shaped hole in the hood of his car where a push rod had blown through like a bullet. "You can walk home and wait for Travis Tritt to climb in your window with a bouquet of roses," he yelled. "But don't wait for me."

She started down the street, then turned and shouted back to him, "When you gonna grow up?"

"When I'm old enough to."

Bonita continued toward her rental house in the next neighborhood. Wesley turned and went into the kitchen. The old man was at the table, home from his supermarket, sipping a glass of iced tea.

"That's the second engine this year, Wes. How many can you afford?"

"I know. She got me so damned mad." He fell into a chair. "I think we just broke up."

His father ran a hand over his gray hair and then loosened his tie. "It's just as well. She was common. Her sister who used to check for me on register six was kind of rough. What was her name, Trampoline?"

"Trammie-Aileen," Wesley corrected. "She works for Le Phong now." He put his head down and his red hair fell forward like a rooster's comb.

"Know what I think?" his father asked.

"What?"

"I think you ought to come back cutting meat in the store. You were the fastest trimmer I ever had. With a rolled rump, you were an artist."

Wesley held up the nub of his left forefinger, and his father looked out the window. "I want to do something else for a while, Daddy."

"I think you'll be safer cutting meat for me here in Pine Oil than off driving for that gravel company. You don't have the disposition for that."

Wesley's face became as tight as a rubber glove. "You mean I'm reckless, don't you?"

"You just got to find a girl who'll calm you down. Only thing'll do that is a good girl and time."

Wesley put his head back down in his hands. "I don't want to hear this."

"Well, when's it gonna happen? You're twenty-four and been through eight cars." His father took a swallow of tea and softly grabbed a fistful of his son's hair. "That old Tempest wasn't any good, but it was transportation."

"I can afford Lenny's rusty T-Bird. It's for sale."

His father clamped the coppery strands in his fingers, an old game, his way of saying, "Calm down. Come back to earth." Then he said, "I'll get you a better car if you come back to work for me."

Wesley pulled free and moved toward the window. "I've got to go roll some gravel. I'm good at it."

"I don't like you running those tight schedules."

Wesley leaned on the wooden window frame and watched a wisp of oil smoke rise from the puncture in his hood. "The construction folks want the rock quick. If we can't get it to them when they need it, someone else gets the contract."

His father rubbed his eyes. "Your boss is making money on your lack of patience. You need to slow down and find a girl who thinks there's more to life than fast cars and cowboy music."

Over the next month he made more runs than any other driver at the gravel pit. His boss, old man Morris, pear-shaped, with skin like barbecued chicken, told him, "Boy, you're a natural."

"A natural what?" Wesley asked, stepping up into a blue Mack.

The old man spat on a wheel rim. "A natural way to get my rock moved faster than Ex-Lax."

Each day, his truck clipped a minute off the time to the big casino site in New Orleans, but each fast trip shaved a little off his nerves, the way the road wore down tires to the explosive air at the center of things. He couldn't help the urge to sail across the twenty-four-mile-long causeway over Lake Pontchartrain like a road-bound cargo plane weighted down with many tons of pea gravel. A big sedan might be in the right lane doing sixty-five and he would be coming up from behind at ninety, water showering up from his wheels, a loose tarpaulin flying over the forty-foot trailer wild as a witch's cape. Near his left rear mud flap there'd be another car, and the time to change lanes was exactly then or the people in the big sedan would be red pulp, so after one click of his blinker he would roll out like a fighter plane, road reflectors exploding under his tires like machine-gun bursts.

He used his recklessness like a tool to get the job done. After every twelve-hour day, he would tear out of the gravel pit in his rusty Thunderbird, spinning his wheels in a diminishing shriek for half a mile. The road turned through worthless sand bottoms and stunted growths of pine, and the car would surge into the curves like electricity, Wesley pushing over the blacktop as if he were teaching the road a lesson, straightening it out with his wheels. When he would charge off the asphalt at eighty onto a gravel road, he would force the low sedan over a rolling cloud of dust and exploding rock as though he were not in danger at every wheel skid and shimmy of slamming into a big pine like a cannonball. For Wesley, driving possessed the reality of a video game. After thirty miles, he would skid to a stop, a half ton of dust boiling in the air behind him.

His destination was a dented sea-green mobile home parked in an abandoned gravel pit. He would pull at its balky door until the whole trailer rocked like it was caught in a hurricane, and finally inside, he would sit at his little kitchen table and watch his hands shake with something beyond fatigue.

One morning at six o'clock he was awakened by an armadillo rummaging in his kitchen. The animals were all over the place and had come in before. Wesley soft-kicked it through the open door frame like a football and watched it land in a pit of green water on the other side of his car. He sat down to listen to a radio talk show coming from the AM station in Pine Oil.

"Wouldn't you say that giving a man the death penalty for stealing two cows is a bit excessive?" The host's voice was pleasant and instructive.

"If they was *your* cows, sweetie, you'd want him to fry like bacon," a tubby voice said.

Wesley forced himself to eat breakfast, and sometime between the cereal and the orange juice, he began to relax. The woman announcer's voice was smooth as a moonlit lake, and he remembered meeting her at the store when she did a remote from the meat aisle during Pine Oil Barbecue Days. After breakfast, he sat on the galvanized step below his warped door frame, folded his hands, and rested his chin on his knuckles. He wondered how fast he would be driving in another month.

Wesley watched a lizard race from under the step. When the pit around the trailer had been operating, years before, a watchman had lived here. Spread over it for two hundred acres were green ponds shaped like almonds or moons or squares. To the south was an abandoned locomotive, its wheels sunk into the sand. Shards of machinery and cable lay about as though rained down from the clouds. He had lived in the center of the wreckage for six months and not one person had been to see him. He needed a new girlfriend—his father had said it—one who would make him go to the movies, barbecue hamburgers over a lazy fire, read magazines with no girlie pictures in them. He remembered the woman on the radio.

Turning up the ivory-colored Zenith left behind by the watchman, he listened to Janie, dealing with the farmers' wives. She ran from six to twelve, starting each program with a simple question, such as: "Do you think people should send money to TV evangelists?" or "Should the federal government spend more on welfare?" Many of her callers were abusive or made inflammatory statements far beyond the boundaries of simple ignorance. Most, Wesley decided after weeks of listening to the program, were people too stupid to be trusted with jobs, so they just sat around the house all day thinking up things to call the radio station about. He turned up the volume.

"Hello, you're on the air." The voice laid hands on him.

"Miz Janie," a high-pitched old-lady voice whined.

"Good morning."

"Miz Janie?"

"Yes, go on. Today's topic is the library tax." The voice was seasoned with a bright trace of kindness.

"Miz Janie, ain't it a shame what the law did those poor boys down in Manchac?"

"Ma'am, the topic is the library tax."

"Yes, I know. But ain't it a shame that those poor boys got put in jail for killing birds?"

"You're referring to the Clemson brothers?"

"That's right."

"They killed over two thousand Canada geese," she said, not the least hint of outrage in her voice.

"Birds is all," the old lady said. "Them boys is people. You can't put people in jail for what they do to birds."

Wesley balled up his fists and glared at the radio, remembering

Elmo, his pet mallard from childhood.

"Ma'am," the smooth voice said, "if everybody killed all the geese they wanted to kill, soon there'd be no more geese." Wesley searched from some bitter undercurrent in the voice but found not one molecule. The announcer gradually guided the old woman through a long channel of logic that led to the day's topic, the library tax.

"Miz Janie, everybody wants to raise our taxes. It's hard to make ends meet, you know."

"This tax is twenty-five cents a month." That was slick, Wesley thought.

"Well, it's the principle of the thing," the old voice complained. "Seems like we're paying people just to sit around and read when they ought to be out doing something else. If everybody would quit hanging around the library and get out on the highway picking up trash paper instead, we'd have a clean community, now wouldn't we?"

Wesley glared at the dusty radio. But the lady announcer continued to speak with honesty and openness until the woman on the line lost interest and hung up.

The next caller was an old man. "What the hail we need to spend money on a damned library for? Let them what wants to read go down to Walgreen's and buy they own magazines. The old library we got's plenty enough for such as needs it."

The next caller agreed with the millage proposal, but then a straight-gospel preacher came on the air and told that only one book ought to be in the library, and then another voice said he wouldn't mind voting for the millage if they got rid of the ugly librarian. "I mean, if they want to renovate, let's *really* renovate and get rid of the old warthog at the front desk." The announcer, her words like April sunshine, explained that Mrs. Fulmer was a lovely person as well as a certified librarian. Wesley turned up the radio, got out the brushes and Comet, and scrubbed his trailer like a sandstorm, wondering whether the announcer was single and trying to remember what she looked like. Her voice made her seem young, in her mid-twenties maybe, like he was. Then the phone rang, and he was called for two runs to New Orleans.

Down at the pit, he drew King Rock, a vast expanse of red enamel and chrome, the soul of the gravel yard. The foreman swung his gut out of the scale shack and climbed onto the truck's step, shoving his bearded face through the window. "If you can't push the son of a bitch to New Orleans by nine," he said, "you better keep going, hock the truck, and leave the country."

Wesley pulled a steel bar from under the driver's seat, got down, and walked around the rig, beating the tires as if he was angry with them, testing for flats. It was an extra-long trailer heaped with wet gravel. Wesley drove the rig onto the twisting two-lane blacktop, stomping the accelerator at every shift of the gears. He couldn't make himself think about the danger, so he again chose to see the windshield as a big video-game screen he could roar through with the inconsequence of a raft of electrons sliding up the face of a vacuum tube. The challenge was time, and he would lose if he drove a real road. He checked his watch—five after eight. The New Orleans site had to mix cement by nine or send a shift of workers home. King Rock loped under his feet like a wolf after deer.

Wesley streaked past a speeding Greyhound bus at the bottom of a grade, cut into the right lane, hit a curve, and felt the heart-fluttering skitter of nine tires trying to leave the ground. "Good God," he said aloud, surprised and frightened. But when he came to a straight section, as empty and flinty as a dull lifetime, he raced down it. He turned on the radar detector and thought of the two trips he had to make. The order had come in at seven: triple money for a load before nine in downtown. He was the only man who could make the ride.

Soon the truck was singing up to eighty. Wesley tapped his trailer brakes and drew ghosts of smoke from his rear tires. The video game had to be perfect now, for any mistake would cause a fierce yellow flash on the screen, the loss of a man.

He saw pines swarm past his window until he rose over the crest of Red Top Hill, the descending road tumbling away from him, deserted and inviting speed. He tried not to think about how far he could go; he just rode the machinery as though it were only noise instead of iron and rock, and when he slid into the curve at the bottom of the hill, he was not really alarmed at the rear of the stopped school bus ahead with its silly tin signs flopped out and a dozen children strung across the highway.

Wesley stood on the brakes and hung on the air horn while his tires howled and a cumulus of blue smoke rolled up behind. Gravel hammered the roof of King Rock's cab, and he could hear the treads tear off the tires. He fell out of his video game when he saw the faces of the children, real kids whose only mistake in life was to cross a road ten miles down from a greedy man's gravel pit.

The truck slid, and the trailer wagged from side to side. The hair on Wesley's arms bristled, the muscles in his legs cramped. Finally, like a child recoiling from a father's slap, he closed his eyes tight and yelled, not seeing what happened as his truck dove past the bus.

When he opened his eyes, the rig had begun to slide off the blacktop and into a roadside slough. The bumper bit a ton of mud that surfed over the windshield and roof, and the truck stopped at last. Wesley's arms and legs felt rubbery and bloodless. His head turned to the all-seeing expanse of his side mirror, which would at least miniaturize the disaster behind. No one lay in the road, though several children were cowering behind the bus. Three or four heads popped up out of a roadside ditch, and he found comfort in the fact that they were looking in his direction, that perhaps there were no bodies to see. Wesley jumped to the ground, where he heard his tires hissing in the mud, and began running limp-legged to the bus. A river of powdered rubber lay on the roadway, and the air stank. The grammar school kids picked themselves up and stood silently on the grassy roadside, and he could see that no one was hurt. Standing next to the bus, trembling and accused by the young eyes, he felt a presence behind him and looked into the face of the driver, a veteran gray-haired housewife who watched him through the vent window as though he were a snake creeping on the highway. "They'll ticket you, and you'll be back on the road again soon as you clean your pants," she said, her face quivering with anger.

When the parish deputies showed up, they handcuffed him, and Wesley panicked, twisting against the steel loops as he sat in the backseat of the cruiser. His movement was taken, and all he could do was squirm and try not to consider what he had done. No one talked to him except to utter quick, bitten-off questions, and he longed for a helpful voice. When the deputies unlocked the gnawing cuffs at the jailhouse, Wesley shook out his arms like wings warming up for flight.

His boss claimed a favor from the sheriff and made his bail. That night about eight, Wesley drove down to Pine Oil as slowly as he could bear, found out where Janie Wiggins, the radio announcer, lived, and went to her apartment building. He was as shaky and light-headed as a convert come from a tent meeting. When he knocked on the door, a blond woman about thirty years old answered.

"Miz Janie?" he asked.

The woman examined him politely, trying to place him. She had a pleasant face that was a bit round, and bright, alert eyes. "Do I know you?" she asked, her voice just like the one on the radio.

"I'm Wesley McBride. I met you in the meat department at McBride Mart." He picked up his left foot and shined the top of a loafer on the back of his slacks. "I'm one of your...well, fans." He briefly wondered if announcers on five-hundred-watt radio stations had fans. "I've always wanted to meet you again."

Her mouth hung open a bit, and he could see she felt complimented. "You're the guy who does the fancy-cut rib racks. Well, I'm glad to meet you, Wesley, but I guess you ought to come by the radio station if you want to discuss advertising."

"I don't work for the store anymore. I've got a new job, and I'd like to talk to you a little about it now, if that's all right with you. Maybe we could meet at the coffee shop down the street and sit a while."

She looked at him harder now, studying his features. "Talk about what?" He liked the way she ticked off her words like a northerner.

"I want to know about how you're so patient with people." He had never once in his life thought that he would say such a thing, and he turned red.

She looked at him carefully for a moment, shrugged, and told him she would meet him for a cup of coffee in a half hour. Before she closed the door, he saw that her apartment was nearly bare, had blond paneling, cottage-cheese ceiling, rent-to-own furniture, a nubby couch.

At Slim's Coffee Hut Wesley began to tell her about himself, how he was always impatient, even as a kid, but how over the past year he'd been losing control. He showed her his shortened finger, told her about his driving and about the school bus. His hands began to sweat when he mentioned the children, and he put his palms on his knees. She reminded him of a nurse the way she listened, like someone trying to comprehend symptoms. It occurred to him that she might not be able to tell him anything.

"Let me see if I understand," she said. "You want to know how I can be patient with the folks that call me on the air?" He nodded. "Well, I've got bad news for you. I was born patient. I just don't see the point in getting angry with anyone." Wesley frowned. Was she suggesting he had some sort of birth defect? He looked down and saw grains of masonry sand in the penny slots of his loafers. His boss, old man Morris, had given the sheriff two loads of driveway gravel to tear up Wesley's tickets, and he wanted him back on the road in a few days. Wesley wondered how long it would be before he killed someone.

"I'm sorry to bother you so late," he said, looking into her eyes and giving her the easiest smile he could manage. "It's just that I've been sort of waiting for things to turn around in my life. Right now, I got the feeling I can't wait any longer."

"Oh God," she said, her face crinkling like crepe paper, burgundy flushes coming under her eyes. "Don't say that."

"Say what?"

"That you're tired of waiting for things to turn around." She put a hand palm up on the table. "My favorite uncle used to say something close to that, over and over. Nobody knew what he really meant until we found him on his patio with a bullet in his temple."

Wesley straightened up. "Hey, I ain't the kind for that."

She stood awkwardly, almost upsetting her water glass. "I found him. You don't know how that made me feel. The missed connection." She stared out at the street, and he saw a flash of panic in her eyes. Her expression made him think of something his father used to say: that good times never taught him one crumb of what bad times had. "Come on," she said, "I want to show you something." He followed her out, and in the middle of the block she made Wesley get into the driver's seat of her car, a boxy blue Checker, a civilian version of a taxi.

"Where'd you get this big old thing?"

"My uncle," she explained, settling in on the passenger side. "He said it was slow, relaxing to drive, and one of the only things that brought comfort to his life." She rolled down the window. "He left it to me in his will."

"Where we going?" Wesley asked.

"Just drive around Pine Oil. I want to watch you." So he drove down the main street a mile to the end of town as she directed. Then he drove back on a parallel street, then west again, until he had done every east–west street in the checkerboard village. She told him to pull over at the edge of town at the Yum-Yum drive-in, a cube of glass blocks left over from the fifties.

"How'd I do?"

"Awful," she said.

Wesley thought he had never had a milder drive. The heavy Checker had floated over the city streets as though running on Valium. "What'd I do?"

"You rode the bumper on two elderly drivers," she told him. "Then you signaled for dimmers from two cars who had their low beams on. And Wesley," she said in her flutelike voice, "six jackrabbit starts, and at the traffic light you blew your horn."

"The old lady with the bun didn't move when the light changed."

Her face rounded into a tolerant smile. "Wesley, this is Pine Oil. Nobody blows his horn at someone else unless he spots a driver asleep on the railroad track. That woman was looking in her purse and would have noticed the light in a second. And where were *you* going? To a summit meeting?" She put her hand on his shoulder like a sister. "You've got to pay attention to how you're doing things." Her voice held more touch than her hand.

The fat woman wedged in the little service window of the Yum-Yum stared at them. "Okay," he said. "I'll try most anything." Janie then bought him a deluxe banana split, and even though he told her he hated bananas, she made him eat it with a flimsy plastic spoon.

Later, she made him drive the whole town, north to south, from poor brick-paper neighborhoods next to the tracks to the old, rich avenues of big drowsy houses. Janie lay back against the door, twisting a strand of hair around a finger. Finally, she asked him to take her home. When he pulled up to her apartment and turned off the motor, the quiet flowed through him like medicine.

"How do you feel, Wesley?" she asked with that voice.

"Okay, I guess. Just tired." He felt he had dragged her huge car around town on a rope slung over his shoulder.

"You did better." She straightened up and looked out over the long hood. "I have no idea what's wrong with you. I just want you to know that, and I really don't think you need to see me again." She smiled at him politely. "Just be patient like you were when you were driving tonight. You have to wait for things to turn around."

That's that, Wesley thought, as he helped her into the late-night air and walked her to the apartment.

The next morning he was sitting in the door of his trailer, drinking a cup of instant coffee and eating a Mars bar, wondering if he could get a job on the railroad, or even go back to work for his father. He heard the rattle and snap of gravel and saw Janie's navy-blue Checker lumber toward him through the mounds of gravel and sand. Swinging the door open quickly, she dropped from the front seat, fluffing out a full leaf-green skirt. "Wesley, you have got to be kidding."

"Ma'am?"

"Why're you living in a place like this? You can do better."

He nodded slowly, taking the last bite of his candy bar and staring at her. "My boss rented it to me the day I was hired. I guess I thought it came with the job." In daylight, she was prettier, though he could see better the cautious cast of her eyes.

"It wasn't easy locating you, let me tell you." She looked around at the junk as if to get her bearings, then settled her worried gaze on him. She was direct and moved precisely, unlike any woman he'd been around. "Can you take a ride now?" He saw the white arm move out from her side.

He put down his coffee cup. "I reckon so. Where we going?"

She smiled. "I like the way you say 'reckon.'"

Where they went was out on 51, the sluggish two-lane that bisected the parish. She had him pull up at a Stop sign and wait. A pickup truck rattled by, and he started to pull out. "Not yet," she said.

They waited five minutes, watching lumber trucks and motorcycles pass. Janie craned her neck and studied the southbound lane carefully. Finally she saw something that seemed to draw her interest. "That cattle truck," she said. "It's perfect. Get in behind it."

Wesley stared at the tinged sides of the slowly approaching trailer. "Aw, no," he pleaded.

"Follow it to Pine Oil," she commanded as the truck packed with heaving cows rocked by. He pulled into the wall of stench and began to follow at forty miles an hour. After five miles, he begged her to let him pass.

"No," she said. "You'll remember this trip for the rest of your life and realize that if you can wait out this, you can wait out anything." She turned her face to the side of the road, and the sunlight bounding off the hood brightened her high cheeks and made her beautiful. "A road is not by itself, Wesley, even if it's empty. It's part of the people who live on it, just like a vein is part of a body. Your trouble is you think only about the road and not what might come onto it."

He made a face but followed in silence, down through Amite,

Independence, and a half a dozen redbrick and clapboard communities with countless red lights and school zones. Arriving among the low tin-and-asbestos buildings of Pine Oil, he was white-faced and nauseated.

"You look awful," she said, leaning over, her green eyes wide. "Does being patient upset you this much?"

"No, ma'am," he lied.

"Well, let's see." She had him drive to Wal-Mart and stand in the longest line to buy a can of paste wax. They went over to her apartment, where she told him to get busy waxing the car. For three hours she sat in a folding chair under a volunteer swamp maple growing by the street, watching and occasionally calling for him to go over spots he'd missed. "Polish slower," she called. "Rub harder." Wesley thought he'd like to sail the green can of wax a block down the street and tell her to go to hell, but he didn't. His face began to develop slowly in the deep blue paint of her car.

Later, she set him in a straight-back chair in her plain living room and made him read a short story in *The Atlantic* and then talk to her about it. To Wesley, this was worse than following the cattle truck. He stared down at the glossy page. What did he care about a Chinese girl who couldn't make herself look like Shirley Temple to please her mother? Then Janie drove him home and they sat in the Checker outside his trailer. He leaned over and kissed her, long and slow, once.

"Wesley," she began, "what did the story in the magazine mean to you?"

"Mean?" he repeated, suspicious of the word. "I don't know." He knew what she was doing. She was trying to make him patient enough to think.

She asked him again, this time in her nicest radio voice. He told her about the Chinese girl's guilt and about her will to be independent. They talked for an hour about the story. Wesley thought he was going crazy.

The next day he did not see her, but he did listen to the radio. The topic was how to get rid of weeds in the yard. One caller, a wheezy old man, recommended pouring used motor oil along fences and sidewalks.

"But Mr. McFadgin," Janie began, using her most patient voice, "used motor oil is full of toxic metals such as lead."

"That's right, missy," the old man said. "Kills them weeds dead."

Wesley listened to her program for three hours and did not become enraged once.

The following night she called him to meet her at the Satin Lounge, a sleepy nightclub for middle-aged locals next to the motel. In a blue dress with a full skirt, she looked like a schoolteacher, which was all right with Wesley. They talked, Wesley about his father trying to control his life and Janie about her uncle, how he had raised her, how he had left her alone. They ordered a second round of drinks, and Janie did not test him for patience for an hour. Then someone played a slow number on the jukebox, and she stood up and asked him to dance. "Now slow down," she said, after they had been on the floor about ten seconds. "This is not a Cajun two-step. Barely move your feet. Dance with your hips and shoulders." He felt the controlling movement of her arms, of her soft voice, and realized that she was leading. After a while—he didn't know how it happened—he was leading again, but slowly. He felt like a fly struggling in sap, but he willed himself to dance like this all the way through the lengthy song.

Later on, two men sat at a table next to them. One was round and bearded, wearing a baseball cap with *Kiss My Ass* embroidered across the crown. The other, a short man with varnished blond hair, stared at Janie and once or twice leaned over to his companion, saying something behind a hand. Wesley watched him walk over to their table. The little man smiled, showing a missing tooth. He asked Janie to dance, and when she replied in a voice that made being turned down an honor, he scowled. "Aw, come on, sweetie. I need to hug me some woman tonight."

"I'm sorry, but I don't want to dance right now. Maybe someone at one of the other tables would enjoy your company." She smiled, but it was a thin smile, a fence.

He grinned stupidly and leaned over the table, placing his hands down on the damp Formica. "That sounds like a line a crap to me, sweetie."

Wesley caught her glance but couldn't read her face. He figured she would want him to stay calm, to avoid an argument, to sit expressionless and benign, like a divinity student. Maybe this would be another test, like polishing her mountain of a car.

"We really would like to be alone," she said, her confident voice weakening. The man smelled of stale cigarette smoke and beer. He looked at Wesley, who did not move, who was thinking that her voice was betraying her.

"Looks like you are alone," he said, grabbing her wrist and giving it a playful tug.

Wesley was sitting on his emotions the way he used to sit on his little brother in a backyard fight. When he saw Janie's wrist circled by a set of nubby fingers, he said in a nonthreatening voice, "Why don't you let her go? She doesn't want to dance."

The blond man cocked his head back like a rooster. "Why don't you just sit there and cross your legs, little girl."

Wesley looked down at the table as Janie was towed over to the tile dance floor. He relaxed in his fury and watched them. The little man couldn't jitterbug, his steps had nothing to do with the music, and he cramped Janie's arms on the turns. At the end of the song, he pulled her close and said something into her ear. She pushed him away, and the little man laughed.

When she stormed over to Wesley, her face was flushed, her voice a strained monotone. "I am so embarrassed," she said, staring straight ahead. "Why didn't you do something instead of just sitting there like a worm?"

Wesley felt a rush of blood fill his neck. He imagined that the back of his head was ready to blow out. "Do you know how hard it was for me to sit here and not pop him one in the face?"

She rubbed her right arm as though it hurt. "I felt so awkward and helpless while he was limping around out there."

"I was being patient. The only thing that would've made the little bastard happy is if I'd whipped his ass and gotten us all pitched out on the street or arrested."

She seemed not to hear. "I needed help and you just sat there." She stirred her drink with a swizzle stick but did not lift it. "I felt abandoned." She looked down into her lap.

Wesley's face was red, even in the dim light of the Satin Lounge, and the muscles in his neck rolled and twitched. He told himself to hold back. She wanted him patient and slow. "Hey, no harm done. It's over."

Janie stood up, sending her chair tumbling, and slammed her purse on the table. "Right," she yelled. "It's over."

By the time he paid the tab and ran into the parking lot, all he saw were the crimson ovals of the big Checker's taillights swerving around a distant curve. In the hot night air hung the sound of her uncle's car grinding through its gears, gaining momentum as though it might never stop.

The next morning he called Janie four times at the station, and each time she hung up on him. He sat on the sun-warmed iron steps to the trailer and tried to figure out why she was so upset. He had done what he thought she wanted him to do. He looked over at the abandoned locomotive buried axle-deep in the sand and shook his head.

Around eight o'clock the telephone rattled. Big Morris, his boss, was on the line. "Hey, boy. Mount that T-Bird and fly over here. We got called on a full load of masonry sand for the south shore by nine-thirty."

Wesley stared through a cracked window at his ten-year-old car. "It'll be a pinch."

"C'mon. You can do it."

"Call Ridley."

"He went through the windshield yesterday over in Satsuma. Be out for three weeks. Listen," Big Morris said with the cracked and weathered voice of an old politician, "you're my man, ain't you? You're the fastest I got."

Wesley looked at the warped and mildewed trailer, then out at the junk stacked around it. "I think I'm going to lay off driving for a while."

"What? You're good at speeding gravel, son."

"I know. That's why I better quit."

Two weeks later he was cutting meat in his father's grocery store, doing a fine job trimming the T-bones and round steaks, though now and then he jammed the slicer when he hurried the boiled ham. It was a new store, and the cutting room was pleasant, with lots of fluorescent lights, red sawdust on the floor to soak up the fat, and an auto-parts calendar on the wall showing Miss Rod Bearing. He always worked the one to nine P.M. shift, but today he had to cover the morning stretch. While he was in the back pulling meat out of the cooler, he noticed a familiar voice on the janitor's boom box, and he stopped, a rib cage cocked under his arm, to listen to Janie. She was dealing with Raynelle Bullfinch, a motorcycle club president from up near the Mississippi line.

"Who cares if we don't put no mufflers on our hogs, man," Raynelle growled. "Last time I looked, it was a free country."

Janie's voice slid out of the radio. "The ordinance in Gumwood is limited to neighborhood streets, Raynelle. It wouldn't affect your driving through town."

"Yeah, well, what if one of us wants to take a leak or something, and we have to buzz in off the highway? Those fat cops in Gumwood will jump on us like bottle flies."

"You don't think anyone should mind being inconvenienced by your racket?" The voice was a little thinner, and Wesley arched an eyebrow.

"Hey, everybody has to put up with some BS."

"Yes, but ugly noise is—"

"Aw, what the hell do you know, girlie. You never rode a Harley. You never get out of that radio station."

"Yes, but—"

"You got a leather jacket?"

There was a second of dead air. "Why would I want one?" The voice was flat and poisonous. Wesley leaned closer to the radio.

Raynelle shouted out, "What?"

Another second of dead air, and then Jamie's voice splintered, tantrumlike and shrill. "Why would I want to dress like a bull dyke who thinks the highest achievement of Western civilization is a stinking motorbike that makes a sound like gas being passed?" Wesley dropped the rib cage, then caught it up quickly at his ankles and hoisted it onto the cutting table.

"You bitch," Raynelle screamed.

Janie said something that made Wesley sit back against the meat, hold his nub, and stare at the radio. Just then, his father came through the back door, shaking rain off his hat.

"What you frownin' at, Wes? You look like somebody just had a accident." He began pulling off a raincoat.

"Aw hell, I don't know," he said. Janie played a commercial and then broke for the national news. Turning on the band saw, he positioned the ribs, watching the steel flash through the meat.

The next morning Wesley tuned in the local station on a new stereo in his apartment. A male voice filled his living room, an old guy with a scratchy throat who hung up on people when they disagreed with him. Wesley was surprised, the way he'd felt when something unexpected had come into the road in front of his gravel truck. He called the station and talked with the secretary, but she wouldn't tell him anything. For two mornings he listened for Janie but heard only the disgruntled voice, a sound rough and hard-nosed, a better match for the backwoods folks of the parish than Janie could make herself be. He called her at home, but the phone had been disconnected. He went to her apartment, but it was being cleaned by a Vietnamese woman who said she was getting it ready for the next occupants. Finally, he stopped at the station, which was upstairs over Buster's Dry Cleaning, and found the manager in his littered office.

"Hey, I'm Wesley, a friend of Janie. I wonder if you could tell me how to get up with her."

The manager, a tall, square-shouldered man in his sixties, invited him to sit down. "I'm kind of curious about her whereabouts myself. After she lost control with a caller the other day, she just jerked the headset out of her hair and threw it. She ran down the stairs with this damned angry look on her face and I haven't seen her since."

"Does she have any relatives around here?"

The manager looked at his desk a long time before answering. "She moved here with an uncle when she was a kid. He had to raise her, don't ask me why. She never mentioned any parents."

Wesley bit his cheek and thought a moment. "She told me about the uncle."

The manager shook his head and looked across the hall to the broadcast booth. "She was the best voice I ever had. I don't know what happened. I don't care about what she did the other day."

"She sounded great all right." The two men were silent for a moment, savoring Janie's words as though they were polite touches remembered on the back of the neck.

"I wish I could tell you something, Wesley, but to me, at least, she was mainly a voice. It did everything for her—it was her hands and feet." The manager leaned closer to him and narrowed his eyes. "After she lost her uncle, I listened to her, and she didn't sound any different." He motioned to a dusty speaker box over his door. "But if you looked in her eyes, you could see how everything but that voice had been taken out of her. Do you know what I mean?"

"I think so," Wesley said, standing up to go. He tried to picture her walking in and out of the studio's dowdy tiled rooms, but he couldn't see her.

The manager followed him to the door and put a hand on his back. "She sounded like she knew it all, didn't she?"

"She could give advice," Wesley told him, "but she couldn't follow it." Together they stared through the soundproof glass at a fat man scratching his bald liver-spotted skull with the eraser of a pencil, an unfiltered cigarette bobbing on his lips as he berated a caller.

He looked for her off and on for six months, writing letters and calling radio stations throughout the South. Sometimes he'd be cutting meat, hear a voice by the display cases, and go out and search the aisles. His father tried to match him with one of the cashiers, but it didn't work out. One evening he was helping the old man clean the attic of his house on Pecan Street when they found a wooden radio behind a box of canceled checks.

Wesley studied the Atwater Kent's dials and knobs. "You stopped using this before I was born. You reckon it still works?"

His father walked over to where Wesley knelt under a rafter. "Don't waste your time."

"Let's plug it into the droplight there." He stretched to the peak of the low attic.

"You won't get anything. You need a dipole antenna."

Wesley pulled a wire from the back and attached it to an aluminum screen door propped up sideways under the rafters. "Didn't you tell me these old sets would bring in Europe?"

His father sighed and sat Indian-style in the attic dust next to Wesley. "You're crazy if you think you'll find her on that," he said. They watched the ivorine dial build its glow, heard a low whine rise as the screen door gathered sound from the air. Outside, it was sundown, and all over the country the little stations were signing off to make room for the clear-channel fifty-thousand-watt broadcasters coming from Del Rio and New Orleans, Seattle and Little Rock. Wesley turned the knob slowly, the movement of his fingers like a clock's minute hand.

"This thing's got some power," Wesley said.

His father shook his head. "All you'll get is junk from all over the world, especially at night. What's that?"

"*Bonjour* is French. Are we getting France?"

"Maybe Canada. It's hard to tell." For ten minutes, as the roof timbers ticked and cooled above them, they scanned the dial for used cars in Kansas City, propaganda in Cuba, Coca-Cola in someplace where children sang a clipped language they had never heard before, the voices coming clear for a moment and then fading to other tongues even as Wesley kept his hand off the dial, the radio tuning itself, drifting through a planetful of wandering signals. And then, a little five-hundred-watter from another time zone where it was not yet sundown skipped its signal for a moment over Pine Oil, Louisiana, and Wesley heard a woman's liquid voice as she ran the tail of a talk show off toward nightfall.

"Oh, it's usually not as bad as you think it is," she was saying.

A sour voice answered, an angry sound from the inner city. "You're not in my shoes. How do you know what I feel?" Somewhere lightning struck, and the words began to stutter and wane. Wesley grabbed the walnut box and put his head down to the speaker.

His father let out a little groan. "It's not her. Don't be such a fool."

"I can't know how you feel," the announcer said. "But are you saying there's nothing I can tell you?"

The response was lost in a rip of static, and the woman's voice trembled away from Wesley's ears, shaking like his father's dusty hand pulling back on his hair.

CHARTING THE TERRITORIES OF THE RED

William Gay

When the women came back from the rest area, slinging their purses along and giggling, Dennis guessed that someone had flirted with them. He hoped they'd keep their mouths shut about it. He was almost certain that Sandy wouldn't say a word, but you never knew about Christy.

Well, we got flirted with, Christy said. She linked an arm through his and leaned against him, standing on his feet, looking up at him. The sun was moving through her auburn hair, and there were already tiny beads of perspiration below her eyes, on the brown, poreless skin of her forehead. She smelled like Juicy Fruit chewing gum.

Dennis unlaced his arm from hers and stepped back and wiped his wire-rimmed glasses on the tail of his shirt. He was wearing jeans and a denim shirt with the sleeves scissored out at the shoulders. He glanced at Wesley. He put the glasses back on and turned and looked at the river. Moving light flashed off it like a heliograph. I guess we need to get the boats in the water, he said.

Wesley had both of Sandy's hands in both of his own. Her hands were small and brown and clasped, so in Wesley's huge fists they looked amputated at the wrists. Who flirted with you? Wesley asked.

Sandy just grinned and shook her head. She had short dark hair, far shorter than Wesley's. Wesley was looking down into her sharp, attentive face. The best thing about her face was her eyes, which were large and blue-green and darkly fringed with thick lashes. The best thing about her eyes was the way they focused on you when you were talking to her, as if she was listening intently and retaining every word. Dennis had always suspected that she did this because she was deaf. Perhaps she didn't even know she did it.

Sandy had once been beaten terribly, but studying her closely Dennis could see no sign of this now. Perhaps the slightest suggestion of aberration about the nose, a hesitant air that she was probably not even aware of. But her skin was clear and brown, the complex and delicate latticework of bones intact beneath it.

Nobody was flirting with us, she said, smiling up at Wesley.

If they did, you flashed them a little something, Wesley said.

If I couldn't get flirted with without flashing them a little something I'd just stay at the house, Christy said. She was giggling again. The big one said his name was Lester, she told Wesley. But don't worry, he was ugly and baldheaded.

Lester? What the hell kind of redneck name is Lester? Was he chewing Red Man? Did he have on overalls?

You know, Wesley's not the most sophisticated name I ever heard, Christy said. Nobody's named Wesley, nobody. Do you know one movie star named Wesley?

It occurred to Dennis that Christy might be doing a little flirting herself, although Wesley had been married to Sandy for almost two years and he supposed that he was going to marry Christy himself, someday sooner or later.

I don't know any movie stars named anything at all, Wesley said. I'll make him think goddamn Lester. I'll Lester him.

Wesley wore cutoff jeans and lowcut running shoes with the laces removed. He was bare to the waist and burnt redblack from the sun so he looked like a sinister statuary you'd chopped out of a block of mahogany with a doublebitted axe. He'd been in the water, and his jeans were wet, and his hair lay in wet black ringlets.

Nobody was flirting with anybody, Sandy said carefully. She enunciated each word clearly, and Dennis figured this as well was because she had been deaf so long. Now she had an expensive hearing aid smaller than the nail of her little finger, and she could hear as well as anyone, but this had not always been so.

Are you all going to get the boats and stuff? Christy asked.

Let's get everything down from the camp, Dennis said. We can pick the girls up here.

They followed a black path that wound through wild cane, brambles, blackberry briars. It led to a clearing where they'd spent the night. On the riverbank were sleeping bags and a red plastic ice chest. Dennis began to roll up the sleeping bag he'd slept in with Christy. Sometime far into the night he had awoken, some noise, a nightbird, an owl. Some wild cry that morphed into Sandy's quickened breathing as Wesley made love to her. He wondered if Wesley still beat her. He looped a string around the sleeping bag and lashed it tight. When the breathing had reached some frenzied peak and then slowly subsided to normal, he had turned over, being careful not to wake Christy, and gone back to sleep. He turned now and tossed the sleeping bag into one of the two aluminum canoes tied to a hackberry depending out over the river.

When the canoes rounded the bend through the trailing willow fronds, Dennis saw that a red four-wheel-drive Dodge truck had backed a boat trailer down the sloping bank to the shallows. On it were two aluminum canoes that might have been clones of the ones Dennis and Wesley were rowing. Two men were in the bed of the pickup, two men on the ground. The man unbooming the boats did indeed have on overalls. He was enormous, thicker and heavier than Wesley. He wore the overalls with no shirt, and his head was shaved. The top of his head was starkly white against the sunburned skin of his face, as if he'd just this minute finished shaving it.

Son of a bitch, Wesley said.

This is by God crazy, Dennis said, but Wesley had already drifted the canoe parallel with the shore and was wading out. Don't let this canoe drift into the current, he said over his shoulder. He went up the bank looking at Sandy and Christy. Sandy's face was as blank as a slate you'd erased, but a sort of constrained glee in Christy's told him what he wanted to know. He turned to the men grouped about the red truck.

Lester, I heard you were trying to hit on my wife, he said.

The bald man was turned away, but they were so close Wesley could smell the sweat on him, see the glycerinous drops seeping out of the dark skin of his back. The man had a malignant-looking mole the size of a fingertip between his shoulders, where the galluses crossed. The man fitted a key into a lock clasped through two links of chain securing the canoes. The lock popped open, and he freed the chain and locked the hasp through another link and pocketed the key. He turned. He looked up at the two men in the back of the truck and grinned. At last he glanced at Wesley.

This electronic age, he said, and laughed. I reckon it's been all over the news already. He wiped the sweat off his head with a forearm and turned to inspect the women. They'd seated themselves on the bank above, and they were watching like spectators boxseated before some barbaric show.

Which one'd be your wife? Lester asked.

Faced with the prospect of describing his wife or pointing her out like a miscreant in a lineup, Wesley hesitated. Sandy raised her arm. That would be me, she said.

Did I hit on you? Say anything out of the way?

No. You didn't.

The man looked Wesley in the eye. He shrugged. What can I say, he said.

Hey, loosen up, good buddy, one of the men in the truck called. He turned and opened an ice chest and began to remove cans of beer from it. He was bare to the waist, and he had straight, shoulderlength hair that swung with his movement when he turned from the cooler. He tossed a can to Dennis: Unprepared, he still caught it onehanded, shifted hands with it. One for the ladies, the man said, and tossed them gently, one, two. When he pitched a fourth to Wesley, Wesley caught it and pivoted and threw it as far as he could out over the river. It vanished without so much as a splash.

Lester looked up at the longhaired man and grinned. Not his brand, he said.

Don't try to bullshit me, Wesley said.

I wouldn't even attempt it, friend, Lester said. He turned to the boat, his back to Wesley, as if he'd simply frozen him out, as if Wesley didn't exist anymore. He unlooped the chain and slid the canoes off the sloped bed into the water. The two men leapt from the bed of the truck and with the third began to load the boats with ice chests, oars, boxes of fishing tackle. They climbed into the canoes and headed them downstream into the current. Lester turned to the women. He doffed an imaginary hat. Ladies, he said.

Wesley seemed to be looking around for a rock to throw.

Let it go, Dennis said.

I could have handled them, Wesley said. All that fine help I had from you.

Dennis turned and spat into the river. Hellfire. You didn't need any help. You made as big a fool of yourself alone as you could have with me helping.

I ain't letting them shitkickers run over me, Wesley said. Hell, I got a good Christian raising and a eighth-grade education. I don't have to put up with this shit from anybody.

But Wesley's moods were mercurial, and he seemed to find what he had just said amusing. He repeated it to himself, then looked toward the girls. Let's get organized, he said. As soon as Jeeter Lester and his family get gone we'll start looking for that Civil War cave.

He waded out to the canoe containing the red cooler. But first let's all have a little shot of that jet fuel, he said.

Dennis was watching Sandy, and a look like apprehension flickered across her face and was gone. No more than a sudden shadow of a passing cloud. Wesley had removed the lid from the cooler. He had somewhere come by an enormous quantity of tiny bottles of Hiram Walker. They were the kind of bottles served on airlines, and Wesley called them jet fuel. He was fumbling under the sandwiches, dumping things out. Jet fuel, jet fuel, he was saying.

I'm sorry, Wesley, Sandy called. I left that bag setting on the kitchen table.

Wesley straightened. Well it'll do a whole hell of a lot of good setting on a table fifty miles from where I am, he said. He sailed the lid out over the river like an enormous rectangular Frisbee.

I said I was sorry. I really am.

Regret is not jet fuel, Wesley said. He hurled the cooler into the water. Everything went: cellophaned sandwiches, a sixpack of Coke, apples bobbing in the rapid current. A bottle of vin rosé.

Shit, Dennis said.

Wesley came wading out of the river. Sandy and Christy were buckling on lifejackets. Dennis glanced sharply at Wesley's face. He stood up and put his folded glasses into the pocket of his denim shirt.

I don't think you're supposed to be throwing crap in the river like that, Christy said.

Oh no, Wesley said. The river police will get me.

Dennis was staring out at the lighthammered water. Lester and his cohorts had drifted out of sight around the bend. Now where is this famous Civil War cave? he asked.

Supposed to be somewheres close, Wesley told him, relaxing visibly. He turned to the women. Can you all handle a canoe?

I can row as good as you can, Christy told him. Maybe better.

You all check out one side of the river and me and this fine defender of Southern womanhood'll look on the other. Check out every bluff, look for anything that might be a cave. It's supposed to be about halfway up. If you find a cave, sing out as loud as you can and we'll be there. OK?

OK.

And keep those lifejackets on. If you have to take a leak or just whatever, do it with the jackets on.

I'm not sure I can do that, Christy said. She turned and gave Dennis a look so absolutely blank it could have meant anything. It could have meant, You showed common sense staying out of that argument he had. Or it could have meant, Why the hell weren't you backing him up?

Wesley was looking out across the river. Goddamn it's hot, he said. Did anybody see where that beer hit?

They drifted with the current, and Dennis shipped the oars, only using one occasionally to steer clear of trees leaning into the water. Huge monoliths of black slate and pale limestone towered above them, ledges adorned with dwarf cedars twisted and windformed. The river moved under them, yellow and murmurous, flexing like the sleekridged skin of an enormous serpent.

Snipes, Wesley said suddenly.

Dennis thought he meant some kind of bird. He was scanning the willows and cane; he had a mental picture of some kind of longlegged bird, one foot raised out of the water, a fish in its mouth.

Where? he asked.

Wesley by God Snipes, Wesley said. Ain't he a movie star?

Yes, he is.

I'll have to tell Christy about that when we catch up. They're done out of sight around that shoal yonder.

After a while Wesley told him again the story of the Civil War cave.

The guy always called it that, the Civil War cave, as if the entire Civil War had been fought inside it. He said it was where Confederate soldiers hid out one time. You can't even see it from the ridge; you have to find it from the river. He said there was all kinds of shit in there. Artifacts. Old guns, lead balls. And bones, too, old belt buckles. He didn't even care, can you feature that? Said the guns was all seized up with rust.

In the lifetime he had known Wesley, Dennis had heard this story perhaps a hundred times. He had his mind kicked out of gear, coasting along, listening to the river mumbling to itself. He thought of the look on Sandy's face when Wesley turned from hurling the cooler into the river, and he thought about gauges.

Once, long ago, on one of the few occasions when he had been blind, falling-down drunk, it had occurred to Dennis that life would be much simpler if everything had a gauge on it, the sort that on an automobile measure the temperature of the engine and so on. If the brain had a gauge you would know immediately how smart a certain decision was. You could start to act on it, keeping an eye on the needle all the time. You could proceed, pull back, try another approach. If the heart had one you'd know how in love you were with somebody. And if you could read their gauge...you could live your life with one eye on the needles and never make a foolish move.

Dennis had made several foolish movements in his life, but he had never wavered in the conviction that Wesley had a gauge in his head. It measured how close he was to violence, and went from zero into uncharted deep red, and every moment of Wesley's life the needle hovered, trembling, on the hairline of white that was all that stood between order and chaos.

Dennis had long ago quit going to bars with Wesley. At a certain point in his drinking, as if a thermostat had clicked on somewhere, Wesley would swivel his stool and survey the room with a smile of good-natured benevolence, studying its contents as if to ascertain were there inanimate objects worth breaking, folks worth putting in the hospital.

Six months after he married Sandy, he had eased into the bedroom of an apartment in the housing project and studied the sleeping faces of Sandy and a man named Bobby Joe Seales. He had slammed Seales full in the face with his fist, then turned his attention to Sandy. He had broken her arm and nose and jaw and shifted back to Seales. The room was a scene of carnage, folks said, blood on the floor, blood on the walls, blood on the ceiling. He had ripped the shade from a lamp and used the lamp base as a club, beating Seales viciously. Folks came screaming, cops. Dennis did not hear this story from Wesley, or from Sandy, but he had heard it plenty of other places, and Wesley stood trial for aggravated assault. The son of a bitch aggravated me, Wesley had said. So I assaulted him.

Seales had been on the Critical List. Folks always spoke of it in capital letters as if it were a place. A place you didn't want to go. Don't fuck with Wesley Deavers, folks said. He put Bobby Joe Seales on the Critical List. It looked like they'd been killing hogs in there.

Did you hear something?

Dennis listened. All he could hear was the river, crows spilling raucous cries from above them, doves mourning from some deep hollow he couldn't see.

Something. Sounded like yelling.

Then he could hear voices, faint at first, sourceless, as if they were coming from thin air, or out of the depths of the yellow water. Then he heard, faint and faint: Dennis. Dennis.

They've found it, Wesley said. He took up his oars and turned the boat into the swift current. Let's move it, he said. The voices had grown louder. If this is the right cave we'll map it, Wesley said. Make us up some charts so we can find it again.

The river widened where it shoaled, then began narrowing into a bottleneck as the bend came up. Dennis could feel the river quickening under him, the canoe gaining urgency as it rocked in the current.

Dennis. Dennis.

I wish she'd shut the hell up, Dennis said.

All right, all right, Wesley yelled. We're coming.

That must be one hellacious cave.

But the cliffs had been tending away for some time now on this side of the river, and when they rounded the bend they saw that the bluffs had subsided to a steep, stony embankment where Christy and Sandy were huddled. Dennis couldn't see their canoe. They were on their knees and still wearing life jackets, their hair plastered tightly to their skulls. Sandy was crying, and Christy was talking to her and had an arm about her shoulders.

Now what the fuck is this news, Wesley said, and Dennis felt a cold shudder of unease. He remembered something Dorothy Parker had purportedly said once when her doorbell rang: What fresh hell is this?

They tipped us over, Christy said. Now she began to cry as well. Goddamn them. They were waiting for us here and grabbed the boat. All four of them, two boatloads. They tried to get us into the boats with them and when we wouldn't go they got rough, tried to drag us. I hit one with an oar, and that baldheaded fucker tipped us over. They took the boat.

Wesley seemed actually to pale. Dennis could see a cold pallor beneath the deep tan. It seemed to pulse in his face. Sandy, are you all right? Wesley asked.

She can't hear, Christy said. When we went under it did something to her hearing aid, ruined it. Shorted it out or something. She can't hear a thing. I mean not a goddamned thing.

Oh, Wesley cried. He seemed on the threshold of a seizure, some sort of rageinduced attack. Eight hundred fucking dollars, he said. Eight hundred dollars up a wild hog's ass and gone. I'm going to kill them. I'm going to absolutely fucking kill them.

Wesley made twelve dollars an hour, and Dennis knew that he was mentally dividing twelve into eight hundred and arriving at the number of hours he had worked to pay for the hearing aid.

Where's the other oars?

I don't know. They floated off.

I'm gone. I'm going to kill them graveyard dead.

He turned the boat about to face the current.

Hey, Christy called. Wait.

Stay right here, Wesley said. And I mean right here. Do not move from that rock 'til we get back with the boat.

Let them keep the goddamned boat, Christy screamed, but Wesley didn't reply. He heeled into the current and began to row. He did not speak for a long time. He rowed like a madman, like some sort of rowing machine kicked up on high. I'll row when you get tired, Dennis said. Fuck that, Wesley told him. After a while he looked back and grinned. How dead am I going to kill them? he asked.

Graveyard dead, Dennis said.

Wesley hadn't missed a stroke rowing. After a time he said. There will be some slow riding and sad singing.

Trees went by on the twin shorelines like a landscape unspooling endlessly from one reel to another. A flock of birds went down the metallic sky like a handful of hurled slate. Dennis guessed by now the Lester gang was long gone, into the tall timber, their canoes hidden in the brush, laughing and drinking beer, on their way back across the ridges to pick up their truck.

What were you going to do, back there, kick my ass?

Dennis was looking at the sliding yellow water. What?

Back there at the camp when my jet fuel was missing. You got up and folded your little glasses and shoved them in your pocket. You looked for all the world like a schoolteacher getting ready to straighten some folks out. You think you can kick my ass?

I wouldn't want to hurt you, Dennis said.

Wesley laughed. How long have you known me, Dennis?

You know that. Since the third grade.

Third grade. Have I ever lied to you?

I don't know. How would I know that? Not that I know of.

I never lied to you. So I'm telling the truth now. I'm going to kill them. I'm going to kill them with an oar, not flat like I was paddling their ass, but sideways like I was chopping wood. I'll take their heads off. Do you want out? I'll ease over and let you out.

The boat hadn't slackened. The oars dipped and pulled, dipped and pulled, with no variation in their rhythm. The boat seemed to have attained its own volition, its own momentum.

No, Dennis finally said, and he knew with a cold horror that Wesley was telling the truth.

Do you really think I'd stop long enough to let you out?

You never lie.

No.

I can ask you the one right question and you'll lie.

Ask it then.

But before he could ask it, Wesley suddenly shouted. A hoarse cry of exultation. Dennis looked. They were aligned on a sandbar far downriver, three of them, the three canoes beached on the shore like bright metallic whales. Tiny dark figures in attitudes of waiting, watching them come.

Shouts came skipping across the water. Now he could see that Lester had his hands cupped about his mouth like a megaphone. It took you long enough, he yelled.

Wesley might not have heard. He was leaning into the oars, the muscles in the arms that worked them knotting and relaxing, knotting and relaxing.

They stood like the last ragged phalanx of an army backed to the last wall there was. They each held an oar. When the boat was still twenty feet from the shoreline Wesley bailed out. Oar aloft like God's swift sword. He seemed to be skimming the surface, a dark vengeful divinity the waters would not even have. He knocked Lester's oar aside with his own and drew back and swung. The oar made an eerie, abrupt whistling. Blood misted the air like paint from an exploding spray can. Lester went to his knees clutching his face, blood streaming between his fingers. Wesley hit him across the top of the head, and a vulval gash opened in the shaven flesh. Dennis slammed the long-haired man backward, and he stumbled and fell into a thicket of willows and wild cane. He advanced on him, swinging the oar like a man killing snakes. An oar caught him across the biceps, and his left arm went suddenly numb. He turned. A man with a fright wig of wild red hair and clenched yellow teeth broadsided him in the shoulder with the flat of an oar just as Wesley broke his own oar across the man's back. Wesley was left with a section half the length of a baseball bat. The redhaired man was going to run through the cane, and Wesley threw the stub of the paddle at him.

The longhaired man had simply vanished. Dennis had driven him into the cane, and he'd just disappeared. Dennis was almost giddy with relief. It seemed over before it had properly begun, and it had not been as bad as he had feared it would be.

Lester was crawling on his hands and knees away from the river. He crawled blindly, his eyes full of blood, which dripped into the sand below him.

Wesley picked up a discarded oar and walked between Lester and the growth of willows. He had the oar cocked like a chopping ax. Lester crawled on. When his head bumped Wesley's knee he reared backward, sitting on his folded legs. He made a mute, armsspread gesture of supplication.

Wesley, Dennis yelled.

Kill this motherfucker graveyard dead, Wesley said.

Dennis crossed the sand in two long strides and swung onto

Wesley's arm and wrested the oar from him. Wesley sat down hard in the sand. He got up shaking his head as if he'd clear it. He crossed the sandbar and waded kneedeep into the river and scooped up handfuls of water and washed his face. Lester crawled on. Like something wounded that just won't die. When he was into the willows he struggled up and stood leaning with both hands cupping his knees. Then he straightened and began wiping the blood out of his eyes. Dennis lay on his back in the sand for a long time and stared into the sky, studying the shifting patterns the clouds made. Both arms ached, and he was slowly clasping and unclasping his left hand. The bowl of the sky spun slowly clockwise, like paleblue water emptying down an endless drain.

He could hear Lester lumbering off through the brush. Wesley came up and dropped onto the sand beside Dennis. Dennis had an arm flung across his eyes. He thought he might just lie here in the hot weight of the sun forever. His ribs hurt, and he could feel his muscles beginning to stiffen.

I wish I hadn't quit smoking and I had a cigarette, Wesley said. Or maybe a little shot of that jet fuel. Chastising rednecks is hot, heavy work, and it does wear a man out so.

Dennis didn't reply, and after a time Wesley said, You ought to've let me kill him. I knew you weren't as committed as I was. I could see your heart wasn't in it. You didn't have your mind right.

He was dragging off like a snake with its back broke, Dennis said. What the hell do you want? Let it be.

We need to get these boats back to where Sandy and Christy are. Damned if I don't dread rowing upstream. Bad as I feel. You reckon we could rig up a towline and pull them along the bank?

I don't know.

You don't think they'd go back to where the girls are, do you?

I don't know.

We better go see. No telling what kind of depravities those inbred mutants could think of to do with an innocent young girl.

Dennis suddenly dropped an arm from his eyes and sat up. He

could hear a truck engine. It was in the distance, but approaching, and the engine sounded wound out, as if it were being rawhided over and through the brush. He stood up. The truck seemed to be coming through the timber, and he realized that a road, probably an unused and grownover logging road, ran parallel with the river. They know this river, he thought. The fourth man went to get the truck. Through a break in the trees chrome mirrored back the light, the sun hammered off bright red metal. The truck stopped. The engine died. Immediately Dennis could hear voices, by turns angry and placating. They seemed to be fighting amongst themselves, trying to talk Lester either into or out of doing something. A door slammed; another or the same door slammed again. When he looked around, Wesley had risen and gathered up two of the paddles. He reached one of them to Dennis. Dennis waved it away. Let's get the hell out of Dodge, he said.

We got to get the boats.

To hell with the boats. We got to move.

Something was coming through the brake of wild cane, not walking or even running as a man might, but lurching and stumbling and crashing, some beast enraged past reason, past pain. Wesley turned toward the noise and waited with the oar at a loose port arms across his chest.

Lester came out of the cane with a .357 Magnum clasped both-handed before him. It looked enormous even in his huge hands. Lester looked like something that had escaped halfbutchered from a meatpacker's clutches, like some bloody experiment gone awry. His wild eyes were just black holes charred in the bloody suet of his face. The bullet splintered the oar and slammed into Wesley's chest. Wesley's head, his feet, seemed to jerk forward. Then Lester shot him in the head, and Wesley sprung backward as if a springloaded tether had jerked him away.

Dennis was at the edge of the canebrake running full out. He glanced back. The pistol swung around. He dove sideways into the cane, rolling, and running from the ground up as the explosion showered him with sand, the cane tilting and swaying in his bobbing vision. The horizon jerked with his footfalls. Another shot, shouts, curses, men running down from the truck. He'd lost his glasses, and trees swam into his blurred vision as though surfacing at breakneck speed from murky water. Branches clawed at him; a lowhanging vine hurled him forward like a projectile blown out of the wall of greenery. He slowed and went on. He could hear excited voices, but nobody seemed to be pursuing him. He went on anyway, his lungs hot as if he moved through a medium of smoke, of pure fire. The timber deepened, and he went on into it. He fell and lay across the roots of an enormous beech. The earth was loamy and black and smelled like corrupting flesh. He vomited and lay with his face in the vomit. He closed his eyes. After a while the truck cranked and retreated the way it had come, fast, winding out. He raised his face and spat. There was a taste in his mouth like a cankered penny, and he could smell fear on himself like an animal's rank musk that you can't wash off.

When he finally made it back to the sandbar, the first thing he did was hunt his glasses. They were lying in the cane where he'd dived and rolled, an earpiece bent at a crazy angle but nothing broken. He put them on, and everything jerked into focus, as if a vibratory world had abruptly halted its motion.

Wesley was on his back with the back of his head and both hands lying in the water. He looked as if he'd flung his arms up in surrender, way too late. Dennis looked away. He took off the denim shirt and spread it across Wesley's face.

He dragged one of the canoes parallel with the body and began trying to roll Wesley into it. Wesley was a big man, and this was no easy task. He was loath to touch the bare flesh, but finally there was no way round it and he picked up the legs and worked them across the canoe and braced his feet and tugged the torso over into it. The boat lurched in the shallow water. By this time he was crying, making animal sounds he did not recognize as coming from himself. He threw in two oars and, running behind the boat, shoved it into deeper water. When he climbed in, he had to sit with a foot on either side of Wesley's thighs in order to row. In the west the sinking sun was burning through the trees with a bluegold light.

Twilight was falling when he came upon them, a quarter mile or so downriver from where they'd been left. They were straggling along the bank, Christy carrying what he guessed was a stick for cottonmouths. He oared the boat around broadside and rowed to shore. He waded the last few feet and dragged the prow into the bank, turned toward the women. They were looking not at him but at what was in the boat. All this time he'd been wondering what he could say to Sandy, but he remembered with dizzy relief that she was deaf and he wouldn't have to say anything at all. There didn't seem to be any questions anyway, or any answers worth giving if there were.

Christy's face was a twisted gargoyle's mask. Oh no, she said. Oh, Jesus, please no.

Dennis sat on the bank with his feet in the water. Rowing upstream had been hard, and he had his bloody palms upturned on his knees, studying the broken blisters. Sandy rose and climbed down the embankment, steadying her descent with a hand on Dennis's shoulder. She stood staring down into the boat. She knelt in the shallow water. Dennis stood up and waded around the boat and steadied it. He looked curiously like a salesman standing at the ready to demonstrate something should the need arise. He could hear Christy crying. She cried on and on.

Wesley lay with the bloody shirt still flung across his face. He lay like a fallen giant. Treetrunk legs, huge bronze torso. Sandy took up one of his hands and held it. The great fingers, thick black hair between the knuckles. She held the hand a time, and then she began folding the limp fingers into a fist, a finger at a time, tucking the thumb down and holding the hand in a fist with her own two hands. She sat and looked at it. Dennis suddenly wondered if she was seeing the fist come at her out of a bloody and abrupt awakening, rising and falling as remorselessly as a knacker's hammer, and he leaned and disengaged her hand. The loose fist slapped against the hull and lay palm upward.

He thought she might be crying, but when he looked up her eyes were dry and calm. They locked with his. Nor would she look away, as if she were waiting for his lips to move so she could read them.

We've got to get him out of here, Christy sobbed. A road somewhere maybe; somebody would stop.

Nobody answered her. Dennis wasn't listening, and Sandy couldn't hear at all. He wondered what it would sound like to be deaf. What you'd hear. From the look on Sandy's face across the body of her fallen warrior he judged it must be a calm and restful sound, the sighing of a perpetual wind through clashing rushes, a lapping of peaceful water that never varies or ceases.

GHOSTS IN BLUE AND GRAY

Juliana Gray

They will not let us go, the old dead.
They loom from roadside markers, museums, names
of weary families. Entire fields
are filled with them. We cannot turn around
without tripping headlong over them,
banging our knees, stubbing our toes on the dead.

Not even the water is safe, the rivers clogged
with history, the bays cluttered with wrecks.
We dragged the *Hunley*, that absurd submarine,
into the air, and emptied out the silt.
Then we found their tarnished buttons, their teeth,
scraps of cloth, even the salted bones.
In the gun turret of the *Monitor*,
a skeleton held fast, waiting for
the living to discover him whole.

How to free ourselves of them? How
to shed their dust, their claptrap sabers and scrip?
Antietam, Vicksburg, Shiloh—could we just
stroll among the monuments and say
in resolute tones, "Enough, please,
enough, we have had enough of you"?
Most likely, they would not listen; and if they did,
some of us might miss them. Some of us
would sift through channel silt, fingering
the soil, weeping over buttons and bone.

SHRIMPERS

Juliana Gray

They leave the Gulf before the sunlight sparks
the waves, and drive their trucks up the interstate
to Birmingham and Gadsden and Anniston
and us. The gravel pops beneath their wheels
as they turn into the same empty church
parking lot, and stop beneath the same
shady oak that shelters them each year.
They hang their signs, light a smoke, and wait
for us to come in our station wagons and vans,
hauling coolers and sweaty bags of ice.
The placid men wear clean shirts and shorts,
but still they reek of fish and salt and blood
as they scoop their catch onto scales and pour the mass
in our outstretched coolers. By noon, the trucks
are empty. They hit the breakfast bar at Shoney's,
taking luxury in scrambled eggs,
biscuits, gravy, glistening bacon strips,
all theirs for the easy taking. Then back in the trucks
and south again, to the Gulf, the boats, and home.

And we, in our inland houses, seem to hear
the ocean as we clean the pearly shrimp,
beheading, peeling, choosing which to freeze
for winter gumbo, and which to cook today.
And now and then, a hand that plunges down
into the icy brine emerges full
of something unexpected: urchins, squid,
some tiny unnamed fish the shrimpers' nets
had blindly caught. The children gather round
to stare, to touch, to hold the mystery,

the treasure valued more for its surprise.
They marvel at the shrimpers, who seem to take
no notice of the things they live among,
the miracles they haul into the air.

I'LL FLY AWAY

Wayne Greenhaw

O n Friday morning, Mama called.
Her words were soaked with despair. "He's not doing well, son. They had to restrain him yesterday. He tried to hurt himself." Daddy had tried to leap from a third-floor balcony of Bryce Hospital for the mentally ill. He decided he could fly. For years he had wanted to.

After his first stay at Bryce's, I drove him to the Meadowbrook Golf Club. He had a Schlitz and watched his friends play gin rummy. He asked me to drive around through the neighborhood before going home. Smiling, he said, "Wouldn't it be great to open your wings and take off, like a bird?"

After Mama called, I drove the hundred miles north to Tuscaloosa.

Entering the house, I looked around at all I had known, but it was foreign, heavy with the perfume of childhood, strains of heartache, echoes of emotional poverty.

I put my bag on the single bed. Above, an Alabama Crimson Tide pennant on the wall. Below, a faded photograph of me and my old friend Jake Sims at Boy Scout camp. Jake's eyes were too happy to have been burned alive in the jungles of Vietnam while his platoon listened to his mournful cries throughout the night. On the bedside table I was a stranger in a white dinner jacket, holding Mary Russell Caldwell on my arm at the senior prom. She was too pretty and pert to have been tortured by the big C that spread through her body until she withered away to nothing by age twenty-four.

Hearing the door of a car slam, I tore myself from memory.

At the front door, her voice caught in her throat. Then she managed, "Harold's dead." I opened my arms and folded them around her, hearing her whimper, feeling her tears against my neck. "Oh, Mama," I said, and she shook like a leaf in the wind.

After a while, we sat at the kitchen table, and she told me how he'd taken too much medication. She frowned and shook her head. "How can you do that in that place? It looks like they'd keep a close watch on…on the patients."

I nodded. I felt drained, void of feeling. Whatever had been no longer existed, like the lady next door whose name I could not remember, a person who had meant so much when the world thought of me as a boy. How can you forget the name of someone whose picture you carried in the edge of memory for years? Whose body and spirit made you ache in the middle of the night? Who made you suffer endless hours? But her name, and even most of the memory, was gone.

After Mama called my brother, Donnie Lee, who was living somewhere in the Texas Panhandle, I found myself saying that Daddy had gotten lost from the real world.

Mama stared at me through filmy red eyes. Her brow wrinkled and she shook her head and, in a scratchy high-pitched voice, said, "His constitution was always weak."

I looked at her, wondering. My father had had the constitution of a bulldog. He'd eat anything. On a week-long sales trip through Alabama's Black Belt, where he called on every barber and beauty shop, my brother and I watched as he ate Possum brand sardines out of a can and a wedge of rat cheese cut from a giant hoop and pickled pig's feet that made my skin crawl when he sucked between the toes. He washed it all down with an ice-cold Dr Pepper. On the way to the next town, Daddy smoked a pack of Kools with his left arm, burned red, stuck out the window of his year-old Chevrolet.

I awakened from a deep sleep and looked around the darkness of the strange bedroom, feeling like a giant in a land of midgets. I'd overgrown the narrowness of the bed, the low ceilings, the room, the house. The apartment I shared with roommates in Montgomery was huge, cut from an antebellum mansion, with eighteen-foot ceilings and gigantic rooms, and I had a king-sized bed.

Wide awake, I suddenly remembered the woman next door, Edna Williams, and I saw the outline of her panties tight against the thin material of her housecoat as she leaned forward on tiptoes to pin her husband's sleeveless undershirt to the clothesline. When she winked at me, her eyes bright with promise, I shivered and my insides weakened. I closed my eyes again, thinking about her as I had years and years ago.

The next morning, drinking coffee, I asked, "Do you know whatever became of Edna Williams?"

"Why, no," Mama said. "I don't know. She and her little girl moved off somewhere. I heard she got married again."

"I was just wondering," I said.

I tried to remember the child. I only remembered the woman and her backside and her winsome wink, and I remembered the awful sound of her screaming, "Noooo!" through a rain-soaked morning after she heard that her husband, Ralph, had been killed in a car wreck. Mama had told me she was pregnant, making the tragedy even worse. After that, the memory of her was only a vague recollection.

On the way to the funeral home, I said, "I was thinking about Edna Williams last night. I was thinking about the terrible way she kept crying out, 'No,' all morning after her husband died. It was so sudden."

"Like with Harold," Mama said.

I thought: No, not like Daddy. Daddy's death was not sudden. Daddy was gone a long time ago. Looking at Mama staring out the window and hearing her almost inaudible sigh as I turned into the parking lot, I knew she had not seen Daddy as I had. I had given up on him. Until yesterday, she held hope for his emergence once again as the man she'd loved and married. I had moved on to a new time and a new place.

We made it through the morning with the funeral director. Back home, a lady from the church brought platters of food: a half-dozen freshly thawed casseroles, two different kinds of deviled eggs, potato salad, green-bean salad, English pea salad, cheese-and-raisin salad, a sackful of yeast rolls, and a mountain of fried chicken. I was halfway finished with my second drumstick when the front door burst open and my brother's voice called, "Am I at the right place?"

Mama rushed out and threw herself into his arms. "My baby," she uttered, kissing his neck as he lifted her from the floor. "Mama, Mama, Mama," he said.

He grabbed my biceps and squeezed, saying, "Brother," his voice breaking as he gazed into my face, seeing my aging as I saw his: tiny crow's-feet fanning from the corners of his eyes, deep furrows lining his long forehead, a girth that had expanded from a youthful athlete's narrow, hipless middle to a beer drinker's gut, and a hesitancy in his speech, as though he'd been thinking about this moment over the last five hundred miles, and now didn't know quite what to say. He was my brother and her son, but there was an unfamiliarity of growth, an absence of three years, a flash of time when years of love and loss and sorrow and happiness all filtered down to now.

We stood there, touching, feeling far apart and uneasy, grasping for each other across a sea of quiet turbulence. "Mama," Donnie Lee said. "I'm sorry." He ducked his head and buried his face in her narrow shoulder and thin neck.

"I know, baby," Mama said, and held him while I stood stone-still until he raised his head and dug a handkerchief from his pocket.

"I've got some coffee made," Mama said.

"There's piles of food," I said.

"I just want to hit the bed and sleep like a zombie," Donnie Lee said. Then he blinked and said, "There's nothing to do, is there?"

"Not until tonight," Mama said. "Visitation from five to seven at the funeral home."

Donnie Lee glanced toward me and I nodded. "Wake me at four-thirty," he said, then disappeared into the house.

Mama and I sat in silence in the semi-darkness of the kitchen and sipped our coffee and listened to his snoring.

At four-twenty-five, I shook his shoulder. "Donnie Lee" I said. He mumbled something, pulled away, looked into my face. Recognizing, he said, "Oh."

He swung his legs off the bed. He said, "I'm not Donnie Lee anymore. I'm just plain Don," then stumbled into the bathroom.

At ten to five, we rode to the funeral home. I drove. My brother sat next to me. Mama sat like a statue in the back. The first out of the car, she moved across the parking lot.

Don and I hurried to catch up.

Inside the room with muted lighting and piped-in music, we led her, like a waltz in slow motion, toward the open casket. She gasped a tiny breath deep in her throat. I felt her grip tighten as Daddy's profile came into view.

He did not look like himself. His features were too sharp: his nose too long, his chin jutting upward, his throat without wrinkles. His skin pale gray and wax-like.

From Mama's other side, Donnie Lee uttered, "Uh-uh," in disbelief.

Then the faint light shone on the white scar zigzagging from the left edge of his placid lips to the bottom of his chin.

For the first time in years he looked peaceful.

"Daddy," I said.

Mama's grip tightened again.

"Daddy," Donnie Lee said, the same way I'd said it, but more lonely and desperate, seeking, searching, the second syllable breaking.

A shudder went through us like a wave of electricity. We quivered together.

When we felt the presence of others behind us, we parted.

I fetched a box of Kleenex, brought it to Mama, and Donnie Lee took a wad.

In the next hour, people came. Faces appeared in the door and floated toward us, mouthing words of grief, taking our hands, explaining themselves and how they knew Daddy. Kinfolks came from north Alabama where Daddy had been born and raised. Aunts and uncles and cousins we saw only at funerals or an occasional wedding hugged us and kissed Mama on the cheek. They shook their heads and looked sad. They were all sincerely empty and counterfeit in their grief.

A salesman who'd known Daddy years ago appeared at the door. I thought Mama was going to wilt. Donnie Lee and I grabbed for her, holding her. The man stepped to her and said his name. "He loved you so," she whispered, as he took her small body in his grip and rocked back and forth. Momentarily, she backed away and they held each other at arm's length, looking at each other through their tears. "Boys," Mama said finally, "this is Alva Gibbons, your father's best friend." I'd met the man once, out on the road with Daddy, but I never thought of him as Daddy's best friend.

Alva, a tall, bald man with a pink hue to his skin, cleared his throat and said, "We traveled together for years and years, meeting up at places like Greenville and Enterprise, Montgomery and Selma. I sold dry goods. Like Harold, my line fell short somewhere in the late fifties, and I had to move to selling cars." His eyes shifted to Mama. "Ella and I still live in Anniston, and I sell for the big Chevrolet dealership up there. I haven't seen Harold in six, seven years."

"Harold was partial to Chevrolets," Mama said as she guided him toward the coffin. Moments later, he wept and Mama put her arm onto his shoulder.

Mama's cousin, Ray Hassell, appeared in the doorway like a magician. He smiled like he was considering a joke. A wiry man, slender and short, he had ruddy skin and a glint in his eyes. The last time I'd seen him he'd been wearing a wide-brim hat cocked over his right eye, shading that side of his face. He had a thin mustache that clung to his upper lip. He'd been up at Granddaddy and Nanny's in the country at Samantha, a community where many of the Hassells were born and raised, where they hunted coons in the swamps and killed hogs in the winter and farmed corn and hay in the summer, made gardens, and got along like they'd gotten along since the first Hassells came over from the poor farmland of southern Ireland more than a century ago. Ray still had that Irish flair about him. No bigger than Mama, he didn't mope and drag his feet. He stepped spryly.

There was a sharp crease in his chocolate-brown trousers. His beige shirt was open at the collar. He wasn't ashamed of being the only man in the room without a tie. He stepped to Mama and gathered her into his arms and picked her up off the floor. "Damn, Myrt, you're still light as a cloud." Mama rapped Ray playfully on the shoulders with both hands. "Ray Hassell, you're a sight," she said. She hugged him and kissed his cheeks. "The wind's slapped your face," she said. And he said, "That's what happens when you're welding on a pipeline in the Alaska chills. It's cold as the devil up there."

"I thought the devil would be hot," she said.

For a moment, I thought she'd forgotten Daddy.

Instantly, she turned with Ray to the coffin. Ray said, "I hate to look at dead people. Folks always say how natural they look. But ol' Harold don't look natural at all. He was natural when he was stepping around, funning people, playing tricks, and having himself a big time. When he was talking up a storm, conjuring a sale or two."

"Ray, you always had a way of speaking the truth," she said, gazing down into the container that held my father.

Momentarily, they turned back toward me and Donnie Lee. Mama eased away from her cousin. She greeted others. Several from the Elks Club came in and shook her hand. A woman from the church hugged Mama and glanced at Daddy. It seemed to me there was more disdain in her eyes than sympathy. She spoke to us. I shrugged. I didn't commit to her. I couldn't. Donnie Lee turned away.

Mama threw me a look.

Ray sat in the corner opposite the coffin. It seemed as though he was watching us. As the evening wore on, I became more and more aware of his eyes.

At the end of the second hour we prepared to leave. At the front door, Mama turned to Ray. "Do you have a place to stay?"

He nodded. Then, like an after-thought, he said, "Would y'all like to have dinner with me? I remember this place downtown, The Fish Basket, had fresh seafood brought up from the Gulf."

Mama glanced toward us. Neither of us uttered a sound.

"There's a world of food at the house," Mama said. "More than me and the boys could ever eat."

"You always liked shrimp, Myrt," he said. "Sautéed in garlic and butter."

For the first time in two days, Mama smiled. She glanced into our faces. "Boys?"

"Thomas? Donnie Lee? Wouldn't y'all like some shrimp or oysters? Maybe some red snapper from the sea?" Ray asked.

At the sound of his name, my brother glanced toward me. "Sounds fine to me," he said, holding the door open while Mama stepped out. Ray moved after her. I followed.

The Fish Basket was a storefront café down from the pool hall where Donnie Lee and I used to hang out, seduced by the staccato sounds of solid balls, the mechanical action of a tapered stick through powdered fingers, words peppered with profanity as the cue ball struck at an angle that gave geometry a new meaning.

Entering, the fragrance of strong herbs surrounded us. Even before we were seated against the wall covered with student artwork, fanciful abstracts of meaningless shapes, the light lifted the veil of sadness that had shrouded us. Mama's pale face brightened. Her eyes lightened. Her nose, too big for her face, flared with the rich smells.

Ray ordered a bottle of chilled Blue Nun. Mama waved away the offer of a glass, but Ray told the waiter to put it down. "She may like a taste with dinner," he said, offhandedly.

Mama smiled, not protesting.

Ray and Donnie Lee and I raised our glasses. Ray offered a toast. Looking at Mama, raising his heavy steel-gray brows, he said, "Myrt, sure you won't have a taste with us? We're drinking to Harold."

Mama shrugged, holding her smile. "Well…" she said, "just a little." Ray poured.

She touched her glass to ours.

"Harold was one of the most alive people I ever knew," Ray said. Donnie Lee and I frowned.

"Harold was light on his feet," Ray continued.

I noticed Mama held her glass to her lips, but she didn't swallow.

"For a large man, big-boned and heavy through the middle, he walked like a dancer, barely touching the floor. When he talked, his words flowed. He was exuberant."

I nodded. I'd never thought of Daddy like that.

"Harold's words were never boring. They sang. They told a story. They hit the nail on the head. He never beat around the bush. He could've been a songwriter, if he'd known music."

Between sips, my brother's eyes focused on our old cousin. I didn't think he knew Ray as well as I—and I had been with him only two or three times. When I was a kid, spending the night with Nanny and Granddaddy, Ray came with a frayed old pasteboard guitar case from which he'd extracted a cheap pawnshop instrument and played ballads and sang in brittle off-key notes. I remembered his voice, raspy and not-so-clear, singing in the night about a cowboy whose love was leaving and would never return. His was a plaintive voice remembered from more than ten years ago.

As Donnie Lee glared at him, Ray said, "Harold was a poet. Small-town people knew him and loved him. Everywhere he went he spread a joyful view of the world. People loved to see him come."

"He was crazy as a lunatic," Don blurted.

Mama looked into her younger son's face in the bright overhead light like she was seeing him for the first time.

Ray didn't disagree. "That's part of being a poet. He sees things different, from a different slant, not like ordinary people. Ordinary people are a dime a dozen. Harold was something special."

Don frowned, like he was looking into a carnival mirror that reflected distorted images.

"Blessed with a poet's vision, you're tortured without having the slightest idea what makes you the way you are."

"I think that's bullshit," Don said.

"Son!" Mama said.

"Well..." Don said. He looked toward me.

My eyes shifted back to Ray.

"Harold acted the fool sometimes," Ray said. "That too was part of his personality."

"He was a fool most of the time," my brother said.

"You father loved the road," Ray said.

"That's why he left us all the time," Don said.

"He was eaten up with loneliness, driving on the highway by himself, every mile longer and longer. He got so lonely he tried to escape by coming home and being close to y'all, but finding himself fenced in by what he had been doing all of his life: a traveling salesman. He didn't know anything else. His office was his car. He bounced from barbershop to beauty shop, bringing people a smile and a bright word. Folks knew him in every little town in his territory. They loved to see him coming. For a moment or two, his joy was theirs to share, before they went back to cutting or washing hair. Can you think of anything more monotonous? When he left them, he left his mark. Right now, all over small-town Alabama, people are missing him. They're thinking back on the memories of him, the story he told them the last time he visited, the picture of his sons that he painted for them.

"I rode with him a time or two way back. I'd come in from one of my trips out west. I'd have some time to kill. Back then, that's what I thought you did with time: kill it or while it away."

He took another swallow and poured more wine.

Don and I glanced at each other. He blinked away a tear. I felt one coming.

Mama held her glass for another drop or two.

"I enjoyed my time with Harold," Ray said. "When we got back from a week on the road, I'd take the memory of his stories with me. His words kept me company many a night.

"Sure, he was crazy." He grinned, showing teeth crooked from birth and yellowed from tobacco. "He was crazy in the best way I know: it came natural to him. Hell, we wouldn't be sitting here now, talking about him over a glass of wine, if he was a everyday Kiwanis Club asshole who attended church every Sunday and patted little children on the head and told mamas their little babies were cute. There was nothing hypocritical about your old man. Say what you will, he was a damned interesting guy."

"He thought he could fly," I said.

"What's wrong with wanting to fly?" Ray said.

"You can kill yourself," Don said.

"Or you can soar like an eagle, in your own way."

"He enjoyed talking about it," I said. I told them about the time he said he really wanted to fly.

Jovially, Ray said, "I bet that's what he's doing right now. I bet he's flying high above the treetops, hearing the wind sing in his ears. He's gliding along pretty as you please, belting out that old song, 'I'll Fly Away,' with the birds and the angels singing harmony."

Don gave him a skeptical glance but said nothing.

Mama nodded. A smile filled her face. "I'll drink to that," she said, lifting her glass. We all brought our glasses up and touched them with a clink.

As we drank, I noticed that Don's scowl had not vanished.

Later, after we dropped Ray at his motel, after Mama went to bed, Don and I had one last nightcap.

We sat at the kitchen table. I leaned forward and stared into my brother's shaded face. His eyes looked tired, his face weary.

"How's Texas?" I asked.

"Like anywhere else," he said.

I was the one who stayed close to home. I was the one who always talked about traveling. I went to Mexico for the summer, to Greece for a short holiday, to London on a stolen weekend.

It was he who put miles and miles behind him to settle down with a new family in a new place, trying to escape this town, this house, this kitchen.

"That old man is still as full of shit as he was when we were kids," he said.

It took me a moment to realize he was talking about our cousin Ray.

"Yeah," I said. "I guess he is."

Later, I lay awake in the narrow bed, thinking that I believed in Ray. I believed in his words, his bullshit. I believed in the idea of thinking you could fly, if only for a moment.

The next day, sitting next to Mama on the front pew, I raised my voice to sing with all of the congregation, "I'll fly away, oh glory, I'll fly away," our collective voice just as out of key as I remembered Ray's voice that night when he sang with the old guitar.

After Daddy was put into his grave and the preacher sprinkled dust onto his coffin, it was Don who pointed out that Ray had not made it to the funeral.

Mama said, "I don't reckon he could stand it."

Don looked at her, frowning.

I shrugged.

"Some folks just can't stand to attend funerals," Mama said.

"Then why'd he come to begin with?" he asked.

Mama gazed at him incredulously.

That night, when we were alone again at the kitchen table, Don shook his head. "I don't guess I'll ever understand people," he said.

"How's that?" I said.

"Ray came all the way up here from south Georgia. He came all the way, two or three hundred miles, then he didn't bother to attend the funeral."

"Mama's probably right," I said.

"But he came all that way."

"He saw us. He saw Mama."

"You mean...?"

"He cared enough to want to see us and let us know how he felt about Daddy," I said.

He stared into the glass he twisted back and forth in his hands.

"It's strange," he said.

Two mornings later, on my drive south to Montgomery, I thought that it wasn't strange at all.

MATERIAL

Donald Hays

They were in Erin's bed making love when it happened. Across the room from the bed was a window to the back yard. When Harper was there, Erin always kept the curtains closed. But this time, according to what Messier later told the police, there was an opening, an inch or two, through which he could see. The window itself was closed. There was a screen outside it. Messier managed to cut through the screen without either Erin or Harper hearing him. They didn't hear anything until Messier crashed through the window itself.

When Harper saw him, Messier was already on the floor, shattered glass all around him. Erin was on top of Harper, astride, facing his feet—in about the most compromising position imaginable. But they were so startled that neither of them moved. Erin screamed, but only after Messier scrambled to his feet.

It was cold out, so Messier was wearing a jacket. That protected most of his body from the glass, but his face and neck were punctured and sliced, and the cuts had started to bleed. He held an opened pocket knife in his bleeding right hand.

"Bitch," he said. He didn't shout. His voice was cold. He just spoke the word.

"Martin! Damn you! Go away!"

At first, the name meant nothing to Harper. Then he remembered. Still neither he nor Erin moved. Messier stared at them. "Who's this?" he asked Erin. "Your father?"

"Go away. Leave me alone. You have no right." Her voice was calm, measured.

She got off Harper. She stepped onto the floor and walked to Messier. She was naked and fearless. He didn't move, just stood there bleeding. "Get out, Martin. Go right back through that window and get out of my life forever."

He looked for an instant as if he might do just that. But then he grabbed her and threw her down and lurched toward Harper. Harper didn't move, didn't make a sound. He merely lay and, as if he were a disinterested, mildly curious observer, watched the knife blade slice three times across his chest. Later he would remember thinking that Messier would kill him. But even that thought was objective, a mere recognition.

Then he heard Erin scream again. She was standing behind Messier. She hit him with something—it turned out to be a vase—and jumped on his back and clawed at his face, and he bucked and turned and threw her off him. He looked down at her. "You're bleeding," he said. "Call 911." He walked across the room and sat down in the ladder-back chair beside her dresser.

None of them said anything for a moment. Messier's rage seemed spent. Apparently he had done what he had come to do. Now he seemed to be waiting stoically for whatever was going to happen next.

Erin, still sprawled on the floor, stared across the room at Messier. Harper looked at her, at Messier, who was the picture of patience, resignation. Harper looked down at himself. It occurred to him that he should pull the sheet up over his body, but he didn't. *None of us knows what to do,* he thought. *Each of us is waiting for one of the other two to do the next thing.*

Harper became aware of being aware. He noticed the way Messier sat in the chair without slumping, staring straight ahead, his palms resting on his thighs. He noticed the way Erin, on the floor, surrounded by slivers and shards of window and vase, lay on her hip and thigh and braced her torso with her arms so that she seemed to be resting briefly before pulling herself the rest of the way toward Messier. He noticed the way the shadow of Erin's head fell across Messier's lap. He was still a writer, after all; he noticed things. And for an instant he was pleased with himself, felt a pulse of pride that even under these circumstances his eye was cool, accurate, reportorial. Then Messier turned his face toward Harper, studied him for a moment, his dark, disdainful gaze running the length of Harper's body, foot to head. Harper felt himself being analyzed and dismissed. The pride Harper had felt a moment before vanished and was replaced by a mixture of shame and resentment.

Erin stood and looked at her hands. They were bleeding. There were bits of glass in them. She began pulling them out, dropping them to the floor. Her feet were bleeding, too. The backs of her legs. Her buttocks. Carefully, one by one, systematically—from her hands, her feet, left leg, right—she removed the splinters of glass.

It must have taken fifteen minutes anyway. It was like something out of a dream. No one said a word. Messier didn't even seem to be paying attention.

When Erin had finished picking all the glass from herself, she looked up at Harper and said, "We'd better do something about that cut." Only then did Harper become aware of himself again. Only then did the cuts begin to hurt.

Blood had oozed from the wounds, covered his stomach, and stained the bunched-up sheets beside him. They went into her bath-room. Erin dabbed blood from his body with a towel. "I don't think it's deep," she said. "But you need to go to a doctor, the emergency room."

Harper told her no, he'd just put some alcohol on it. She got a bottle and some cotton balls from the medicine cabinet and treated the cuts. Then Harper did the same for her. Again it took a good while. The alcohol caused each of them to wince and jerk a bit, but neither of them spoke. They stayed there until their wounds quit bleeding. It might have been half an hour.

When they returned to the bedroom, Messier was still in the chair. He didn't seem to have moved. Why hadn't he left? Why didn't he leave now? Odd, but now, for the first time, Harper was afraid of him.

"I called 911," Messier said. "I had to. They're coming."

"Go on, Martin. Get out. I don't want you here when they come."

"I'm sorry," he said. His voice was resigned, sincere. "I can't help it. I can't do it any other way."

Erin shouted at him for a while, then calmed down and tried to reason with him. If he stayed, he'd be arrested, go to jail. It would be much worse on him than on her and Harper. She didn't want any more trouble. She just wanted this to be over.

He seemed to listen carefully to everything she said. When she had finished, he told her again that he was sorry. He had to stay.

She told Harper to get dressed and leave. "There's no reason for him to be here," she told Messier. "I want to keep him out of it."

He shook his head. "He can go. But if he's not here, it'll just look worse for him. It'll look like he left you with a maniac. I have to tell them what happened."

"You bastard," she said.

"Maybe you ought to get dressed, though," he said. "That might look better. They'll be here any minute."

Harper got dressed, but Erin didn't. She sat on the edge of the bed and waited. When the doorbell rang, she wrapped the bloodied sheet around herself and went to answer it. They followed her into the bedroom, two medics and a couple of cops. The medics checked everyone's wounds, told them they'd be all right, but advised them to go to the emergency room for treatment and tetanus shots. Then they turned them over to the cops and left. One of the cops asked Erin what had happened, and she told them. Then he turned to Harper, who confirmed what she had said. He asked Harper's name, and Harper gave it to him. Harper told him he'd never seen Messier before. Messier told him that everything the others had said was true. "But they were fucking when I saw them," he said. "They left that out. I wanted to marry her. He's an old man, and she was doing this to me."

The cops took Messier to the emergency room and then to jail. After they were gone, Erin began to weep. Harper took her in his arms and guided her to the bed. They lay there together. There was blood on the bare mattress. They held each other. They didn't speak. Harper never wanted to leave. The world was outside her door. Harper didn't want to be in it again.

After a long time, she said. "Do you want to make love? It won't be the same again."

So they made love again. They began slowly and carefully, each of them cautious about the other's wounds, but by the end they were wild, ravenous. Harper had never been more aroused. He lost himself on the bloodstained bed.

Once or twice a year, Harper placed a story in a literary journal, usually one edited by an acquaintance—or even, sometimes, a former student—but it had been twelve years since the publication of his second novel, which had sold fewer than two thousand copies, never gone into paperback, and been remaindered after six months. He'd written two novels since then, both of which had been rejected by all the New York houses, as well as several university and regional presses. He tried to console himself with the familiar litany of excuses: bad agents, bad editors, bad luck. He could—and sometimes did—go on and on about the corporate, bottom-line nature of American publishing. Like most failures, he nurtured his resentments. But he knew the truth: the world is what it is, and he had failed in it.

He made his living as a writing teacher, and he was good enough at that. He could run a workshop, edit other people's stories. He knew the basics of form and structure, the tricks of point of view. He could take apart a Cheever or a Chekhov story and show you how it worked, how the pieces fit together. He taught bright, talented students, recruited from all over the country for the graduate writing program. Each year, they gave Harper high evaluations, and a reasonable number of them had gone on to publish books of their own.

Erin Hughes was twenty-five, a year less than half Harper's age. A brilliant young woman, the most gifted, Harper believed, of all the students in the graduate writing program. She was in her last year in the program, and Harper was directing her thesis. The stories in the thesis were, line by line, beautifully written, and Erin had a rare gift for form. They began where they should begin, ended where they should end, and moved efficiently and intelligently, scene to scene, section to section, from conflict to closure. Several of them had been published in minor literary journals. The only thing wrong with the stories was that they weren't very interesting. Her characters took few real risks, led quiet, conventional lives, with minor disruptions. Harper told her that the stories were plenty good enough as thesis material, that they might even be good enough to be published as a collection, but that she could do much better. She was being too cautious, he told her. Terrible things happened to people, he said, wonderful things, too, all the time, even to the citizens of the shaded suburbs she wrote about. Fear, rage, greed, lust could cause apparently good people to behave monstrously, to betray the people and principles they held dearest. And the worst people—Klansmen, killers, child abusers—were sometimes capable of love, tenderness, perfect sacrifice.

"I know that's true," she said. "Intellectually, I mean. But I haven't experienced it. Haven't felt. People almost never surprise me. I know it's me and not them, but it's the truth. I worry about it. Maybe I'm not open enough to be a writer."

Harper assured her that she was wrong. He told her that we tend to spend the early years of our adulthood categorizing people. After that, we begin noticing the exceptions. Then we see that everyone is an exception. She was already at the second stage, and she was still very young.

She said that maybe she should join the Peace Corps or something, seek out experience, material. He told her she could do that if she wanted, it probably wouldn't hurt, but it wasn't necessary, you didn't have to go to Bosnia to be a writer, you just had to pay close attention to what was right around you. "It's not the material. It doesn't need to be exotic. You just have to be open to—curious about—the here and now. Make yourself available to life, ordinary life. It's the artist's eye and ear and mind that matter. And it's paying attention to what everyone else takes for granted—ordinary betrayals, everyday adulteries—that makes the artist." Then, feeling pretentious even as he did it, he quoted Henry James. He told her to be one of those on whom nothing is lost.

Twice a week, in late afternoon, she came into his office for a conference. On Tuesdays, they discussed her thesis. On Thursdays, she came in for the readings course she had set up with him. After the first three or four weeks, they'd walk together to Alberti's, the brew pub at the edge of the campus. They'd sit there over beer or wine or coffee for maybe an hour and talk. She told him about her family, her childhood, her boyfriend, Martin Messier. He was doing graduate work in architecture. She liked him well enough, maybe even loved him, but was a little frightened by his possessiveness and by his rare but fierce anger. She had broken up with him, but he wanted her to give him another chance, and she was tempted—there was so much good in him.

Harper sympathized with her but never gave her any advice more practical than that she should be careful. Mostly, he told her about his wife, his son. He thought talking about his family would protect him from temptation—or, more accurately, help her protect herself from him. He meant it as a warning: I'm a married man, I have a son, I love them both. But of course—and on some level he must have known at the time that it would have this effect—it drew her closer to him. By mid-October, they were meeting in her apartment.

She lived in a duplex whose back yard adjoined the parking lot behind the used-book store on Taft Street. A tall, vine-draped wooden fence surrounded the back yard. Harper would park in the bookstore lot, open the gate in the fence, enter the seclusion of the yard, and go up to her back door. Very convenient and, he thought, about as safe as such things can be.

Anyway, after the first couple of weeks, he never worried much about getting caught. Oh, he had no intention of leaving Kate—or of arranging to get caught so that she would be provoked to leave him. He was convinced that in every practical way, the affair with Erin made him a better husband to Kate. He took her out more, to dinner, to the movies. They spent a couple of weekends in St. Louis, going to the art museum and to the symphony. He made love to her more often, and with a tenderness and passion he hadn't consistently felt for her in decades.

And by November the same sort of thing was happening with

Erin and the architect. They were dating again, and she said they were better with each other than they had ever been. She said the only reason she hadn't let him move back in with her was that it would end her arrangement with Harper. She could see herself someday marrying Messier.

Harper and Erin used to lie together in her bed and talk, lightly, about all that. They agreed that each person in any pair of lovers should be, simultaneously, one of another pair of lovers. The second relationship should be modeled on theirs. It should be carefully regulated, carefully protected from any outside intrusion, perfectly private, but the couple themselves should be completely open with each other. Each lover should be free of any but the most immediate commitment to the other. They should be rational romantics.

The story was in the local paper two mornings later. Neither Harper's name nor Erin's was mentioned. But at the college that day, one of the students in Harper's fiction workshop—a young man Harper liked a lot—came into his office and told him that Messier had called each of the women in the class to tell them about the affair Harper had had with Erin and to warn them that they had better be wary of him, he was a sexual predator. And when Harper got home that afternoon, Kate was sitting at the kitchen table, the newspaper open in front of her. Messier had called her, too. She said he had been thorough and matter-of-fact. He told her he had become suspicious of Erin because she would never agree to see him on Tuesdays or Thursdays. She told him it was because of her thesis and the readings course she was taking from Harper in his office during those afternoons and because she wanted to keep those evenings free so that she could go home immediately after the conferences and work for hours on her thesis. Those were her nights, she told him. They could share the other five nights. This sounded fishy to Messier, so he called Harper's office a couple of times during the hours when she had told him she would be there. No answer, of course. After that, he had come by several times and knocked on the office door.

He didn't say anything about this to Erin for a while—weeks. She had already broken up with him once because he'd been so possessive, and he didn't want to risk losing her again. And they were getting along so well at the time, better than they ever had, that he kept telling himself that he was just being paranoid about those Tuesdays and Thursdays. He did ask her once whether she and Harper always met in Harper's office. No, she told him, they almost never met there. The phone was always ringing, students would knock on the door. So, to keep from being interrupted, they met anywhere but his office— the union, the library, Alberti's. That satisfied Messier for a while, and they kept getting along better and better.

A couple of days after Christmas, she flew with him up to St. Paul, where he was from, and they had a wonderful week, a perfect New Year's Eve. His parents had really liked her. She had liked them, too. He thought about asking her to marry him then, but he didn't want to rush things. Instead, he asked her to go to Paris with him over spring break. They'd go to Chartres, too, Mont-Saint-Michel. He'd give her the architectural tour. She liked the idea. She had never been to France. He decided he'd propose to her in Paris, in the evening, on the Seine, behind Notre Dame.

But when the spring semester started and the Tuesday-Thursday routine resumed, suspicion started gnawing at him again. One Tuesday he followed Harper from his office and watched him get in his car and drive away. He knew Harper wouldn't be driving to the union or the library or anywhere else on campus. So he rode his bicycle to Alberti's. Harper wasn't there. Then he rode past Erin's place. He didn't see Harper's car on the street in front, so he went around to the back. There it was. He stood there astride his bicycle for a while, trying to decide what to do. Then he went home. The next afternoon he and Erin went to a bargain movie together and afterwards had a pizza. Then they went to her place and made love. It disgusted him. It would've been different if he had thought she loved Harper. That would've been hard for him, he could've understood that, accepted it, kept his respect for her. But she didn't really care for either of them. It was just a game to her. Sex and lies. And he knew

Harper had to know that he, Messier, was in love with Erin, wanted to marry her. He could imagine them laughing at him, at his sincerity, his earnest love.

That Thursday, he was ready. He hid across the street, in the arts center parking lot. He watched Harper park his car, get out, open the gate, and go into the yard. Then he waited a few minutes and followed. He went to her bedroom window and watched. And then, well, maybe it was wrong, certainly he had acted without thinking, but he had done what he had to do.

It took Kate a good ten minutes to tell Harper all that. She was as thorough and matter-of-fact as she'd said Messier had been.

She stared at him calmly, coldly after she finished. Harper didn't know what to say. He told her he was sorry.

She said, "I despised him when he was telling me all that. I told him I didn't want to hear any of it. I told him he had no right to call me like that. I told him he was an awful man. And you know, Jack, I think I was right. I think he may be an awful man. He must be. But I couldn't hang up. I couldn't stop listening. I knew it was all true. Every word. I knew he wasn't a liar. And when it was over, I felt just like he did. I was disgusted. With you. But even more with me. I feel like a fool. Everything I believe in is a lie." She stopped and stared at him hard. "Goddamn you, Jack. Goddamn you."

Harper reached across the table for her hand. She drew it away. "It is all true, what he said. Isn't it, Jack? Don't lie to me now."

He sat there for a moment. Then he began, inadvertently, to nod. "Yes," he said. "It's all true. He wasn't lying."

She started crying then, and Harper told her that he loved her, that he had always loved her, that what he had done had nothing to do with that.

She raked the back of her right hand across her eyes. "I want you to leave. I want you to get what you need from the house and leave. I don't want to see you now."

Harper started in again—he was sorry, he loved her, he always had, always would, she had to believe that—but she stopped him.

"No. Get out, Jack. I can't do this now."

Harper kept telling himself that if he'd be contrite and patient, Kate would take him back. Just last year, a woman they both knew well—she taught French at the college—had left her husband after twenty-five years because she discovered he was having an affair with a student. Kate had told Harper at the time that she thought Ann was making a mistake. "A fifty-year-old man making a fool of himself over a young woman. I mean, Jesus. Maybe there should just be a standard punishment for that. Make the bastard stand naked in a public square for a day or so. That should cure everyone of desire." She grimaced, shook her head. "But you don't end a marriage over it. She's letting her pride do her thinking."

In February, just a couple of weeks after Messier came through the window, Kate arranged to meet Harper at Alberti's. After she told him she had filed for divorce, Harper reminded her, as gently as he could, of that conversation. He didn't point out that she had been right, that Ann was now sorry she had insisted on getting the divorce—she was alone and lonely and her ex-husband was, by all appearances, happily remarried. Kate knew all that. But what she said in response was, "I have to live with my pride. I don't have to live with you."

That night Harper called and asked their son, Colin, who was then finishing up a film degree at Cal Arts, to fly home and talk to Kate about reconciling. Reluctantly, Colin agreed. It did no good. If anything, it hardened Kate's resolve. She accused Harper of emotional blackmail, of trying to use her own son against her. And Harper agreed. She was right. It was wrong. He shouldn't have put their son in that position. But he was desperate, he told her. He didn't want to lose her. He didn't know what else to do. Please understand.

Harper didn't contest the divorce, which went through in what seemed to him record time, becoming final in April. A few days later, he called Kate. He had thought that then, after the clean break, they might begin again, a slow courtship, a gradual rediscovery of each other. He didn't say that, of course. He merely asked her out to lunch.

She was as fierce as ever. She told him she wasn't about to become one of those middle-aged divorced women who, just because they can't get anyone else, start fucking their ex-husbands. "If I get that desperate," she said, "I'll hire a gigolo."

For the first couple of weeks after Messier came through the window, Harper and Erin stayed away from each other as much as possible. On the phone, she said that Emily Burns, chair of the architecture department, had told her that if she were to file a grievance against Harper for sexual harassment, she could count on a lot of support from the faculty. Erin said she hated that, and hated the way people looked at her at the university—as if she were a whore or a victim or both. She didn't know what she wanted to do. Maybe she should just leave, get away. She could finish her readings on her own, and her thesis was already finished, really. She could come back for the defense. Harper told her he would do whatever she wanted. He said he didn't want her to be hurt. She told him she'd think about it and call him back in a day or so.

When she called him the next night, she said she didn't want their affair to end this way. She would graduate in May. She'd be leaving after that, going to Europe for the summer and then moving to New York. Her departure would bring the affair to a natural end. That had always been their plan. She thought it would be a mistake to let Messier change that.

Harper agreed, mostly because now that, for the time being anyway, he had lost Kate, he wanted to keep seeing Erin, but partly because he was a little afraid not to do whatever she wanted. She had enormous practical power over him. At any moment, for any reason, she could bring him before the gender police.

She seemed to understand what he was thinking. "Look," she said, "you don't have to. I know it might not be smart for you to be seeing me now. You have a lot to lose, I know."

"No. I want to. It's all right."

"What I'm saying is that you don't have to be afraid of me. What we've had together, it's meant a lot to me. I won't do anything to hurt you, I promise."

So they resumed the affair. Harper, who had been living in the Chief Motel since Kate had ordered him out of their house, rented an apartment in a complex in Rogers, twenty miles north of Lafayette. Erin spent most weekends with him there and at least one night during the week. Twice during the semester, they spent a long weekend in Kansas City, four hours away—stayed at the refurbished Savoy, took in movies at the Tivoli, ate ribs at Arthur Bryant's, spent, each time, their Sunday afternoons at the Nelson-Atkins, beginning and ending their tour before the Caravaggio *John the Baptist*. Harper wanted to say something about the painting that would connect it to their affair, their lives. But the words never came. They stood and looked.

They still sometimes tried to pretend they existed on an island they had themselves created. But it didn't work. Maybe, Harper sometimes thought, it would have been different if they hadn't stamped a termination date on the affair. As it was, he sometimes felt as if he were serving time, making a point, performing a duty. It was good duty, God knows, a tender sentence. Each of them became more and more expert with the other's body. They went about their love-making with an artisan's skill, a craftsman's competence. As lovers, they were, Harper thought, more proficient than passionate. It was as if they were being careful not to lose their heads. Too often, as he lay with her after sex or faced her over breakfast or even stood beside her before the Caravaggio, Harper felt that they were trying to hold onto something they'd already lost. There was a sweetness to those times, Harper thought, but already it was the sweetness of regret. He realized that what he regretted was the loss of that time, the months before Messier came through the window, when, he now believed, they might still have let themselves fall in love.

Near the end of April, Kate called and said they needed to have a talk. "It's Colin," she said. "Nothing serious. Don't worry. He's all right. But I think we should talk."

Harper could see everything working out. In less than a month, Erin would be in Europe. And now here was Kate calling him, needing to talk. Surely their shared history would sooner or later bring them back together. He offered to drop by after his undergraduate workshop late the next afternoon. She didn't think that was a good idea. She'd meet him at that brew pub, Alberti's, just off campus. That would be convenient for both of them.

When Harper arrived, she was already in the corner booth facing the door. There was a glass of white wine on the table in front of her. Harper ordered a pale ale at the bar and, when it was drawn, carried it to the booth. "Kate," he said as he sat down. He smiled, nodded. "How are you?"

"They're really good-looking, these kids," she said, opening a hand. "Bright-faced, friendly. They don't seem as driven to be tormented as we did at that age."

Harper turned sideways in the booth and looked around. He turned back to Kate. "Well, the writers aren't here yet," he said.

She smiled. He thought that might be a beginning for them, but then she got right to the matter she had come to discuss. Colin had just gotten another DUI, his second in the past six months. He hadn't been very drunk, .09, which wouldn't even be legally drunk here. There in California, though, he'd have to go to court. He would need a lawyer. He'd have to pay a fine, he didn't know for sure how much yet, but his friends were telling him it would be at least a thousand. "He'll certainly have his driver's license suspended for at least a year. He'll have to go to alcohol counseling classes all that time. And he'll have to be on probation." She sighed and then shook her head. "That's if he's lucky. He could go to jail."

"Jail?" Harper said. "Jesus!"

"That's why I wanted to talk to you. We'll make sure he has a good lawyer. I want him to learn his lesson, but I want to do everything we can to keep him out of jail."

"Sure. I'll talk to him. I'll pay for everything."

She nodded. "Thank you." She sipped her wine. "I think you should call him. He needs his father now."

"Sure," he said again. He leaned back, put both hands, palms down, on the table, and shook his head. "Fucking California," he said. He was about to say something about O.J. being able to decapitate people and get by with it while Colin faced jail time by having a couple of beers. Before he could, though, he saw Kate's eyes widen in apparent alarm. He turned to see what she was looking at, and there was Messier, walking toward them.

When Messier reached their booth, he nodded down at each of them, then said, "I know I'm probably the last person either of you wants to see right now. But I wanted to apologize to both of you. It was wrong, what I did, Professor Harper." He turned his face to Kate. "And Mrs. Harper, I shouldn't have called you. I heard about the divorce, and I couldn't help thinking that maybe if I hadn't called it wouldn't have happened."

Harper wanted the son-of-a-bitch to just shut up and leave. But Messier kept standing there, waiting for something—absolution, Harper supposed. Then Kate said, "No. I think it would've happened sooner or later. Anyway, I'm glad you called, Martin. I'd rather know than not."

Martin, Harper thought. *She's calling him fucking Martin.*

"Well," Messier said. "I still wish it hadn't happened."

Harper watched Kate nod.

"Professor Harper..." Messier had extended his hand, wanting to shake Harper's. Harper looked up at Messier, glanced around the place, turned back to Kate. She was glaring at him. He gazed down at the proffered hand again. Then he shook it.

Messier thanked him, then said, "And I want to wish you all the best with Erin, Professor Harper. I really do. She's great. Please take good care of her, all right?" He gave Harper a brotherly, good-loser nod, then turned and walked out of the place.

"Well, wasn't that nice?" Kate said. Then she left, too, leaving Harper with the wine and the beer and the bill.

A couple of weeks later, Erin defended her thesis. All three people on the committee—Harper, Andrew Cunningham, and Simone Persons—praised the stories at length and in detail. They told her they expected to be reading her stories in the best magazines and journals soon. They told her they looked forward to reading her collections, her novels. They told her she had a chance to be a writer who mattered to the world. They told her that if there was ever any way any of them could help her in the future, they'd be honored to do so. She thanked them. She told them how much she had learned from each of them. It was all, Harper thought, very professional.

Afterwards, the committee took Erin down to Alberti's to buy her the ritual celebratory drink. As soon as he stepped inside the door, Harper saw Kate. She was sitting in the same seat in the same corner booth she had been in the last time he saw her. She was drinking white wine again. She was talking to someone. Harper couldn't tell who it was, could see only the back of a man's head, a hand, a pint glass of dark beer. Then Kate saw him. Her eyes widened. She nodded, but didn't smile. Mere recognition was all she offered. The man across the booth from her leaned forward and out and looked at Harper. He nodded. He smiled. It was Messier.

Harper soldiered on, chin up, through the celebratory drink and then through the tag end of his affair with Erin. She spent three more nights with him at his apartment, and they had a final weekend in Kansas City. He helped her pack her things. Books, CDs, and clothes, mostly. All of it fit in the back of her Civic. Harper told her he envied that. He could hardly remember that kind of freedom.

Just before she drove away, he borrowed her camera and took a photograph of her standing next to the car. He handed the camera back to her and said, "Mail one back to me, all right?" She said she would. He thought she would take a picture of him then, but she didn't.

They held each other for a long moment. Then he stepped back and studied her face. Her eyes were wet, but she didn't weep. With the tips of his fingers, Harper brushed strands of her hair away from her forehead. He kissed her on the forehead, the cheek, the lips. "I love you," he said.

"No," she said. "Don't." She kissed him sweetly. She told him she'd write. She thanked him for everything. She got in her car and drove away.

In the days that followed, Harper drank. When he woke, around noon usually, he'd sit at the kitchen table and drink a beer. Then he'd brush his teeth, shower, shave, and dress. After that, he'd pack his little six-beer cooler with tall boys and go for a drive. He never knew, when he left the apartment, where he'd go. Sometimes he drove north into Missouri. Sometimes he drove east toward Mountain Home or Calico Rock. Sometimes he'd go south to Lafayette, circle the campus, drive down Fulbright past the bookstore and Erin's old duplex. Sometimes he'd just pass slowly on by. Sometimes he'd pause a few seconds. He never let himself stop for long. From there he'd go up School to Maple, which he'd follow into the historic district and past his old house—Kate's house now. As he went by, he'd turn and look, some irrational part of him expecting to see Messier sitting, smiling, on the screened-in porch, having a gin and tonic with Kate.

But Harper never saw Messier again. Not in the flesh. He kept thinking he'd get a letter from Erin Hughes—and a print of the photograph he'd taken. But the weeks went by and there was nothing from her. Maybe it was just as well. By the time school started again in late August, he was more or less back to normal—or as normal as he could be without Kate. He quit the drinking and the driving. He bought a two-bedroom farmhouse just outside Prairie Grove, just north of the Civil War battlefield and only twenty minutes from campus. He liked it there. He fell back into the routine of teaching. The new students in the program that year seemed talented and interesting. One of them—Alicia Luhan, a beautiful Oregonian— told him one evening when the whole class was having an after-work-shop beer at Alberti's that she had chosen to come to this program because she had so admired his first novel. He thanked her and tried to say something clever and self-effacing. But he was foolishly, child-ishly pleased by the compliment. He told himself to be careful. He'd been talking to Kate again—mostly about Colin, always about prac-tical matters. Still, they were friendly again. There might be a chance. Harper didn't want to piss that chance away.

The fall semester went by and most of the spring. Harper gave himself to what he thought of as routine virtue. He talked to Kate every week or so on the phone, and once a month they had dinner together, usually at the Thai place on Mountain. She was always friendly, but never more than that. One night in March she told him that she was seeing another man, a lawyer Harper didn't know. It was serious, she said. She liked him a lot. For the first time, Harper knew that he had lost her.

In April Harper was sitting in his office checking his email when Simone Persons came in. "Harper," she said, "have you read this?" The new *Paris Review* was in her extended hand.

Harper shook his head, shrugged. "No."

"Well, maybe you should. Erin Hughes has a story in it."

She left the journal, and he read the story.

It was about their affair. It was written from his point of view, a close third-person. She presented him as a sympathetic failure, a slightly ridiculous over-the-hill writer. There were two extended scenes between the Harper character (Archer in the story) and his wife (Mary). Harper couldn't remember telling Erin much about Kate, and he was almost sure he'd told her next to nothing about their private conversations, but the dialogue between them in the story was uncannily accurate. Erin herself—called Maeve in the story—came across as the least sympathetic character. She was using her teacher to broaden her experience. The affair was for her, finally, nothing more than material.

Harper was first hurt, then impressed, then hurt again. He told himself to let it go. It had ended nearly a year ago. It didn't matter now. Anyway, that's what it meant to be around writers. Sooner or later, you'd be reduced to material. And surely one of these days he'd write about Erin, too.

The next week Harper got another copy of The *Paris Review* in the mail. Erin had sent it to him. Inside the journal, marking the page on which her story began, was an envelope. Inside that were two photographs. The first was the one he'd taken of her just before she drove away. On the back of it she'd written:

"A writer is one on whom nothing is lost."

Thanks,

Erin

In the other photograph—and there was nothing written on its back—she was sitting at a table in an outdoor café in what Harper thought might have been the Luxembourg Gardens. She was smiling at the camera and holding a glass of red wine out at arm's length, as if toasting the viewer. A man was sitting beside her. He too was smiling. He too held up a wineglass, though his glass was not held up as high or out as far as hers, as if he had joined the toast belatedly or reluctantly.

It was Messier.

WATERWALKERS

Bret Anthony Johnston

As Hurricane Alicia drifted north-northwest up the Gulf coast from Veracruz, Mexico, Sonny Atwill stood outside McCoy's Lumber hanging NO PLYWOOD signs in the windows. A gray, blurring rain blew over the parking lot, diffusing the headlights of cars waiting for empty spaces. Horns blared and bleated. In addition to plywood, the store was low on batteries, masking tape, flashlights, kerosene lanterns, bottled water, sandbags, and propane. Originally the Hurricane Center had predicted that Baffin Bay, Texas, would bear the brunt, but revised reports had it heading for Corpus Christi, making landfall that evening. Sonny believed the storm would veer south, go in around Laredo; he'd projected its course with a grease pencil on his laminated hurricane map.

When he came back inside the store, the crying woman was sitting at the bottom of a rolling ladder in the cabinet fixtures aisle. She had her face cupped in her hands. He thought to sidestep the hassle and let someone else explain that the store was sold out of everything she would need. This was what he'd learned over the years: Stay out of it. He was fifty-nine, retired from Coastal Oil Refinery, working ten hours a week at McCoy's because his doctor wanted him to exercise. Usually he was off on Friday, but when the shipment had unexpectedly arrived last night, the manager had ponied up ten sheets of plywood plus regular pay to clock in this morning. The woman kept her back to him as she stood. Leave her be, he thought once more, let the husband come; yet he was drawn to her, reluctantly compelled to suggest other lumberyards and offer the possibility that the storm would spare them. Then, hurriedly, she turned and their eyes met. "Sonny," she said. He took a single unintentional step backward, emptied and suspended inside a chastening quiet.

"My sister," Nora finally said, but then fell to weeping again. She wore a white scoop-neck blouse, faded jeans. In twelve years, she'd lost ten, maybe twenty pounds; her ring finger was naked. Sonny knelt beside her, vaguely hearing the announcement that McCoy's would close in fifteen minutes; suddenly he was awash with a potent, gathering urgency. Whenever excited, his son used to say butterflies were tickling his palms, and now that seemed the perfect description. Nora wiped her eyes and said, "My sister has huge windows."

For years, he had thrown hurricane parties. Named storms hit four and five times a season, and he cleaned out the garage and fried flounder and invited people from the oil refinery. They sat in frayed lawn chairs and drank Schlitz, watching a storm's edge cut off the horizon like a charcoal sheet, and playing cards—Mexican Sweat, Texas Hold 'em, Stud—until the wind howled, then they slipped into plastic ponchos and danced. He'd mounted a radio over the workbench (to hear the Oilers lose while he fiddled with the lawn mower) and they listened to tapes—Anne Murray, George Jones, Johnny Rodriguez. Once, the Kmart sign had cartwheeled through the yard. A man from the refinery had brought Janice Steele to the party, then she'd borrowed Sonny's phone to call her sister. When the storm broke up and the others left, Nora stayed.

That was 1972, the year he was named supervisor of an eight-man crew. He was thirty-one, Nora twenty-six. She shelved books at the library while attending the community college at night; she aimed to earn her teaching certificate. They had been together a few months when he bought the house he'd been renting on Shamrock Street. She moved in, filling the rooms with her expensive, honeyed shampoos, hanging ivies and matted photographs. Each Sunday they drove to an open-air restaurant on the Laguna Madre and ate baskets of shrimp and hushpuppies. One night she said, "*Take all away from me, but leave me Ecstasy.*"

Her voice was so low and cool that his heart stuttered. He asked, "Does that mean you want another beer?"

"It means I want you to marry me."

The wind lifted a corner of the red-checked tablecloth, raising it gently from the slatted table then dropping it again; waves sloshed heavily against pylons; the smell of batter and fish and salt-splashed cedar; the divine heat in his chest, like a ray of light refracted in a jewel.

The weather slacked off after McCoy's closed. Sonny followed Nora to her sister's on Del Mar Street. The talk-radio station he liked was overrun with storm coverage: Authorities had taken down traffic lights around the harbor and were evacuating boats from the bay; Alicia's sustained winds topped 115 mph; the Navy was tying down vessels in mooring systems and deploying others to sea; ferry service had been halted, soon rising tides would close off Padre and Mustang Islands. Residents were advised to bring in pets, to stock up on canned goods, caulk bathtub drains and fill them with water.

She drove slowly, her brake lights blinking like Morse code. Traffic was bottlenecked at the freeway; shoe-polished windshields read "Help Us Jesus" and "Go Away Alicia!" The city's south side was flooding. Corpus seemed transformed, like a dream version of itself from which a somnolent atmosphere had been cast off; wind made street signs tremble. What he felt behind the wheel was a long-dormant vulnerability, an encroaching raw exposure. When he had offered Nora his plywood—it lay in his truck bed, under the camper—she had accepted by saying, "So here we go again."

Del Mar was a wide, palm-lined street, a quarter mile from the bay. The house was a five-bedroom with a French garden and greenhouse that Sonny had helped build; Janice grew orchids. She was summering in Italy—"with some Guido," as Nora put it—so she was house-sitting. Janice was an attorney who had never married and when Sonny had passed the house in intervening years, he believed a place so large would depress you to live alone in. Years before, he'd moved into an all-utilities-paid duplex and put the money from the Shamrock house in mutual funds. He wondered if Nora had avoided Shamrock since she'd been back, or if she'd seen the newly painted trim, the garden trellis and oak saplings, the lush elephant ears she'd never been able to grow.

He reversed into the gravel driveway, doubting he could finish boarding up before the sky opened again. The house looked larger, the windows higher. Nora had calmed; maybe she'd popped a nerve pill. She greeted him with a familiar distractedness, an improbable air of casual lightness as if she'd just returned from shopping and needed to get some milk into the icebox. Her rejuvenation disappointed him, as did how quickly she disappeared inside. He'd hoped she might ask his opinion on Alicia, maybe even tear up again. He buckled his tool belt and switched out the bit in the cordless drill he'd borrowed from McCoy's. He hoisted each sheet of plywood onto his thigh, held it to the house with his left hand, then screwed the sides, corners, top, bottom. Twice the drill twisted and caught the flesh between his thumb and finger. He took breathers between gusts, and each breath felt like a spear in his ribs. Hammers banged on nearby streets; a circular saw whined; a woman started calling for a pet named Scooter. Sonny tried not to stomp the snapdragons and budding hydrangeas, but that proved impossible.

And not unexpectedly he heard Max—the memory of his voice still strong and viable, like a clear radio signal. They could've been sitting in the Shamrock kitchen, the boy's elbows propped on the newly laid-in countertop, an evening when they studied for the merit badge test. He was eight, fawn-skinned and sharp-cheeked like Nora, fascinated by windmills and in the habit of climbing into their bed after they'd gone to sleep. Recently he'd been prone to lying, was in fact currently grounded for it. The restriction opened up the after-supper hours to tie knots and practice splinting broken limbs and to review the history of the Karankawa Indians, the first inhabitants of south Texas: Members of the tribe stood over six feet tall, wore no clothes, and were known cannibals; they slept on dried palms, tattooed themselves from head to foot, and smeared the inside of their leaky pottery with asphaltum that had washed ashore. Sonny asked Max for the translation of the tribe's name.

The boy filled his cheeks with air, pouting, stalling, then he exhaled. He said, "Waterwalkers."

"No," Sonny said. "Dog raisers."

"But also Waterwalkers," he said. "They can also be called Water-walkers."

At Janice's, the drill twisted again, and Nora said, "Guess you didn't need help."

Her voice made him feel cornered, ashamed. She had changed into a loose sweater, a fisherman's hat, and old sneakers. He'd liked her in the scoop neck and wished she hadn't taken it off, though maybe that was precisely why she had.

"Small potatoes," he said. It was not something he'd said before, and he had no idea where it had come from. His heart was still pumping hard. His face felt raddled, his mind dull-witted; he regretted that he hadn't shaved before work, that he'd worn such a wrinkled shirt.

"That one would've been a bugger," he said.

The front of the two-story house across the street was more glass than brick.

"Architects," she said. "Remember? The Christmas party."

"That's all a blur for me. The old noggin mixes things up lately."

"I doubt that. But if you're serious, at least you held out longer than I did."

He returned to the plywood, cranking down already tight screws. He wanted to shy away from solemn conversations.

"The first storm of the season, in August, and it just turned Category Four."

"Welcome home," he said, but the words sounded laden, riven with an inappropriate, boastful enthusiasm. He said, "We'll get some wind, but she'll spare us. There'll be a good haul of shrimp behind the weather."

"Alicia. They always pick pretty names for the first ones."

She had believed this since he'd known her and had always cited the first storms—Ayla, Antonio, Amelia—to evidence her point. That she still observed it pleased him.

A kettle whistled inside Janice's kitchen, a room where he'd carved beef for holidays, Super Bowls, the funeral. The night of the architects' party, he'd crossed the street for more gin and spied Janice bent over the butcher-block table, the architect biting her neck and groping her breasts.

A stiff breeze riffled the palms near the street. Across Ocean Drive, the sky faded downward by degrees, violet to lavender to oyster silver, until at last it softened into a seam of sallow light on the horizon.

Nora said, "I boiled water. I thought some tea might take our mind off things."

Once, he'd seen Janice in the clubhouse of Oso Municipal Golf Course. She'd played nine holes with partners from the law firm and sat at the bar drinking screwdrivers. Raking her fingers through her hair and leaning back to expel plumes of smoke, she resembled Nora. The men around her burst into laughter at a joke she made while fishing through her purse. One of them said, "That *is* a hole in one," as she started for the door. Sonny thought he'd escaped her, then she shuffled over to his booth. He was finishing a Reuben—gratis, like his rounds, because he maintained the course's carts and sprinklers on weekends—and he was reading about Karankawas.

He said, "These fellas used to slather themselves with mud and shark grease."

"Injun Old Spice," said Janice. Her eyes were red-rimmed, her lips slow.

"Repelled mosquitoes," he said. "They also talked—communicated—with their mouths closed."

"So do those lawyers." She pointed at them with her chin.

Her hair was cropped, highlighted white and gold. Not a style Nora would ever wear, so having confused the resemblance irritated him. He'd intended to carry on about the Karankawas, explain how they'd tie lanterns to a mule's neck and lead it in circles on darkened beaches to attract vessels at sea. A captain would read the distant light as a buoy and steer his boat toward the harbor he assumed it marked. By the time he realized his mistake, he'd have struck the outer sandbar and the naked Indians would emerge with spears. But now all of that seemed trivial and Sonny explained nothing. He heard himself say, "I haven't gotten a word in a while."

Immediately he wished he'd not mentioned Nora and at the same time wanted Janice to spill what she knew. For a while, he'd received postcards and late-night weepy calls from Nora. He told her that he'd not contested when Coastal proposed the early retirement; she said she missed hearing surf reports on the radio, missed good chalupas. He resisted the urge to call her Honey or Love or No-No. They never spoke of Max. Then the communication dwindled, and a blankness set in—a disorienting malaise born anew with each hour, as if not reporting his actions to Nora, not even *planning* to report them, stripped them of any significance. She had lived in Michigan, Arizona, Nebraska, and North Dakota, locales untouched by the ocean, and he knew she'd never return to Corpus. His days were incurably wide and ponderous, and at night he fought phantom jealousies of other men.

After the retirement, he'd moved through life like a fugitive, trepidatious and worried he'd meet someone from the old times. If he glimpsed an acquaintance in the supermarket, he lingered on a far-off aisle or abandoned a full cart of groceries and fled to his truck. If someone caught him, at McCoy's or Oso or a pre-dawn bait stand, his veins surged with dreadful eagerness. Those mundane encounters left him utterly unsure of his identity. No longer a father, no longer a husband. And though he felt on the verge of some old, indolent connection—maybe they felt that, too—he'd erected such sturdy walls, perfected such inconspicuous deflections that the conversations passed without even the slightest revelation. The men told him about the refinery hub, which plants were producing more barrels per day, who had passed on and who was stealing compressors to sell out of his garage; they avoided mention of families. Sonny spoke of golf and fishing; he told them he was living the life he'd always worked for.

Janice ran her tongue between her teeth and lips. She was older than Nora by five years, but people had always thought her younger.

"She's working at a bakery. In Ann Arbor," she said. "But that's yesterday's sad tune, I want to hear about good old Sonny."

He said, "I put one foot in front of the other, like a good soldier."

"And the ladies? Still need a stick to keep them away?"

He washed down the last of his Reuben and wiped his mouth with a napkin. Lois Whipple was at her house, slow-cooking a roast, vacuuming, and curling her hair for tonight. He'd been seeing her for two months, but already he smelled the relationship rotting on the vine.

"No," he said, "mostly they stay away on their own."

That same afternoon his shoulder numbed. On the sixth green, he recognized the tingling in his fingers and sharp punches in his chest with an almost grateful, razor-like clarity. In his mind was the image of a fist squeezing an aorta, of a child clenching a water balloon, dreading and courting the moment it bursts. He replaced his putter, sat down and waited.

Gusts started breaking branches off trees, Del Mar was pooling. Tallow leaves eddied in tight circles above the gutters. No doubt boats had been pulled from the marina, trailered into parking lots and vacated streets. An early, slatey dusk descended. If Sonny waited much longer, he'd be marooned through the storm.

"I never got my degree," Nora said cheerfully. "Never transferred my credits. I just enrolled willy-nilly."

They sat at the butcher-block table, opposite each other on wicker stools. She had brought in Janice's grill, the redwood patio furniture and potted plants—azaleas, macho ferns, a bromeliad. The grill smelled of sodden ash. Six jugs of water sat on the counter, beside a new fire extinguisher.

"Nursing classes mostly," she said. Her eyes went to the abrasions on his thumb, which immediately started throbbing. "We're not wired to remember what hurts us. Our bodies have no memory for pain."

Then she winked: "Biology 101."

"You'd make a keen nurse. Or *will* make, you'll finish soon enough." Then because he couldn't stop himself, he added, "The college just expanded its nursing program here."

"The hospital was the first place I went when I got back. Isn't that typical? The place still smells the same. What did we use to say?"

"Iodine and clover."

"And that hideous mural, Jesus and the Jackass."

A clap of thunder rattled the windows. Nora had always closed her eyes during heavy thunder, as if it saddened her. Opening them, she looked embarrassed. He thought she might be wearing contacts; maybe her vision had deteriorated over the years. How did he look to her now? Had Janice described him from Oso? As a shell, a ghost, as a man who'd lost his religion? Or did she afford him that cruelest kindness—*he's holding up fine*. Nora had coped with the events one way and he'd done it another. While he burrowed, she fled.

Yet here they were. The wind straining against the house, rain like pebbles on the plywood. Holding her gaze was impossible, but he stole glances. With one, he noticed the silken line of her neck; with another, the cleft of her lips; another, the creases on her knuckles. Over the years her speech had hastened, her words had acquired the occasional unfamiliar diphthong—she pronounced "about" like a Canadian. He stayed guarded, flexed against whatever else had changed, ready to absorb how her presence would dissolve his memories, like water on sugar. Still, an anticipation buoyed him. He liked being in the room with her.

A flow of memory rushed just beneath the waking world, like a frozen-over stream; if he wanted, he could punch through the ice and let the current drag him under. Max had stayed here once, sometimes twice a month, and his aunt had ordered pizza, rented movies Nora wouldn't allow at home. He'd always adored Janice, behaved best for her. She had opened her house after the funeral—men and women from the refinery had crowded the stark halls. Many of the artifacts Sonny had discussed with relieving, unprecedented thoroughness still lined Janice's shelves—a framed scrimshaw and wood giraffe from Kenya, an antique clock from Paris, a bronze statuette from Athens. Commanding one wall was an enormous chiaroscuro of a policeman studying his reflection in a parking meter: Max's favorite.

Nora had started talking about the hurricane again. Sonny said,

"I think she'll miss us."

She smiled, then peered into her mug. "You're that same man."

"Same old Sonny."

"Still chasing storms on your little map?" She laughed a small, breathless laugh. A chinaberry tree's soaked limbs whipped the house, a metal trash can rolled across the street. He paced to the front door, daring himself to imagine a more unlikely, more longed-for night. What else, he wondered, do you remember? What else do you want to know? Probably she wondered if he still searched out information on the Karankawas, but she kept such questions to herself. Were they in his duplex, the various Karankawa books stacked in his breakfast nook and around his bed would have prickled his flesh with shame. She stood behind him briefly, touched his shoulder like a woman in a crowd, then returned to the kitchen. Brown soupy water was inching up the yard. His truck, reversed in, was up to its headlights. The weight of her hand lingered, an imprint in drying cement.

Nora hadn't wanted Max to go to Camp Karankawa; he'd never been away from home for anything close to a week, and a tropical storm was brewing in the Gulf. Meteorologists predicted it would turn and head out into the ocean, but she had undertaken a benign, half-hearted campaign to discourage the trip. ("You could go next year," she said. "You'll be older.") Still, she allowed herself to be convinced that if other scouts were going, if the camp opened despite the weather, then he should go, too. He wanted his merit badge, and he'd been grounded for the last week, so the trip must have seemed a beacon. *He's just at Janice's*, she began telling herself, trying to dismantle his absence into manageable increments. But nothing—not work or cleaning or sleep or conversation—could fill the void; nothing could deliver the nights swiftly enough. She tried distracting herself, her mind and body—restaurants with tasseled menus, candlelit baths, ice cream, letter writing, aerobics. Most of the ideas paled, though, and those that didn't—soaking baths and mint chocolate chip—invigorated rather than relaxed her. Both letters she wrote were to Max.

So she felt relieved and vindicated—Sonny had described her as "plucky"—when three days later Max called for them to fetch him. His stomach hurt; he didn't like the beds; mosquitoes bit him at night; he'd pulled a deer tick from his shoulder. The scoutmaster said Max had a slight fever, but mostly his interest in the camp seemed to have waned after he'd earned his Karankawa patch. Then the home-coming became a double relief because the storm—now Hurricane Fay—had stalled, organized, and was churning back toward the coast. Forecasts anticipated that storm surges would bring tides fifteen feet higher than normal; rain, up to an inch every hour. She'd told herself not to throw a fit, not to demand they drive up and abscond with their embarrassed son, but now that he wanted to come home, she knew she'd been right all along.

Or so Sonny had imagined.

The doctors diagnosed the boy with a flu that was making the rounds; Nora had taken him the day after his return. Sonny intended to meet them there, but a fire had started in the heater of the refinery's No. 4 platformer, then the boss ordered a weekend shut-down because of Fay. When Sonny arrived home that afternoon, Max said, "They didn't give me a shot." And Sonny said, "No? Well, we'll have to go back."

That night, the wind squalled. Max was asleep on the couch, his fever rising with the evening. Now that he was home, Nora wanted, ironically, inappropriately, to make love. She liked sex during storms, always had, but Sonny also knew Max's being back had returned Nora to herself, and whole again, her body was yearning. And didn't being parents sweeten intimacy anyway? Didn't their lovemaking benefit from the pleasure of escaping accumulated responsibility? Rain in her hair, vodka on her lips, the lovely, briny smell of her sweaty neck, they were nearing that moment when they would forget mortgages and storms and summer colds for a few seconds, the moment when they'd be brilliantly freed from their senses, but she paused and said she wanted to move the boy into his room. "Stay here," she said, the words slow as honey.

What a time for Sonny to recall the raffle tickets: Max wears a dress shirt, creased slacks, loafers that blister his ankles—church clothes. White sunlight dapples the street, a thick wind stirs leaves as he walks; maybe he rehearses his speech. He carries a notebook to record the donations and raps on neighbors' doors. The pitch is that someone will be drawn at the end of the fund drive—Frasier Elementary needs money for a new gymnasium, playground equipment, fish tanks and fish—and the winner and two guests will fly, with the top-selling student, to AstroWorld in Houston. He relays the information with the eager, distracted seriousness of a boy whose feet do not yet touch the linoleum under the chair. He accepts cookies and Cokes, kisses on the cheek and handshakes along with the cash; he does not accept checks. He wads the money in his pocket, then proceeds down the block, trying to meet his goal before his father gets home for supper.

What did Nora's screaming sound like as Sonny waited in their bed, how to describe that voice that ripped through the reverie and made his heart knot and turn over in his chest? A wounded wild animal? A hiccupping, impossible attempt to call his name though she's started to hyperventilate? A barbed, throat-tearing screech? Are there no words for such afflicted noise?

Max wouldn't wake. In Sonny's memory, time had warped; by the moment he'd kneeled beside the boy, his mind processing the limp arms, the awful surprising weight of an unmuscled, unconscious child, Nora had already been told that ambulances were caught in the weather. She argued irrationally, or hyper-rationally, with the dispatcher, but Sonny had slipped into chinos and bolted outside to start the truck, struggling to shut out the sudden, overpowering fear that it wouldn't crank. Despite himself, he noticed the mailbox gaping open; a cedar plank in the fence had sunk inches below the rest, their welcome mat floated down the street. There was the consideration of whether to cover Max with something—a garbage bag?—and shield him from the rain, then the decision instead to take a towel and pat him dry in the truck. After Nora situated herself in the passenger side, he scooped Max from the couch, keeping him swaddled in the blue afghan, and cradled him out into the storm. Ducking outside, Sonny thought: Breathing, he's breathing. He did not think to put on his shoes.

A constant sluice of water, the harsh, labored squeak of worn-down wipers. Wind slammed the truck like waves. Nora talked: *Daddy's getting us there.* His foot slipped from the accelerator, his forearms and wrists burned from fighting the steering wheel, water dripped from his hair into his eyes, mouth. *Are you cold? Want more blanket?* The wiper blades wouldn't clear fast enough, each sheet of water replaced by another. He drove in second gear, shifted to third, then back to second. Rain skidded over the pavement, made it appear clean, soft. *Pretend we're on a boat, a ferry.* The engine bogging, bogging, almost choking out under the water. *Remember the ferry? The jumping fish? Remember the Flippers? Sure you do.* He deliberated everything at once; what to do if the engine quits; which streets to take; alternate routes if necessary; what to tell the doctor; in what order. *You're the good one. You're okay. We love you. I'm sorry. I'm sorry.*

Had he opened his eyes? Nora said she thought he had for a second, but she'd turned away, believing they'd missed a turn. Max's face seemed trapped in the glow of streetlamps—a jaundiced gray. They hit deep, hidden puddles and new potholes that jarred the truck and bounced each of them hard on the bench seat. Sonny wanted to slow down, wanted to speed up. Each minute squeezed in around them; they were at the bottom of a well, losing oxygen. Palm trees bowed. The hospital seemed impossibly far; each intersection left him panicked, sick with indecision. Though he retraced their course in his mind and found no mistake, he convinced himself he *had* taken a wrong turn. The city looked foreign, a maze of Möbius streets that disappeared behind the truck and led nowhere. He had no idea where he was, where he'd taken his fraught, desperate family, but just as he started to confess, the hospital towers came into view, each distant window ablaze with a promising amber light.

The opportunity to leave Janice's passed like a secret. Curtains of rain slapped the north side of the house; the metal garbage can clattered at the top of a driveway; wind slipped between the plywood and windows, whistling, threatening to pry them apart.

She remembered the hurricane parties differently. No radio, no dancing in the garage, no lawn chairs or slickers. She placed the same friends not in the garage but around the kitchen table, playing dominoes. She had come *with* Janice, not after. A sign *had* sailed across the yard, but she recalled it coming from a nearby gas station—called Kum-and-Go—not Kmart across town. She told him this sitting in the front room, on a sofa upholstered in Italian silk. Waves of uneasiness rolled over Sonny; he fought back discouragement, a stubborn disbelief. For years he'd thought—fantasized really—of meeting her again, of happening upon her in an airport or catching her eye in a dark restaurant. He heard himself deliver beautifully aged, devastating orations. He'd had nightmares, too; in one, he stood beside her bathtub and threw a plugged-in television into the water and watched her convulse. Now his words got tangled before he spoke them, his thoughts jettisoned down regrettable tangents.

"I should admit I remarried," she said. "A groundskeeper at a cemetery. I was snapping pictures of headstones for a photography class. He was pulling weeds and called me maudlin."

"I needed that word for a crossword puzzle last Sunday," he said. This was true, but more than anything, he wanted not to hear about this man. From now on, he knew the word "maudlin" would recall this uneasiness, the specific gravity and matter of the moment—a framed French cigarette advertisement on the opposite wall, the faint, candied smell of cinnamon, the thrum of pelting rain, Nora studying her bitten-down nails. He checked her fingers again, expecting a ring to have appeared. Nor did he want to tell about the women he'd dated—a divorced waitress, a pacemaker programmer, a veterinary technician—each more familiar than the last, each another version of the same woman.

Nora said, "We've not spoken in two years, the groundskeeper and I. He believes I used him. His term is 'emotional tampon.'"

She laughed, then he did.

Outside, the wind picked up the garbage can and hurled it against

Janice's garage door. They both started at the sound, then recovered, as if someone had unexpectedly entered and exited the room. She said, "Still think it's going to miss us?"

A gentle lilt had crept into her voice, a beseeching tone fringed with playfulness, as though this would become their private joke.

Sonny had taken solace in the completeness of her grief. Her devastation reassured him; he thought, *This makes sense.* She cried and vented, accepted sympathy and acted alternately hostile and distracted. Then, once the obligations were completed, family and friends delivered back to their jobs and homes, she locked herself in Max's room and refused to leave.

He set trays of food outside the door—she wouldn't retrieve them until he showed himself through Max's back window. When the phone rang, she picked up the extension in the room; she used his bathroom, dried herself with his towels, squeezed into his T-shirts. She detailed these things through the door—the wood still plastered with superhero decals and postcards from Janice's travels—while Sonny waited for all of this to end, trusting that something would snap and they'd be liberated from such desolation. But sustaining her became his new project. Her despair so steeled him that he was afraid to upset that balance, and he savored the comfort of again counting on something. The worst feeling, far worse than he could have anticipated, was that tending to her distracted him from Max's absence, that he toiled to sustain her because he'd failed their son; in his darkest moments, he accused himself of employing her hopelessness to pull himself out of the sludge. Or he believed, as never before, that people incurred punishments of the soul.

On the third day she said, "I found a notebook under his bed." Then, after a moment: "He had a little girlfriend. Nikki Palmer. She has a pony named Sprinkles."

He knew her immediately. "Blonde. From the assembly."

"Right!"

He imagined Nora clutching the notebook against her breasts, gazing up to recall Nikki Palmer beside Max, swaying and singing

"Home on the Range." He'd worn a cowboy vest fashioned from a paper bag, decorated with crayon zigzags and a tin-foil sheriff's star. He was pigeon-toed and off key and so beautiful Sonny had to squeeze his eyes closed.

Nora said, "She's a looker! Our little heartbreaker."

And what became clear hearing her voice, bubbling and proud and hopeful for that which would never be, was that he had already lost her. When they had heard the word *meningitis*—they were standing before the hospital's surreal, childlike mural of Christ feeding a donkey on a plane of blond sand—Sonny sensed a grotesque race beginning and that he was suddenly responsible for their outrunning a stalking, paralyzing chaos. A thing like this either bound people together or drove them apart, but now he knew she was gone. Maybe he'd leave lunch outside her door—already it had become *her* door, *her* room—and she'd never answer; maybe tomorrow he'd wake to find her car and clothes gone; maybe in an hour she'd waltz out and they would live together another ten years without exchanging an unkind or meaningful word; maybe she'd cinch Max's paisley tie around her neck and kick his desk chair out from under her.

"Hungry?" he asked.

"Ravenous," she said, still bright. "Is there more cereal?"

"For supper?"

"Doesn't it sound delicious? I have a real taste for sugar lately."

In the kitchen he mashed enough sleeping pills to knock her out and sifted them into the bowl. Within the hour he lifted the door off its hinges, loaded her into the truck, and returned to the hospital.

He tried bringing her back, with kindness and romance, with promises and memories and plans and pleas, but she always seemed just beyond reach. Nora seemed to think he wanted her to recover—the word now spurious, blasphemous—wanted *them* to recover, and that galled her. But he'd abandoned that dream as he'd abandoned the refinery; when he left for work, he drove to the National Seashore and passed the hours among the mud flats and saltwater marshes. When he returned in the evenings, still under the pretense of a completed shift, she ranted and collapsed, threw accusations and insults and skillets, while all along he was becoming too severe in an unanswerable resistance. No, recovery was not what he wanted; he wanted them to go down together—man, woman, child. But life at home lurched and creaked; love turned into a cross-threaded bolt. He proposed moving from Corpus, and finally that's what she did, alone. The divorce was swift; she wanted nothing except for the marriage to end.

He carted their furniture and housewares, the clothes she'd left and even a few of Max's long-discarded toys onto the lawn and sold them to neighbors and strangers. (After the first plastic tractor sold, he rescued the other toys.) When only piles of blouses and skirts lay on the lawn, he sold the lot for eight dollars. Crystal and antiques went to an auction, yielding more than he'd expected; he sold the Shamrock house after a year in the duplex. Then a deadly void opened, a steep, widening channel across which he still heard her voice and saw her visage, but trying to ford the space would kill him sure as cancer. Days came when he could feel Nora's presence, as if she'd arrived in Corpus for a visit, but hadn't yet called. Sometimes he heard her saying his name, others he glimpsed her zipping by in traffic. Once he saw her at the cemetery, kneeling beside the headstone. He made his way to her, thinking how fittingly peculiar the scene was, right from a movie. Maybe they'd have an innocuous conversation to counter the melodrama; maybe they'd try vainly to recover their old selves by racing to bed; maybe they would speak of him, laugh about the raffle tickets.

Janice, not Nora. He felt stifled, shot through with frustration. She said, "Would you believe I haven't been here since the service?"

His mind hadn't indulged such optimistic murmurs when he approached her in McCoy's. She didn't look familiar enough to start his gut's swirl of exquisite agony, yet once he recognized her, he couldn't blot out the feeling that the boy was with her, hiding behind the discounted shower stalls, waiting.

The electricity blacked out. Wind and thunder coupled with darkness and lightning to give Nora enough courage—or fear, or pity—to nestle into his shoulder on the couch. Had he been standing, the smell of her hair, more oily than fragrant, would have buckled his knees. Water poured from the roof. Safety candles flickered on the coffee table. Sex crossed his mind, a breaking light of dangerous possibility, and the notion sent his heart racing; he hoped she couldn't feel it. He was unsure where to lay his hands, afraid to disturb the delicate air that was so mercifully tempered with her apprehension. Neither said anything, not even when she began to weep quietly into his chest. What, finally, could be said? Drifting to sleep, he imagined the candles igniting a gas leak; as the storm blew outside, he half-wished it would turn the house to scrap.

No memory of retiring to Janice's room, but he found himself there—clothed, muscles stove-up, on top of the down comforter—waking, then tumbling back into sleep. A ragged dream: strolling with Nora through endless aisles of boats anchored in downtown streets. The vessels are on sale. A cluster of Karankawas, naked and wet and towering with cane-pierced lips, browse as well. Nora worries the sale hasn't started yet; she puts her hand on his shoulder, and it stays there while they walk, as if she's blind. She says, "It's nice you're here." When he woke, she was not beside him, though she had been. He feared that whatever ease they'd enjoyed the night before, whatever comfort the storm had forged between them, would have vanished now, that the morning would have let the air out of Nora's lovely need. The dent in her pillow filled him with an intractable dread, a dispiriting expectation of discovery.

She was watching the news, perched in front of a portable television. She wore a jaunty blouse and skirt of Janice's. Even these years later, he saw the clothes were borrowed.

She said, "They keep showing pictures of a drowned armadillo."

"Good morning to you, too."

"And film of the island. Turned-over boats, missing roofs," she said. "We slept through the worst of it."

His heart swelled: We.

The boarded windows dimmed the house, and the plywood's still

being there pleased him. The room smelled of a velvety, sweetly nauseating perfume. She had opened the front door and the sun filtered
in, a new light made brighter and more poised by the saturated lawns.
Broken, waterlogged branches littered the street. A drenched basset
hound trotted along the sidewalk, ambling past neighbors clearing
detritus. From down the block, a woman's ecstatic voice, "Scooter!
Scooter!" The dog stopped, perked its ears, then loped homeward.
Across the street, the architect inspected the taped X's on his tall
windows; he was smaller than Sonny remembered, bald now. Wet
leaves were plastered to the truck. On television the meteorologist
advised viewers not to leave their homes; power lines were down and
conditions were ripe for flash floods, lightning, funnel clouds, and
tornadoes. Defeat weighted his voice; Alicia, his lover, had left him.
A map showing the storm's trajectory clicked on the screen. The eye
had hit between Corpus and Kingsville; Sonny's prediction couldn't
have been more wrong.

Nora poured coffee. He thought to say he only drank decaf, or to
tell about the afternoon on the sixth green that had predicated the
change, but he refrained. That day he'd enjoyed a fleeting cogent
relief: Max wouldn't hear of this, wouldn't have to slog through an
autopsy and funeral, wouldn't have to wonder about his father's pain
or be mired in regret or recover. And he'd wondered when Nora,
wherever she was, would receive the news. Now he accepted the
coffee because he already felt weakened before her, felt scattered and
drugged, and if she hadn't noticed his vulnerability yet, he didn't
want to lay it bare.

"I've learned to make crepes." Then as if worried she'd over-
stepped her boundary, she exhaled and slouched against the corner.
"Or you probably need to get to work."

"We'll open at noon, if at all." More likely, he had phone mes-
sages asking him to come to work. He said, "Tomorrow everything
will go on sale."

"Sonny..." She paused. Over her shoulder, he saw grackles in the
yard, hunting beetles and earthworms. Two greenhouse windows were

broken. Stalks of banana plants were snapped. She said, "Nothing."

He could've pressed, maybe she even wanted him to, but he let it go. Let it go because whatever she would say could have destroyed him, the words could have instantly unraveled the perfect lace of the night. The threat proved enough. Since finding her in McCoy's, he'd ignored how the corners of her eyes, tight and slightly, elegantly, upturned, resembled Max's. He'd ignored how after she left a room the air faintly carried the boy's powdery scent. Over the years, Sonny had naturally fitted himself to this role—grieving father, abandoned husband. Now such identities seemed self-aggrandizingly thin. And he realized the reason he'd skirted all the grave conversations had nothing to do with a fear that Nora would cave in again, but that he would. After she'd left, breaking down remained his one terror and he'd clung to it like a lifeline.

She said, "This morning I remembered when they wanted to cut off our power, on Christmas Eve. You called and convinced them to leave it on, so we could light the tree for Max."

How long since he'd recalled that night, how long since he'd heard the name spoken aloud? She said it with such ease that Sonny felt cleaved from himself. And he knew she said it every day; like a prayer or confession, it absolved her.

"It was their mistake," he said. "We were square."

"That's what you always said. That was always sweet of you."

On television an anchorman interviewed a Port Aransas couple who'd lost everything. Missing person reports were coming in; bridges were washed out. Sonny didn't want to hear this and didn't want Nora to either. He said, "The newsman's a short fella, but you wouldn't know on television. He comes into McCoy's."

She cupped her hands around the coffee cup. A blush rose in her cheeks. Despite the clammy air that comes after storms, she looked cold and he expected her to shiver. Then, like that, she did. The room's brandy-tinged light and the air's fleeting, inexplicable scent of winter gave him the feeling of having crawled through a tunnel, of emerging to find Nora waiting for him. When she wasn't looking, he found his eyes could linger seconds longer than yesterday.

She said, "Janice told me you worked there. I was looking for you."

To his surprise, his answer didn't surprise him at all. He said, "I know."

The ferry engine chugged, turning over a frothy wake of the olive-hued water between Corpus and Port Aransas. They were due at a picnic for Coastal employees, the annual affair designed to build morale. In the truck bed was an ice chest with beer, mustard potato salad, peeled shrimp, cornbread. Nora and Sonny had bathing suits on under their clothes; Max wore his outright. He'd been grounded for a week and would remain so until Sunday, when he left for Camp Karankawa. But they had agreed he should be allowed to go to the picnic; they recalled how he'd loved last year's tug-o-war and sack races, how he'd caught a lightning bug in his mouth and the insect continued firing its harmless light on his tongue. Despite their best intentions to stay strict this week, their resolve had wavered. Nora had admitted to letting him watch cartoons after school, and Sonny confessed to telling Max his initiative would pay off in his adult life.

No raffle, no fund drive, no prize flight to AstroWorld. A neighbor had been boasting about his school's fund drive, so Max had invented his own campaign. He had pulled from the firmament the failing school budget, the depressed playground equipment, the impromptu district meeting that had so swiftly initiated the raffle. He'd already canvassed the neighborhood, come home, and situated himself in his room to denominate bills when Mrs. Dixon called Nora. She'd said, "I need him selling Avon!"

Sonny hoisted him onto the ferry's guardrail, kept his arm around Max's middle. He needed a haircut, the wind blew back odd strands that tickled Sonny's neck, cheeks. Before the raffle, he was consumed with scouting, with securing his Karankawa Badge, and before that he'd been a dramatist, drafting a play each afternoon, then casting his parents in after-supper productions. He'd written of mobsters and kings and aliens and pirates, and Sonny always felt that he'd not done the parts justice; nightly he'd seen his son be disappointed by his parents. But he'd also felt in a luster, shining in the boy's reflected light. When he'd arrived home from the refinery and found Nora hanging up with Mrs. Dixon, she'd smiled and said, "Your son."

"Looky here," she said now, leaning over the port side. "Dolphins."

Porpoises, actually, four or five racing beside the boat, cameling their backs and jumping out of the water and diving in without splash. They were dusk-colored—one almost black—their bellies glistening pink in the sun. Nora, he knew, was offering an olive branch, trying to rouse Max from sullenness. This was her way. Whereas Sonny waited for the smoke to clear, she lowered her head and barged in. Such grace, such luminous disregard for graveness had always thrilled him.

"Flippers," Max said. "Flippers!"

That is such a short float across the channel; usually most of the time is spent in traffic, waiting to get to the landing, but within a minute, Max was growing antsy. Oh, youth. Hadn't he just gotten a haircut? Sonny felt certain he had. He imagined the coming week when he and Nora would have the house to themselves, and he ignored how restricting Max had been its own reward, keeping him at home, with them. This seemed something he'd admit one day, perhaps when Max had a son of his own. When will that be, he wondered. When will I have to wait to see you? As the ferry neared the dock and the captain sounded the great horn, as the pod of porpoises banked off to race the opposite boat and Sonny helped his wife and son back into his small truck, their time together threatened to pass within a breath.

A Season of Moles

Jack Kerley

Reverend John Harlan Dewitt glared at the balled-up letter on his desk pad. Reading it moments ago, he'd involuntarily crumpled it in his fist. He closed his eyes and ran slender fingers through dark hair, wings of premature gray at the temples. "Madness," he whispered, first softly, then with anger, his voice filling the small office behind the sanctuary. Dewitt shook his head, smoothed the page flat, and read again. Not the whole letter, but a single phrase midpoint in the text.

In accordance with revised doctrine, all church teaching must immediately and without question emphasize the inerrancy of Biblical text. To deny this will result in...

Dewitt stood abruptly and walked to the window, letter in hand. Through the glass—four clear panes poured a hundred years previously—the morning shadow of the church fell across sun-bright grass, spearpoint steeple poking the neighboring woods. The lawn between church and trees resembled a green and perfect carpet from a distance, but up close disturbances showed; it was a season for moles and their burrows veined the grass. Dewitt couldn't bring himself to harm the creatures. Maybe they aerated the soil or something. They had a purpose, according to Ecclesiastes, a time and reason.

He heard an approaching vehicle, then watched a red pickup pull from the gravel road to the parking lot, a hardware store in its bed: lawn edger, rake, shovels, pitchfork, cans of paint, tubs of caulk. A ladder clattered in the rack as the truck shivered dead in a cloud of dust. Groundskeeper, handyman, and church elder Galen Tucker pushed from the pickup and strode to the church, red face screwed tight against the sunlight. Dewitt's office door was half open, and Tucker entered unbidden. The groundskeeper was in his early fifties, slight in stature and apparently carved from flint, all angles and edges and deep-cut hollows. He wore a white shirt buttoned full and khaki pants tucked into black Wellingtons.

"There's more digging out there today than yesterday, moles."

Dewitt glanced out the window. "Looks the same to me, Mr. Tucker."

"That's 'cause you ain't worrying over them. I don't feel like I'm watering the lawn, I'm watering moles."

Dewitt tried a smile. "Maybe you'll drown them."

Tucker's eyes tightened. "I've got poison in the truck."

"You set out poison last year, Mr. Tucker. Here they are back."

Tucker stared at Dewitt, then dropped his eyes to the page in Dewitt's hand. The groundskeeper smiled with his teeth, as if tasting something agreeable.

"Might that be a letter from the national committee, Reverend?"

Dewitt looked at the letter, then at his visitor. "How do you know that, Mr. Tucker?"

"I'm a church elder. On the list that gets them letters. Maybe even I got mine 'fore you got yours."

"I take it you have an opinion, Mr. Tucker? On the letter?" It was impossible, Dewitt knew, for Galen Tucker to not have an opinion.

"I'm all for it, Reverend, what that letter says. People either believe exactly what's in the Book or fry in Hell. No scooting around. That's unerrity of the Word."

Dewitt quarter-folded the letter, started to put it in his pocket, then dropped it on his desk. "*Inerrancy*, Mr. Tucker. Which I support, though I believe inerrancy rises from hearing the overall message posited by scripture, and growing toward correct—inerrant—spiritual decisions. I see my job as opening ears, not enforcing doctrine."

Tucker yanked a small black Bible from his back pocket, striking it with a yellowed fingernail. "What's in my hands is what God meant it to be, and that's nothing more than exactly right. Ears don't need to listen to you—it's all said here. Ain't no room for different."

Dewitt heard his teeth grind. He took a breath. "For over a hundred years this church allowed a degree of latitude within a system of core beliefs, determined through individual congregations. I believe in that autonomy, Mr. Tucker, and in reconciliation through similarities, not perceived differences."

Tucker's eyes slitted. "Simular ain't the same as same. Bible don't leave room for elsewise. Now that it's been said by the committee, young preachers that don't hear ain't long for their jobs."

Dewitt felt his fists clench. "Individual and highly personal interpretations leave room for—"

"I got work to do." Tucker turned his back on Dewitt and started through the door, halted by a middle-aged woman framed in its opening. The groundskeeper paused and stared. The woman's eyes turned to the floor and her face reddened. Tucker grunted displeasure, then marched away, the pine floor echoing his boot heels.

"Mrs. Jessup?" Dewitt said. "Please come in. Goodness, I haven't seen you in—"

"I ain't disturbing nothing, Rev'rent?" Marjorie Jessup's eyes split the difference between crossing the threshold and retreating. "I was just walking by and thought to have a word if you wasn't busy. I can come back tomorrow."

Jessup lived miles across the rolling, wooded hills. There were crescents of sweat beneath her arms, and her dusty shoes were scarred by stones. Dewitt guided the woman to a chair, his light touch bidding her sit. "Something's on your mind, Mrs. Jessup. It's written on your face. Please tell me."

She closed her eyes. A quiver took her hands and she stilled them by clutching the faded blue cotton of her dress, squeezing and releasing. Dewitt heard the high scream of a lawn edger outside as Tucker renewed his thrice-weekly battle against disorder: mowing, edging, yanking nascent dandelions as though each insulted his existence.

Jessup said, "I don't want to pass on my troubles."

Dewitt slid a chair from the wall and sat beside her. "It's why I'm here. Tell me what's wrong."

"It's my boy, Rev'rent. Little Ray. You don't know him; he was gone 'fore you came."

"What happened?"

"My poor lamb died four days ago in Memphis. Trying to get money from a store."

Dewitt paused, the words sinking in. "Robbery?"

A tear striped her cheek. Jessup fumbled a tissue from her sleeve, dabbed. "He got born without enough air for his brain, the doctors said. It made him do things didn't make sense. When he was eight some older kids told him you could eat mud like food. He ate it and ate it. He came home and threw up mud acrost the floor. I said, it's all right, baby, it's all right. I held him tight until the mud stopped coming out." Jessup paused, palmed growing tears from her face. "My baby didn't know enough to keep from eating mud. Or anything else. Now he's sunk in Hell, burning like a bunch of sticks."

Dewitt scowled. "What?"

"He never gave himself over, Rev'rent. I know he didn't. We never got my poor broken baby baptized in the name, neither. We was always moving, never set. When Ray's daddy passed, Little Ray and me came here. He ran off five years back, just seventeen. And now he'll rot in Hell. I heard it from someone who knows."

Dewitt narrowed an eye. "Who might that be?"

Her eyes went to the window. The howl of the edger beat on the glass.

Dewitt said, "Tucker?"

"He's got an ear everywhere. I didn't tell but three-four people and Mr. Tucker found out. He come to my house the other night to tell me Ray's soul was gonna scream until time stopped."

In the two years since coming to the midsized rural church—his first full-fledged appointment—Dewitt knew all the Galen Tuckers in the congregation. Older, though not always, hard-set and vocal about it, they seized upon misfortune as proof of God's eternal bookkeeping, a collection of debts and debits always owed by someone else. Tucker had probably enjoyed a fine and satisfying supper before visiting Mrs. Jessup, fuel for his evening's message.

Dewitt pressed Jessup's hands between his. "Ray was wounded at birth, Mrs. Jessup. His wound prevented acceptance in a normal manner. God knows this."

"Mr. Tucker says God hates Ray for staying turned away. He says it's in the Book."

"Listen to me, Mrs. Jessup. That's simply wrong. God is not an engine of anger. He is—"

A motion at the window caught Dewitt's eye—Tucker driving a pitchfork into the mole mounds. Dewitt crossed the floor and tried to open the window, forgetting the groundskeeper had painted it shut. Dewitt banged on the panes.

"Mr. Tucker. Mr. Tucker!"

The man continued jabbing angrily at the ground. Dewitt hurried outside, Marjorie Jessup ghosting his footsteps.

"Mister Tucker!"

Tucker removed his hat, wiped sweat from his brow, turned slowly to Dewitt.

"Say what?"

"Leave the moles be, sir. I told you that not fifteen minutes ago. Please respect my wishes."

Tucker struck again at the burrows, then spat on the grass. "You want the moles to mess up the place, I'm done. For today, leastwise."

The groundskeeper threw the tool in his pickup and climbed into the cab. He glared at the pair, then drove off in a spray of gravel, stones clattering against the clapboard slats of the church. Dewitt put his hand over the woman's shoulder and drew her close. They walked in silence across the lawn, studying slight embossments in its surface, the occasional eruption where a tunnel broke the grass. Dewitt pushed flat a burrow with his shoe, watched it rise like a sponge when he lifted his foot. He'd never seen a mole. Did they come up at night?

Jessup studied the rebounding soil. "You think it's just a few blind moles scratchin' through dirt, Rev'rent? Or is it like a city down there? Before he was high as my waist Little Ray kept a jar of dirt and ants. They'd dig a couple tiny holes up top..."

Dewitt nodded. "But beneath the dirt a webwork of passages."

Jessup turned to Dewitt, her eyes alight with hope. "What you started to say inside, Rev'rent—my baby Ray is safe in heaven? I think so, too, and I believe you'd be the one who'd know."

Dewitt looked down the road, the groundskeeper's dust a gray cloud above the gravel. Now that inerrancy was codified, the Tuckers would gleefully document perceived lapses by Dewitt, transgressions communicated to the hierarchy. Warnings would arrive. Enough warnings and he'd be gone.

But the Marjorie Jessups would remain.

Dewitt gathered and measured his words. "Yes, Mrs. Jessup. Ray's safe. It's the honest, perfect truth. But for right now—just a little while, I hope—the truth about Ray is a truth between you and me and God."

Marjorie Jessup stared into Dewitt's eyes, then thought for a long moment. A sad and understanding smile crossed her face.

"It's the mud again, isn't it?

Dewitt took Jessup's hand, squeezed it. She held tight for a moment, then turned away and headed down the road. The dust of Tucker's truck had settled, appearing to have been burned away, like fog beneath a rising sun. Dewitt watched until Jessup disappeared behind the trees, her face serene in the light. *A time for everything,* Dewitt thought, nodding to himself, *a season.* He took a deep breath and crossed the lawn to the church, stepping dance-lightly over gentle hints of moles, careful to not disturb their quiet, subterranean industry.

BIRDLAND

Michael Knight

Between the months of April and September, Pawtucket, Rhode Island, is inhabited by several generations of African parrots. A millionaire and philanthropist named Archibald brought a dozen or so over from Kenya around the turn of the century and kept them in an aviary built against the side of his house. A few days before his death, in a moment more notable for generosity than good sense, he swung open the cage and released the birds into a wide summer sky. According to eyewitness reports, the parrots made a dazed circle beneath the clouds, surprised by their sudden freedom, and, not immediately seeing anything more to their liking, lighted amid the branches of an apple orchard on the back acreage of Archibald's property. There, as is the habit of nature, they flourished and have continued to thrive for more than ninety years. But in September, when winter creeps in from the ocean and cold air kindles hazy instincts, the parrots flee south for warmer climes and settle here, in Elbow, Alabama, along a slow bend in the Black Warrior River, where perhaps they are reminded of waters, slower still, in an almost forgotten continent across the sea.

I know all this because The Blond told me it was true. The Blond has platinum hair and round hips and a pair of ornithology degrees from a university up in New Hampshire. She has a given name as well—Ludmilla Haggarsdottir—but no one in town is comfortable with its proper pronunciation. The Blond came to Elbow a year past, researching a book about Archibald's parrots, and was knocked senseless by the late August heat. Even after the weight had gone out of summer and the parrots had arrived and football was upon us, she staggered around in a safari hat and sunglasses, drunk with the fading season, scribbling notes on the progress of the birds. She took pictures and sat sweating in the live-oak shade. They don't have this sort of heat in New Hampshire—bone-warming, inertial heat, humidity thick enough to slow your blood. She rented a room in my house, the only room for rent in town. At night, we would sit on the back porch, fireflies blundering against the screen, and make love on my grandmother's old daybed. "Tell me a story, Raymond," The Blond would say. "Tell me something I've never heard before." The Blond is not the only one with a college education. "This," I said, throwing her leg over my shoulder, "is how Hector showed his love to Andromache the night before Achilles killed him dead."

The only TV for miles sits on the counter at Dillard's Country Store. Dillard has a gas pump out front and all the essentials inside, white bread and yellow mustard and cold beer. Dillard himself brews hard cider and doubles as mayor of Elbow. He is eighty-one years old and has been unanimously elected to eleven consecutive terms. On fall Saturdays, all of Elbow gathers in his store to watch the Alabama team take the field, me and The Blond and the mayor and Mae and Wilson Camp, who have a soybean farm north of town. Lookout Mountain Coley is the nearest thing we have to a local celebrity. These days, he stocks shelves in the grocery and mans the counter when the mayor is in the head, but thirty-five years ago, he was only the second black man to play football for the great Bear Bryant and once returned a punt ninety-nine yards for a touchdown against Tennessee. The Crimson Tide is not what it used to be, however, and we all curse God for commandeering our better days. Leonard and Chevy Foote, identical twins, have the foulest mouths in Elbow, their dialogue on game day nothing more than a long string of invective against blind referees and unfair recruiting practices and dumbass coaches who aren't fit to wipe Bear Bryant's behind. The parrots perch in pecan trees beyond the open windows and listen to us rant. At night, with the river curving slow and silent, they mimic us in the dark. "Catch the ball," they caw in Mayor Dillard's desperate falsetto, "Catch the ball, you stupid nigger." Mayor Dillard is an unrepentant racist and I often wonder what the citizens of Pawtucket, Rhode Island, must think when the birds leave us in the spring.

The Blond is still working on her book. She follows the birds from tree to tree, keeping an eye on reproductive habits and the condition of winter plumage. Parrot, she tells me, is really just a catchall name for several types of birds, such as the macaw, the cockatoo, the lory, and the budgerigar. Common to all genera, including our African grays, are a hooked bill, a prehensile tongue, and yoke-toed claws. The African parrot can live up to eighty years, she says, and often mates for life, though our local birds have apparently adopted a more swinging sexual culture due to an instinctive understanding of the rigors of perpetuation in a nonindigenous environment. Her book will be about the insistence of nature. It will be about surviving against the odds. One day, says The Blond, she will return to Paw-tucket, as she had originally planned, and resume her studies there. She mentions this when she is angry with me for one reason or another and leads me to her room, where her suitcase still sits packed atop my grandmother's antique bureau. And the thought of her leaving does frighten me to good behavior. I can hardly remember what my life was like without her here, though I managed fine a long time before she arrived. Seven months ago, when March finally brought her to her senses and the birds began to filter north, The Blond and I were already too tangled up for her to leave.

My grandmother left me this house upon her death. It isn't a big house, just a one-story frame number with a sleeping porch and a con-verted attic, which is where I make my bed, but it sits high on red clay bluffs, and, when November rain has stripped leaves from the trees, you can see all the way to the Black Warrior. Here, the river bends like a folded arm, which is how our town came to have its name. In the fall, we sit mesmerized and enraged by the failings of our team, the dark water litters Dillard Point with driftwood and detritus, baby carriages and coat hangers, kites and high-heeled shoes. When the game has ended and I need an hour to collect myself, I wander Mayor Dillard's land, collecting branches that I carve into parrot figurines and sell from a shelf in the window of his store. We have birdwatchers by the busload in season and, outside of the twenty dollars a month I charge The Blond for room and board, these whittlings account for my income. But I don't need much in the way of money any more. Years ago, my family owned a lumber mill and a loading dock by the river so the company could ship wood to Mobile. My great-grandfather torched the mill in 1939 for insurance, and gradually, a few at a time, people drifted downstream for work until there was almost no one left. The Blond wonders why we still bother with elections since there are fewer than a dozen voters and Dillard always wins. I tell her we believe in democracy in Alabama. I tell her we have faith in the American way.

Neither does The Blond understand our commitment to college football. Ever the scientist, she has theorized that a winning team gives us a reason to take pride in being from Alabama, and, with our long history of bigotry and oppression and our more recent dismal record in public education and environmental conservation, such reasons, according to The Blond, are few and far between. I don't know whether or not she is correct, but I suspect that she is beginning to recognize the appeal of the Crimson Tide. Just last week, as we watched Alabama in a death struggle with the Florida Gators, our halfback fumbled and she jerked out of her chair, her fists closed tight, her breasts bouncing excitedly. She had to clench her jaw to keep from calling out. Her face was glazed with sweat, the fine hairs on her upper lip visible in the dusty light. The sight of her like that, all balled-up enthusiasm, her shirt knotted beneath her ribs, sweat pooling in the folds of her belly, moved me to dizziness. I held her hand and led her out onto the porch. Dillard's store is situated at a junction of rural highways, and we watched a tour bus rumble past, eager old women hanging from the windows with binoculars at their eyes. The pecan trees were dotted with parrots, blurs of brighter red and smears of gray in among the leaves. "Catch the ball," one called out, and another answered, "Stick him like a man, you fat country bastard." She sat on the plank steps and I knelt at her bare feet. "Will you marry me?" I said. "You are a prize greater than Helen of Troy." She looked at me sadly for a minute, her hand going clammy in mine. The game was back on inside, an announcer's voice floating through the open door. After a while she said, "I can't live here the rest of my life." She stood and went back inside to watch the rest of the game, which we lost on a last-second Hail Mary pass that broke all our hearts at once.

The Blond won't sleep a whole night with me. She slips up the drop ladder to my attic and we wind together in the dark, her body pale above me, moonlight catching in her movie star hair. When she is finished, she smokes cigarettes at the gable window and I tell her stories about the Trojan War. I explain how the Greeks almost lost everything when Achilles and Agamemnon argued over a woman. I tell her that male pride is a volatile energy, some feathers better left unruffled, but she only likes the stories for background noise. She is more interested in the parrots, a few of whom have taken up roost in an oak tree beside my house. If there is a full moon, the birds are awake for hours, calling, "Who are you?" back and forth in the luminous night; "Why are you in my house?" According to The Blond, old Archibald was deep in Alzheimer's by the time of his death and was unable even to recognize his own children when they visited. She goes dreamy-eyed imagining the parrots passing these words from generation to generation. Before she returns to her bed, she wonders aloud why it is that the birds learned such existential phrases in Rhode Island and such ugly, bitter words down here.

Sometimes, Lookout Mountain Coley gets fed up with Mayor Dillard shouting "nigger" at the TV screen. Having played for Alabama in the halcyon sixties, Lookout knows what football means to people around here and he restrains himself admirably. But when they were younger men and Mayor Dillard crossed whatever invisible boundary exists between them, Lookout would circle his fists in the old style and challenge him to a fight. They'd roll around in the dirt parking lot a while, sweat running muddy on their skin. Nowadays, he presses his lips together and his face goes blank and hard like he is turning himself to stone. He walks outside without a word, watches the birds across the highway. He wolf-whistles, the way parrots are supposed to, and speaks to them in ordinary phrases. "Pretty bird, pretty bird. How about a little song?" After a few minutes, Mayor Dillard shakes his head and joins Lookout beside the road, 142 years of life between them. We focus our attention on the game so they can have some time alone to sort things out. No one knows for sure what goes on between them out there, but they return patting each other on the back, making promises that neither of them will keep. Mayor Dillard offers a public apology each time, says he hopes the people of Elbow won't hold this incident against him come election. He buys a round of bottled beers, and Lookout accepts the apology with grace, waving his beer at the TV so we'll quit looking at him and keep our mind on simpler things.

Her first season in town, The Blond was appalled by these displays. She is descended from liberal-minded Icelandic stock, and she couldn't understand why Lookout or any of us would allow Mayor Dillard to go on the way he does. She sprang to her feet and clicked off the television and delivered an angry lecture welcoming us to the "twentieth-fucking-century." Her fury was gorgeous, her face red, her thighs quivering righteously beneath her hiking shorts. She tried to convince Lookout to report Mayor Dillard to the NAACP and, short of that, to run for mayor himself, arguing that because he was a minor sports celebrity he might have the clout to unseat an incumbent. But Lookout told her he wasn't interested. He shook his head gravely and said, "Uneasy is the head that wears the ground, miss." Though I know she would be loath to admit it, the words don't offend her so much any more. You can get used to anything, given time. Some nights, however, when she is moving violently over me, she grits her teeth and says, "Who's the nigger, Raymond? Who's the nigger now?" I understand that her indignation is not aimed directly at me, but that doesn't make those nights any easier. I twist myself sleeplessly in the sheets when she is gone.

Raymond was my father's name. I am the only child of a land surveyor. My mother died giving birth, and my dad wandered farther and farther afield looking for work until, finally, he never returned. I was thirteen when he disappeared, left here with my grandmother and the house. She paid for my education with nickels and dimes, millions of them, hidden in Mason jars beneath her bed because hers were old notions and she trusted neither banks nor the long-term value of paper money. "That's ancient history," she said, when I told her what I was studying. "You ought to be thinking about the future." She loved this town and hoped that I would bring my learning home and give something back. She made me promise before she died. But all I have given unto Elbow is driftwood parrots and The Blond. Everyone knows she lingers here because of me, and no one is quite sure how they feel about that.

A few days ago, she found a parrot nest in Wilson Camp's defunct grain silo and spent a whole day sitting against the wall, watching the mother feed her babies regurgitated pecans. I panicked when I returned from wandering Dillard Point and found an empty house, waited on the porch and watched the road for cars, but she never showed. I don't have a phone, so I drove from house to house, stopped by to see Lookout, swung past the Footes' mobile home, whipped the town into a posse. I prowled country lanes until I saw her Jeep parked beside the Camps' most distant field. When I didn't spot her right away, I suspected the worst. This deserted road and vacant field are like horror movie sets, the silo rising from the ground like a wizard's tower. I called her name, but only the parrots answered back. "Who are you?" Their voices were flat and distant. "Catch the ball." Then, faintly, I heard her voice, a stage whisper coming from the silo, and when I crawled in beside her, she shined a flashlight on the nest and I could see the baby birds, their feathers still slick and insufficient, heads wobbly on their necks. The Blond threw her arms around me and wept and pressed her lips against my collarbone.

Mayor Dillard has a deal with his counterpart in Pawtucket, Rhode Island. On one Saturday in the fall and one in spring the towns combine in celebrating Parrot Days. In October, the mayor of Pawtucket flies south on his constituents' tab. He stands outside the store, where Lookout has rigged a hand-painted banner, delivers a short speech, and has his picture snapped for the record, his limousine idling beside the grandstand. Then he continues on to New Orleans, where he spends a few days whoring and playing at being a bigwig. Dillard takes a similar trip in May, which we do not begrudge him, and winds up in Atlantic City; once, Lookout had to drive up there to bail him out of jail. Our octogenarian mayor, it seems, was chasing showgirls down a hotel hallway wearing only an Indian head-dress and screeching "Polly want a cracker" at the top of his lungs. Such, I suppose, are the prerogatives of power.

Mayor Dillard always arranges it so that Parrot Days fall during an off week for the Crimson Tide. This year, we gather in the parking lot and offer gifts to the Pawtucket delegation, my figurines and jugs of hard cider and a red plastic hat shaped like an elephant head, and listen to the visiting mayor give his speech. The parrots jeer at him from the trees. "Run, darkie, run," they call, and he pretends not to notice. The Blond is disappointed with the day. She wanted more from these proceedings, wanted something meaningful and real, but most of us are grateful for a break from football this year. Six games into the season and already we've lost four. Another stinker and Bama is out of contention for a bowl. We'd settle for anything at this point: Taco Bell Aloha, Sun America Copper, even the Poulan Weed Eater over in Louisiana.

Elbow, Alabama, is easy enough to find. Take Highway 14 north from Sherwood until you come to Easy Money Road. Bear east and keep driving until you're sure you've gone too far. Past a red barn with the words "His desire shall be satisfied upon the hills of Gilead" painted on the planks in gold letters, past a field where no crops will grow, past a cypress split by lightning and full of vivid, loquacious birds. This is modest country, and nature has had her steady way for years. My house is just a little farther, over a hill, left on the gravel drive. Someone filched the mailbox years ago, but the post is still standing, headless and crooked. All our mail is addressed to Dillard's Country Store. In the evenings, when the sun dangles like molten glass over the river, we ride into town and Mayor Dillard presents us with news from the world. Once a month, the Footes hang their heads and grit their teeth, a stew of shame and desire running in their veins because their subscription to *Titty* has arrived. The Camps get postcards now and then from Wilson's brother Max and his other brother, Andre, whose marriage broke up years ago. Lookout gets religious pamphlets and sports recruiting news, but letters never come for me. I no longer have connections beyond the boundaries of our town. The Blond dawdles nearby when Mayor Dillard passes out the mail, her hair sweat-damp against her neck. She cracks her knuckles and goes for nonchalance. She has, it seems, applied for a government grant. She wrote the proposal without telling me and will head north in spring if her funding comes through on time. We are sitting at a picnic table behind my house eating PB&J when she announces her intentions. I force down a mouthful, ask her to marry me a second time, but her answer is the same. She covers my hand with hers, looks an apology across the table. The Blond holds all of history against me. When it is clear that I have nothing else to say, she stands and walks around the front of the house. I find her staring up into the trees at a pair of fornicating parrots. "Don't mistake this for love," she tells the birds. "Don't be talked into something you'll regret." She watches unblinking, her arms crossed at her chest, her vigorous legs shoulder-width apart. I ask her why she stayed last spring, why she didn't follow the parrots when they left Elbow for the season. She tells me she was broke, that's all. She would have vanished if she'd had the cash. I remind her that she paid her rent, that she was never short of cigarettes and oils for her hair. "Shut up," says The Blond. "I know what you want to hear."

When I was fourteen, Hurricane Frederick whipped in from the Gulf of Mexico, spinning tornadoes upriver as far as Elbow. Dillard's store was pancaked and a sixty-foot pine fell across the roof of my grandmother's house. My father had been gone almost a year, and we huddled in the pantry, the old woman and I, and listened to the wind moving room to room like a search party. The next day, she sent me to town to borrow supplies and see if everyone was all right. Telephone poles were stacked along the road like pickup sticks. But the most terrifying thing of all was the quiet. The parrots were gone, the trees without pigment and voice. We thought they had all been killed, and to this day no one is certain where they spent the winter, though The Blond has unearthed testimony for her book regarding strange birds sighted in the panhandle of Florida during the last months of 1979. We rebuilt the grocery, and my grandmother turned her roof repairs into a party, serving up cheese and crackers and a few bottles of champagne she'd saved from her wedding. Despite our efforts at good cheer, and exempting New Year's Day when Bear Bryant licked Joe Paterno in the Sugar Bowl, a pall hung over town until Lookout spotted the birds coming back, dozens of them coloring the sky like a tickertape parade.

Our river is named for the Indian chief Tuscaloosa, which means Black Warrior in Choctaw, and when I was a boy you could find arrowheads and chips of pottery buried in the banks. Now, as I make my way along the shore, the river offers up Goodyear radials and headless Barbie dolls. Parrots dance from branch to branch above me. I remember Calypso casting a spell to keep Odysseus on her island, and I want to teach the birds a phrase so full of magic that The Blond will never leave. At night, she types her notes and files them away on the chance the government will respond to her request. It's warm enough still, even in October, that we leave the windows open, air grazing her skin and carrying her scent to my chair in the next room. I whittle and listen to sports radio and wish I had a phone so I could call all the broadcasters in New Jersey who have forgotten how great we used to be, how we won a dozen National Championships, how Alabama lost only six games in the first ten years of my life. To listen to them talk, you'd think they'd never heard Bear Bryant was on a stamp. I pace the floor when I get agitated and shuffle wood shavings with my feet. I talk back to my grandmother's Motorola portable. When I make the fierce turn to my chair, I see The Blond standing in the doorway, her hands on the frame above her. She smiles and shakes her head. "You people," she says. "When are you gonna put all that Bear Bryant stuff behind you? That's all dead and gone." I cross myself

Catholic-style and look at her a long moment, my heart tiny in my chest. She is wearing a man's sleeveless undershirt and boxer shorts, her hair pinned behind her head with a pencil. I would forgive her almost any sacrilege for the length of her neck or the way she rests one foot on top of the other and curls her painted toes. "I thought you liked football," I say. She crosses the room and puts her hands on my cheeks, kisses the spot between my eyebrows.

I want to tell her that the past is not only for forgetting. There are some things, good and bad, that you shouldn't leave behind. According to the record books, Bear Bryant didn't sign a black player until 1970 because the state of Alabama was not ready for gridiron integration. A decade earlier, however, he recruited a group of Negro running backs who were light-skinned enough to pass for white. They hid their Afros beneath helmets and bunked in a special dorm miles away from campus. They were listed in the program under names Bear himself selected. Lookout Coley's playing name was Patrick O'Reilly.

Every now and then, Mayor Dillard will set his ancient reel-to-reel on a card table and show black-and-white movies of Lookout's punt return against the rear wall of his store. He ordered the game from a sports memorabilia company, and we sit in the grass after dark, watch the image break around chips in the paint, press beer bottles against our necks to ward away the heat. There is Lookout, sleek and muscled and young, ball dropping into his arms, shifting his hips side to side, giving a Tennessee defender a stiff-arm to take your breath away. The image flickers as he shakes and shimmies toward the sideline, then he breaks upfield, his back arched with speed, the rest of the world falling away behind him. The movie is without sound, and Mayor Dillard rewinds the touchdown over and over. Lookout, streaking backward in front of the Alabama bench past his exultant teammates and granite-faced Bear Bryant, then forward again toward the end zone, all swift and silent grace. None of us has ever done anything so wonderful in all our lives. Chevy Foote whispers like he has witnessed a cosmic event. "Old number 41, man, you sure could fly." Crickets murmur in the underbrush. Lookout weeps quietly, and

Mayor Dillard throws an arm over his shoulder while the film clicks softly and plays itself out against the backdrop night.

I ask The Blond why the parrots keep returning to Elbow, and she says it's instinct, plain and simple. We are sitting on the riverbank with our feet in the water. The Blond slips into her academic's voice as she tells me that because the birds are native to equatorial Africa, because their food supply of seeds, nuts, and fruit dries up in the Rhode Island cold, they are obliged to embark on a southerly migration in order to survive. "It's a miracle *Psittacus eritacus* endures in this country at all," she says and lies back on the ground, crossing her hands behind her neck. There is a parrot perched on a cypress branch across the river watching us with the side of his head. I find a stone on the bank and skip it across the water in his direction, and he screeches and flutters his wings at me. "Run, darkie, run," he says. "Why are you in my house?" The Blond squenches her lips disapprovingly and closes her eyes, and I run a fingertip along her hairline until the furrows in her brow go smooth. "But why here?" I say. "They could live anywhere in the world." The Blond lifts herself up on her forearm, her hair falling over her eyes, and opens her mouth to speak before she realizes that, for once, she doesn't have an answer to my question.

In the second quarter of the Ole Miss game, a freshman quarterback named Algernon Marquez comes off the bench for Alabama and throws a pair of touchdowns before the half. For nine minutes, as our team works to tie the score, we are beside ourselves, leaping about Dillard's Country Store, pitching our bodies into each other's arms, but at the break we fall silent, fearing a jinx, and cross our fingers and apologize to God for all the nasty things we have said about him in the recent past. Even The Blond wants to bear the suspense in quiet. She carries her cigarettes outside and sits smoking in her Jeep. I stand behind my parrot sculptures, watch her through the window, as she eyes real birds across the road and pretends she is above all this. But I know otherwise. The Black Warrior winds forty miles down from Tuscaloosa, and The Blond is hearing faint cheers on the watery wind. The second half, God bless, belongs to Alabama. Our defense is inspired, our offense fleet and strong. Algernon Marquez isn't Joe Namath, but he is more a dream than we could have hoped, "a no-name wonder from Letohatchee," says the announcer, "whose only goal in life was to play for the Crimson Tide." I wonder how it would feel to have achieved all your aspirations by your eighteenth year. A bus full of Delaware parrot lovers rolls up while the score is 35–17, and Mayor Dillard gives them whatever they want for free.

That night, I tell The Blond Andromache's story—how, after Hector's death, she was made a slave to Pyrrhus, the son of Achilles, but grew to love him a little over time. "She was happy in his house even though she never guessed it could be true," I say, sitting on the bed with my back propped up. The Blond is naked, still flushed from our coupling. "I'm pregnant," she says. "I can feel it in my bones." She traces concentric circles on her stomach with a finger, the parrots frantic beyond the windows. The Blond bolts upright and looks at me, like she wants to see something behind my eyes. I'm just about to haul her into my arms and waltz her joyously around the room when she slaps my face, leaving an echo in my head. I watch, too stunned to stop her, while she jumps up and down on the wood floor, landing hard and flatfooted each time, shaking window panes, sending ripples along the backs of her legs. She is crying and pounding her knees, and I wrap my arms around her and pin her down. "This is not my baby," she says. "This is not my life," and she keeps shouting until her voice is gone and she has cried herself to sleep beneath me.

There are ghosts in Elbow. Little Hound, one of Chief Tuscaloosa's lieutenants, was betrayed on the banks of our river by Hernando de Soto and his men, shot in the belly, according to legend, then flayed while he was still alive as an example to the Choctaw people. On cold nights, when football season has come and gone, you can hear him chanting a curse against white men in the dark. That old broken-down house on Route 16, the one with the stove-in porch and kudzu creeping up the walls, Gantry Pound murdered his wife and three daughters there because he believed that women were vile creatures and he couldn't bear the smell of their menstruation. According to Wilson and Mae Camp, who live in the next house down the road, an ebullient sorority of phantoms roams the halls at midnight, glad to have the place finally to themselves. Even my house has a ghost. My grandmother swore that she would never leave, and sometimes, when I am hovering on the brink of sleep, I see her watching over me, calling me by my father's name, though I am never sure if I am dreaming.

The day after The Blond declared herself with child, just before I open my eyes, I hear a voice, faint as electricity, but the room is empty. Morning finds me alone, still sleeping on the floor. I check the house to be sure, but The Blond is nowhere to be found. Her suitcase is gone from the bureau, her hair care products vanished from the shelf beside the bathroom sink. I sit drinking coffee on the sleeping porch while the parrots call around me. "Who are you? Why are you in my house?" It is not quite new day yet, and I watch the world come to life, winter buds opening in the light, the river far below hauling water toward the sea. I tell myself that I will give up hope at lunch. And though I hold off eating until two o'clock, I keep my promise and carry a melancholy peanut butter sandwich out into the yard. The grass is cool on the bottoms of my feet. I wonder about The Blond, see her streaming down the highway in her Jeep, sunglasses on her head to keep the hair out of her eyes, wonder if she will put an end to our baby in a sterile clinic or if she only wants to get some distance between history and the child. I want to tell her that even bland Ohio is haunted by its crimes. I want to tell her, while the air is full of birds and the shadow of my house still lingers on the yard, that she is exactly what I need. Behind me, as if on cue, The Blond says, "I drove all night, but I didn't know where else to go." I turn to face her, blood jumping in my veins. There are tired blue crescents under her eyes, and her hair is knotted from the wind. She smiles and smoothes the front of her shorts. I am so grateful I do not have the strength to speak. "I took a pee test in Gadsden," she says. "It's official." The Blond walks over, grabs my wrist, and guides my sandwich to her lips.

Election day is nearing again, November 17. Though he will, as

usual, run unopposed, Mayor Dillard is superstitious about compla-
cency. He pays Lookout overtime to haul campaign buttons out of the
storage shed behind his store and stake *Dillard Does It Better* signs
along the road. He visits each of his constituents in person, bribes us
with hard cider and the promise of a brighter future here in Elbow.
Bird-watching is up, crime down, he tells us at his fried chicken
fundraiser, and each will continue in the appropriate direction if he
is reelected. Things are looking brighter for the Alabama team as
well. We've won two games in a row, and all the Yankee radio per-
sonalities are beginning to see the light. They say our team has an
outside shot at the Peach Bowl, over in Georgia, where we will likely
face Virginia's Cavaliers. But we do not speak a word of this in town.
We hold our breath and say our prayers because hated Auburn is still
looming in the distance, and one false step could bring all this new
hope down around us like a house of cards. At night, The Blond and
I drink nonalcoholic beverages beneath the Milky Way. We have
reached an acceptable compromise: spring in Rhode Island, fall back
here, until she is finished with her study, but she will give birth in
Alabama. Elbow will have a new voter in eighteen years, and The
Blond has convinced Lookout to contend for mayor himself one day.
He will not run against his friend, he says. Too much has passed
between them. But it won't be long before Mayor Dillard gives in to
time, and Lookout Mountain Coley can sweep injustice from our
town like an Old West sheriff. My life purls drowsily out behind me
like water. Parrots preen invisibly in the dark. I shuttle inside for
more ice and listen to The Blond spin stories about our unborn child.
Her daughter, she says, will discover a lost tribe of parrots in the wilds
of Borneo and invent a vaccine for broken hearts. She will write a
novel so fine no other books need writing any more, and she will
marry, if she chooses, an imperfect man and make him good inside.
And maybe, if the stars are all in line, our daughter will grow up to be
the hardest-hitting free safety who ever lived.

AUNT MARIE

Mack Lewis

Aunt Marie would see the old, dead dog, and then she would know how he hated her. She had come to stay with him, and she slept in his mother's bed. He knew she did not care for him, and Gilbert hated her.

"Know what?" he asked, lying across the bed in his sister's room and looking out the second-story window.

"What?" asked Leyla. She sat in her dressing gown before the mirror. On the table before her was an assortment of creams and powders of varying colors.

"When my daddy gets home, I'm gonna have him run her off," Gilbert said.

The house was surrounded by ashes, with fallen leaves gray over the ground.

"Gilbert!" she scolded.

"Yep," he said, "I'm gonna hand him the broom and have him run her down the road."

"I've told you not to talk like that," Leyla said. "Now hush."

"Hey, look at that old dog laying down there," Gilbert said, looking to the street.

"Where?" she asked. Leyla spread a flesh-colored cream over her face. She looked intently into the mirror, turning her face first to the right, then to the left.

"In the gutter," he said.

"Whose dog is it?" she asked.

"Nobody's now. He's dead," Gilbert replied.

The sky was clouded gray with smooth, low-hung clouds.

"Oh, that one," Leyla said absently. With a tissue she removed the cream from her skin.

Holding the curtain open, Gilbert looked at the swollen brown-and-white carcass. His face brightened suddenly, and he sat up on the bed.

"Maybe he ain't dead," he said. "He's smiling. See? Like this," and he drew his lips tight back over his teeth.

"He is?" she said, pondering her face in the mirror. "That's nice."

"And his legs are stiff like this." He fell over on the bed and extended his arms and legs. Gilbert grinned again. He seized a pillow and pressed it to his chest. "And he's swollen like this," he said.

"Really?" Leyla asked and then glanced toward him. "Gilbert! Stop that! Get up! I don't know what to make of you. Get up!"

"He's fat like Aunt Marie," he said. Gilbert frowned at the name. He rolled onto his stomach and looked out the window again. "What does it mean?" he asked. She had picked up a brush and was running it through her hair. "Say!"

"What?" she demanded, irritated, turning to him.

"What does it mean that dog laying dead down there?" he asked.

"'What does it mean?'" she repeated, slumping in the chair before the mirror. "It means…. You're a strange little boy. It doesn't mean anything really."

"Yes," Gilbert insisted. "Yes, it does. Aunt Marie said she didn't know what they meant leaving that old dog dead out there."

"Oh," Leyla sighed. "She meant they should have put him somewhere. Buried him or something." She turned back to her face in the mirror.

Maybe Aunt Marie would want him, he thought, laughing to himself.

"Does she like dogs?" Gilbert asked.

"Well, you know she doesn't," his sister said.

"Maybe she likes them better dead," he mused.

"Uh-huh, she would. Less trouble to her," Leyla mumbled, spreading the lipstick over her lips.

"I hate her," Gilbert said, rolling over onto his back. "Do you hate her?"

Leyla dropped her hands into her lap. "Yes, I believe I do. Yes, I do."

"I'll have him run her off," he said angrily. "Just wait 'til my daddy gets home."

"Gilbert!" she snapped, scowling toward him. "I've told you over and over to stop talking that way. You do not have a daddy. You never saw him. He's not coming here."

Aunt Marie doesn't know how much she's hated, Gilbert thought, but I can show her.

Aunt Marie would sit barefooted on the porch and spread her legs upon the banisters. The boys passing by, some of them Gilbert's friends, would stop and point between her legs and laugh at her. They made up names for her and for what they saw, and sometimes they called them out. She ignored them at first, but when she'd been drinking beer and belching aloud, which grew more and more frequent, she'd call them names in return and scold them for looking up an old woman's dress. Sometimes she would chase them, grab up her switch and hobble down the sidewalk behind them. They'd turn and run backwards, bickering with her like blue jays teasing an ancient cat.

Gilbert laughed, too, at first. The boys that were his friends laughed to him about her, and he laughed, thinking the novelty would wear from the old woman. But it did not, and eventually they began walking by his house just to see her. They went out of their way to walk in front of the porch. Even some of his classmates that did not live in the neighborhood came by his house. The boys would ask her for beers and cigarettes; they dared each other to go kiss her. She continued to scold them. When someone suggested to Gilbert that they all go ask Aunt Marie for cigarettes, he told them she didn't smoke, but dipped snuff. This information had not had the effect he had intended. They were not put off but howled with laughter and raced off to torment the old woman. Gilbert had asked her not to sit on the porch like she did, and not to drink beer and dip in public. She did not hear him. And as if to spite him, she would put her teeth into the pocket of her dress and talk to him with her tongue slipping between her gums. Gilbert was defeated by her. He began to dread going to school. He went in late and walked straight home afterwards. When he tried to joke with his former friends, they inevitably turned the conversation upon the old woman, and he ceased joking with them at all.

Aunt Marie had perhaps saved him from some social difficulty when she came to stay, but he did not recognize this. It was just as well, because she had saved him through no charity of her own. She had traveled eight hundred miles by bus to her sister's funeral and, being tired afterward and seeing no reason to travel another eight hundred miles back, had sat down to stay. Aunt Marie did almost nothing. Gilbert's mother had been fastidious and busy. She went to work when he went to school, and she was always home in the afternoons. He had taken her for granted, the fussy woman who helped him dress, and who read to him and helped him into bed. He had thought Aunt Marie would be like her, and handed the old woman his favorite storybook. "Read me some Uncle Remus stories, Aunt Marie," he said. Gilbert assumed she would read to him, although she was fat and would not hold him.

"Who's this old nigger?" Aunt Marie asked, looking at the illustration inside the cover.

"That's him," Gilbert said brightly. "That's Uncle Remus."

She handed the book back to him. "I ain't readin' no stories about no nigger."

His mother had been warm and soft. She held him against her breast as she read to him. When it was cold, she opened her robe and let him nestle warm inside it. Gilbert slept with his mother on those nights. Aunt Marie was old and fat and drank beer upon the porch. She did not bathe very often, and he never slept with her. She snorted and sniffed horribly. Aunt Marie could smell nothing. Gilbert had asked her not to make such awful noises, but she continued, saying that she'd had an operation that left her sniffing and without her "smeller." She wasn't interested in what he thought. She wasn't interested in him or anybody. Aunt Marie wanted to be left alone.

Gilbert came down the stairs and walked onto the porch. She sat with her legs spread upon the banisters.

"E'ning, Gilbert. Have you had any supper yet?" Aunt Marie asked, her eyes red and glassy from the beer.

"No, ma'am," he replied. "There ain't any clean dishes."

Gilbert picked up a tennis ball and bounced it to the porch. It struck on an angle, rebounding against the wall and flying back to him.

"I don't know what's the matter with me these last few days," she said, "but I just don't feel like cooking."

"You don't ever," Gilbert said, glancing at her. She had not moved. He threw the ball over and over.

After a while she said, "Well, when you're old as I am, you won't either."

He threw the ball harder and harder against the wall, closing his fingers around it as it thudded into his palms and smashing it into the wall again.

"But I do need to go in and wash those dishes," she sighed.

"Probably take four hours," Gilbert said, "the way it looks." He glanced toward her again. She sat unmoving.

"Yeah," she replied.

"Everything in the kitchen's dirty," he told her. Gilbert stopped throwing the ball and turned to her. She had pulled her feet from the banisters and sat forward in the chair. He stared angrily at her, waiting.

"You're right. I believe I'll just get me another bottle of beer and watch TV instead," Aunt Marie said. She picked her teeth up from the porch rail and slipped them into her mouth.

It began to rain. Gilbert started throwing the ball again. Aunt Marie walked to the door.

"Where's your sister?" she asked.

"Gone," he said.

"Well, tell her not to be making too much noise upstairs, with her room right over mine," the old woman said from beyond the door.

Gilbert did not try to make her understand. He threw the ball once more and stopped. He turned and looked across the street. The rain fell heavily. He stood immobile for a moment, then walked down the steps and into the yard. The grass was soggy with the water. The rain hammered against his back and head and soaked his clothes as he walked from the yard and across the street.

Gilbert stood over the dog for some minutes. It did not smell so awful; surrounded by the rain it didn't. The water swirled black, cascading through the gutter, eddying around it, spinning the leaves against its stiffened limbs. Gilbert leaned down, grabbed it by the tail, and pulled. It was surprisingly heavy, lying half submerged in the gutter. His hand slipped; the hair pulled free from the skin. He seized the tail again, this time with both hands, and pulled backwards. It came up from the gutter and slid stiffly behind him. The rain ran down Gilbert's face and into his eyes. It raged against the black road and hammered into the trees. He pulled the dog slowly across the road. The stench was coming from it then, rising from the wasting skin and entrails into his face. Gilbert slid it from the street into the yard. They were in the hedgerow then, moving laboriously through the grey autumn leaves, Gilbert panting and heaving, the dog grinning into the night. The tail was nearly devoid of hair. It had been rubbed and pulled away as the boy heaved and stopped, and heaved and stopped, dragging the dog a few feet each time over the soggy grass. Gilbert held his breath; then he gasped for breath. The odor from the decaying body was stifling. The rain covered his face, ran streaming down his cheeks. He wanted to cry. He was going to be sick, and he could not go on.

But he had it under her window then, under the high first-story window beyond his reach. Gilbert released the dog and ran from it. On the back side of the house he stopped and leaned trembling against the wall. He could smell it on his hands, but he hated Aunt Marie. She did not care for him, and she slept in his mother's bed. Aunt Marie didn't know how much he hated her, but he could show her. She had sat upon the porch and ruined him. Gilbert took the stepladder and leaned it against the house under her window. He climbed up and opened the sash and, crawling down, stood looking at the dog. He slowly leaned over and, sliding his arms around the carcass, lifted it from the ground. Gilbert held it around the midsection, so that the head was directly below his and the rotting back was against his stomach. He could not hold on. The extended, stiffened legs caught in the rungs of the ladder. The body threw him out of balance. The stench was overpowering. He tried going up the ladder with his back against the rungs, inching his way up. He made it to the top, but as he turned around, the dog pitched from his arms, its head striking a lower rung, and flipped to the ground. Gilbert crawled down and seized it by its front legs. He pulled it into a sitting position. With it facing him, he pushed it up on the lowest rung. The dog sat grinning at him. Gilbert forced it up another step. Then another. He pushed it up ahead of him until it was at the window. This time Gilbert worked it inside but, being afraid it would make too much noise falling in, closed the sash behind its forelegs.

He ran crying around the house and slipped in the back door. He could hear the television blaring in the front. He went to Aunt Marie's bedroom and turned on the light. The dog had slid backwards in the window, but its legs had stopped its descent, one against the window and the other against the wall. Its smell was awful, filling the room and choking Gilbert. He grabbed the dog once more around the middle. He pulled it in silently, working the hind legs in so that they did not catch against the outside wall. He dropped it lightly on the floor and dragged it across the room toward Aunt Marie's bed and, with a final heave, swung it up onto the mattress. He turned then, when his work was finished, and walked hurriedly from the room.

He went to the bathroom and undressed. His clothes were covered with the hair and dirt and rain, and he rolled them up and threw them into the closet. Gilbert bathed and felt better. He trembled, but he was excited. He had done it. She had come to stay with him, and she had ruined him. She was not his friend. Aunt Marie did not care for him, and he hated her. She had not known how much, nor just what she had done to him by doing nothing, but now she'd know. She would be screaming shortly. He had left her dozing before the set and had gone up to his room, but she'd be crying before long. Gilbert lay across his bed and tried to read. He listened for her. He tried to be patient, but he could not be still. The excitement was unbearable. He rose, walked a few feet down the stairs, and sat down.

Presently Aunt Marie staggered by the stairs. Gilbert crept down after her. She walked into her room, leaving the door ajar. He heard a gasp or a muffled cry as he neared the room. Aunt Marie stood with her back to him.

"Well, for Pete's sake," she said, standing over the unmade bed. "How'd you get in here?" she asked the dog. She looked closer at the carcass lying on its side on her pillow. "Why, you're dead. What in the world? Gilbert!"

He ran upstairs to his room and waited as long as he could bear. She called him again. When he came back down she had opened another bottle of beer.

"Gilbert, come here," she said. "Looky here." She pointed to the dog. The stench within the room was overwhelming. Gilbert grew sick again. "Reckon how he got in here?"

"I don't know," he said.

She walked over to the bed and tried to wiggle one of the legs.

"He didn't come in here by himself," she said.

"No," Gilbert replied, staring intently at her.

"Must have been one of them blame young'uns," she said, leaning over the dog.

"No, it wasn't," he said.

She glanced at him. "How do you know?"

"'Cause I did it," Gilbert said. She'd see now. When she realized how he hated her, she would be screaming and asking him why.

"What?" she asked.

"I did it," Gilbert said, backing against the wall. Why wasn't she crying? Didn't she understand what he had said?

"Why, Gilbert!" Aunt Marie said. "That's not even funny."

"I hate you," he said, his voice choked and faltering. "See? Don't you see?"

"But Gilbert—"

"I hate your guts!" he screamed. His entire body trembled. "I hate you! I hate you!"

"Why, it probably stinks, too," she said.

He collapsed against the wall and cried.

The old woman was silent for a moment. She looked at Gilbert and she looked at the dog. She drank from her bottle of beer. "You don't hate me," she said, walking to Gilbert. Aunt Marie leaned over him and with her index finger tapped him lightly on the head. "I know you miss her. I ain't bothered you, though. I been careful not to boss you. Why," she added. "I ain't even mad about that old dog in my bed. I ain't mad. Come on now." Aunt Marie stood up. She turned and walked to her bed once more. "I'll get him out in the morning. Whew! He looks ripe!"

Gilbert stood against the wall staring at her. The old woman had been unmoved. *What is she?* he thought, looking at her then with curiosity. *It's all over and she didn't even mind the dog. I couldn't make her see. She just doesn't care.*

"Go on to bed now," Aunt Marie said, pushing him lightly from the room. She closed the door behind her, closed in the grinning dog. "Gilbert!"

"What?" he asked, turning on the stairs.

"I'll sleep on the extry bed in your room," Aunt Marie said, mounting the stairs after him.

"You what?" asked Gilbert, wondering at her, his voice high.

"Yep, I'll sleep in your room with you," she said, going past him. He did not move. "There ain't no covers on this bed," she called from his room. "You bring me a blanket up when you come, son."

Gilbert descended the stairs in a helpless fury. He went to the front porch, trying to think what had happened. He did not understand. He had tried to reject her, ruin her with his anger, and now she would be snoring in the bed next to his. There was no way to get even with her. She just didn't care. Soon Leyla would be home. He considered his sister for a moment. She'd know about the old dog as soon as she walked in. She wasn't like Aunt Marie, was she? "No," he said in a low voice. "Leyla will be angry. Yes, I'm certain she will be very angry."

Yesterday My Father Was Dying

Chip Livingston

Yesterday my father was dying, and he asked me why—in a voice so hoarse and dry I had to lean in close to hear him—why I flew two thousand miles. I asked myself: about the odor from the cracked shell of his skin; about his breath, which smelled as if he'd crawled from underneath the house, or drifted up from oceans' depths, like the one I flew across, only to borrow the truck he could not drive, and race to a gas station for cigarettes, when I had not smoked in years.

I sit out on his front porch swing, another thing untouched since I've been here, and watch a trail of ants raise a cricket from the ground. Paralyzed, and I hope numbed, she drags her egg stick along the cement like a broken magic wand, her feelers twitching uselessly as they lift her up and carry her—like the clumsy paramedics hauling my father to the funeral home.

We're all alone, I thought, that cricket and my father's wife and me. And we can't grasp what carries us. It isn't grief, at least not mine, that moves us to another's house, for days or weeks, a time of strangers leaving chicken made in casseroles, and frozen, labeled with dates, names, and numbers, like toe tags, so we know where to return the clean dishes and Tupperware.

I sit and smoke, watching the insects scale the bricks, not knowing if the cricket laid her eggs, or where the ants will carry her, or if I give a damn what they do with my father. How would I know what he wanted? I wasn't here, and we weren't close. His wife should know better than to ask me if I care if she buries him in her hometown three states away; or if she keeps the urn; or if I want to share his ashes.

Though maybe I do.

There is a hint of rain in this morning's humid air, and the ants have moved the cricket to the concrete's edge, where she teeters before falling in the weedy flower bed.

I find their nest: the sand hill's higher on the western side, to keep the rain from rushing down and flooding them. The hole, too small to fit the carcass underground, is perfect for a final cigarette.

THE WATCH

Jonathan Odell

As dusk fell on Delphi, a large part of the black population was holed up in Tarbottom, a cluster of unpainted and tarpapered shacks wedged in a crook of Hopalachie River. Though most people were at home, the quarter was graveyard quiet. After returning from their jobs in the field or in the white households, most families silently disappeared into the darkness of their shacks, doors and windows shut tight against the mounting frenzy up in town.

The few inhabitants not tucked away in their homes sat in solemn watch out on their porches, some holding guns, talking low, periodically looking off into the gathering dusk, eyes glancing nervously toward the crest of the hill, where the road left Delphi proper and descended into Tarbottom.

So naturally it was those out on their porches who were the first to see his approach. From above them, he emerged from the twilight as an almost imperceptible, diaphanous shimmer against the gathering gloom. As he neared the shacks, his form claimed the shape of a small boy, but no one spoke to him. Surely if he had appeared on some other night, someone would have called out.

But on this evening, doors carefully cracked open, men in their porch chairs leaned forward, mothers reached out for their own children, counting heads. By the time the specter reached those in the first few houses, they had already judged the boy to be light-skinned. They could see that he was pitifully dressed in nothing but a raggedy pair of one-gallused overalls, so oversized the bib fell well below his frail chest, leaving it exposed, and as he progressed, stumbling determinedly forward, the boy's denim-concealed feet punched at the fabric with each step. The only evidence he left in the fine, powdered dirt were the snake-like tracks of the leggings dragging behind him. He looked neither to the left nor to the right at the houses that lined the road, only straight ahead, as if his eyes were focused with all his might, squinting furiously, on a spot down by the river.

And still no one called out to him. After all, the boy had come to these people in a time of in-between, when their world hung in the balance and none could be sure what his advent meant, which way it could throw the scales. Some found themselves wishing that Reverend Hart was on hand, for there seemed to be something biblical in the boy's approach, descending upon them today of all days, something that harkened to that night the killing angel passed over the houses of Pharaoh's slaves.

But others saw nothing but a white-trash child, somebody who was likely to bring white-trash grownups and unthinking violence into their homes. Tonight, they reasoned, even a wandering boy could set off the old unquenchable thirst. After all, who had not seen the two monstrous electric generators on the flatbed truck parked next to the courthouse, resting there, mute, until midnight when they would be aroused for a taste of colored blood? Would one Negro be enough? they wondered. These were the first to shut their doors against the sight.

As the boy continued his advance down the dirt track, the whispering began.

"That a white boy?" a few asked.

"Could be maybe. Could be high yaller, too."

"Got skin like a copper cent. Could be Choctaw."

"But he look yaller-headed."

"Who's he be?"

"Don't take after nobody from round here."

"Nobody from *up there*, neither," someone remarked with scorn, gesturing with a nod toward town.

"What's the matter with his eyes?" another asked.

"They all squinched up. Like he still got the sun on his face."

The boy, as if just now realizing he was being watched, squinted up at the porches, in what appeared to be a detached, critical attitude, all the more baffling considering he couldn't be more than seven.

But still no words were exchanged between the inhabitants of Tarbottom and the intruder. Not even a nod. Yet no eye left him, even as the boy squinted back and forth between the houses, rejecting what he saw, continuing his progress straight toward the river.

When Gran Gran saw the boy, she stilled her hands from combing out the girl's plaits. "Well, what in this wide world?" she said after the boy had passed by her porch. She dropped her hands to her lap.

"Don't look like nothin in this world to me," her elder son Marvin, replied, shaking his head, flipping a cigarette into the yard in the direction of the boy.

"Don't look like nothin to me neither," Violet quickly agreed, annoyed that the boy had stolen away the old woman's attention. She plucked the comb from Gran Gran's fingers and began tending her own hair. "Ouch," she cried, emphasizing the consequence of Gran Gran's negligence.

But the old woman's eyes were still on the boy. "Now I done seed all manner of creatures wandering down in here," she mused. "Half-starved dogs and a runned-off mule, and onced I seed a fox. But I ain't never seed nothin the likes of this chile. I reckon that boy near-bout starved to death. You see them ribs sticking out and them raggedy coveralls?"

"No, ma'am," her other son, Freeman, answered, "but did you happen to see them little possum eyes peerin up at me? That thing so ugly gives me the willies."

"Some kind of ugly!" Violet said fervently.

"Where his momma be?" Gran Gran asked none of them in particular, straining forward in her chair, her rheumy eyes fighting the deepening dusk.

"Devil ain't got no momma," Marvin answered.

"White folks been coming from out in the county all day long," the other son said. "Prob'ly belong to some of them."

"It's the fever," the old woman said. "The white folks sho got the fever tonight. Gone crazy with merriment." She nodded solemnly.

"You right, Freeman. They got the fever so bad, could of forgot one of they own."

Violet stepped in front of the old woman, intentionally blocking her view. "Tell about the fever, Gran Gran. Tell about the fever the white folks get."

Acting like she hadn't heard Violet make mention of her white mother, Gran Gran waved the girl aside and eased up out of her chair. Then she gazed back up the road, from the direction the boy had come.

"Now, Momma, let that boy be," Marvin insisted. "Take a lesson from what you jest said. That fox you talkin bout come down here with the rabies and them dogs was eat up with the mange and the worms and the mule blonged to a white man what 'cused me of horse thievin. That act of mercy come close to landin me in jail."

"Leave the boy lone," Freeman said. "No good gone come of it. Not on this day, no way."

But her sons' words were wasted. Without further discussion, Gran Gran carefully managed the porch steps and then limped down the road on her cane, following in the boy's tracks. She was not alone. As if struck by the same note of compassion for suffering animals, other women were climbing down off their porches and heading toward the river after the boy, their own children tagging after them.

Violet did not move. What hurt her most was the sympathy the old lady showed for this motherless thing...this boy...this stray. Whatever it was, she would have no part of it.

Stubbornly she watched as Gran Gran followed the boy into the mist gathering down by the river, until, unable to see her any longer, Violet bolted down the steps after her.

By the time they got to him, the boy was already standing at the water's edge, staring off upstream, as if he could see through the trees around the bend. The group stayed back for a moment, taking in the sight.

Up close, Violet was sure he was the vilest thing she had ever witnessed. He was a crazy quilt of colors, in combinations she had never seen before. His nose was flat and his lips full, so that for a moment she was tempted to consider him a colored boy. But the blond hair and the pinkish skin with rusty freckles told a different story. And she noticed something else. Even as they stood enveloped in the dank of the river, the boy stank to high heaven.

But the boy seemed oblivious to her judgments. His focus was unbroken, and so intent, the women peered expectantly up the river, trying to track his gaze. For a moment, Violet wondered if the boy was waiting for something waterborne to wind its way down the snaking river to fetch him.

Looking back at the women, Violet saw that they were still and quiet, their eyes now on Gran Gran, waiting for her to make sense of it all.

And finally she spoke. "Chile, where's yo peoples at? Is you lost?"

But the boy ignored her, not breaking his gaze up the river. For a while there was no sound but the rush of water and the whir of insects rising to meet the night. The first fireflies of the season began to tentatively dot the woods across the river.

Again Gran Gran spoke, her voice stronger. "Where's yo momma, boy? I know she be worried."

But still he squinted upriver, as if that was where the answer to her question lay. And to reinforce this impression, he suddenly pointed upstream.

Violet followed the direction of his finger, but saw nothing but a river spinning to silver in the early night. Then she searched the faces of the other women, wondering if perhaps they had seen something she had missed. But they only shook their heads, confused, like her, at the meaning of the motion.

A woman almost as old as Gran Gran asked, "Can't you speak, boy?"

But the boy wouldn't look at her either. Impatient, the same woman reached out and roughly shook his shoulder. He flinched, and she quickly drew back, as if bitten.

"That boy's been skinburned," Gran Gran said, understanding

now. "That why he so reddish." Then she carefully lifted the unbroken strap of his overalls. Even in the dim light, the shielded band of skin on his shoulder glowed white. There were clucking noises from the crowd.

"He really is a white boy," Violet whispered.

For the first time, the boy turned away from the river. He looked up, directly into Violet's face, wide-eyed.

She gasped at what she saw. The boy's eyes were the color of dank tree moss, but that wasn't all. His eyeballs jittered violently—as if they were struggling desperately to free themselves from their sockets. It sickened Violet to think that his frequent squinting might be the only thing keeping the boy's eyes in his head. Her stomach went queasy and she turned away.

Violet wasn't the only one repulsed. "Lord a mercy," she heard several of the women exclaim as they reached for their children.

"The demons is dancing in them eyes," someone said.

Gran Gran waved at them to hush and leaned down on her stick to the boy. "Ain't you got a name, chile?" she asked.

He said nothing, refusing to even look at her. Instead, he kept his fluttering gaze on Violet.

"He done choosed you, Violet," Gran Gran said solemnly. "Look on him."

When she dared to look his way again, he was squinting hard, his eyes once again hidden, studying her behind the slits.

"Tell it to her, then," Gran Gran said to the boy.

He glanced quickly at the old woman and then up the river for a moment as if considering. Then he returned his gaze to Violet. To her, he uttered one single sound, a resonant, one-note rumble of the throat. "Ahhhhhhd," was what it sounded like to Violet.

"Odd," she repeated quickly, without thinking.

There was a faint upturn of the boy's lips, toward a smile almost, and his strange green eyes once more flitted in Violet's direction, much, she thought, like the wings of a crazed moth battering against a lit window.

"That what he said, 'Odd'?" Gran Gran asked. She looked around at the other women, who shook their heads, confirming nothing.

"Sho is that," Gran Gran finally said with a sigh. "If it be one thing, it be that."

The boy turned away from Violet and back to the river, looking once more upstream. Again he pointed.

The little assembly stood in silence for a long moment, studying the boy, contemplating his identity, shifting through his scant testimony—an indiscernible growl, a pointed finger, devil eyes, colors that coalesced in such a way as to nearly cause a congregation of mothers to withhold sympathy.

Finally it was Gran Gran who spoke. "Violet, you take the boy back up to the house. He trust you. Get him some food. And tend to his skinburn. Wipe it down with cream out the milk pitcher."

"Ain't you comin, Gran Gran?" she asked, the idea of touching the boy turning her stomach.

The old woman shook her head. "I reckon I'll stay down here for a spell," and then turned toward the river.

As the women began back to their homes, Violet carefully plucked the boy's finger, like she would a bait worm, barely touching it, lest his hideous discoloration spread to her like mange. But he willingly submitted to her lead, keeping his eyes on her now and nothing else.

Halfway up the track, Violet turned to face the river once more. The leaves of the trees along the water's edge had begun their sighing in the evening breeze. She could hear the night birds boldly calling to one another. And there on the bank stood the old lady, like a cypress, still and silent, her ancient head turned upstream, as if she had taken up the boy's watch.

Later that night, as Violet held the lantern, Gran Gran tucked the freshly cleaned and fed boy neatly between the two grown men, who were fully dressed with cigarettes lit, their pistols loaded and under their pillows. When she was leaving the room, Violet caught sight of the boy's face. He was staring up at her, as if appealing to her, those green eyes all a-twitch. For an instant, she thought he looked small and helpless, a little boy lost in the valley between two mountains. But then she carefully shut the door between them.

Violet was awakened from her sleep by a deep, resonant moaning. At first she thought it might be the snoring of Marvin or Freeman or perhaps another wordless, inhuman cry from the boy. She got up from her bed, careful not to wake her Gran Gran, and tiptoed to the men's door, pushing it ajar. When she peered into the moonlit room, she saw that the boy was missing. The sorrowful moan rose up again. This time she reckoned it farther away, sounding more like the prolonged expression of sadness from some great animal.

After stepping onto the porch, she could tell that the groans were coming from over the rise, carried down into Tarbottom on a coolish May breeze. The sound caught in her chest and vibrated there. Trembling, she stood in the night air, dressed only in a flour sack shift. Violet held herself tightly, suddenly remembering the hulking machines on the flatbed truck. She recalled the man's impassive face at the barred window of his cell, staring down upon them. His moment had come, and now she trembled for him.

On the porches, she saw silhouettes of men with guns, ready to sound an alarm if the fever should spread. She heard the groan once more. This was no time to be outside in the open, and now the thing had gone missing. For certain, Gran Gran would blame her if anything happened. Reluctantly, in bare feet, she took off for the river.

When she found him, he was standing on the water's edge, almost radiant in the moonlight, looking off upriver, still waiting. At once Violet became furious with him. The burden he was putting on her now felt intolerable. The special treatment he was getting from Gran Gran was unforgivable. She hated this boy—this stray.

Violet crept up behind him slowly, soundlessly. If he was aware of her presence, he didn't let on. When she was close enough to hear his breathing, she reached out her hand, ready to snatch him by the neck. She wanted to shake him, yell at him. She wanted to make him cry. Her extended arm shook with rage.

But then she hesitated. The boy was stone still, and his concentration was so intense, it was as if he were putting his entire soul into this effort.

There was only one thing she knew of that required this much single-minded diligence. Violet, for so long a watcher of roads, a disciple of reappearance, understood now that the boy was not merely waiting. He was casting his prayers into the river like nets. She pulled back, awed to have found another so like herself. Another one who had been left behind.

In the distance the groaning surged once more. The boy turned to her, calmly, as if he had known of her presence all along, only his eyes trembling. Hesitantly, she reached out with both arms and touched the boy lightly on his shoulders, and to her surprise, he stepped into her embrace. He touched his face to hers.

Gran Gran's words came back to her. "He choose you, Violet." She felt a warm rush over her body. It was true. For the first time ever, Violet was the one who had been chosen, not the one left behind. The boy remained motionless in her arms as if he desired to be nowhere else in the world but with her.

Violet closed her eyes and whispered into his ear. "I the one you choosed. Ain't that right? Nobody else," she said. "Just me. Promise it." Her arms ached for his answer. The boy slowly nodded, rubbing his cheek against hers.

For a few moments, she held the boy gently, protectively, marveling at how small he felt in her arms, how he trusted her without reserve. She felt his breathing on her skin, his heart beating against her own chest. He was hers and the thought intoxicated her.

Suddenly she tugged him closer. For up the hill, the groaning of the generators had ceased, only to be replaced by the swell of a thousand voices, united in a roar of jubilation.

They held tightly to one another. Finally, as the cheering gave way to the surging spring fullness of the river and the screeching of nesting night birds and the rustle of new growth in the trees, Violet wondered if the fever had finally passed.

ATTENTION JOHNNY AMERICA! PLEASE READ!

Jack Pendarvis

I am sending this to your publication of _____ and I hope that you will print it. I cannot afford to pay for it as an advertisement of blank amount per word. This is a subject that everyone is talking about today, and that is Johnny America. He is the mysterious crusader who has sprung forth from our imaginations much like a colorful character in a comic book so they say. But as everyone knows he is for real 100%. I have seen his costume up close and it appears to be blue shiny and scaly. I am only mentioning certain details to lend myself credibility. Why am I writing, is to explain that Johnny America has made a mistake about me personally and to make a public statement that I would like him to leave me alone. That is not to scorn any of the great things he has done for our community. But isn't it possible that anyone can make a mistake? That is all I am saying.

I have been out of work because some logs fell on my leg. The doctor says I should move around somewhat. In the past I have enjoyed walking to the grocery store and purchasing some things to make for dinner. When my wife came home she was pleased to find the smell of cooking in the house, and it made me feel like I was contributing some thoughtfulness to our relationship.

On one such day I was returning from the store with two bags of groceries when who should spring out of nowhere but Johnny America, who I did not know it was him at the time, just some gaudy dressed person who looked exciting to me, like there was a parade or celebration nearby.

He told me that I was very clever but one day I was going to slip up. Then he hit me in the stomach very hard causing me to drop my groceries and kneel on the ground in great pain, also landing on my bad knee.

I was made aware that this was the real Johnny America for to my surprise blue flames shot out from beneath his cape and he flew amazingly to the top of a neighboring building and scampered agilely away.

My reaction was bewildered. For a long time I was scared to get off the ground.

Needless to say I did not cook dinner but sat in the apartment trying to figure all the ways I might have made Johnny America upset. Some awful things raced through my mind, things I have done that I am not proud of. Talking a lot when I am drunk in a blaring and inconsiderate manner. I also have greed and sloth and many other unlikable qualities.

When my wife arrived home I told her my tale. She became agitated and threatened to put an announcement on the telephone poles of our neighborhood, warning of vigilante activity as she called it. She began to draw one such object, displaying the talent as an artist she had exercised in college. The stinging sarcasm of her wording and drawing caused me to become alarmed. I did not wish for the boat to be rocked where Johnny America was concerned. My wife expressed it as me taking a beating and thanking the beater for the privilege. In a rude manner I snatched her paper away and tore it into many ribbons. There were other ways I could have expressed myself better without violence and censorship. This led to a terrible argument. There were many recriminations. We got so tired of arguing that it actually put us to sleep.

Exactly one week and one day after my first adventure I again encountered Johnny America in the same surprising manner. I was dismayed, for he seemed purposeful and his face was stern.

I thought I told you to stay out of this area, he said. Decent people live here, he went on. He emphasized the word decent as if to imply that I was not decent. I had no groceries at the time to drop, being on the way to the store rather than coming from it, but he harshly blackened my eye explaining that he would give me something to remember him by. Once again I was preempted from clearing my name by seeing him blast off in a cloud of amazing blue flame.

This night I cooked dinner as usual and made as if all was well. My bruise I explained by saying that my bad knee had buckled and I had stricken my head upon the divan. My wife was solicitous and we had a pleasant evening. That night there was a televised report that Johnny America had stopped a gas leak in a shopping mall just before it was about to blow up numerous innocent people. I could not reveal the complicated nature of my thoughts, which were, How can a man so good and true act in a manner so mistaken where I am concerned? All those people whose life he saved tonight could not care less if he gets it wrong about one man, so ran my troubling thoughts. If he killed me even, I continued to think, would everyone believe that Johnny America knew best? Apart from my wife I tried to imagine others who would rally to my side and there were none that I could think of right away, a fact that filled me with emotions.

One night I awoke to see Johnny America climbing into our bedroom window. He held a rag over the face of my sleeping wife. I suppose it was chloroform to prevent her from awakening from the beating he then gave me. He took me to the kitchen, dragging me along by pinching my neck in an uncomfortable manner. He wrapped two small potatoes and a lemon in a dishrag and hit me on the chest, stomach, back, and buttocks area several times in a harsh manner. Without a word he left me lying on the floor. I do not know if he again sped away on a chariot of blue flame but I suspect such was the case.

My wife did not believe my tale of what had happened. The manner of beating had been constructed as I now believe so as not to produce bruising upon my body and therefore to further discredit me. The ironical thing of it was that now my wife seemed to doubt anything I had said about Johnny America at all. When I mentioned my blackened eye as evidence she referred scoffingly to the divan.

Please do not print my name or current location, which is not my usual home. I cannot afford to stay here too much longer. I can no longer sleep with any success. My wife is with a distant relative of hers whose relationship and name I shall not mention for safety. Things are not going too well with us. I do not blame Johnny America for that, or for anything else, for he is just doing his job and my marital problems are of my own making. Maybe Johnny America has done me a favor by bringing to my attention an atmosphere of marital dis-comfort that has been boiling beneath the surface all along. I cannot blame him for that! In fact I should thank him! My only request is that he will place a personal ad in this publication that announces his intention not to beat me any more. If you mention what was in my grocery bags that first time you knocked me down, I will know for sure it is you.

In conclusion thank you for your many efforts on behalf of the community. Good luck with your future endeavors. You have my sup-port 100% Johnny America!

THE OLD PRO AND THE OPEN

Brewster Milton Robertson

In memoriam: Slammin' Sam Snead and Papa Hemingway,
may they rest in peace.

He was an old pro who played late and alone on the Golf Course and he had gone eighty-four tournament rounds now without taking a birdie. In the first forty rounds a young amateur had been with him. But after forty rounds without taking a birdie the young amateur's parents had told him that the old pro was now definitely and finally *snakebit*, which is the worst form of unlucky, and the boy had gone at their orders to carry the clubs of another pro who had taken three birdies in the first round the first week. It made the boy sad to see the old pro come in each day, and he always went down to help him carry his clubs and his equipment into the pro shop rack storage. The weathered leather bag was scarred, and the faded knit club head covers were worn and stretched and, white, they looked like a flag of permanent surrender.

The old pro was lean and gaunt and his skin had the look of leather. There were deep wrinkles at the corners of his eyes, and the back of his neck was reddened on top of the tan from being too many years in the sun. His hands were heavily callused and they seemed ancient. Everything about him was of another age except his eyes, and they were the same color as freshly mowed, double-cut greens and were clear and undefeated.

"Old pro," the young amateur said as they made their way around the practice green and up the steep hill to the bag drop by the pro shop, "I can caddy for you tomorrow. My man did not qualify. Is it too late to work as your caddy?"

"No, it is not too late, but there is still time to get the bag of one of the luckier young pros. You're better off with one of them. Tell me, does your father know you are here with me every day? Your father forbade you to caddy for me. He believes the unluck is with me. A boy should always listen to his father."

"I have spoken to Papa. He has given permission for this one time. My man has taken the rest of the month to play abroad. We have made some money," the young amateur said. "Let me carry your bag. I can club you like I used to do. You always said that I chose the clubs the best, remember?"

"I remember," the old pro said. "All right. Tomorrow we will go together."

"Good, I will go with you and clean your clubs at the place of the Motel. But first can I offer you a beer on the Terrace?"

"Why not?" the old pro said. "Between golfers."

They sat for a time on the Terrace. Some of the golfers made fun of the old pro behind his back, and he was not angry. Others, of the older professionals, looked at him and were sad. But they did not show it, and they simply nodded and spoke politely of the fast condition of the greens and the promise of good weather. Still, none of them would sit with them.

"It is true. They all believe the unluck is with me now," the old pro said.

"It does not matter what they believe, old pro. They forget too soon the big ones that you took in the other days. Then you took many of the birdies and the ones of the most difficulty, the eagles," the boy said.

"Can you really remember that or did I just tell it to you?" The old pro smiled.

"I remember everything from the time I first saw you hole it from the rough on seventeen at Pebble on TV. Tomorrow you will make them all remember."

"Thank you for your confidence," the old pro said. "I wish I was so sure as you."

The old pro looked at the young amateur with sunburned, loving eyes and did not protest. He was too simple to wonder when he had attained humility, but he knew he had attained it and he knew it was not disgraceful and it carried no loss of true pride.

"Come, let us get the clubs and go to the place of the Motel," the young amateur said. "I will polish your clubs until they shine like mirrors. Tomorrow has the promise of a good day for the golf. Tomorrow the unluck will leave you."

The old pro knew it made the young amateur happy to clean the clubs and check their condition. There was nothing wrong with the way they cared for his clubs in the shop of the club professional during the week he had been playing the daily rounds that were allowed for practice. The head professional had once worked for him in the old days. Everywhere there were many of those he had taught, and they loved him. He valued their respect and carried it with him nestled close to his heart like the young corporal in 'Nam who had carried the fat little puppy inside the blouse of his fatigues tucked under his arm with the grenades.

They picked up the clubs from the rack at the bag drop. At the place of the Motel they ate the chicken from the café the poorer pros called "the greasy spoon" while the young amateur cleaned the clubs, and they talked basketball.

"Who was the greatest?" the young amateur asked. "My father says Larry Bird was the greatest."

"Hah! Because your father is from Boston. If your father had been from Los Angeles, he would say Worthy or The Magic or this new Kobe Bryant was the best."

"Who then?" the boy asked.

"Jordan. No one has ever been as good as this man called Jordan."

"And the best golfer is you. You are still as strong as a well rope."

"Thank you. I hope tomorrow does not prove you wrong," the old pro said thoughtfully. "I may not be as strong as I once was, but I still know how to maneuver the ball in the wind and around the difficulties. And I never take defeat as my partner."

"I must bid you goodnight now," the young amateur said. "You need to go to bed. I will meet you early at the place of practice. You will be well rested in the morning."

For a time after the boy had left, the old pro sat and thought about the Golf Course. In his reverie he was a knight and the Golf Course was a great green dragon. To slay this monster was his lifelong quest. This great green dragon held captive the many birdies and the rare ones, the eagles, that could be taken by only the most skillful and the very brave.

And the lucky.

The old pro looked at the old bag of weathered kangaroo hide that held the gleaming deadly clubs of steel that are called irons and the solid trustworthy clubs which in the good old days were called woods and were constructed with heads of persimmon. Now, they were made of metal. In the hands of the most skilled these trusty weapons hit the ball long and true. He knew he had not lost his skill. Unlike many of the older pros, it was not the yips that plagued him. Truly the unluck had been visited upon him.

Tomorrow he would go early to the practice area to work away the stiffness. Then he would be worthy to do battle with the great green dragon. Setting the clock for seven, he turned out the light, and in a short time he was asleep. In his sleep the old pro dreamed of the other days. Once before the unluck had been visited upon him. That time he had not taken a birdie in fifteen tournament days. Then he had gone to play at the Augusta. There the great green dragon had yielded to his skill and cunning, and he had taken many of the birdies that the Augusta guarded with fierce pride and determination. Finally on the last tournament day he had taken two of the eagles. There had been nothing of the unluck with him then. It had been then that the father of the young amateur had come to him and asked him to teach the boy his skill.

At seven the old pro woke. Methodically he showered and dressed. He took the bag of clubs to the car. At the house that is for the club members he ate the fine brown eggs and a single piece of the good bacon. When he finished he descended the stairs to the shop that is of the club professional and the young amateur stood waiting.

"It is a fine morning for golf. I hope you slept well," the young amateur greeted him.

"I slept very well. I dreamed the unluck was no longer with me."

"That is a good omen. Give me your car keys. While you change your shoes I'll get the clubs and the practice balls and meet you at the place that is for practice."

When he arrived at the place of practice the amateur was already waiting, and the old pro silently set about the serious work of hitting the balls that are for practice. For almost half an hour he hit the practice balls, and when he had finished nothing of his years remained in his muscles.

The young amateur handed the old pro six new balls still glistening white in their cardboard sleeves and picked up the bag with the clubs. The old pro followed him to the green that is for practice. The young amateur gave the old pro the club with the oddly shaped head that is called the putter. Silently, with great concentration, the old pro took the putter and began rolling the balls at the holes cut into the green that is for practice.

Finally the old pro heard his name called over the loudspeaker.

"Come, we are next," the amateur said.

The old pro handed back the putter and smiled broadly. He offered his hand extended outward, palm thrust forward and fingers pointing to the sky in the fashion that the basketball players call the "high five."

"Good luck!" The amateur swung his hand across and slapped the old pro's outstretched palm.

"Fairways and greens," the old pro replied.

The amateur pushed a path through the gallery crowd that encircled the green that is for practice as the old pro followed him to the starter's tent.

"Now we begin again," the old pro mused to himself, "this old war that knows only beginnings and there is no end."

For three tournament days the old pro battled the Golf Course and he still could not take the birdie. Many of the others had taken birdies and two had taken the eagle but each had been forced to give many bogies in return. One by one the old pro had taken the green dragon's pars. He played with much skill and great determination and refused to be defeated.

On Sunday at the first hole that was of the final round of eighteen holes and was a hole of five strokes, the old pro hit his driver straight and true to the center of the fairway. He took from his bag the iron club which bears the numeral four engraved on its sole and struck the ball with much skill and with great courage. With a trueness of flight that speaks of many things and many years, the ball flew to rest finally in the shadow of the flag that is for the marking of the hole.

"Right on!" The young amateur took back the iron club and handed him the oddly shaped club that is called the putter.

Walking onto the finely mowed surface that is for putting, the old pro said to the green monster, "Now, Green Dragon, I will take from you the eagle."

He putted with great care and the ball rolled across a steeply curving surface as twisting and precipitous as the giant roller coaster at Disney World.

The ball dropped cleanly in the cup.

At last the unluck had left him.

With his jaws clenched tightly together in the manner which betrays determination in a man, the old pro renewed his assault on the Golf Course. With the skill and cunning that is the property of only a few, he wrested three birdies from the green dragon before he walked to the teeing area that marks the beginning of the final hole.

When the word spread of his successes the gallery poured from out of the bowels of the great green dragon and thronged the fairway and green of the final hole to watch him finish. There, with cool pre-cision, he took a final birdie so that all might be certain of his skill.

Standing as he held the trophy high above his head, they applauded and shouted. He could hear above the tumult the mur-mured words *skillful, glorious,* and *finesse* and the expression *great credit.* But he did not say anything. He was always embarrassed when he heard these words from the sycophantic TV commentators or read them on the pages of the newspaper that are set aside for basketball.

They were only words. No libraries of words or rooms full of crystal and pewter trophies had any meaning if they were not followed by the presentation of the check.

What good was any of it if afterwards there was not enough money to drink the good beer, drive the fancy car, and have the company of the fine young women?

After it was over and the old pro and the young amateur sat among the envious golfers on the Terrace drinking the beer the boy said and nodded, "You played with much skill, old pro. There is not one here among them with as much skill as you."

"Yes," the old pro shook his head thoughtfully, "and truly I was lucky."

Hard to Remember, Hard to Forget

Dayne Sherman

I can recall Grandpa Hiram Carter sitting in a straight-backed chair on the porch seventy years ago. He drank from a jar of illegal whiskey. His eyes were hollow from a stroke that whittled at his soul. "Boy," he called to me.

I stood in the dirt yard spitting at a red hen. I was playing like I hadn't heard him call. I didn't answer right off.

Papa, Mama, and my little sister Jennie were in Mount Olive at Alford's Dry Goods that morning, a half-hour wagon ride west of our cotton farm in the clay hills.

"Go catch that black dog yonder," he said. Again, I didn't answer.

The old man was ailing, his right arm soft and stuck to his side, limp from the shoulder like a dead fish hanging on a skinning nail. His walk jerked and halted, as if stalled from a lack of will. Papa's sister, Aunt Virgie, had looked after him for a month before she hired L. A. Robinson to carry him out to our house in a Model-T Ford truck; she couldn't live with him anymore. Neither could any of Papa's other brothers and sisters who had taken turns with the old man and given up soon after. Aunt Virgie sent him to live with us.

"I says go catch that dog yonder. Tie him to the fence post."

"Ain't got nary a rope." I stared down at the chicken pecking at nothing in the dirt. "Why you want that black dog?"

I did what a ten-year-old was never allowed to do in 1930. I dared to question a grown-up. The old man was as mean as a basketful of copperhead snakes. I suspected that he was the cause of my two feisty dogs, Buster and Bounce, to come up missing a week after he arrived. His hatred of dogs was paled only by his hatred of humans.

"Ne'er mind why. Go catch that dog and tie him to the fence post. Get your papa's plow line and tie him," he said with a Mason jar sitting between his legs, moonshine he'd sipped on since daylight.

The stray dog had wandered up in late July that summer, a black hound with ears long enough to touch his ebony nose. He was young and full of play, but he had the worst case of mange I'd ever seen. The dog might have once had a solid white coat and you'd never know it for the lack of hair covering his gray-black skin, and he was stinking as if he had rolled in the rotten flesh of a dead cow. The hound, whip-tailed and long-legged, carried a backbone sharp enough to carve a pork roast. I'd sneak him scraps from the kitchen, slop headed for the hog pen. It hurt my eyes just looking at him; the ugliest dog in Baxter Parish.

I eased off to the mule barn and the stray followed me just as he did when I packed a can of scraps, tail wagging. The black-skinned dog pranced behind me all the way out to the yard and over to the house. He wasn't my dog yet because I hadn't named him.

I reached up on the pine wall of the barn and grabbed a loose plow line that wasn't laced to a mule bit, an extra line Papa had hanging on a hook. It was about twelve feet long and made of soft cotton. I fixed the line around the dog's neck with a slipknot, making a leash out of it, and walked back to the yard with the hound. On the porch, Grandpa stared blankly, eyes looking as vacant as the darkened sockets of a dried skull.

"Well," he hollered from the chair, "tie that sonofabitch to the post." I turned around and grabbed the hound's scaly neck and felt sores under my fingers. The blockheaded hound groaned, and I dragged him about a foot to the fence post. The rope was wrapped tightly around his neck. I tied him close to the knotty wood. I didn't know what the old man wanted with that dog.

"Tie him shorter," I heard from behind.

I did, and the dog began to fight, shaking his head and throwing himself back on his haunches, tightening the plow line around his neck, cutting off his wind.

Behind me I heard Grandpa's feet slough down the porch steps. In an instant, before I could turn around, he was upon me. He shoved me away from the dog with his left hand, slamming me to the ground, knocking the breath from my lungs. I couldn't move.

He was atop the black dog with my mother's long butcher knife, a knife Papa forged from a file, the knife she kept keen as a razor in the back of the cupboard. The dog fought and snapped his jaws, jaws clamping like the shut-mouth of a loggerhead turtle. Before my eyes Grandpa was straddling the dog and there was a muted yowl and then the sound of bone cracking and crunching. The dog was cut from ear to ear.

In all my life I have never witnessed anything like the old man's smile, the droopy right side of his month. His joy was full. The crimson spewed into the air and all over his khaki cotton pants and blue work shirt. Not even at Utah Beach in World War II did I see anything like this smile of death. No one else ever beamed like this at the sight of innocent blood.

Grandpa Carter balanced himself there with the dog bleeding, the head dislodged from the hound's neck hanging by a strip of skin, and the knife firm in his left hand.

He looked down on me where I lay in the dirt frozen, the air half-spent from my lungs. "Little Leonard," he said, "you ever question me again, and I'll send you right where I just sent that goddamned dog."

As soon as I got my bearings and could breathe, I picked myself up from the parched ground. I ran through the woods the longest time without stopping, ran as far as the Mullins place on Line Creek Road. I stayed gone 'til almost dark. I knew that his evil would not be quenched. I sat in the crook of a mulberry tree and cried off and on 'til dusk, thinking as much about Buster and Bounce as I did the bloody stray dead in the yard.

When I finally wandered back down the road to our house, Papa, Mama, and Jennie were back home. The wagon was beside the barn, but the red mules stood tied, unhitched, still in their collars and gear at the hitching post on the east side of the house, as if they were awaiting Papa's return. The lanterns were lit on the porch, which struck me with fear. We hadn't got electricity yet and we usually went inside when it got dark; we kept shut-up in the house and washed, and read the Bible or did school lessons. We didn't burn coal oil need-lessly. I could see that the dog was still by the wooden post, unmoved, unburied. I winced. The plow line was attached to the post.

I was at once confused over what was going on and overtaken by dread. Maybe they were out searching for me on foot. This would mean I'd have a thrashing ahead for running off.

As I passed from the dirt road into our yard, I could hear fierce arguing inside the house, my mother whimpering in high-pitched tones, the way she sounded when her older brother died of cancer.

I slipped up the steps. When I opened the door, I saw Papa. His eyes were set on the old man who was reclined on our sitting couch. Mama stood ten feet away watching; little Jennie clutched Mama's dress at the hem.

"That boy killed the dog. Why else did he run off?" Grandpa asked, pointing to me with a gnarled index finger. But the blood marks were black on his shirt and pants.

Papa reached for my shoulder and drew me to him. "Did you do this?"

"No sir. He done it. He cut him with Mama's butcher knife." My shoulder throbbed as I stared up to Papa. I tried not to break my gaze even under the pain of his grip.

Papa released me. Then he lunged at his father. "Rotten bastard. Why do you have to lie? Why do you always lie like a common thief?"

"I ain't never lied."

"You lie like a boldface liar. The blood on your shirt calls you a liar."

Grandpa reached from behind his back and yanked out the bloody knife that he had wedged in the homemade couch cushion. He jabbed the knife at my father and stuck the blade into his overall bottoms. The slit missed the skin on his groin by a quarter of an inch, the metal blade tangling in the loose denim. My father jumped backwards, and the knife fell to the floor, free from the old man's grasp.

"Damn you. Goddamn you to hell," Papa screamed, one second in shock, then in a blind rage. He beat Grandpa across the head and neck with his fists, pounding him into the wood floor of the farmhouse.

Papa sat on top of the old man. He sent me to get the plow line from the post, and I ran out into the yard and untied it from the man-gled hound corpse. When I returned Grandpa Carter still lay in the floor with Papa over him; he was semiconscious, inaudible. We tied him up with the cotton line that had held the dog, tied him the way you'd rope down a piney woods rooter hog in the open rangeland.

Papa stuffed a piece of flour sack into the old man's mouth when he came to, spitting and cursing. He was left curled on the floor jerking, his body in fits, the eyes of him watching as we passed by.

Mama packed his bag. The mules were hitched to the wagon again. After Papa buried the hound in the pasture, we hauled the old man tied up all the way to Magnolia, Mississippi, where we left him at the Con-federate Veterans' Home, a six-hour wagon ride into the night.

Three days later, L. A. Robinson pulled into our yard in his Model-T, a dust sheen covering the black paint. He told Papa that he was there to bring bad news from Aunt Virgie. Grandpa had died in his bed at the home.

But his passing did not cause much of a stir at our place. We didn't even go to the funeral service in McComb City.

I was never saddened by his death like I was by his life. He chose to walk down the lonely road where the bastards of genealogy trod. He died the way he lived, sent to a place formed by his own cruelty and hate, a place burdened with the ruin of wicked men.

A man like Hiram Carter is hard to remember, hard to forget. Dreams' spidery threads catch our memories, and some won't lie still. They writhe and twist, and awaken little boys. And men. My wife's hand on my shoulder in the night, to slow my heart and ease my breathing, says, "There now." But it's never enough.

THE JOY OF FUNERALS

Alix Strauss

I've lied to my mother about where I'm going.

She thinks I'm traveling to Nantucket for a wine-tasting expo, but instead my ticket reads Atlanta. From there, a van will pick me and nine other people up and drive us an hour to Macon, the slums of Georgia.

The Learning Annex has promised a "fascinating and cultural experience for anyone who wants to learn about Georgia's history and is intrigued with historical homes and graveyards." The highlight of the trip is a visit to the Rose Hill Cemetery, where a rambler, a person trained in storytelling and factual history, leads a tour. The brochure says you can point to any of the ten thousand headstones in the cemetery, and the rambler will tell you about the person, how they died, and who their family was.

I've had a love affair with funerals and cemeteries since I was eleven, the year my grandfather died of leukemia. At the chapel, my mother's longtime girlfriends gathered around me in a circle. They sat on gold-colored folding chairs with matching velvet padding and leaned forward, a little closer than normal, their faces open but serious, their legs crossed. Their recently polished nails clicked against stout glasses filled with water, or long-stemmed glasses that held red or white wine. I was telling a story about my grandfather, something that had to do with a trip to F.A.O. Schwarz, and everyone smiled and nodded. I was holding court and I felt very grown up, very important.

Most thrilling was reconnecting with family members I hadn't seen in years, and being introduced to others I'd never met before. In these situations, everyone is included; everyone deserves a chance to say good-bye. The word *family* was tossed around so freely. I was suddenly labeled. Defined. "This is my cousin." "This is my niece, Nina." I sat on people's laps and got hugs from total strangers.

An hour in, I was hooked.

My mother and I meet on neutral ground, the fifth floor of Bergdorf Goodman, and have tea sandwiches. It is here that she tells me how excited she is that I'm taking this trip, insisting it's good therapy for her thirty-two-year-old daughter—the one who's unmarried, unsuccessful, and unfulfilled. She doesn't know my shrink has died, that I've got no one to talk to and have stopped taking my medication. I meet her for cucumber-and-egg-salad sandwiches, and we drink iced tea, and I let her be excited and buy me clothing I will never wear: a red leather shirt/jacket, a jean skirt and a teal knit sweater that zips up in the front. I allow her to make me into the daughter she'd like to have rather than the one she's got. I want to ask her if this makes her happy. Almost lean over the table, motion to her as if she's got a fallen eyelash on her cheek or a small hair out of place and ask if she'll still love me if I never wed. If I never give her grandchildren.

Ten of us are to meet in the boarding area at Delta. We've been mailed orange folders and nametags and it's suggested we wear them out in the open so we can tell one another from the other passengers.

I'm one of the first to arrive. The folder/name tag trick works because I spot Brian immediately. I wave the folder lightly and point to my tag. He greets me with a warm smile and tells me he's a professor at Binghamton who teaches Historical Southern Culture.

Fifty minutes later, I find myself in the window seat sitting next to Myrna and Fred Shultz, a retired couple in their sixties who do travel writing—he takes the photos, she does the text. Sitting across from me are four married women who graduated from Tulane together. They wanted to take a quick getaway from their husbands and children and chose this because, as Barbara said, the ringleader of the pack, they "just couldn't look at another spa." Behind me are two Gothic teens who haven't said much except that they're filming this experience, hoping to have the next Blair Witch Project. We are, at best, a motley crew.

The inn is surprisingly lovely. Old and creaky, just as the Learning Annex guaranteed, it was built in 1812 and is one of the only homes still in its original foundation that wasn't destroyed in the war. My room is called the Marigold and has a canopy bed, fireplace, antique furniture, and small balcony. The bathroom walls are faced with marble. Two large palmetto beetles that appear to be having sex are free of charge.

On our first night, we sit in the parlor and have mint juleps and cheese puffs with artichoke mousse dip. Dinner is served on the porch where we're serenaded by an insect operetta. The night is sticky and balmy, the food rich and heavy, just as Southerners like.

The college foursome doesn't split up. Rather they sit in a row with the boy Goth across from me. Rhoda, spirit of the earth, is on my left, leaving Brian and the retired couple on my right. The owner of the hotel, Walt, and Thomas, the rambler, sit at either head.

Thomas is a true Southerner with boyish charm and eyes that are soft and inviting. His sandy blond hair is tousled, he wears a white shirt and suspenders, which hold up his khakis, and brown buck shoes. His accent is charming. Every time I hear him say, "I reckon it's so," I'm reminded of the rooster from the Bugs Bunny cartoons.

I ask a few questions, trying to impress him with my knowledge of New York cemeteries, mention several celebrities who are buried at the Greenwood graveyard, and we seem to be connecting. I've flirted, he's smiled. I wish I was sitting closer to him, would like to lean forward, wrap a strand of hair behind my ear, and laugh, girly-like.

Breakfast is an exact replica of dinner. It's as if we've slept in our seats; only our clothing selection has changed. Homemade cheese biscuits are waiting for us in the morning along with hot grits, scrambled eggs with bacon and sausage, and thick French toast with fresh strawberries. The male Goth and the retired couple talk about camera equipment. Myrna wants to go digital, Fred fears technology, or as he puts it, "A CD is something I buy at the bank." He laughs as if this is the funniest thing anyone has ever said. The college gals push food around on their plates, each commenting how fattening everything looks. The one in the middle requests that yogurt be added to tomorrow's menu.

At 10:43 A.M. Tom appears with a megaphone attached to a small gray box that he carries over his shoulder.

We take a trolley car to the cemetery and stand, cameras ready, by the massive black gates. Tom raises the sound piece to his mouth.

"Can everyone hear me?"

We all answer yes.

"Do we really need this?"

"No."

Tom smiles as if this is part of his routine. He puts the instrument down by the entrance, explaining that he'll pick it up on the way out, unless a spirit wants it.

"This tour started fifteen years ago. Rose Hill was founded in 1840 and stretches sixty-five acres." He suddenly sounds very professional. "It is home to ten thousand people, including three governors, two United States senators, thirty-one city mayors, and eight congressmen."

The cemetery is ultra-bright, and the sun reveals its true weathered appearance. Even in its dilapidated state, it's beautiful. We pass by a white wingless angel, a little stone girl in a long dress wearing ribbons in her hair, and an owl. Outdoor works of art enclosed in an open-air museum.

The earth is super-dry, and the grass is brown and dying. Nothing lives here but red ants that suck your blood and can kill you. This is what Tom is saying, not to touch or kick the small mounds that spring up every several feet.

"The first thing to note is the typical Italian angels and allegorical pieces that reign above or seem to protect a specific plot. The architecture is reminiscent of the nineteenth century. The details are delicate and finely carved but many are broken or are missing appendages," Tom says. "Footstones and headstones are chipped, beaten by Mother Nature. These monuments were once ornate and ostentatious. Elaboration was the rule. But in 1954 a tornado did horrible damage, and many vandals have had their way with them."

Tom is doing a splendid job. He practically glows with life, a living spirit walking among the dead. I catch him gazing at me, probably because I'm most attentive. I try to nod and flirt while he speaks, but I'm afraid of distracting him too much.

"We begin the first ramble at the Confederate section, home to six hundred men. Here you have very little space between plots. It looks as if the men were stacked on top of each other."

The sun is beating down on us, and my skin feels as if it's burning. The college girls are drinking Evian water they brought with them from New York. Brian is taking notes, and the Goths are still filming. The retired couple are arguing over camera shots and angles.

"Note the typical Southern granite and gray marble," Tom says, hand extended like a game show host. I steal a shot of him with my digital camera. I zoom silently onto his face and click, I've immortalized him. Captured the moment and slowed time down. He eyes me and walks over. At first I think he's going to take the camera away, but he hands it to Brian and ask if he'll do the honors. He puts his arm around me and smiles widely. His body feels hot next to mine, as if it's projecting some of the sun's heat. His head is tilted in my direction and I copy his position, my hair touching his, and grin. And then it's over. He steps forward and Brian hands the small silver square back to me.

"Now if you give your attention to this plot," Tom continues, "you'll notice it belongs to Lieutenant Bobby, a terrier. He was the men's mascot and a cherished pup. His owner, Captain Harris, died on a Monday; the dog took sick and passed away exactly one week later, an hour to the minute that Harris died."

Everyone seems interested, so he moves the group along.

"This is the Woolfolk household, where eight members of the family were axed to death in their beds in 1887. Mr. Flint D. Woolfolk's son, Bill, was charged with the murders. The only one to survive, Bill was found wandering the streets of Macon, bloody and disoriented."

Tom appears sexier as he leads us deeper into the land. His voice gets creepy and quiet during suspenseful parts.

"Here, a fireman's hat, coat, and belt, all made of stone, are draped over the headstone of Kit Tobias, the four-year-old son of a fireman. The irony of this story is that he died in a fire in his home while his father was at work, unable to save him," he says.

The plot is maybe three feet long, outlined by stone planks to show the resting place belongs to a child. I wonder if and when I'll have one. I wonder if anyone visits this child anymore. If his mother grieved for years. If the father contemplated taking his own life, angry at the world for such a sick joke.

There are times when I want to dig up the graves, rip open the coffins, and see the strangers I visit. I want to know the men we're paying homage to, meet the people whom they once loved.

Sometimes I fantasize about parading around the cemeteries, decaying bodies in my arms, families trailing behind me, picking up fallen jewelry, clothing, and body parts. I would place them back in their homes, tell them they are missed, and kiss them all goodbye. I turn to Tom hoping to whisper this into his ear, give a tiny piece of myself up to him, but he is busy answering questions for Brian, who hasn't stopped taking notes and making inquiries since our tour started.

By the third ramble, which overlooks Ocmulgee River, the college posse seem bored and tired, the Tim Burton wannabes are running low on batteries, and the older couple look like corpses, dehydrated and pale. Even their umbrellas can't blot out the sun.

Hours later, we collapse onto the trolley and head back to the inn where fresh lemonade, cookies, and mini cakes are waiting for us.

After dinner Tom and I stroll the neighborhood, and I try to explain my fixation with cemeteries. I walk close to him, knocking my knuckles into his, hoping at some point he'll reach for my hand. I wonder what my life would be like if I moved here, just inhabited the simple, slow way of living. I could be a rambler like Tom, or I could show historic homes, talk in a Southern accent and make perfect grits. In Georgia, I realize, I could be anyone I want. I could start over.

Tom has a sweetness about him, an innocent, untainted American feel. I see all these characteristics in his face as we stand on the stairs of the inn. We stand awkwardly, a light above our heads attracts every bug in the neighborhood. I try not to swat them away while we talk, afraid of ruining the romantic moment.

When he kisses me goodnight, I close my eyes. His mouth is warm and tastes like brandy, our after-dinner drink. The sound of crickets magnifies as I attempt to hold onto the moment.

Intense sunbeams bleed through the tissue-thin curtains, illuminating my room, illuminating Tom. I stare at him in my bed, his body tangled in my sheets. I watch his eyes flutter, copy his breathing, thank God he's next to me.

For the next five minutes I watch him sleep. I inch my finger over the bare shoulder peeking out from the comforter. I move it down to his elbow lightly so I don't wake him, and yet I want to talk to him. I want to see what he has to say in the morning. If we have something, anything in common except for last night. I slide an arm under my head and memorize his features.

A half-hour later, I am seated next to Brian and an empty chair. It's Tom's and everyone is wondering where he is. I slid out of the room this morning, having dressed in silence, afraid to disturb him. I thought I'd take some sliced fruit and fresh muffins up to my room, spend a few more moments with him before we need to go back. I tap lightly on my door before turning the knob, I'm about to sing "good morning," like they do in *Singin' in the Rain*, but the bed is empty, his spot no longer warm. He's not in the shower, and after searching for several minutes, I find no note.

Tom doesn't surface at any of the historic homes we're touring. At the first, I keep eyeing the door while the woman, who's dressed in nineteenth-century garb, gives her opening speech. Distracted, I catch every few words, so I know she's talking about Sherman, the battle of something, and then I see her point to a small black object, the size of a softball. "This is the original cannonball that grand old Sherman fired in the 1800s."

The second house is from 1855 and looks like Tara. The theme to *Gone with the Wind* plays over and over in my head as I picture myself drinking mint juleps, dressed in a pouffy, lacy outfit like our tour lady. Standing on the porch, a fan in my hand, I'd wait for my Tom to come home—on horseback—then we'd waltz into our eighteen-room estate and he'd make passionate love to me on our wooden bed. I think about this as we exit the house, as we board the plane, as I stand in the baggage area eager for the Goths and the college girls to reclaim their belongings (everyone one else did carry-ons).

A Town Car is waiting for the college group when we leave the airport. The Goths decide to shuttle it to the subway, Myrna and Fred live on the Upper West Side and cab it home. Brian is taking Amtrak back to Binghamton but offers to drop me off.

We don't have much to say during the ride home. We agree the trip was interesting and well organized, that we were lucky to have such lovely weather, that we're glad to have gone, but neither of us has the desire to return. I want to tell him about Tom, get his opinion, ask if this is "normal guy behavior," but instead, I watch the meter jump as I listen to the cabbie talking to someone, maybe his wife, as he coasts up an empty Madison Avenue.

When we pull up to my awning, I brush his cheek with mine, a bold move on my part, and thank him for being a gentleman.

My doorman lifts an eyebrow when I enter. He looks at his watch and announces the time, 12:49 A.M. "That's late for even you."

I nod, watch Brian's cab drive off as he fills my waiting palm with mail.

I call my mother in the morning to tell her I've arrived home safely, but when she answers, her voice sounds odd. It's scratchy and softer than normal.

"What's the matter?" I ask.

"Your aunt Delia died while you were away."

"What?"

"Massive heart attack. She was sitting in a restaurant, waiting for Jerry. She was thirsty, asked for some water, and by the time the waiter got back to the table she was dead." She says this like a robot, even-toned and void of feeling.

318

"When did this happen?"

"The night you left."

"Why didn't you call me?"

"We wanted you to enjoy your trip. Anyway, the funeral is today, if you want to go. You could meet your father at work."

If I owned a cat, I'd be holding her.

"He wanted to go in for a few hours. Who am I to stop him? Maybe it's the best place. It will keep his mind busy…"

"If I hadn't called would you have even told me about this?"

"Nina," her voice is impatient, sharp, "don't do this to me today. You know how I feel about your father's family. I have nothing to wear, and I need to go to Greenberg's and Eli's and pick up the desserts."

"Fine, forget it." My voice comes out harshly, surprising both of us, and I hear my mother suck in air at the other end of the phone. It sounds like a balloon losing helium. "Just give me the information and I'll meet you there."

I shower quickly, change into my good black suit, and scan the apartment thinking I've forgotten something. My overnight bag sits exactly where I left it, still packed, waiting by the front door like a child for a parent to come home. Not having time to sift though it for my makeup, I decide to take it with me, thinking I can leave it at my aunt's and put my face on in the cab.

As I search for my keys, the phone rings. I let the machine answer for me, and hear Tom's distinctive drawl breaking though the quietness of my apartment.

"I just wanted to see if you got in okay," he says. There's a long pause and I picture him reading from a manual on Southern etiquette. A numbness comes over me, and I feel as if I've done something wrong. "Anyway, it was nice to meet you…. I mean, last night was nice." His voice is soothing, like hot soup warming my insides. I stare at the machine, then at my watch. I could still pick up the phone, force myself to say something, ask him where he was and why he didn't say goodbye in person. I was owed at least that.

"Well, I guess that's it. Bye."

Putting on makeup in a moving car is hard, close to impossible when you're crying. In a sudden moment of nausea, I ask the driver to pull over, swing open the door, and throw up breakfast and last night's dinner at the corner of 3rd and 94th Street. I consider turning back, going home, drawing the blinds, and hibernating in my bedroom, but feel compelled to pay my respects. I want to see my cousins and uncle, want to feel part of something.

The cemetery is cold, and the walkway is littered with colorful leaves. It's extremely breezy, and the rabbi has to yell over the wind.

"Delia wasn't one for words, so we'll keep this short and simple as she would have wanted," the rabbi says. It feels as if we're doing a *Reader's Digest* version of someone's life. Everyone seems uncomfortable, myself included.

Earlier, there was a big discussion about where my aunt wanted to be buried, in the mausoleum with my grandfather and her mother, or alone in the plot my uncle bought. After much debate we watch in silence as she's lowered into the ground by the silver pulley system. Three Hispanic groundskeepers oversee this process. They're dressed in floral shirts, which remind me of the fallen leaves, and jeans. The contrast is an odd mix to our sea of blacks and blues and I realize this is my second cemetery in forty-eight hours.

The rabbi concludes by explaining the shoveling procedure. Our first good deed is coming here, to help escort the dead to their final resting place. The second is to drop dirt on the grave as a way of letting the soul leave peacefully.

Mounds of dirt, which sit on sheets of asphalt with three shovels standing upwards, are on the left. The rabbi takes the first scoop and we line up in order of importance. No one delegates or directs, people seem to have an innate sense of cemetery etiquette. My uncle is at the head, followed by my cousins, David, Robert, and Vickie, their spouses and children, my father, me, my uncle's brother, his friends, and more family from my uncle's side.

Each of us takes a turn.

The sound of shovel into dirt, dirt onto coffin, back into mound of dirt, builds into an odd rhythm. Familiar, yet non-placeable. My hand grips the round handle. The heaviness of the shovel compounded with the dirt is empowering. The feeling magnifies with each scoop of soil I take. "Rest in peace," I say under my breath as the clumps fall into the hole. "Why didn't I know you better?" is what I ask when my second scoop drops on top of my first.

I watch the line move, notice the smattering of dirt that clings to the men's pants as they walk away. Proof of their involvement. When the last person has gone, David and Robert resume the work like a mechanical assembly line. Vickie ventures forward and takes the remaining shovel and my cousins move in silence. Dirt. Drop. Dirt. Drop. She is masculine and muscular, half man, part woman, maneuvering in an unspoken competition with her siblings. Someone asks if she wants to stop, but she refuses. She is intent on scooping up every last bit.

Afterwards, Vickie and I take one of the limos back to her mother's home. My overnight bag sits between us, her hand resting on top, while silence envelops the extra space.

At my grandfather's funeral, Vickie was out of cigarettes and let me tag along with her in the car to get more. I sat alone, motor running, while she paid for the smokes at the convenience store. I was about to look through the glove compartment when she came back. Like a well-choreographed number, she hit the car lighter with the palm of her hand, unwrapped the box of her Parliaments, tapped the packet a few times on the dashboard, removed a single cigarette in perfect time for the lighter knob to pop out. She rolled down the window, puffed on the cigarette, and started to cry. I didn't know what to do or say, I just sat there watching her as she flicked ashes out the window. Then I reached for her hand, the one that rested on the clutch. I placed mine on top of hers, noticed that her iridescent salmon-colored nails were all chipped and that her skin was dry. She wore silver rings and the tops of my fingers rested on them.

I do this now, but she pulls away. Instead, we glance out the windows and stare at opposite sides of the highway.

It's been over a decade since I've been in my aunt's home. They haven't redecorated in eons and a visual comfort moves through me like a quiet hush. As I hang my coat up in the closet, my grandfather's shivah flashes before my eyes. I remember being here and serving drinks and cold cuts, offering coffee to some of my parents' friends, picking up dirty napkins and empty paper plates and bringing them in to my aunt's kitchen.

Usually, when I crash a funeral, I search for someone to talk to. Anyone whose face looks open and accepting, or who is sitting alone and appears as if they, too, are hoping to connect with someone. It's easier to befriend someone who needs you. To grab them in their dark time, and create a bond when they are weak, tired, and extra break-able. But today, I can sit anywhere. I've earned this right from birth, from the very minute of conception.

The hallway wall is a timeline in pictures. My aunt and uncle's wedding day, Delia pregnant, Delia pregnant with Robert, David and my uncle standing beside her, and on and on. There are no pictures of me or my parents, no snapshots of Delia with my father. At this moment, here in this house, I don't exist. I think of the photos from Macon and have a sudden urge to see Tom, even if he's in digital form. I'm about to dig through my belongings and search for the mechanical unit, but my mother calls to me instead, her voice demanding and pleading. As I enter the living room I see my uncle lean forward and rest his elbows on his knees; one hand covers his eyes, the other holds a shaking glass. His brother is sitting next to him, his hand pressed firmly on his back. David comes over and removes the glass from his father's grip. I watch my mother bite down on her lip and shake her head. My father stands behind her and rests a hand on her shoulder. For the first time in years, I see her take his. She pats it first, then grips his fingers. Things seem to be happening in slow motion, and yet everyone is very still, as if a photographer has said, "Hold please. Now say 'cheese.'"

For a moment, I can't catch my breath. The walls seem blurry, and I feel as if my throat is closing up. I think of Tom, that if I were to die, right here in my uncle's home, he would never know how I felt. Never know I got his message and intended to call him back. That I could hear he was sorry in his deep, twangy voice.

I will myself out of the chair, hear my mother utter my name, then fade as I enter the kitchen, taking refuge in the all-cream room, the Formica countertops, the hum from the refrigerator, the open windows.

I search through my purse, hand shaking like my uncle's, find the tiny camera. It feels cold in my fingers, solid in my grip, and frantically I look for the photo I took of Tom. I forward one to the picture of us. There we are, smiling, appearing happy. I close my eyes and try to visualize him in my mind, see him on the porch of the inn, his hand on the banister, his body lean and healthy. I see myself standing next to him, waiting for a kiss, waiting for my life to start. We look nice together—a city girl with her Southern boy. I mentally resurrect our night, can almost feel his muscular legs touching mine, his thumb, which he placed over my brow and rubbed back and forth while he whispered in my ear stories from his tour that he hadn't gotten to share earlier that day, until I fell asleep.

Delta Airline's 1-800 number is easy to remember, and I dial it now. I'm on hold when Vickie enters the kitchen. Elton John's "Rocket Man" is playing, Muzak-style. Tissues are in her hand and she's slightly wobbly. Her dark-green suit is too tight and too short. She looks as if she's falling out of it. I want to show her the photo of Tom. But I don't. Instead, I wait for the Delta woman to come back to me, my weekend bag at my feet, a credit card in my hand.

Artifacts

Brad Vice

It seems Margaret has been in the kitchen since the beginning of time. Since sunlight she's been cooking—kneading dough for bread, chopping, slicing, measuring out her day on the big oak counter next to the stove. Every few minutes she stops and scribbles ideas on a yellow pad with a grease pencil. The manuscript for Margaret's second book, *Voyages of the Dinner Table*, is due in Birmingham in two days. The book is a kind of gastronomic history with some new creations thrown in, and she is trying to make sure the recipes are perfect before they reach Ann H. Hardy, her editor.

Margaret can prepare nine recipes at once, but it makes her feel more like a juggler than a cook: moving from notebook to cutting board, board to skillet, to oven and back to the cutting board again. By the end of the month the book will have traveled from the desk of Ann H. Hardy into the test kitchens of Southern Progress Publications, where eight highly trained home economists will work in secret to weed out any dishes they find overcomplicated, irreproducible, or "esoteric." That was the word Ann H. Hardy used to describe five entrées that didn't make the final cut for *The Ashevillian*, Margaret's first book.

But Margaret isn't worried about tests now; she's put the corporate kitchens out of her mind. She is summoning all her powers to prepare one of the most "esoteric" dishes in the new book.

She is going to make Chocolate Duck.

She begins by pouring two cups of red wine and two cups of beef stock into a saucepan, then waits for the mix to simmer. While she waits, she pours herself a glass of wine. Wine is something of a hobby for her husband, Dan. He had the carpenter make a rack that stretches all the way around the kitchen, just shy of the ceiling, atop Margaret's cabinets; he got the idea from a magazine. The rack accommodates more than two hundred bottles of wine, cheap Merlots and Cab Sauvs from South America and the Sonoma Valley mostly; a couple of the Italians are worth something. Sometimes she wonders if keeping them here is a good idea: they're too high, and exposed to heat. Dan likes the look of them, though. He says they look like soldiers, all lined up like that.

The dark smell of warm beef and wine makes Margaret think of blood. It reminds her of the Victorian ladies in their corsets and petticoats who used to stroll to the slaughterhouse every afternoon for a fresh glass of it. In the nineteenth century, doctors told housewives that drinking blood staved off consumption. The glass of wine stays on the counter.

Margaret would not have made a very good Victorian. There is something too equestrian about the way she moves through the kitchen. She doesn't bake bread so much as command it to rise and brown.

Margaret comes from a long line of good cooks. She gets her talent from her mother, and her grandmother before her, who came to Asheville to work in a big hotel's kitchen after World War I. Margaret also got her curly black hair from her mother's side of the family; she has not cut it short like most women in their forties. Dan likes this. He likes the fact that his wife looks ten years younger than most of his friends' wives, or at least he used to notice things like that.

Right now Dan is with his mistress—his new car—a used Jaguar with fifty thousand miles on the odometer. He spends most of his free time driving recklessly around the neighborhood, trying not to run over the ducks that wander off the nearby golf course into the road. Dan and Margaret's house is just off Charlotte Street, across from the eighth hole. The country club is known for its aquatic fowl: mallards, geese, even five or six stately swans with clipped wings that swim on the ponds amid all that immaculate green. Dan has given up golf for the car. Before the Jag, he drove an Accord to the office and back, but last week he gave Margaret the Honda as an early anniversary present and bought himself the Jag. He goes for a drive every day after work, most of the time without a word for her before he leaves.

Margaret pulls out a long, sharp knife and slices open a plastic bag of dried figs. She begins to halve the fruit. They look like mummified lips; with each cut an ancient, lurid smile creeps out at her.

She pauses, the knife poised an inch above the cutting board. Today is her twenty-third wedding anniversary, and just now she is caught in a moment of reflection. Reading with her fingers the cuneiform of the wooden board, an artifact passed down from mother to daughter, Margaret moves back in time. She sees the spice caravans of Mesopotamia, the cradle of the dinner table—serpentine lines curving between the Tigris and Euphrates. Camels heavy-laden with saffron and thyme are sailing through the desert toward her and the other anxious wives waiting on the edge of Ur.

Sometimes Margaret wanders the Attic fish markets, far from the philosophers. She knows what they do not—logic breaks down on an empty stomach. Bearded men pry into the secrets of the heavens, but not one of them has invented a philosophy to teach us how to eat well. Prostitutes are moonlighting by the wharf, selling raw, bleeding tuna. The girls' complexions remind Margaret of spoiled oysters.

When Margaret daydreams, she never becomes someone else; rather, she recasts herself in similar roles in various settings. In Athens she is an aristocrat, her husband a powerful rhetorician. His funeral oration for their son has left the citizens numbed and dazed with grief. The entire city-state is in mourning. Not far from the market, merchant ships are slipping into the distance like old friends. The cold blue Aegean crashes on the coast.

Margaret and Dan's son, John, died four summers ago, drowned in the undertow off Cape Hatteras, where they had built a cabin in Rodanthe. John was only a few feet away, waving at his mother, when he was swept away. It took five days for the water to bring him back like a damaged letter, his body found by renters in the aftermath of a nor'easter. Waiting through the storm to look for John had been hard enough, but when he was found and Margaret wasn't allowed to see him, she became hysterical. The seventy-mile-per-hour winds and the violent surf had made the body endure terrible things. Dan had to force Margaret into the car to get off the island. She tasted sand all the way home.

"Damn." Margaret reprimands herself for not paying attention. She adjusts the gas under the wine, which has slipped from simmer into boil. The flames retract like cat's claws. Margaret smiles; she loves this stove. Gas allows for more precision than electric. The stove has a nineteenth-century cast iron design, but the features are pure twenty-first: built-in griddle, two ovens, wok rings, six burners. Each burner is shaped like a star—eight radial fingers instead of the old, round eye. They provide even heat under the entire pan for fast searing or delicate simmering. The liquid settles. She places the figs in the pan—they blossom. Margaret preheats the oven.

In a few moments she makes her way to the refrigerator and fetches the duck. It has already been decapitated, plucked, and placed in a mesh net. Margaret makes short work of the net with a knife. Then she takes two bowls from the cabinet. One she fills with flour. Next to the stove are glass jars filled with staples: bulk peppercorns, sugar, salt. She pours peppercorns into the Turkish coffee grinder. It is old, nobody knows how old; it's one of the items that made the trip across the Atlantic with Margaret's grandmother, all the way from Santorini, a Greek island in the Cyclades. The grinder is over a foot tall and made of solid brass; it is heavy with family mythology. Like the cutting board, it was given to her when she married. It is strong enough to crush bones into flour. Margaret grinds out four table-spoons of pepper.

The salt is low, so she reaches back into the cabinet. There is a little girl on the package, holding an umbrella in one hand and a cylinder of salt in the other. Margaret pours an equal amount of salt into the pepper bowl and then fills the glass container. Before she puts the salt away she examines the package again. Inside the little girl's hands is another little girl, presumably holding salt. Margaret gets drunk trying to count all the little girls who live in her cabinet.

The duck's flesh is smooth, ugly, discolored like a newborn baby. Its cavity is filled with rich fat. After dusting her right hand with flour, she spends about ten minutes ripping this out with her fingers. While she does this, she tries to imagine how the recipe will look in print.

CHOCOLATE DUCK

DINNER FOR TWO

2 cups beef stock or canned beef broth
2 cups dry red wine
1 sixteen-ounce package of dried figs, halved
1 five- to seven-pound duck
1 orange, halved
1 large yellow onion, chopped
4 tablespoons salt
4 tablespoons pepper
4 bay leaves
6 tablespoons Armagnac or Hennessy cognac
3 tablespoons butter
3 ounces Ghirardelli or other quality semisweet chocolate, halved

Ducks were the first domesticated fowl. The Chinese kept them in little huts, like henhouses, over four thousand years ago. Maybe because of the birds' long history of domesticity, the Chinese say that eating duck keeps lovers faithful. There are recipes for roast duck in the ancient Greek cooking guide The Deipnosophist, *or "The Banquet of the Wise," and in many of the household records of the Egyptian pharaohs. But it is in the medieval* Forme of Curey *that we find the definitive method. Duck should be stuffed with sweets: apples, raisins, prunes, quince, figs, sugar, and/or honey are all excellent ingredients for accenting the meat's rich flavor.*

After the invention of the printing press, the Forme of Curey *and other cooking guides were second only to the Bible in popularity. Newer editions of the guide had additional instructions if royalty were going to be at table. If serving duck to the king, a host might want to shred orange rind over the bird's skin, then pour a jigger or two of brandy on the platter and set it aflame.*

Of course, they didn't have chocolate in the Dark Ages, which is one of the reasons they were dark...

"Well, there've been projects like this before," Ann H. Hardy had said on the phone a few months earlier. "Of course we'll give it a shot, but *The Ashevillian* had regionalism on its side, and that's really Southern Progress's bread and butter."

The Ashevillian was written in a matter of days soon after Margaret finished college. She entered UNC-Asheville after John died; Shakespeare seemed cheaper than psychoanalysis. She took twenty-one hours every semester and went summers. After graduation, she wrote poems filled with handsome drowned boys. At night John appeared to her in dreams, with his fair hair and wet blue eyes, dripping in his funeral suit. He described the grand civilizations under the ocean they could have seen together had she only caught his hand in time. She would write this all down in the morning, but when she was done her handwriting looked frail and pathetic. She never showed anyone.

Dan took to staying up drinking wine and brandy until long after his wife went to bed. He looked like Dan, acted like Dan, same big arms and shy smiles, but he ignored her. She persuaded him to come to bed early once, but when he complied it was as if John's corpse were under the sheets with them. Now Dan wanders around the house at odd hours of the night like a ghost, bumping into furniture.

She saw the ad in *Southern Living* for a first cookbook contest, and decided to write down the old recipes and her mother's stories about the wild life she'd led in Asheville. Margaret wrote about the time George Patton stayed in the hotel and showed her mother his ivory-handled .45s, and about Scott Fitzgerald's long nights at the bar when he came to visit Zelda in the loony bin. At the time, Asheville Asylum was one of the best in America; it occupied a nineteenth-century cobblestone mansion only a mile from Charlotte Street. The hotel and restaurant business was nothing if not interesting, but Margaret had never liked it much. Her mother was rarely home (her father died before she was born), and she was often alone.

The Ashevillian won the $1,000 prize and sold ten thousand copies in the Southeast alone. It was going into paperback, and the publisher gave her a $12,000 advance and a two-book deal. The first book had been easy, just a matter of putting onto paper things she'd known all her life; but *Voyages of the Dinner Table* she had researched like a term paper. It was exhausting, and she had to write with the additional burden of knowing that her editor wasn't overly enthusiastic about it.

Margaret cleans the duck fat from under her fingernails with a toothpick. In the back of *Voyages* she has compiled a *Did You Know?* list. Margaret never met a fact she didn't like. *Fact #31: Witches were said to smear cooked baby fat on their broom handles to give them the power of flight. Fact #32: In the sixteenth century, tobacco was often called the "dry drink" and was served after dinner in place of alcohol.* Margaret finds herself fatigued and wanting a cigarette, a habit she refuses to give up—there no longer seems to be a reason. But she will have to hold out until she gets the duck in the oven.

She begins massaging the mixture of salt and pepper into the bird's flesh, inside and out. She's a bit disgusted by the slickness on her hands, and she stops to wash them with steaming water and dish-washing liquid, but they won't come clean. She scrubs until it feels as if the meat will fall away from the bones, but her fingers are still sticky. She gives up.

She goes to the refrigerator again and takes out an onion and an orange. The orange is like its own little world, perfectly round, a reliable fact like the speed of light. Margaret remembers a lot of tidbits from high school. The Earth is approximately twenty-five thousand miles in circumference; to find the circumference of a circle, multiply the radius squared by pi. Margaret divides the orange at its equator. It falls apart. The problem with facts is that they are meaningless in and of themselves. A fact that stands alone is devoid of value; you have to understand everything to make one fact worth something. You always have to keep asking yourself *why*.

Margaret massages the duck with half of the orange. Dan is out there, on the road. He's wearing his aviator shades. The top is down. Maybe he's fighting his way up Black Mountain, or trying to find a long straightaway so he can get the Jag up to eighty, ninety, one hundred. He might even be risking his life trying to hug the sheer curves between here and Knoxville. That's where he went yesterday. Lately he has been taking the car farther and farther, as if he were an explorer preparing for a long expedition, testing the ship, testing his own endurance. Margaret milks the orange for its last drop of juice.

She puts the other hemisphere of orange inside the cavity of the duck. The fruit's puckered navel reminds her of maternity. She can recall every storybook she ever read to John. She finds it hard to remember what she did with herself before he was born. Dan had been a successful architect in Asheville for years before John's birth. They moved to Knoxville while Dan studied at the University of Tennessee, and she'd put him through school by waiting tables. She hated the work; he worshiped her for it because he knew it was a sacrifice, all those loveless soups and entrées meant for strangers. It made her feel like her mother, alone and sucking up to the public for tips.

Anonymity—that was one of the real difficulties in writing a cookbook. How do you cook for someone you've never shaken hands with, much less kissed or made love to? How do you put yourself into your food? That is the question. The Knoxville ordeal was soon over, and Dan got a good job. He designed the two-story Tudor they live in now with the massive kitchen just for her, the big house Margaret always wanted. And for a time this was enough.

Then came motherhood, which was frightening—not just the physicality of it, the moods, the cravings, the nausea (sometimes she still feels phantom pains of John's skull pushing into her spine), but the awesome, holy responsibility of it all. Baby John warmed her heart when he nursed, but at the same time that blind, gnawing mouth made her fear for her life. And when he slept, he slept so quietly. Children always seem like little strangers when they're sleeping, and this made Margaret feel like a pretender as a mother. She told Dan this once, and he laughed at her, but that was before the undertow. Even now Margaret doesn't think of John as dead. It seems more like he's asleep in another room of the house.

Through all this, neither Dan nor Margaret has ever mentioned divorce, and this has given her a little hope, though she can tell there's something sad and dangerous growing inside her husband, waiting to manifest itself. Something that stems from never having had the opportunity to say goodbye to their son, to weep over his body, to touch his little hand inside the coffin. Their lives are like the cabin in Rodanthe, which just sits there by the edge of the cold ocean, boarded up and haunted, waiting for the next hurricane.

Five months ago, the country club called. The greens keeper ordered Margaret to come pick up her husband, who was drunk and causing a disturbance. Dan had clubbed a swan to death with a pitching wedge. By the time Margaret made it around the block, Dan had disappeared. Margaret didn't try to offer an explanation, and the greens keeper didn't ask for one. He'd seen a lot of the world, and was a man not without pity. "Please, ma'am," he said. "Please, ma'am. We can't have this. Keep him at home, whatever you have to do; don't let him come back. If he comes back, we'll have to press charges."

While Margaret minces the onion, she ponders the Middle Ages. Castles, cathedrals, flowing tapestries, knights fighting dragons. John used to tell her he thought a dragon lived inside Black Mountain. The dragon must be very old now, his ancient scales aching. He wishes a knight would come along and kill him; it would be indecorous to die of old age. Only he is afraid there are no knights left.

Even as a girl Margaret appreciated fine things, maybe because her mother never had many. Crystal, china, elegant platters—Margaret has a gift for pageantry, has mastered the art of arrangement. Always after setting the table she is overwhelmed by the heraldry of knives.

Tonight, after dinner, Dan and Margaret are going to a play. They are benefactors of the UNC-A theater, and they receive season tickets. Tonight's performance is A Midsummer Night's Dream, one of her favorites—the fairies are so courtly; the confusion is so well-framed. But it's getting late, and Dan still isn't back.

Margaret wonders to what extent her life with Dan has been staged. Mother, father, wife, husband: the family cast just roles for halfhearted actors. After they built the golf course even the house didn't seem real; the country club turned the neighborhood into an

amusement park. But Dan was happy because it increased the property values. Margaret thinks about all her friends who got divorced
and moved west. Strangers live in their houses. Zelda Fitzgerald's
grand asylum was turned into a real estate office. It seems to Margaret,
at forty-three, that even real estate isn't very real anymore. In a way
even John seems like an actor playing a corpse. For a moment she sees
his body laid out across the kitchen table, surrounded by silver, his
hands crossed under the candles.

Margaret puts the onion inside the duck with the orange and adds
four bay leaves. The onion's vapor will make the duck succulent; the
orange's sugar will caramelize and sweeten the onion. Margaret punc-
tures the duck's flesh with a skewer and puts it in the oven. Everything is almost ready. Richard II's Compound Sallet, garnished with
rose petals and marigolds, chills in the fridge, and Beauvillier's Sev-
enteenth-Century Cheese Soufflé is on the counter. Cream almond
pastries, *darloy*, or maids in waiting, are for dessert. In ten minutes
Dan will either walk through the door with flowers or he won't come
back at all. She sees his car smoldering on the side of the road, safety
glass shattered like teeth around Dan's dead body. She wonders what
she would do with his clothes.

Margaret drinks a glass of wine and smokes. The smoke makes her
feel sad. She feels like Liz Taylor or Veronica Lake in an old movie;
she can only picture herself in sepia tones.

All that's left are the figs, cognac, and chocolate. The sauce has
reduced to only a cup or so. Margaret pushes the movie out of her
head and goes back to work. Over the sink she strains out the figs,
which will be served on the side; she saves the rich liquid, returns it
to the pan and pours in another glass of wine. With a wooden spoon
she rubs the pan to deglaze the caramelized sugar on the sides. She
walks into the living room, where Dan keeps the Hennessy behind
the bar. This is what he drinks when he's up late. He thinks that just
because it's expensive, he is a connoisseur and not a drunk.

She goes back into the kitchen and pours six tablespoons into the
sauce. Then she adds butter and flour to make it thicken. Now the

final touch: the chocolate, semisweet gourmet chocolate. She eats a square. It makes her feel rich and bitter. The foil glimmers. Margaret picks up her knife to halve the wafers of chocolate before she adds them to the sauce. She is going to split the squares down the middle. On the cutting board she holds one between her forefinger and thumb.

Ahhh! the sorrow of a sliced thumb. Blood spills into the grooves of the board. In a strange way Margaret likes this, to have a little blood flow reminds her she's still alive. The cut is deep. There is blood on her apron and on her dress. Blood glints on the foil. She sucks her thumb, and her mouth fills with copper.

She balls her fist and squeezes blood into the sauce. "For salt," she says aloud, and then begins to stir in the chocolate. When it has melted, the pan takes on rare depth. She is trying to find her image in the liquid. Instead she sees the Jag. Dan is driving toward the ocean, accelerating toward Hatteras, the abandoned cabin, and the undertow. She knows she should be running for the bathroom—for gauze, a towel, *something*—but she doesn't. The whole universe swirls about the blue flames of the stove.

By the time she picks up the legal pad and the grease pencil, she has already composed the recipe in her head. She writes with purpose, knows as the pencil graces the page that the prose is succinct, clear, flawless. She will show them; before she is done she will show the interns and strangers in the test kitchen a recipe fit for kings. She will give them the recipe for swan.

This has been simmering in her head for a while, ever since Dan brought home the great white swan he slaughtered. It was a long time before he came back to the house that day. Margaret sat in the kitchen for hours, waiting. She was horrified when he lurched in cradling the enormous bird. The greens keeper hadn't told her that Dan wouldn't let it go, that he'd been holding it all the time they were on the phone.

When Dan walked in, there was blood on his shirt, and somehow there was even blood in his hair. He sat down on the floor like a little kid with the bird in his lap and wept. Margaret knelt beside him and cried too. The swan's beak was crushed; its broken neck dangled straight down. It had bright eyes. She had not known swans were so large. Then she made a mistake; she tried to take it away from him. For a long time they struggled on the floor. But he held on, clutching the bird to his chest with his big arms, refusing to give it up. In the end there was just no way Margaret could take it away from him, and there was just no way he was letting go of the dead thing between them.

DEAR NEIGHBOR

Daniel Wallace

Tony Shusterman was writing a letter.
Dear Neighbor, he wrote.
Dear Neighbor.
The letter stayed that way for a long time—two days, in fact. Finally, though, a kind of inspiration struck, and that evening he began from where he had left off, this time in earnest.

I am writing in reference to the tragic events of late, insofar as they concern your cat, Marybelle. First let me offer my condolences and let you know that if I could take back what happened now I would, but as we are not endowed with this kind of ability (and power), obviously we must accept what has happened and move on. This is by way of saying that I am in large part responsible for the death of Marybelle, and that I'm sorry. I wish things had not gotten out of hand the way they did, and, under different circumstances, things wouldn't have turned out the way they did, I'm sure. But the truth is, I've been under a great deal of stress lately. This doesn't justify my actions in any way. But the fact that I have been under stress—both in my personal life and at work—I think is important. Marybelle is the first thing I've ever killed in my life.

He stopped writing then because he realized, almost as he wrote it, that this wasn't true. Marybelle was actually the *second* thing. The first thing he ever killed was his sister's goldfish, twenty years ago. He had flushed it right down the toilet, an action he assumed eventually killed it. Stress was an issue then too. Seven years old. His parents: splitting up. Yelling. Slamming doors. He was so unhappy then. But it was his sister, a five-year-old, whose feelings appeared to be getting the lion's share of attention. At the time, Tony felt that by killing the fish he would somehow restore the world to the way it had been before all this started happening, that by sacrificing the fish he could make the events that had led to its demise magically disappear.

Of course, nothing of the sort occurred. He got more attention all

337

right—a whack on the butt with the back of his father's hand. And his parents eventually divorced. So killing the fish changed nothing.

It was much the same with Marybelle. Killing Marybelle—which was an accident, sort of—hadn't changed anything either: it only made things worse. He wished he hadn't done it, that the cat were still alive, because, among other things, he wouldn't have had to write this letter.

He dropped the pen onto the small kitchen table where he was sitting and rubbed his cheeks, his eyes. He hadn't been sleeping well, not since what happened with Sally. He woke up three or four times a night, and in that gray world between sleep and waking he thought it was all a dream, that he would turn and find her sleeping happily beside him, and Marybelle still alive. But it wasn't a dream. She had left him, and the cat was dead, and each time he woke it was like a wound opening up all over again. He kind of wished he never slept at all. So he didn't so much, and his work suffered. Tony was a marketing specialist. His marketing was done over the telephone. All his calls were monitored to ensure customer satisfaction. His every syllable, his every breath was either overheard or recorded. It was like living in some nightmare future-world, only it wasn't the future: it was his real life, right now. Which was kind of unbelievable. Eighteen months on the telephone... It seemed both completely improbable and totally inevitable. His father had often compared a man's life to a mouse in a maze, the secret to getting out of it being cunning and persistence. Tony thought this was probably true, but, short on both counts, he had come to a dead end and simply stopped there. So when he said to a woman he had called, "Lady, you wouldn't know a good deal if it bit you in the leg," he was sure this would be noted in his files, and it was, a little chart hanging on a hook on the side of his cubicle. From then on Tony had a very strong premonition that his job was in danger. Every day he felt could be his last. When six o'clock rolled around and he hadn't been fired he nearly ran from the building to avoid the tiny, sunken-eyed Mr. Sellers, who would be the man to do it if it were done, and whose office was the last one he passed on his way out. Getting into his car brought with it a sense of lightness, a feeling of blessed relief.

Tony read over what he'd written. The words wobbled across the light blue lines in a painful scrawl, shoddily cursive here, pitifully printed there. He read down to the place where he said that Marybelle was the first thing he'd ever killed, and he wondered now if he should tell them about the fish. Probably not. He didn't want to give them the idea that he was a serial animal killer. And anyway, since he hadn't actually seen the goldfish die, there was a possibility, however slim, that he hadn't killed it, that it had lived and grown huge and mutant in the sewers beneath the city. Marybelle was different: he had seen her, alive and then dead. He knew exactly what had happened to her.

But the truth is, I've been under a great deal of stress lately.

Something about this part bothered him too. This was true, of course, he *was* under stress—a lot of it. But he wondered if this was information he wanted to share with his neighbors. Admitting to being afflicted by stress somehow made him sound nervous, unsettled—dangerous even. And maybe Tony *was* dangerous. Potentially. But that didn't mean he was going to share his life story with his neighbors.

He really didn't trust them.

He thought of the day they met, just last Thursday, and the altercation they'd had, and he felt the blood go to his head. The thing is, regardless of their place in the maze, they weren't very nice people.

So he crumpled the letter and began again.

Dear Mr. and Mrs. Richards, he wrote.

I realize that we have not had the best experiences as neighbors, but I want to apologize for what happened with Marybelle, specifically regarding the fact that I am largely responsible for the fact that she died. I feel bad about what happened.

Well…not true, he decided upon reflection. He didn't really feel bad about it at all. He wished he hadn't done it, of course, but Tony had a book *full* of wishes, things he wished he'd done and hadn't done, and wishing he hadn't killed the cat was just one of them. Killing the cat had actually made him feel *good* for a moment, better than he'd felt for some time, actually, but of course he could admit that to nobody, ever, and scarcely even to himself. The victory that culminated in Marybelle's death had filled him with a bright, though brief, sense of wonder: wonder at having subdued a foe, of course, but there was also the pure and simple wonder of him, Tony Shusterman, here in this place and time, twenty-seven years into a life, having been down this path and that one, and after all of it finding himself here, in a suburb of a big city, staring at the corpse of a cat, still soft, still even a little warm in his hands.

Not just any cat, though. That was the thing. This cat was one of those weird, possessed, evil creatures, who knew everything you've ever said or done or thought and is there to make you suffer for it, in whatever way they can. The kind of cat who *stared*. The kind of cat who would appear out of the darkness when you least expected it, its eyes *alive with light*, nearly giving you a heart attack, and who somehow found its way into your second-story apartment one night and was resting curled up in a little ball on your pillow, *smiling at you* as you screamed at it to go, get the hell out, but still actually *smiling* that lipless, toothy grin. Tony had never seen a cat smile before. It made his skin crawl. That's when he went for it. That's when everything fell apart.

Truth: the cat had been stalking him for months. It was a truth no other human being would ever believe, but it was the truth, nonetheless.

She had placed herself prominently at every intersection of his life. She slept on the hood of his car in winter, on the rubber mat in front of his apartment door in summer. In the morning, when he left for work, she would be watching him from behind a tree; when he returned she would be there still, positioned to see him when he arrived.

Why Marybelle had chosen him to torture, or for what, he couldn't say. But she was spooky. He couldn't lose the spooky feeling that cat gave him, even though she was dead now. He had never given her food, never scratched the top of her head with the tips of his fingers. Nothing. And yet there she was every day. Tony wasn't abusive. He'd shove her aside with his shoe sometimes, just so he could open his own front door—it's where he lived, for God's sake. But she made a mournful meowing sound every time he did this, as if to suggest *how dare you!*

Tony was more of a dog man, actually. He thought about putting that in the letter too but didn't see how that would matter to the Richards. So he didn't.

I feel bad about what happened. But Marybelle had been acting strangely. Maybe you noticed, I don't know. Her behavior disturbed and alarmed me. So if you believe that what happened has anything to do with what happened between us the other day, you are wrong. It was all about Marybelle. Marybelle and me.

Marybelle and me, he read. *Marybelle and me*. That sounded weird, like they were a couple, a crazy pair.

He crushed the paper and began again.

Mr. and Mrs. Richards,

I can't put into words how I feel about what happened the other day with Marybelle. I wasn't feeling well when I came home, and all of a sudden—

Tony had been kind of drunk. This was the night Sally had left him for reasons he still couldn't fathom. He had gone to a bar to shoot pool and drink beer and not think about himself or his life. He had beer after beer, and for some reason this didn't make him feel any better; it made him feel worse. It made him think of all the dark things in his life, like his mother, who was sickly and living in a retirement community in Fairhope, and his father, who had died ten years ago of a heart attack, and of his little sister, who moved to California and never called anymore. She was like a stranger to him now. Would they even recognize each other, he wondered, if they passed on the street? It was difficult to grasp, how they had all ended up where they had, after having been kids and part of a family.

The same thing would happen to the Richardses one day. This is what he thought as he paused in the composition of his letter and, as the memory of that night came flooding back in every detail, got himself a beer from the refrigerator, the taste of it a kind of simulation of the inebriation of the week before. No, he thought, the Richards were not immune from the ravages of life. Now they had this lovely, perfect family unit, the mom, the dad, the kids, the cat. But one day it would all fall apart. Mr. and Mrs. Richards would grow apart, and get divorced. The girl—Samantha—would grow crazy and wild. Cameron, their boy, would end up in some pointless job and get some sort of disease…maybe a skin disease. Somebody would get sick and die. Maybe all of them would. This is just what happened to people, to people and their cats.

What a day that had been. It was just an hour or so after the verbal fray with the Richardses that Sally came over. They'd been thinking of going to a movie. That was the plan. But something didn't seem right from the beginning. When he kissed her hello, she turned her face a little to one side, so he got part of her lips, the edge of them, and that was all. Then she sat on the couch, distracted, her purse in her lap. Her thin blonde hair looked as if it were tickling her shoulders, and her cheeks were flushed red. He told her what had happened earlier, every detail, down to the pipe Mr. Richards smoked, but she didn't see what he was getting all upset over.

"What do you mean, you don't see?" he said.

"I mean, you're like that sometimes, Tony," she said. "You overreact. Sometimes it's hard to know where you're coming from."

"*What?*" he said.

This was so out of left field it was crazy. Were they even talking about the same thing? He was just telling her what had happened and now she was making some universal judgment on his character. So Tony was like, *What?* The same thing had happened when he had told her about the cat a couple of weeks ago, how he thought it was following him around. She had missed his point completely.

"We need to talk," she said.

And that's how she did it, that's how she broke up with him after six months of some pretty good times together. Bam. And though she tried to explain it, why she was feeling the way she was, none of it really got through to him. The things she was talking about—his anger at the world, his moodiness, the wall inside him she could just not break through—these things were just who he was, and not even all of the time but just some of the time.

He didn't get it. He asked her, "Is there somebody else?" "No," she said, there wasn't anybody else ("I *knew* you were going to ask me that," she said).

"It's just me, then," he said. "You want me to be somebody else."

"I guess?" she said, like it was a question. "In a way?"

"Somebody perfect," he said.

"No," she said. "Not perfect, just…"

"Well, that's what it sounds like to me," he said. "You want somebody perfect. And I'm not. Nobody is. You'll find this out one day. Good luck, Sally. Bon fucking voyage. Have a nice trip."

"Tony," she said.

But he shook his head and turned away. He didn't know what she wanted from him now, now that she'd said all this, but that was all he was willing to do for her then. He found the wall she had referred to earlier, got behind it, and when she left he didn't even turn to watch her go. He just heard her footsteps, every one of them, and the door close, and that was that.

He sat there, still, for a good long time. From somewhere outside he heard a muted, plaintive meow.

It took longer to get drunk than he thought it would. He found he could not drink fast enough. He sat at the bar at Charlie's Que and Brew, and as the warm wash of the alcohol began to suffuse him all his heartaches began to feel as one. Sally, his neighbors, his job: it was as if they were taking up arms against him, as if they were connected in some way. And they *were*. He realized that they were. Maybe his father was wrong and life was more a puzzle than a maze. And if that was the case maybe this was a piece, or three pieces, and if he could understand the connection between them he would stop feeling so bad. So he tried to understand.

His neighbors were the Richardses. The husband, Mr. Richards—Dick Richards, believe it or not, was his name, his parents had actually named him Richard Richards—was a writer of some kind, or said he was. His wife was a social worker. They owned the first house on the block, right beside the apartment complex.

Mr. Richards had seemed nice enough at first. They had waved at each other on occasion, when Tony drove past on his way home from work; Mr. Richards enjoyed a cocktail most evenings, sitting out on his front porch. And then, one day for no reason at all, Dick Richards waved Tony over, and invited him to come up to the porch for a beer. Tony couldn't say no to that. That's when he met the whole family, one after the other: the son, the daughter, the wife, the cat—though the cat, Marybelle, he'd known. All her shit had been going for a while by then. But Tony didn't say anything about it. She had jumped into his lap immediately, and Tony let her sit there, he didn't want to be rude. While Marybelle kneaded into his khakis until her claws dug into his skin, Mr. Richards puffed on a pipe and asked him what he did. And this is when the whole thing between them arose, just like that, when Tony told him he was a telephone marketer.

"I'm sorry," he said. "You're a what?"

"A telephone marketer," Tony said.

Mr. Richards squinted at him, then smiled. A yellowish swirl of smoke poured from his mouth.

"Wait," he said. "You mean you're one of those people who call me during dinner to try to sell me a credit card?"

"Exactly," Tony said. "Not credit cards, though. Free vacations, timeshares, that sort of thing."

They both nodded. Mr. Richards seemed pleased. Because of this, Tony felt compelled to parody himself for his new friend. He brought a hand to the side of his face, with his thumb and little finger extended so that it looked like a telephone.

"*Mr. Richards?*" he said, in a slightly deeper voice. "*This is Tony Shusterman. I hope I'm not disturbing your dinner, but if I could have just a minute of your time. You won't be sorry.*"

Mr. Richards laughed, and stared at Tony for a moment with a growing smile on his face. Then he called for his wife. She was inside making dinner. Tony could smell it. He was hoping they'd invite him to stay.

"Honey," he said when she came out.

Mrs. Richards was pretty. She had long red hair and big green eyes and a nice body for a woman who had already had two kids.

"You're not going to believe what Tony here does," he said to her.

"Try me," she said, wiping her hands on a towel.

"He's one of those guys who sells stuff over the phone."

She cocked her head to one side, as if she were having trouble understanding. But she understood.

"What?" she said. "You mean one of those guys?"

"One of those," Mr. Richards said.

Everybody looked at Tony and smiled.

"Wow," she said. "I've never met anybody who did that before."

"He's got a girlfriend named Sally, he lives alone in the apartments over here, and he's a telephone marketer. Doesn't that sound like—

Mrs. Richards frowned, pensively.

"Maybe," she said.

"What?" Tony said. He was lost completely. "Sound like what?"

"An idea for a sitcom," Dick Richards said, trying not to laugh, though little bursts of laughter popped out, like burps. "You know, a situation comedy. I'm always trying to give ideas to a friend of mine who works at a studio. This sounds like something he would *love.*"

"I still don't get it," Tony said.

"I'd have to talk to you," he said. "Over a beer—my treat. Get some of the details, flesh it out a little. But I think it has legs, don't you, honey?"

She nodded. Then, all of a sudden, she laughed, as if she were imagining a scene from the sitcom.

"It's funny," she said. "It really is."

And suddenly it dawned on him what they were talking about.

"Wait a minute," Tony said. "Are you saying you want to write about me—my life—for a television show?"

"Yes!" Dick Richards said. He gave his pipe a good suck, nodding. "Exactly. What do you think?"

"I think you should forget about it," Tony said.

Mr. Richards raised his eyebrows and shook his head.

"You don't understand," he said. "It would just use your life as the basis for something. It's not like someone would come over there with cameras."

"No," Tony said. "I think I understand. You think my life is funny."

"Of course not," Mr. Richards said, and he exchanged a worried expression with his wife. "Just some parts of it, as the basis for something else entirely."

"Well, it's not funny," Tony said. "Believe me. Not even parts. If it were, I'd be laughing a lot more than I am."

"Tony, please, we've gotten off on the wrong foot here. I didn't mean—

"You know what's funny?" he said. Suddenly the situation was out of his hands. "*You're* funny. Why don't you write a little show about yourselves. Call it *One Fucking Funny Family*. I'd laugh my ass off."

He laughed a little then, to show them what his laughter might sound like. The Richardses looked at him as though he were crazy. And they actually seemed a little scared. Mrs. Richards backed away a little bit, and when one of the kids came to the porch door to see what was going on she said, "Stay inside, honey. I'll be in in a minute."

Tony stopped laughing, and pushed Marybelle out of his lap. The cat, deep in a purring sleep, fell to the porch with a thud. Mr. and Mrs. Richards let out a simultaneous gasp, horrified. Mrs. Richards bent over and scooped the cat up in her arms, and then everyone, including Marybelle, stared at him with fear and pity in their eyes. Tony couldn't even speak. There didn't seem to be anything left to say. He just stood up and walked away, the way Sally would later that evening. Sally, to whom he would tell all of this, and who wouldn't understand, and who would break up with Tony, then and there, and Tony, who would go out himself and drink until he was ready to come back, but not ready for what was waiting for him when he got there.

Because I walk in and all of a sudden I saw Marybelle. She was curled up on my pillow. She had those green eyes looking at me. I don't know how she got in. Maybe through a window, or maybe she had slipped in when Sally left before and I hadn't seen her. But she was all curled up there like she was at home, and after everything that had happened between us, how she had been with me, following me around and watching me every day for so long, I couldn't take it anymore.

"What the hell are you doing in here?" I said to her. "What the hell."

She stretched out then, her front paws, and started away licking at them. Like there was nothing about her being there at all that I might find weird or out of the way. But fuck. "Scat!" I said. "Get out!" And I made some scary noises and threw my hands into the air. This got her attention. But all it did was make her get off my pillow. She started walking toward me. I walked ahead of her and into the living room, where I opened the front door. "Go on now," I said, holding it open. "Get back to your happy little family."

But she wouldn't leave. She sat herself down right there in the middle of the living room and stared at me, the way she did. She meowed. So I took off my shoe and hurled it at her. I missed, but scared her, and she took off into the kitchen. I followed her in there and kicked at her with the foot that still had a shoe on it, trying to get her to come out of there and leave. But it just sent her moving in circles around the table, even when I connected with a solid hit to her midsection. She flew across the room and into the wall, but fell on her feet, and stood there, looking at me.

And that's when I realized: she thought she was better than me. That's what this whole thing was about. She felt it was her job to let me know that, of the two of us, she was the one doing better. She had the nice house, the nice family, the nice life. She was farther along in the maze, and from here on out I would have to run to catch up. So I ran to her, and I picked her up, and took her to the door and threw her as far away from me and my place as I could, just so she'd get the idea that I didn't want her around anymore, not ever.

I guess I threw her too hard. Because when I went out to check on her she wasn't moving, at all. She was just dead. I put her in the gutter, to make it look like a car had done it. But it wasn't a car.

It was me.

So that's the story, Mr. Richards. It occurs to me to say that this is not a sitcom after all, is it? That it's something else altogether. It's like a drama, I think, and I'm the main character in the drama, and this is the part of the story where the guy everybody is secretly rooting for hits bottom, and can't find the way back up.

Tony let it all wash over him, all of it. Then he picked up his pencil, and wrote.

Dear Neighbor, he wrote.

I'm the guy who killed your cat. It's not the first thing I've killed, and, the way things are going, it probably won't be the last. But I'm sorry. I really am—

No.

This wouldn't do.

It was late, he was tired, but he knew this wouldn't do. The words he had written seemed to hover above the paper, shimmering. There was more to it, much more, but it was just too hard to write. So he stood up, leafed through the phone book, and dialed a number. Then he listened to it ring until somebody, finally, picked up, and said hello.

"Mr. Richards?" he said. "Hi, Mr. Richards. Tony Shusterman here, from next door. I hope I'm not disturbing your dinner, but if I could have just a minute of your time."

Mystery Hill

D. B. Wells

Lucinda West hid her medicine under her tongue that morning, and now she did not feel like emptying the sanitary napkin receptacle in the ladies' room at the Mystery Hill Bar and Grill.

"I ain't touching that shit," she told her mom. "That's Dwayne's job."

"You tell her, Cindy," one of the men at the bar said.

"You shut up," Trinh Minh West said. "Dwayne gone," Trinh told her daughter. "You do. Wear groves." Trinh held out a pair of disposable latex gloves.

"I wouldn't stick my hand in there with fifty of those fucking gloves on," Lucinda said.

The men at the bar laughed.

"I'd get fired if I said that," a weary waitress said, delivering a fishtail sandwich with fries. Lucinda growled, baring silver braces piano keyed with blue and red spacers.

"It slide off wall!" Trinh said, putting the gloves in Lucinda's hand. "Just dump!"

Lucinda started to speak but Trinh put her finger to the girl's lips. "No tawkie! Just wawkie!" And she pointed the way to the ladies' room.

When Lucinda returned she took a cigarette from a patron's pack. It angered Trinh when her daughter smoked in the Grill because Lucinda was underage and you never knew when a liquor agent would show up.

"How was it?" one of the men asked.

"Well I ain't busing no more tables, if that tells you anything," Lucinda said. "The sight of ketchup is about to make me puke."

The men laughed and Trinh said something in Vietnamese that required gesturing with both hands.

"Right, right," Lucinda said. "Whatever." She scooped some change from the bar and walked to the jukebox.

Through the window, she saw Jack McAdams' truck rumble into the parking lot.

Jack usually came to Mystery Hill on weekends since he taught at the university during the week. Why was he here on Wednesday? Just to dig in one of his ditches? Was that why he had driven all the way from Lexington in the middle of the week? To dig?

Sure enough, Jack went straight to the trench at the edge of the parking lot and pulled back the tarpaulin.

She wondered if he planned to stay the night.

"Woosinda!" Trinh called. She tapped her watch to signal that it was time for the evening pill.

Lucinda didn't have to be told that. She could tell time. She shot her mom a dirty look and shoved through the swinging door to the kitchen. At the back sink, she shook a single blue pill into her hand. If she went a whole day without her medicine she *might* have trouble sleeping. And trouble sleeping might lead to acting-out behavior tomorrow. And that might lead to an episode. *Might.* The doctor said she would outgrow the episodes and the acting out, and she thought that had already happened. Still the pill had to go somewhere. So it went down the drain.

Lucinda ran upstairs to the rooms she shared with her mother, leaving her clothes where they fell. Before the mirror she brushed her black hair out of the ponytail and looked at herself. It was important to look good and smell good because each day now more and more people wanted to look at her and smell her and because it was about so much more than just being looked at and smelled. It was about being loved and being hated, for beauty was a blade that cut both ways. Lucinda had learned this by watching her mother—who was also beautiful—wound herself time and time and again. But Trinh Minh West was a foreigner and pretty much a dumbass most of the time. Lucinda knew she would wield the double-edged sword of beauty with much greater effect.

She looked out her window. Jack was sitting in the trench looking down. If he looked up he could see her.

Jack McAdams was exhausted. That morning he had driven all the way to the Rainbow House to be at the deathbed of Mother McAdams. The place was filled with past members of the Rainbow Chorus, most of whom Jack knew well, having sung with them during his own rotation in the group, and the endless how-are-you's and what-are-you-doing-now's had drained him.

The Chorus had toured fundamentalist churches throughout Kentucky and West Virginia in the 1970s and '80s, a blue-eyed blonde child anchoring one end, a Negro at the other. In between, children of every skin tone. Mother McAdams' Rainbow Chorus. And each child had a story that Mother sometimes told between songs, droning on her Casio while the featured child stood forth.

Jack stepped to Mother McAdams' bedside. "Oh, Brother John!" Sister Sarah McAdams said, "I don't think she'll ever know you came now."

Jack looked at the bottom of the trench. A meter beneath the surface was the nearly straight edge of an oblong, fire-fractured stone, one of 144 such buried blocks found by an electrical resistivity survey and now marked with little orange flags on wires. Jack glanced down the hill at the village. Many of the older houses were made from the same curiously quarried stone. Just as the Bar and Grill was.

A member of the West family had owned Mystery Hill since before the age of photography, when the blocks still lay in great heaps on the hill overlooking the Red River. After the Civil War, tons of the stones were sold to anyone who could cart them off. Lucinda's grandfather further disrupted the site by shoving the remaining stones around to create a roadside attraction when he built the Grill. Jack could still make out the vine-covered outlines of Cinderella's Castle and Snow White's Bower.

No one from the university would touch Mystery Hill. Everyone agreed something had been there, but the site was hopelessly tainted and working there, Jack was frequently reminded, would do nothing to advance a serious academic career.

Lucinda stepped from the shower. She'd only washed her bottom half. A whore shower, her mother called it. She applied lip gloss and retouched her eyes, blending the corners to accent Asia. She would wear her low risers and a short T and a red silk thong that belonged to her mother.

"Why didn't you tell me Jack was here?" Trinh said in Vietnamese, rushing into the room. "What do you think you are doing? You should let me handle this because I know what I'm doing. You will only get hurt."

"Jack here?" Lucinda said. She looked out the window and saw that he had left the trench.

As a child in Vietnam, Trinh had been an outcast, being the spawn of an unknown American. As a young woman in America, she ended up at Mystery Hill, working for David West, a veteran who'd been in such a hurry to go to Vietnam that he dropped out of high school to join the army. When Trinh got pregnant, David married her. When David died, she got it all.

Jack studied the photographs that David West had hung on the wall of the Grill. Newspaper articles about the mysteries of Mystery Hill. Photos of a teenaged David with a rifle and a twelve-point buck. David by the river with a string of rock bass. Trinh's wedding photos. Pictures of Lucinda at various stages of development.

"Man oh man!" Lucinda said, coming through the kitchen door. "I'm sure glad to see you! I got this big test and I just don't get that stuff at all! Please help me Jack. *Please!* There's a booth by the window. C'mon. It'll just take a second to clean it." They walked to the table and Lucinda loaded the dirty plates and silverware into the bus pan, missing a spoon, which she wiped onto the floor. "Oh, shoot!" she said, and bent to pick it up when *Click-click, click-click!* The spark of her mother's high heels.

"*Jack!* What surprise!" Trinh stood at the end of the bar and let Jack take her in for a second before she started her slow onslaught, serpentine, like shifting liquidification in a simple black skirt. Lucinda looked at her mother, then at Jack. She followed his eyes. Of course. He looked at her mother's legs, at her ankle bracelet and sandals. Of course.

Jack smiled and stood until Trinh sat down. He was always doing stuff like that. Standing until she sat. Opening doors. Generally treating her like she was some kind of royalty instead of some foreigner.

"Whatschu doing here?" Trinh asked, flipping her hair. Lucinda mimicked the gesture perfectly. She slammed the door as she left the Grill.

Lucinda wandered back to Jack's pickup. Jack slept in the truck when he worked at Mystery Hill, running an extension cord from the bar and lighting his campsite with strings of white Christmas tree lights while he wrote on his laptop. Lucinda felt like crying, the Christmas lights were so beautiful, but she held back. She held back by telling herself she was going to get exactly what she wanted—no matter what it took.

Jack couldn't sleep that night because Lucinda had her CD player sitting on the sill of her open window. So he got up and sat against the bed at the tailgate of his truck. The night was moonless and cold but he sat wrapped in his electric blanket and looked at the stars. It was a corny thing to do, but he did it.

He looked up at Lucinda's window. Blue-gray light washed her ceiling. So she was watching TV. No, her computer screen was on. He wished she would turn the volume down a little.

A little after 2 A.M., Jack's cell phone woke him. "John," Sister Sarah cried, "She's left us! Mother has gone to her reward."

Shadows pulsated in the blue-gray window. Lucinda was dancing.

"*Cock-a-doodle-doo!*" Lucinda yodeled. "Room service!" She climbed onto the tailgate with two steaming Styrofoam cups. Jack sat up and rubbed his eyes.

"I put skim milk in it just the way you like it," she said. She sat on the edge of the mattress, her legs outstretched, crossed at the ankles. She had on the Nike sandals she wore in the locker room at school. All the girls on the soccer team carried the sandals in their gym bags and wore them whenever they could even though they violated the dress code. She'd painted her toes last night and took the occasion to admire her work.

"Thanks," Jack said. He looked at her. She was in her uniform. Trinh sold forty acres of burley base after David died and put the money away. Now Lucinda went to an all-girls school in Clay City. "How're you doing in school?"

"I'm a total dumbass. You know that. What's wrong with you?" she asked. "Why you so bleary? Didn't you sleep well last night? Can I ask you a personal question? Did you fuck my mom last night?"

"What?"

"Yes or no."

"Lucinda—"

"You *did!* Why don't you just ad*mit* it? I see the way you look at her! I'm not *stupid!*"

"I *didn't!* Why are getting so angry?"

"Don't give me that superior calm and reasonable bullshit. There's the bus." She slid off the tailgate and slung her backpack over her shoulder. "My mom uses men to get us things, Jack. She's a complete bitch and you're an idiot if you don't see that."

Mother McAdams was laid out in the dining room annex of the Rainbow House since that room was the largest and many people were expected to file by her casket.

Sister Sarah hugged Jack when she saw him. "Oh, Brother John, we're going to sing again! The Rainbow Chorus is going to sing for Mother one more time!"

"Yes, yes," Jack said. "Of course we will." He cycled through the mourners, shaking hands with men and embracing women, until he made it to the periphery of the crowd.

"Frère Jacques," said a man in a wheelchair with braided hair. Beside him was a tall blind blonde woman with a black lab on a handle.

"Peter," Jack said. "Ruth."

Jack learned the two had married and moved to New Mexico,

where Peter had reclaimed his Apache identity, most noticeably in the form of silver and turquoise.

"I need a smoke," Ruth said, and the four of them went out on the porch. Cars were parked in the yard and lined the road in front of the home. A steady stream of people came down the driveway.

"So that's your van with the New Mexico plates," Jack said. "That's a long drive."

"We started when we heard the end was near," Ruth said, lolling her head from side to side. "We wanted to make sure she was dead."

"Did you see the obituary, John?" Peter said. "It was so full of crap." Peter tried to light Ruth's cigarette. "Quit lolling, dear. You know, that story she told about me? A bunch of baloney. If she really wanted to help me when I was a kid she could've just sent my mom a few bucks every month. She didn't have to adopt me. She just needed a red skin to fill a slot in her rainbow."

"I can't believe how some of these people are deifying her," Ruth said.

Jack nodded. "It's almost like they knew someone different from the person I knew," he said.

The parking lot of the Mystery Hill Bar and Grill was full of loggers' trucks when Jack pulled in just after sunrise. He'd got up and left the Rainbow House early so he wouldn't have to talk to anyone. They had all stayed up late the night before talking and he was talked out.

Jack didn't go into the Grill, though the smell of bacon and eggs tempted him. Instead he walked to the banks of the Red River, then downstream to where Tug Creek joined in. He turned up the creek and walked the short distance to the abandoned homestead of Hollis Brown. It was six miles from the Grill if you went by the road, less than a mile if you walked along the river.

Though the house had burned twenty-seven years ago, it was not hard to find the site. Around the place where the house had stood were blades of iris, the planting of Hollis's wife, Hazel. And there was Hazel's headstone. And her daughter Ann's. Both made of the local soft sandstone. Somewhere on the other side of the field, Hollis lay in his grave.

He had been a fool to farm this narrow strip of land that lay in shade so much of the day. He was trying to get away from the world, trying to find a place where the Bible could win its battle with the bottle. The milk cow struggled and the chickens barely held their own against the foxes while, season after season, Hollis creased the steep ground trying to coax a crop of corn. Then his thirteen-year-old daughter turned up pregnant by one of the local boys, and that seemed to signal the unraveling. Still Hollis hung on for three more years, flood following drought, listening to whatever whispers came from the forest until one October day they told him to bring everybody home.

Hazel had her throat slit. Eighteen-year-old Ann had multiple wounds to her arms and hands. Jack thought he had some authentic memories of that day. The house was burning and his dog had been killed. He remembered the cow was bleeding and making a sound. And he remembered his mother, but not her face. Never her face. He'd looked up her picture in an old middle school yearbook, but the tiny black-and-white face smiling back at him, her head put at an unnatural angle by some photographer, rang no bells in Jack's mind.

"Run," she had told him. "Run from Grandpa. Just run."

Lucinda West woke up late Friday morning since she wasn't going to school. At around 11:30 she slipped on her flip-flops and went down to the bar. Her mother brought her hot chocolate and a scrambled egg with cheddar cheese and wheat toast.

Trinh spoke to her daughter in Vietnamese, telling her that she shouldn't come down to the bar in her pajamas anymore.

Lucinda responded that the only thing that stuck out was her hands and feet.

"Can't you smell it?" her mother said. "Smell the air now. That is the smell of all of these men thinking of you in bed."

"I'll just leave then."

"Don't leave, but wear your housecoat the next time. Please don't leave. I want to talk to you. Please sit down."

Lucinda sat back down. Then Trinh helped someone at the cash register, then she filled coffee cups, then she went back in the kitchen.

"What were you two talking about?" a man in a John Deere hat asked.

"How fucked up you look."

The men at the bar howled.

"What going on?" Trinh said, swinging through kitchen door with a glass of orange juice and a napkin. "What Woosinda say now?"

Lucinda took the pill from the napkin and washed it down with the juice.

"The fall is the most beautiful time of year," Trinh said as she looked out the window. "I think the leaves must be at their golden peak today."

"I would like to lie in the sun awhile," Lucinda said.

"Take phone," Trinh said.

Jack enjoyed the mindless work of excavation. It was a job that required no concentration and only a little observation. The easy physical monotony provided a release for him.

Lucinda came out on the deck in her bathrobe. At first she did not see him and then, when she did, she raised her hand timidly and looked as if she might not come out into the field and talk to him at all. But she did, walking slowly like she could at any minute change her mind and go back.

"What are you doing home today?"

"Suspended."

"Suspended?"

"I went off."

"What did you do?"

"I went off, I told you. *God!*" Her mane was held high on top of her head by several twisted elastic bands that sheathed the hair into a high cresting wave.

Jack went back to his digging.

"It was all your fault," she said, sitting down and dangling her feet in the trench.

"My fault?" He looked up but her face was lost in a halo of sun.

"I'm just kidding," she said. "I cussed out Mrs. Pugh."

"I guess that would get you suspended."

"That wasn't even what done it." She moved her feet up to the side of the trench so that her knees came out of the robe.

That was when it happened.

That was when Jack noticed Lucinda's feet.

He looked at her feet. He looked at them for a long time. He didn't know how long. They were still a child's feet, though her nails were fiery red and perfectly aligned, little to big, big to little on the side of the trench. Looking at the toes of Lucinda West, he could almost imagine them as some mythic artifact, some glimmering ruby tiara that had graced the brow of Cleopatra, perhaps, or Helen of Troy. Jack looked at her feet. Someone else might laugh, but for Jack McAdams, Lucinda's feet were the most beautiful sight he'd ever seen. He had a desire to hold them. To kiss them.

"—when Father Larry said they might make me ride the *short* bus, the one for the retarded kids, well I hit the ceiling, let me tell you. You're looking at my feet! You *are*, aren't you?" She tensed her toes against the side of the trench, causing the skin nearest the nail to blanch ever so slightly. This must be an epiphany, Jack thought.

She lowered herself into the pit and walked the length of the trench, her toes leaving pearl-sized indentations in the soft soil. She stepped on Jack's knee and pushed herself up out of the trench. Her robe fell open and she let it be.

"You like that, don't you? That's okay. I want you to like it. See, I've been thinking, and I want to make some changes," she said. "I want you to put me above all others, especially my mom." She saw that he was troubled in that uneasy, adult way, thinking about right and wrong. She knew he was about to offer some responsible reason for rejecting her. But it was too late for her to turn back. She would just have to win anyway. "I want you to put me above all others for all time," she said before he had time to speak, "and in each and every way. Okay?"

Jack McAdams could have saved himself, perhaps, if Lucinda West had not at that moment brushed her hair behind her ear. He might have been able to answer differently had she not bitten her lower lip.

GIMPLE AND ODUM

James Whorton, Jr.

Wallace Gimple was a large and physically powerful man with wavy white hair and a permanently sunburned face. He was also deeply shy—some would say backward—but an old sense of duty compelled him to be present at Sylvester Odum's wife's funeral. He had hoped to slip away after the visitation and before the chapel service, but something unexpected happened: Sylvester Odum grabbed his arm and would not let go of it. Gimple had shaken hands with almost the whole family and thought he was home free, but now he had no choice but to stay there alongside this small, odd, frightened widower who had a piece of gauze the size of a seed packet taped to his neck.

Odum clung to Gimple throughout the eulogy and the hymns and the graveside service as well. Afterwards, Odum's sister-in-law asked them both to join the rest of the family at her home, but Odum declined. Gimple was too abashed to speak. He walked Odum to his car, a white four-door Oldsmobile, and Odum got in.

Gimple gave a long sigh, very glad to have his arm back. Odum gazed into the steering wheel then cocked himself over and pulled out his wallet. He handed Gimple a photograph of a grinning dark-haired woman with small, bright eyes. Gimple studied the picture and did not know what to say or do. This was the woman they had just now buried.

"Everyone liked Nan," Gimple said.

Odum frowned. He took the picture and put it back in his wallet, and then he swung his door shut and drove off.

It was not until Gimple was headed back to his truck at the other end of the parking lot that he noticed several old women nodding their heads at him. A man he'd never met squeezed his shoulder and thanked him for being there.

"I used to work with Sylvester," Gimple said.

"We didn't know he had a friend left in the world," the man said.

Sylvester Odum was not an easily likeable man. He used his deep voice very slowly, not as though he was deliberating but as though he was tempting you to finish his sentence for him, which however he would not have liked, had you done it. There was a strangeness about him. The wet-sounding bass notes emanated from his small neck like the call of a bullfrog from a posthole. His face was craggy, and his skin was powdery white. He had thick, rather sensuous lips. His hair was curly and black, and through his curls the white skin of his scalp could be glimpsed. What he had was not a receding hairline but an overall thinning of the hair.

He had recently been forced to retire from the Osborne paper mill in Kingsport, Tennessee. They had moved him off the plant floor five years earlier, and now at age seventy he was considered too dangerous even to answer the telephone. His retirement reception took place in a break room at the end of first shift on a Friday. Gimple had retired from the Osborne on disability after injuring his back there, and from what he had heard, the break room was not exactly packed for Odum's sendoff. Odum gave a speech of only a few words that nonetheless went on for several minutes.

On the Monday following the reception, Odum had flipped his Snapper Comet on the slope in his front yard, pinning himself with the thirty-inch blade humming just near his right hip. Nan was in the house with Swap Shop blaring, and in time Odum would have slid into the blade to have his hip hacked to pieces, except that a neighbor girl who was home sick with an ear infection had seen the accident from her bedroom window and ran over and cut off the ignition. Then she telephoned everyone she knew, and the story wound up on page three of the Kingsport *Times-News*. The bandage on Odum's neck covered a spot where the muffler had burned him.

Wallace Gimple had never especially liked Sylvester Odum, but he did feel a loyalty to the memory of his friend Charlie Odum, Sylvester's younger brother, who was killed while on leave during the Korean war. The week after Nan was buried, Gimple took Odum to Hardee's for breakfast.

Several of them met there regularly. On that particular morning, Ned Douthitt kept shaking his head. Someone asked him why, and he said it was because his hair felt good. Someone asked him why his hair felt good and he said it was because he had borrowed his candy-eating son-in-law's conditioning rinse, which cost nine dollars a bottle.

Roger Bone said, "Don't shake your hair over my food, please." He was eating biscuits and gravy.

Ned asked Gimple what brand of conditioner he used. Possibly he was teasing Gimple, who washed his hair with Ivory soap whenever something got in it. Afterwards he used a half-teaspoonful of Tiger Rose men's hair dressing from a quart bottle that he had bought in a barbershop a number of years earlier. The dressing was strictly to make the hair stay in place better after he washed it. He said none of this, though, because he had just taken an enormous bite of biscuit.

Ned moved on and said, "Odum, what brand of conditioner do you use?"

Odum set his white fork down on his tray and stared at Ned. He said very, very slowly, "I don't like to discuss a matter of hygiene at the table."

Ned was already a jittery person, and sitting through Odum's molasses-like sentence was a special chore for him. Still he waited for Odum to finish before yapping back, "It's not like I asked you to describe your colonoscopy."

Odum's small jaw snapped shut.

Roger Bone said "Yuck, Ned." He pushed his Styrofoam plate away.

Odum sat as still as an ivory statuette. Hardee's was packed full with many tables of retired people using their loudest voices, but the men's table was quiet.

Then Ned, whose best and worst qualities were one, namely that he didn't know when to stop, said, "I'm talking about the hair on your head, and that's not really hygiene, I don't think. I'm simply saying that I like this type of conditioning rinse a lot. I like to look good if I can. Some of you men, like you, Gimple, are still in the 1950s when it comes to your hair. Gimple wears a comb-over and he's not even bald. Why do you do that, Gimple?"

"I always combed my hair like Daddy did," Gimple said.

"But your daddy was baldheaded!" Ned said.

Roger Bone, who wore a flat-top, laughed and pulled his cap on. He took his leave, and then Ned did the same, which left Gimple and Odum sitting side-by-side with two empty seats across from them. Gimple rose to move to Ned's seat, but before he was all the way up Odum caught him by the sleeve. Odum held the sleeve pinched between the thumb and first finger of his right hand.

Odum took a long yet shallow pull on his coffee, then set the cup down with care. "How many wives has Ned Douthitt had?" he asked.

"Three," Gimple said.

Odum looked off toward the left-hand cash register. Despite his large white ears it seemed as though Odum did not hear words directly but absorbed them through the skin, slowly, as a night crawler absorbs oxygen. He said, "Ned is embarrassing himself."

"He didn't seem embarrassed," Gimple said.

"He doesn't know it."

"I wish I didn't know it when I was embarrassed," Gimple said.

"Men's grooming is a private subject," Odum said. "Men who discuss their grooming haven't outgrown the diaper stage."

Gimple was too distracted to follow Odum's point. He knew it couldn't be true, but he had the impression that Odum had spoken without opening his mouth.

"That's not how I was brought up," Odum said. "There's a lot of things I don't choose to talk about. The reason I don't choose to talk about them—"

Here he stopped in his sentence and swiveled ten degrees in his seat to face the right-hand cash register. His white thumb and finger still pinched Gimple's sleeve.

"—is that there is no need for me to talk about them. A man who prefers to talk is like a woman."

By accident Gimple caught the eye of a man at the next table. This man was wearing a fluffy sweater. Gimple looked away quickly.

"When a woman talks," Odum continued, "it's a part of her

charm. The sound is cheerful. Another quality that I like to see in a woman is neatness."

His voice was impossibly deep. The weather itself did not have a deeper voice than this diminutive man's. Gimple patted his own cheek, wondering if he was about to black out.

"But for Adam there was not found an help meet for him," Odum droned. "And so He made him an help meet for him."

Gimple stood up suddenly, surprising Odum, whose thumb and finger held their pinch even after the sleeve had been yanked from between them. Gimple seated himself on the other side of the table. Just that little bit of extra distance between himself and Odum was such a relief, he wanted to sing.

For the next couple weeks Odum attended breakfast every morning. Why, no one knew. He did not seem to enjoy it, and at times he seemed to endure it like a purging flame. He ate cinnamon-raisin biscuits and sipped coffee with whitener and absorbed the talk and would occasionally offer one of his slow, discouraging opinions. If anyone interrupted him, he would stop in the middle of his sentence and refuse to speak again for the rest of the morning. Gimple came to regret the well-intentioned gesture of bringing his old friend's elf-like brother to breakfast. Ned and Roger regretted it too and let Gimple know.

Ned traded chrome at antique car shows, which he claimed was a viciously cutthroat business, and one morning he repeated a story about loading up after a show in Arden, North Carolina, and discovering that someone had maliciously unfastened the latch on the hitch of his utility trailer. Only gravity held the hitch to the ball.

Roger Bone said, "You or your boy had forgotten to latch it that morning on your way in."

Ned said, "No, by God, we were sabotaged. I locked it down myself before we left Kingsport."

"Maybe, maybe not," Roger said.

"If you'd ever hauled a trailer over the mountain on the old highway, you wouldn't say that, Roger. Hell, I'd sooner have little

Odum pull my trailer than to have you pull it."

Odum had been watching his coffee lid, and now his head pivoted slowly and he looked at Ned.

Ned went on. "He may flip a mower, but he knows more about trailering than you do, I'd say."

Odum was frozen like a spigot now. His stare was firm. Ned glanced at him and then away.

"I'd say Odum would have remembered to latch the hitch," Roger said.

Ned opened his mouth to speak, but Odum cut him off, saying, "The reason I am small is because I didn't get much to eat when I was little."

Ned laughed, blinking. He said, "Well, hell, everyone suffered back in them days, Odum. My people lived off suckerfish and walnuts."

Odum said, "You're big, Ned. You had good nutrition when you were young."

"We done okay. Hell, don't be touchy, Sylvester."

No one would have called Odum intimidating, but he did possess the ability to make others uncomfortable. He continued to stare at Ned with a stare that conveyed this message: *While I am not moving toward you, I am also not backing away.* His power consisted in being stationary. Ned, because his own ego required it of him, also did not move for the next twelve minutes but continued talking about the unrelated subject of deciding to buy matching brass locks for all of the outbuildings on his property. No one cared, including himself, but he was running out the clock. After twelve minutes he rose and left Hardee's. Roger Bone followed.

Odum looked back to his coffee. His right hand rose to touch the bandage on his neck. Gimple moved to the other side of the table and stared at Odum's plate, empty except for some streaks of sugar glaze and a single raisin.

The next morning Ned did not come to breakfast. This might have been interpreted as a victory for Odum except that Odum did not come either. For Gimple it was a great relief. Roger had been to a flea market outside Knoxville and found, for sale there, a three-quarter-inch Milwaukee drill motor that had been stolen from his shed eight months earlier. He knew it was his because he had etched his name into the housing with an engraving pencil. According to Roger, he'd announced to the dealer that he was taking his drill motor home with him, and after an exchange of mild threats he did so. It was a very pleasant breakfast with no tense moments.

Gimple was shy, but he treasured the company of his few old good friends. After breakfast he got to thinking about Charlie Odum, the sidekick of his teenage years. Many, many days they had walked through the woods with one .22 rifle between them, talking about things that Gimple had never talked about since. Then he thought of the other Odum, the one still living, and he felt anxious, as though he was being Sylvesterized from a distance. That afternoon he went to Odum's house. He went up the steps and rang the bell then quickly stepped backwards off the small porch and onto the walkway.

No one came to the door. Gimple waited a full minute and then another half.

He had the sensation that someone was watching him. He looked along each of the five front windows of this long, low, brick-faced house. The brick was a sandy color, which to Gimple seemed like the color of brick a person would choose who thought he was better than other people. Then the weather-stripping crackled on the front door, and the door opened an inch.

From the front walk Gimple said, "Hello?"

The door opened no further.

Gimple was unsure what might be required or expected of him at this moment. Not knowing what else to do, he walked up the steps and took hold of the doorknob. He pushed lightly. Something was blocking the door from the other side, however. That something was a hundred and ten quivering pounds of Sylvester Odum.

Gimple said, "Odum? I'm going to the knife show."

There was no answer. Gently, so that the tensed Odum would not lose his balance and fall into the door, Gimple let go of the knob.

Gimple said, "Do you want to ride with me?"

A small deep voice from behind the crack said, "I guess I'll stay here."

"I thought you had wanted to go to the knife show this afternoon," Gimple said.

"Did we say definitely?"

"I don't guess so."

"I'll stay here," Odum said.

Gimple got back in his truck and drove to the fairgrounds himself, glad to be spared the company of that rude miniature Abraham Lincoln. At the knife show he bought a German Boker Indian Head pocketknife with three blades. He got it for eighteen dollars because one of the blades was broken off halfway. All afternoon he was trying to place the strong odor that he had smelled coming out from behind Sylvester Odum's front door. It made Gimple think of embalming fluid, although he was not sure he had ever smelled embalming fluid. He had come into contact with many harsh chemicals at the paper mill over the years. What Odum might be up to in there he could not imagine, nor did he care. He had made his overture and been rebuffed, and Gimple was not a man to force himself in where he was not wanted.

The following week Bill Chenery showed up at breakfast. Bill had a mannerism that Gimple enjoyed: whenever he told a story, when he was at a point where something had to be explained for the rest of it to make sense, he would diagram a square on the table top with his two index fingers. No matter what he had to explain, he would illustrate it by drawing a square. This was a little thing to look forward to whenever Bill got going.

Bill had not been to breakfast for some time, so certain stories were repeated for him. He was told about the "little Odum" remark. Ned defended himself. "People are overly sensitive," he said. "I'm sorry I said it, but Odum is little. I don't think I said anything wrong."

Roger Bone said, "Odum is overly sensitive, but you are underly sensitive."

Bill said, "I think for Odum, Nan was the—" He stopped to think of a word.

"She wasn't a nut like him," Ned said.

"You know they found her on her back in the hallway with a shopping bag on her head, and a basket of laundry at her feet," Bill said. "And Odum was froze like a zombie on the sofa."

"She had a bag on her head?" Ned said.

"On her hair," Bill said. "She was fixing her hair, maybe. Look here. The other day, my grandson cut and raked Odum's lawn."

"As long as Odum's not trying to cut it himself," Roger said.

"Odum left his pay in the mailbox."

"Somebody will steal that money," Ned said.

Bill leaned in and raised both hands to get everybody's attention. "No, here's what I'm saying," he said. "Odum is in the house. He is home. But he will not come out the door to pay my grandson."

Gimple, who had been waiting happily to see Bill draw a square on the table, was now troubled. Later he brought up the subject with his wife. "Nobody has seen Sylvester Odum," he said.

His wife, Raye, was grooming one of her dogs on a towel in the middle of the living room floor. It was a heavy dog of medium height with a dense, wavy coat of light-colored fur. It was a mixed breed. The dog lay on its back with its legs splayed in four directions and the long, blood-red side of its tongue showing. Raye pushed a set of buzzing electric clippers up the dog's chest in neat overlapping rows. Her manner was assured and efficient, even a little rough. The dog could not have trusted its own mother more than it trusted Raye with these clippers. The towel was spread directly under the ceiling fixture and Gimple could see bits of dog fur, lighter than air, rising.

Raye's own hair was long and straight, knife-blade gray. She frowned contentedly at her work, rubbing her flat hand over the soft, trimmed fur. She said without looking up, "Someone should check on him, then."

Once a long time ago, Gimple had watched a man shoot himself.

The man's name was Scobie, and he lived by himself in a cave in the woods. He had a mule that he kept padlocked to a tree at night. Scobie traded guns, and he had a .36 caliber Colt revolver that he claimed had been used in the War Between the States. He wanted twelve dollars for it. Gimple asked him was it loaded and Scobie said no and in a flourish of salesmanship held the barrel up to his own hand and, smiling, blew the side of his hand off.

That was in Scott County, Virginia, in 1948. In 1982 Gimple's father shot himself deliberately because he had cancer of the throat. It was his choice. Only then had Gimple married. To be alone was too hard. Small things, when you're alone, become big things, and big things become intolerable. In the nineties when the Commonwealth of Virginia was slowly taking action to eminent-domain his home— the home he'd grown up in and never left, except for two years in Korea—there had been evenings when Gimple had contemplated carrying his twelve-gauge to Richmond and taking out some lawyers and VDOT officials. You can't win against the government, but you can decide how to lose. Raye had been there, though, to laugh the proposition down. Her laughter came early enough in the thought process that he could still benefit from it. He considered and saw she was right. Virginia pushed down the old house, blasted the rock, and widened the highway to four lanes plus a bike path. Gimple and Raye moved to Tennessee where there is no state income tax and you do not have to have your vehicle inspected. They still bought their groceries on the Virginia side, where the sales tax is lower.

Now Gimple drove his truck to Odum's house, parked it in the driveway, and went to the door and knocked. He let fifteen seconds go by and knocked again and hollered, "Odum, it's Wallace Gimple. Open up if you would."

The weather-stripping crackled and the door opened an inch, then wider. There was Odum. It was dark in there, and he was wearing a long bathrobe. Gimple said, "I'm here to check on you, Odum. Why haven't you come to breakfast?"

Odum muttered something Gimple could not understand.

"Maybe you should let me in," Gimple said.

Odum backed up, pulling the door open and standing aside. Gimple stepped into a tiled foyer with a brass chandelier overhead. There was a smell of cinnamon and oranges, very strong, and also a scorched smell.

Gimple followed Odum into the living room. Odum was wearing leather slippers, and under his long blue bathrobe he had on starched and ironed jeans and a plaid shirt. He had a stiff, high-crowned cap on his head with the Osborne logo. On his face was a week's white stubble. He looked ill.

Gimple had made up his mind to say certain things, so he started. "Some people are worried about you, Odum," he said. This was an exaggeration, but Gimple felt it was necessary.

Odum sat down on a long plush sofa. He reached for the remote and switched off the television.

"No one has seen you," Gimple said.

"I only go out late at night," Odum said.

Gimple didn't like this room. The chair he sat down in was new and stiff, and the carpet was so clean it shimmered. In the adjoining dining area there was a formal table with candlesticks. Over the buffet was a large portrait of Sylvester and Nan Odum. Nan had a round face with small, bright-blue eyes, and in the picture she smiled delightedly. Sylvester was also grinning in the picture, but in a way that Gimple had never seen him do in real life. He looked like he was being skewered. Husband and wife had the same tight, glossy curls on their heads in the same shade of walnut-husk black. They even had the same hairdo, except that Sylvester's was short on the sides.

When Gimple looked down from the portrait, which was two and a half by three feet in size, Odum was looking back at him. It was a look similar to the one he had given Ned Douthitt at Hardee's on the morning of the "little Odum" remark—a look of tungsten immovability and warning. Possibly there was a touch more of hatred in the look this time, Gimple thought, but that could simply have been the difference between seeing the look aimed at Ned and at himself.

Odum said in his rumbling bass, "If you laugh at me, I will never forgive it."

"Why would I laugh at you?" Gimple said.

Odum lifted his hand and pulled the cap off, revealing something completely new. Instead of the tight glossy curls, he had hair that pointed. Like the wires in a wire brush, each strand stood apart, and the kinks in each hair matched the kinks in those near it. Though the hair had been sparse before, it was now downright spotty. Odum's scalp showed through bright pink, and instead of black, his hair was a brownish purple, as though berries had been pushed into it. The magenta stripe along the top of his forehead also lent itself to that impression.

Gimple looked away quickly.

"I can't face people," Odum said.

Gimple searched for something to say. "Let's see what's on television," he suggested.

"I'm absurd," Odum said. "My head looks like a peeled beet."

With effort Gimple looked at the hair once more. He couldn't tell whether it was wet or dry. "Did you just now wash it?" he said.

"No."

Gimple shuddered. "What in the hell happened?" he said. "Did you do that yourself?"

Odum pressed his lips shut. He was sitting very straight. His bandage was gone, Gimple noticed, and there was a shiny dark blotch where it had been.

"Cut it off and start over," Gimple said.

"What if it never grows back?"

"I don't care. You're better off."

"It's easy for you to say that," Odum said slowly. "You have a nice head of hair."

Gimple covered his face for a moment. He had never been told that, not even by Raye, and even if it was true he didn't want to hear it from Odum.

"I need to get you out of this house," Gimple said. He stood up.

"You need to get away from these fumes. What's burning?"

Odum took an aerosol can from the floor by the sofa and sprayed cinnamon and orange smell. He said he had just now burned some frozen potatoes in the oven. He'd had nothing but frozen potatoes and tea all week.

"Let's go somewhere and get you a meal," Gimple said.

"I can't leave like this."

"Maybe Raye will cook you something."

"Thank you, Wallace. No."

"We'll drive through someplace then," Gimple said. "Put your cap on your head."

Odum did it and changed his bathrobe for a jacket, and he ducked out to Gimple's truck. They rode in silence, looking for a place to get food where no one would know them.

Gimple was mortified. He made only quick glances at Odum, who sat up very erect like a pointer. Gimple could see the wiry, purplish hairs coming out from under his cap. He wished the cap were a full helmet.

If someone has to have that hair I am glad it's not me, Gimple thought. He felt it deeply, and he was grateful that he had never made the mistake of trying to tamper with his hair. It amazed him, the humiliations men bring upon themselves. Then he thought with a pang of his old dear friend Charlie Odum, long gone, killed with a knife in Tokyo by an Australian in a fight over a girl whom Charlie died claiming he was in love with. This was the story according to an American MP who was present at the scene and whom Gimple had spoken to some weeks later. It was not the version that had been sent home to the Odum family, of course. The truth would have tested them needlessly. Charlie was a talkative, big-hearted kid who had never had a single date back home. Maybe he really had been in love with that girl. The MP had referred to her as a prostitute. Gimple had often referred to Rayelene Musselwhite as "the dog lady" until one day he found he could not live without her. In a way, the world was like a dressing room of the kind they used to have at J. C. Penney, with a small plaque below the full-length mirror which warned that a store employee was on the other side watching to make sure you did not shoplift. Once when Gimple was in his thirties he had gone to try on some slacks at J. C. Penney and, forgetting that the mirror was see-through, he locked the door, removed his pants, stuck out his elbows, and flatfooted. He was nimble on his feet but far too shy to dance in public.

When he came out of the dressing room the salesman was smiling, and Gimple saw what he had done. A grown man in his thirties! He paid for the slacks and left, and he had not gone into a J. C. Penney since.

They rode north out of Kingsport on what Gimple still thought of as the new four-lane, although it was by now years old. He drove this road with a mixture of love and resentment. The love part seemed to intensify with the passage of years and the enfeeblement of his capacity for anger. It was late November and had rained hard over the weekend after a dry spell. All up into the hills along the road the damp, amber-colored leaves lay on the ground, giving a velvety smooth appearance, and the bare trees were like gray bristles. Fall in these hills was a melancholy and beautiful change. If you had done your cutting, splitting, and stacking through the summer then you could look forward to some rest in the short days to come.

Gimple liked driving his truck. Odum sat quietly, in deep thought maybe, or maybe he was just glad to be out of his house with its different strong smells all reminding him of his solitude. He had eaten half of an Arby's sandwich, and now he closed the rest of it in its wrapper and placed it back in the bag.

They came to a traffic signal outside Gate City, Virginia, and Gimple pulled off to the right, into the parking lot of a strip mall with a grocery store, a pawn shop, one empty storefront, and a beauty salon with pink blinds in the window. Inside the glass, an artist had painted the head of a woman with yellow hair like Veronica Lake's. The sign said "Hair By Betty." Gimple had passed here some months ago, and he remembered the window and that head, with its beige-colored face and sleek hair. He pulled the truck into a parking spot.

Odum stared at the empty storefront and then at the pawn shop to the right of it. "Pawn shop's closed," he said.

"It's Tuesday," Gimple said.

Odum turned and looked at him, then past him. "I'm not going in there," he said.

"They'll be strangers," Gimple said.

"That's not the point," Odum said.

"What'll it hurt?"

"You don't know what it will hurt," Odum said. "You don't understand this at all, Wallace."

"I guess I don't," Gimple said.

Odum shrunk. "I could have been a better husband to Nan," he said.

"I'm sure you could've," Gimple said.

Odum snapped his head around and shot his heating glare at Gimple.

"You're not perfect," Gimple said. Quickly he leaned across Odum, diverting his face and holding his breath, and he shoved the truck door open. "Now go on," he said.

Odum didn't move, so Gimple took ahold of his forearm, as meatless and hard as a dog's leg, and pushed. He would not have been surprised if Odum had whipped out a pocketknife then or even reached over and tried to claw his eyes. But Odum did not resist. He got out of the truck and let Gimple lead him into Betty's.

That chemical smell was there. A skinny girl was massaging someone's head at the sink, and a big woman sat at a desk by the door. She wore a yellow sweatshirt with glitter on it. Her hair was tall and wide, and her nails were enameled. She looked up and at the same time Gimple stepped backwards to block the doorway, so Odum could not run out. The woman asked if this was a stickup. Gimple did not realize that she was joking and he said no. Then she cackled, startling him.

"He needs his hair seen to," Gimple said.

Odum was looking at the floor. Betty asked, "Can he talk?"

"Yes," Gimple said.

With a great deal of huffling Betty shoved herself up and out from behind the desk. Her sweatpants matched her sweatshirt. They were tight, and Betty was a big fat lady with shaking, dimpled thighs. She stepped up close to Odum and as though it were no more momentous an action than uncapping a jar of Rolaids, she took Odum's cap by the bill and lifted it off his head.

Odum's hair quivered like carded wool. Betty showed her teeth. It appeared that she was beginning to understand the situation. She turned Odum so she could see in back, and then she sat him in a chair. There was not so much as a potted plant for a person to hide behind in the small salon. The woman who'd been getting her head massaged now sat up to look, and the skinny girl watched with suds on her hands. Betty said, "What exactly were you trying for, when you did this?"

Odum opened his mouth, but nothing came out. The posthole was dry. Gimple went to his side and whispered to him, and Odum cocked himself over and pulled out his wallet and showed Betty the small picture of Nan with her curly black hairdo.

She took it from him and studied it closely, then propped it on a little shelf below her mirror. "Don't let me forget to give this back to you, honey," she said.

She began flicking her nails through Odum's hair, loosening it where the cap had pressed it down. Odum shut his eyes and submitted. Gimple took a seat by the wall and after a few minutes, the mood of alarm subsided. Like other embarrassing moments, this one would pass. The women chattered not very quietly, pretending that the men didn't hear them, except once when Betty turned to Gimple and asked him if he was next.

"No thank you," he said. "I've got somebody I go to."

She nodded once. "*Barber Joe*," she said. All three of the women laughed.

It was Raye, in fact. She'd been tending his hair for the last twenty years. That thought, plus the thought that she was at home right now more than likely with a dog beside her legs, caused Gimple to feel a sharp and almost painful stab of fondness for her. He noticed Odum's two black shoes, size sixes, both pointing straight toward the ceiling from the small swivel footrest on the chair. He found himself quietly humming.

ABOUT THE AUTHORS

MATT BAGGETT sells houses in Nashville's historic neighborhoods and urban lofts in reclaimed factories and neglected buildings downtown. He participates in the Writer's Loft at Middle Tennessee State University. He is focusing on the short story form. An earlier poem was included in the *Red Mud Review*. Matt has a five-year-old son.

NIKKI BARRANGER lives six miles north of Covington, Louisiana. He graduated from Yale, practiced law for a number of years, and now writes plays, poetry, short stories, and novels full-time, assisted by four cats and a Yorkie. His few fans and justified detractors may reach him at nikkibar@aol.com.

MARLIN BARTON is from the Black Belt region of Alabama. His collection of short stories, *The Dry Well*, was published in 2001, and a first novel, *A Broken Thing*, was published last year. His stories have appeared in such journals and anthologies as *The Sewanee Review*, *The Southern Review*, and the O. Henry collection.

BARRY BRADFORD is a playwright, minister, and librarian who lives in Chattanooga, Tennessee, with his wife, Becki, and son, Cameron. Scenes from his play *Dead Towns of Alabama* were read at the Alabama Shakespeare Festival as part of the Southern Writers' Project Festival of New Plays in 2003.

RICK BRAGG is the author of the best-selling memoirs *All Over but the Shoutin'* and *Ava's Man*, as well as a collection of newspapers stories, *Somebody Told Me*. While a reporter for *The New York Times*, Bragg won the Pulitzer Prize for feature writing.

MATTHEW BROCK lives with his wife, Amber, in Oxford, Mississippi, where he is a student in the M.F.A. program at the University of Mississippi (Ole Miss).

MARY WARD BROWN, often referred to as the "first lady" of Alabama letters, is the author of the nationally acclaimed *Tongues of Flame* and a collection of short stories, *It Wasn't All Dancing*, from which her selection here is taken.

GRAYSON CAPPS is a thespian-turned-blues musician, with a B.F.A. from Tulane. His recent self-titled solo album was released in the spring of 2004. He also provided songs for the John Travolta film *A Love Song for Bobby Long*, the story of which was based on his lyrics and an upcoming MacAdam/Cage novel by his father.

JAN CHABRECK is an English as a Second Language teacher in Mandeville, Louisiana. She also teaches English for Southeastern Louisiana University. Her short stories have been published in the *Kansas Quarterly*, *Verbatim*, *A Chapbook*, and *Gambit*. She lives in Lacombe with her husband.

BROCK CLARKE teaches creative writing at the University of Cincinnati. He's published two books: a novel, *The Ordinary White Boy* (Harcourt, 2001), and a short story collection, *What We Won't Do: Stories* (Sarabande, 2002), the latter of which won the Mary McCarthy Prize in Short Fiction. He's had stories published in *The Georgia Review*, *The Southern Review*, *New England Review*, *Five Points*, *Mississippi Review*, *New Stories from the South*, and elsewhere.

DOUG CRANDELL is the 2001 recipient of the Sherwood Anderson Foundation Fiction Award, as well as the River City/Hohenberg Award. In 2004 a memoir, *Pig Boy's Wicked Bird*, will be published by Chicago Review Press, and Ludlow Press will bring out his first novel. His essays and stories have appeared in *Smithsonian Magazine*, *The Sun*, *Glimmer Train*, and elsewhere. He lives in Smyrna, Georgia.

JOE FORMICHELLA's "Bayou Canot" is excerpted from his novel *The Wreck of the Twilight Limited* (MacAdam/Cage, 2004). His work has also appeared in *Grasslands Review* and *The Yalobusha Review*. He lives in Fairhope, Alabama. He is now writing *Here's to You, Jackie Robinson*, a book set for release in the spring of 2005.

TIM GAUTREAUX has published two collections of fiction, *Same Place, Same Things* and *Welding with Children*, as well as two novels, *The Next Step in the Dance* and, most recently, *The Clearing*. His work has appeared in *Atlantic, Harpers, GQ, Zoetrope, Best American Short Stories*, and *O. Henry Prize Stories*.

WILLIAM GAY is the author of the novels *The Long Home* and *Provinces of Night* and the short story collection *I Hate to See that Evening Sun Go Down*. He is the winner of the 1999 William Peden Award and the 1999 James A. Michener Memorial Prize and the recipient of a 2002 Guggenheim fellowship. He lives in Hohenwald, Tennessee.

JULIANA GRAY is the author of the chapbook *History in Bones*, published in 2001 by Kent State University Press. She teaches at the University of Alabama and during the summers teaches a poetry workshop at the Sewanee Young Writers' Conference and works on the staff of the Sewanee Writers' Conference.

WAYNE GREENHAW's first novel, *The Golfer*, was published in 1968. He has completed a screenplay of his fourth novel, *The Long Journey*, set in north Alabama in 1919. *The Intruder*, a suspense novel of the closing days of World War II, is scheduled for publication early in 2005. He lives in Montgomery, Alabama, and San Miguel de Allende, Mexico.

DONALD HAYS is the author of *The Hangman's Children*, a novel, and the editor of *Stories: Contemporary Southern Short Fiction*. He is associate professor of English at the University of Arkansas and a lifelong Cardinals fan.

BRET ANTHONY JOHNSTON's fiction has been published in such places as *The Paris Review* and *New Stories from the South: The Year's Best 2004 and 2003*. "Waterwalkers" is from his first collection of stories, *Corpus Christi*, published by Random House.

JACK KERLEY is a former advertising writer who lives in Newport, Kentucky. His first novel, *The Hundredth Man*, was published by Dutton in 2004, the second scheduled for 2005. When not writing, he spends a goodly amount of time in the southern Appalachians, searching for the perfect trout stream.

MICHAEL KNIGHT is the author of a novel, *Divining Rod*, and two collections of short fiction, *Dogfight & Other Stories* and *Goodnight, Nobody*. He lives with his wife, Jill, and daughter, Mary, in Knoxville, Tennessee.

MACK LEWIS is a 54-year-old building contractor who wrote "Aunt Marie" as an undergraduate assignment in 1974. The story won a prize for short fiction at the Southern Literary Festival, and Lewis subsequently published in *Negative Capability*, *Sands*, the *DeKalb Literary Arts Journal*, and others. He found completing construction projects far less difficult than completing works of art.

CHIP LIVINGSTON's fiction and poetry have appeared recently in *Brooklyn Review*, *Cimarron Review*, *Ploughshares*, *Rosebud*, *Blithe House Quarterly*, *Crazyhorse*, and *This New Breed: Gents, Bad Boys and Barbarians 2*. He grew up on the Alabama border in Molino, Florida, but now lives in New York City.

JONATHAN ODELL is a native Mississippian. His first novel, *The View from Delphi*, was released by MacAdam/Cage in June of 2004. Jonathan recently co-founded an institute dedicated to facilitating dialogues across race. He lives in Minneapolis, Minnesota.

JACK PENDARVIS is from Bayou La Batre, Alabama. He wrote the theme song for Cartoon Network's *Popeye Show* and the score for the feature film *Dropping Out*.

BREWSTER MILTON ROBERTSON is a member of the National Book Critics Circle and Southern Book Critics Circle. He has been twice nominated for the Pushcart Prize and Best American Essays. His novels are A *Posturing of Fools* and *The Grail Mystique*. His Golden Eye Literary Prize–winning debut novel, *Rainy Days and Sundays*, is optioned for film.

DAYNE SHERMAN is a former high school dropout from Natalbany, Louisiana. In fall 2004, MacAdam/Cage will publish his novel *Welcome to the Fallen Paradise*. When he's not working as an assistant professor at the college in his hometown, he's writing another Baxter Parish novel and a collection of stories. "Hard to Remember, Hard to Forget" is a one-story chapbook published by Over the Transom. Dayne can be reached through his website at www.dayne sherman.com.

ALIX STRAUSS's articles have appeared in *The New York Times*, *The Daily News*, *Time Magazine*, *Men's Health*, *Marie Claire*, and *Self*, among others. Her fiction has been published in the *Hampton Shorts Literary Review*, the *Idaho Review*, and *Quality Women's Fiction*. The story "Shrinking Away" won the David Dornstein Creative Writing Award. She has been featured on several morning shows discussing lifestyle and food trends. *The Joy of Funerals: a novel in stories* was published by St. Martin's Press. She lives in Manhattan. You can e-mail Alix at alixtjof@aol.com.

BRAD VICE was born and raised in Tuscaloosa, Alabama, and now teaches creative writing at Mississippi State University. His stories have been published in *The Georgia Review*, *The Southern Review*, *Hayden's Ferry Review*, *The Greensboro Review*, *The Carolina Quar-*

terly, The Atlantic Monthly, New Stories from the South, and *Best New American Voices*.

DANIEL WALLACE is the author of three novels, *Big Fish* (1998), *Ray in Reverse* (2000), and *The Watermelon King* (2003). His stories have been published far and wide in many magazines and anthologies, including *The Yale Review, The Massachusetts Review, Shenandoah*, and *Glimmer Train*. A screenplay, *Timeless*, is being produced for Universal Pictures. *Big Fish* is now a major motion picture, directed by Tim Burton from a script by John August. Daniel lives in Chapel Hill, North Carolina, with his wife, Laura, and his son, Henry.

D. B. WELLS is a pen name. The person behind the name lives life in as much anonymity as possible in Kentucky.

JAMES WHORTON, JR.'s first novel, *Approximately Heaven*, was published by Free Press in 2003. He was raised in Florida and Mississippi and studied at the University of Southern Mississippi and Johns Hopkins. He lives in East Tennessee with his wife and their daughter.

ACKNOWLEDGMENTS

One good thing about *Stories from the Blue Moon Café* coming out each year is that when I forget to thank you for helping me in some way get the book out, I get a shot at correcting my omission.

So, last night, I'm standing before a crowd of people thanking them for their interest in the Fairhope Center for Writing Arts, for throwing in their time and money to renovate our Wolff Writers' Cottage in Fairhope, for donating furniture and artwork so the place is comfortable and looks good. Rick Bragg is standing beside me, our guest of honor, about to move into the place and become our first writer-in-residence.

Someone nearby pokes me and whispers, "Thank the mayor and city council…." They leased us the historic little cottage for a dollar a year, and the mayor's in the crowd. With that little reminder, I don't goof.

But everybody's standing there enjoying seafood gumbo and beverages while I'm talking and I forget to thank the person responsible for the food and beverages. That would be my wife. Thanks, Diana! For that, and for the room you make in our family life for the work I do on this book. And my boys, John Luke and Dylan. They seem to miss me when I'm on the road peddling the anthology. And my daughter Emily who tells people up in Tuscaloosa to buy the Blue Moon Café Book.

Then there's the rest of my family, who still admit they're kin to me even though this book has cussing and violence and sex and grotesque stuff in it. My thanks to them. That would be Mama and my brother Frankie and my sisters Sandra and Missy, and Joe and Carolyn, and Kendra, and the rest of my in-laws. God, I gotta mention Nanny. She's 92 and still reads a book a week, and especially likes our collection of Southern writing.

And I do appreciate our Mississippi send-off for each new issue of *Stories from the Blue Moon Café*: John Evans at Lemuria Bookstore in Jackson, and Bill Kehoe and the rest of John's staff; Lyn Roberts and

Jamie Kornegay and the gang at Richard Howorth's Square Books in Oxford. Then I couldn't get by without Martin Lanaux, Bookseller, and Jim Gilbert at Over the Transom Bookshop—he helped me ramrod this book to get it out on time; Scott Naugle at Pass Christian Bookstore; and Ilse Krick at the Fairhope Public Library. Booksellers and bookpeople everywhere are the only reason this book exists. Period.

Newspaper people who tell their readers about us, John Sledge, Curt Chapman, Jerry Mitchell, they're to be thanked. And all the book critics who don't throw rocks at us.

I'm grateful to the writers in this book and the two previous Blue Moon Café anthologies, especially Rick Bragg, Tom Franklin and William Gay, and Bev Marshall; the debut novelists, Joe Formichella and Dayne Sherman, keep pumping me up. Suzanne Hudson and Frank Turner Hollon still get in on that act, too.

Thanks to all the great organizers and staff people at the South's literary and book festivals who keep asking us to bring our Blue Moon Café Gang to their events, like Serenity Gerbman in Tennessee, Laura Hudson in North Carolina, Brenda McLain in South Carolina, and Paul Willis in New Orleans. Wanda Jewel and the gang at Southeast Booksellers Association get a nod, too.

The writers who've come to Fairhope for our November literary slugfest, Southern Writers Reading, which gave rise to this anthology, know a debt of gratitude is owed to Skip and Nancy Jones, Lynn and Cori Yonge, Rick and Debbie Kingrea, Nancy Ursprung, Ann Davis, Cynthia Staggers, and Cindy McBrearty. And Johm Borom at Faulkner Community College and Phil Norris at the University of South Alabama. Guy and Terra at the Gumbo Shack top off our evenings on that great weekend. Mac and Gina Walcott stepped up to the plate when the plate was in danger of being lost under red silt, and knocked it over the fence. Bless them. Then lastly, but not leastly, my friends at MacAdam/Cage. David You-Da-Man Poindexter, Patty Me-Boy Walsh, Scott Big-Hugs Allen, and Dorothy Carico Smith, Kate Nitze, Melanie Mitchell and Tasha Kepler.

GRAYSON CAPPS

It was Grayson's music that bookended the sessions for Southern Writers Reading in 2001, the very event where this anthology series, now in its third volume, was born. Our Troubadour Extraordinaire, we called him then—and he's been traveling with us ever since: playing at the Lemuria bookstore launch of the first *Blue Moon* book; at various readings in my store, Over the Transom; not to mention encoring at SWR in 2003. So it's only fitting that his music and lyrics now grace the interior of the Café proper. You may now sample some tracks plucked fresh from his first solo album, *Grayson Capps*.

—*Sonny Brewer*